HAZARDOUS
SPIRITS

HAZARDOUS SPIRITS

A NOVEL

ANBARA SALAM

TIN HOUSE / PORTLAND, OREGON

First US Edition 2023
Printed in the United States of America

Manufacturing by Lake Book Manufacturing
Interior design by Beth Steidle

Library of Congress Cataloging-in-Publication Data

Names: Salam, Anbara, author.
Title: Hazardous spirits : a novel / Anbara Salam.
Description: First US edition. | Portland, Oregon : Tin House, 2023.
Identifiers: LCCN 2023025059 | ISBN 9781959030133 (paperback) |
ISBN 9781959030218 (ebook)
Subjects: LCGFT: Novels.
Classification: LCC PR6119.A38 H39 2023 | DDC 823/.92—dc23/eng/20230523
LC record available at https://lccn.loc.gov/2023025059

Tin House
2617 NW Thurman Street, Portland, OR 97210
www.tinhouse.com

DISTRIBUTED BY W. W. NORTON & COMPANY

1 2 3 4 5 6 7 8 9 0

In loving memory of
Rebecca Grove Munson

HAZARDOUS
SPIRITS

SUNDAY
25th NOVEMBER, 1923

EDINBURGH

I.

EVELYN WATCHED ROBERT SLEEP ON THE CHAISE longue, his face buried in the tufting. Suddenly squeamish about getting too close to him, she tossed the silk throw in his direction and withdrew to the hallway, where she stood with her back pressed against the staircase. What was she supposed to do? Telephone for a doctor? A minister? His hair had been cut that morning, and it was a little too short. It made his cheeks seem overly full, lending him the smug air of someone who'd recently placed a winning bet on a horse. But still, he looked *normal*; he didn't look like a man who had just announced that he could speak to the spirits of the dead.

The reflection of her face stared back from the windowpane on the far side of the parlour. Her lips were almost white, a smudge of grease on the collar of her blouse. As she put a finger to the stain, the curtain fluttered, and Evelyn jumped, pressing herself even harder against the staircase. Robert had always been open-minded, the type to chat to a peddler at a tram stop, to accept a leaflet from a street-corner fakir, but this? She pictured Robert's expression of hectic excitement, the dampness gleaming at his temples.

"And the voices give me messages," he had said, his eyes jittering.

Evelyn was waiting for a joke that hadn't arrived. "I don't understand."

"Well, they aren't really voices. More like a sort of swirl."

"A swirl?"

"A swirl of suggestions, symbols. At first, I thought I was losing my mind!" He laughed, and Evelyn shrank back. "But it's not so unusual after all. There's lots of ways spirits communicate—returning lost items, butterflies, special numbers. I've been researching."

"What do you mean, researching?" Evelyn's voice was strained, the back of her neck prickling.

"Researching my gift."

"Gift?"

"The gift of understanding the spirits." He turned to stare at the curtains. "The spirits of those who have died."

And now there he was, spent and snoring. For Evelyn, it felt like the disorientation after an accident. With a before and an after and no way to go back. Robert was the one who always knew how to make things right, to think practically, to be rational, reasonable. He was an accountant, for heaven's sake! Evelyn peered across the room. The window on the far side was fixed at the latch, and yet the curtain was moving, the peacock pattern rippling, all by itself. She felt her panic growing, a zeppelin inflating in her throat. Grabbing the first coat that came to her hand in the hallway, she let herself out of the house.

It was dark outside, the streetlamps smudgy baubles of light in the misty evening. Not until she was halfway along the front path, did Evelyn realise the coat she had seized was, in fact, a summer gabardine cloak she'd intended to donate to the Salvation Army. On the other side of the road, Mrs. Wrigley's housemaid was walking her beagle, and she nodded politely. Evelyn swallowed—what if the housemaid could already sense the peculiarity, pulsing out of her? Now aware she was hatless, Evelyn bunched up her cloak and began to run. Breathless, she arrived at Kitty's house and pounded on the door.

Jeanie, Kitty's maid, answered. "Mrs. Hazard, good evening," she said, her eyes travelling over Evelyn's attire.

Without waiting for an invitation, Evelyn pushed past her into the hallway. "Where is Kitty? Upstairs?"

"No, Mrs. Hazard." Jeanie licked her lips. "Mr. and Mrs. Fraser are in the dining room."

Evelyn marched along the corridor and stopped at the dining room door. From outside, she heard conversation, and through the gap in the hinge, silver candlesticks glittered. Kitty never used the Mairibank silver unless she was entertaining.

"Who else is here?" she hissed at Jeanie.

"Mr. and Mrs. Wheeler are dining here tonight," Jeanie said. "Shall I let Mrs. Fraser know you are expecting her?"

"Yes." Evelyn stepped from foot to foot, and dared to put her face around the door. The wallpaper was red-and-black velvet damask, which Evelyn had always found far too heavy, and in the dim light, it took Evelyn a precious two seconds to locate Kitty at the far end of the table. She was wearing her pink Callot Soeurs evening dress, the pearls around her neck shining in the glow from the polished candlesticks.

Jeanie cleared her throat, and Evelyn pulled back.

"Mrs. Hazard? The parlour is available, if you like."

"Fine." Evelyn hurried next door where a fire was burning in the grate, and a card table and four folding chairs had been pulled into the middle of the room, ready for a game of bridge. She paced the narrow aisle between the sofa and the table.

"Evie?" came Kitty's voice.

Evelyn flung herself at her sister so violently she almost bowled her over. Kitty patted her on the back, and then gently levered her away. "What's wrong? Your coat—your shoes!"

Looking down, Evelyn now saw that she was still wearing her Turkish house slippers. "It's Robert," she said, and began to cry. "He's gone insane."

Kitty's hand flew to her pearls, and even through Evelyn's distress, the primness of the action chimed in a way she would later identify as funny. Kitty glanced over her shoulder to the doorway, where Jeanie was wearing a practised blank expression. "Fetch Dr. Greitzer," Kitty said.

Jeanie nodded with the indecent haste of someone thrilled to find themselves perpendicular to a drama.

Kitty gestured to the sofa. "Tell me what's happened. What do you mean, insane?"

Evelyn sniffed into a handkerchief she had recovered from the cloak pocket. "He called me into the parlour, and I thought he was going to complain about the purse I bought for your Christmas present—" Evelyn stopped. "Oh, and now the surprise is ruined."

"Never mind that. What has he done? Has he . . ." Kitty's face flushed. She lowered her voice to a whisper. "Has he struck you?"

Evelyn bristled. Even insane, her husband wasn't *that* insane. "No, it's nothing like that." She wiped her face with the handkerchief; now realising it wasn't at all clean. She swallowed. "He thinks he's hearing voices, whispers in the house."

Evelyn could see Kitty was working hard to compose her expression. "Like Mrs. McFlitt?" she said eventually.

Mrs. McFlitt had been their neighbour back in the old days, when they lived at Mairibank, before what Papa referred to, euphemistically, as the "big move." She had begun knocking on the delivery side door, demanding access to documents in the cellar about the soldiers who were "hounding" her.

"I don't think so," Evelyn said. "He doesn't seem forgetful. He says he's been performing, performing"—she took a deep breath—"investigations into voices of the dead." Evelyn sobbed into the handkerchief. Somewhere outside of her body she was both amazed and appalled that she was making such a scene.

"Katherine?" Alistair, Kitty's husband, was standing in the doorway, his napkin in hand.

Kitty shot him a look that was equal parts warning and promise, and Alistair grimaced. "Ah," he said. "Right you are then," and discreetly, he closed the door.

Evelyn's throat burned. The easy domesticity of Kitty's house—the candlelit supper, the freshly laid fire, the look of complicity between her and her husband—it was all so cosy it was nearly painful. "I shouldn't bother you," she said, standing up. "You're busy."

"Don't be ridiculous." Kitty pulled her back down to the sofa. "When Dr. Greitzer gets here, we'll have Robert all patched up in no time. He likely needs some rest, that's all. Where is—is he—he's not in the cellar, is he?" Kitty said, fiddling with her necklace.

"He's napping."

"Napping?" Kitty winced, and Evelyn felt a thrill of horror run down her spine. What *was* he doing napping at seven on a Sunday evening? How was everything so awful when the day had begun so regularly? It was providential revenge—she had been a fool to think normality would last.

"Let me fix you a brandy, shall I?" Kitty crossed to the cabinet in the corner and returned with a tiny, tulip-shaped glass of brandy, so delicate and pretty that the strangeness of the occasion was thrown into terrible relief. Evelyn drank it in one mouthful. Through the wall she heard the scraping of a chair in the dining room.

Evelyn wiped the handkerchief along her face. "What about the Wheelers?"

Kitty wrinkled her nose. "Alistair can bore them silly about the latest fashions in model trains," she said, and Evelyn gratefully received the mild rebuke, since it was the closest Kitty could come to admitting her own husband's eccentricities.

Kitty's expression became serious. "Now tell me, what exactly has he been saying about these voices?"

Cautiously, Evelyn probed the conversation she'd had with Robert. She didn't want to collect too much information from that hour, so she scraped shallowly across her recall. "He thinks he's acquired a new talent—a knack of receiving messages. From—" Evelyn paused to listen for Jeanie's footsteps. "From people who have died."

Kitty was making a valiant effort at keeping her face still, but nevertheless, her lip twitched. After a moment, she let out a breath. "Well," she said. "Well. That's probably nothing to worry about."

"Really?" Evelyn blinked at her, and the rosy vision of her sister flitted through a prism of tears.

"Yes," Kitty said doubtfully. "He's grieving, that's all."

"But no one has died," Evelyn said. Then they exchanged a horrible look, because, of course, everyone had died.

"I mean—nobody has died recently," Evelyn said.

Kitty looked down at her knees. "Dolores?" she said, quietly.

A cold pebble lodged in Evelyn's windpipe. The room tilted. "Evie!" Kitty was holding her wrist. "Shall I get the salts?"

Evelyn shook her head, but the room was listing. The mention of Dolores was almost too much. It was tapping the fracture in a pane of glass. She collected all of her senses into not shattering.

"Let me get you more brandy."

Evelyn fixed her vision on a loose thread in the carpet. "No, I'm fine."

"I'm sure it's not anything to do with Dolores," Kitty was saying. "That could hardly be called recent. I shouldn't have mentioned it."

"It's fine," Evelyn said with some effort. She met Kitty's eyes. "It can't be to do with Dolly, can it?" The panic began building again, a more byzantine kind now, an ornate, intricate terror with interlocking elements. "It's not possible, is it? He's not, somehow—"

"No," Kitty said, steadily. "Absolutely not." She gave Evelyn a long, hard look.

Evelyn came back to herself. "No, of course not." Kitty was watching her with alarm, and she felt a flush of mortification. She dug her fingers into her palms. Older sisters weren't supposed to collapse. Some kind of example she was setting. "I'm sorry," she blurted out.

"Nothing to be sorry about." Kitty patted Evelyn's hand. "Now, remember that first month in Edinburgh, when Mama kept losing things?"

Evelyn settled on a memory of her mother plugging a pipe under the scullery sink with a woollen stocking. Papa was back at Mairibank, overseeing the sale of the estate, and the weekend girl had gone home. As the stocking grew swollen with water and transferred the leak in a new direction, Mama had sat on the floor and cried. It wasn't quite forgetfulness, but it was close enough. "Yes," she said.

Kitty frowned, unconvinced. "Remember, she put her shoes on the wrong foot, and only noticed on the way back from the park?"

Still, Evelyn had no memory of these events, and her ability to summon up other moments of humiliation was compromised. "Well, after Dr. Halligan prescribed her that vitamin tonic, she was right as rain again."

Now Evelyn remembered the vitamin drops. The bottle was crafted from thick brown glass, and was deceptively heavy. The tonic had to be dispensed through a special pipette. The fragile instrument, the spidery float of the bubbles of tincture dissolving in a glass of water—the ritual of administering the drops had transfixed her. She held on to the image of the heavy brown bottle. "Do you mean it could be a vitamin deficiency?"

A line of concentration appeared on Kitty's brow. "Certainly. After all, scurvy is a vitamin deficiency."

Evelyn nodded seriously.

There was a knock on the door. Jeanie put her head around. "Dr. Greitzer is arrived," she said, opening the door wider so he could enter.

Dr. Greitzer was dressed in a black woollen overcoat, drizzle pearling on his hat. Evelyn stood to shake his hand, and the reassuring sturdiness of his grip, plus the memory of the brown glass bottle of tincture, brought her back to her senses. She became painfully aware she was wearing a stained gabardine cloak and Turkish house slippers.

"Mrs. Fraser, Mrs. Hazard." Dr. Greitzer stood next to the card table. "How can I be of assistance?"

As he unbuttoned his coat, Evelyn saw he was wearing a dinner jacket, and a fresh wave of shame rolled over her. He had been at supper when she'd rung for him.

"Please." She put out her hand to stop him from removing his overcoat. "We'll have to go to my house, it's my husband."

"Bobby?"

"Yes," Evelyn said, although he hated being called Bobby. "That's right." She glanced at Kitty. "He has some kind of vitamin deficiency, I believe."

Dr. Greitzer looked almost disappointed. "Very well. After you." He motioned towards the door. Evelyn fastened her cloak and glanced behind her, where Kitty was following. "Please, I'll be fine now. You should go back to your guests."

"Absolutely not. Let me get my coat."

Evelyn kissed her on the cheek. "Really, don't worry." She felt much calmer now. How embarrassing that she had made such a fuss! Thank goodness the Wheelers hadn't witnessed any of it. And Kitty, she had done so well, keeping her head, telephoning the doctor, the brandy. Evelyn felt a surge of pride for both of them; for Kitty for being so level-headed, and for herself as Kitty's tutor.

Kitty studied Evelyn's face. "I'll call over first thing tomorrow."

Evelyn smiled. "Apologise to Alistair for me."

She followed Dr. Greitzer into the corridor, and Jeanie let them out, wearing a sulky, almost thwarted expression. It had begun raining, and Evelyn's gabardine was soon spotted with water. Dr. Greitzer offered her his umbrella, and gratefully she took his arm. In silence, they walked along Inverleith Row towards her house. And as she watched puddle water soak into her slippers, Evelyn thought of Dolores, of Granny and Grandpapa, of their neighbour's son Stevie, of Dugald Grear, of Alistair's brother, Sydney, of rows of boys in army greatcoats, queuing up in heaven to speak to Robert, like the line for the telephone at the post office.

* * *

EVELYN ENTERED THE HOUSE first, opening the door quietly. Now that Dr. Greitzer was involved, she was almost worried Robert would be back to normal. What if when they went in, he was the picture of decency: smoking a cigar, mildly nodding his head along to the gramophone? As she crept along the corridor, Evelyn crossed her fingers, hoping that he would be where she'd left him, slack and sweaty against the chaise longue. And indeed—there he was. His mouth was open, a thread of dribble smudging the velvet. Evelyn was gratified to see Dr. Greitzer's brow furrowing.

"Shall I wake him?" she whispered.

Dr. Greitzer took off his coat and hat. "Please."

As Evelyn nudged Robert, she took a moment to register that what she had taken for a dinner jacket was, in fact, a tuxedo. Dr. Greitzer must have been at a very nice function indeed to need a tuxedo on a Sunday evening.

"Darling," she said, squeezing Robert's shoulder, "I've brought the doctor to attend to your fever." When it came to Robert, she had discovered that it was better to make a suggestion in advance, and guide him into the desired outcome.

Robert stirred. "My fever?"

"Yes, that's right." She raised her eyebrows suggestively at the doctor, who gave her a slight, understanding nod.

Robert sat up, and Dr. Greitzer took a seat next to him on the chaise longue. "Evening, Bobby. Tell me, how are the chickens coping with all this rain?" he said, snapping a thermometer out of his case and sliding it into Robert's mouth.

Evelyn was taken aback by this familiarity. How did Dr. Greitzer know about Robert's chickens? Perhaps he didn't mind being called

Bobby after all. An oily, uneasy anticipation coated her ribs, and she slipped out of the room and went into the kitchen. She wiped the table, and then the counter, and peered into the larder. What if the doctor wanted to stay for supper? It would indeed be proof of a vitamin deficiency if she were left to cater to him. Ignoring Marty's inventory list tacked to the wall, she began unpacking the shelves, lining the counter with jars of Bovril and tinned sardines, Crawford's biscuits, bags of flour, jars of peach jam, searching for something that she was sure she'd know when she saw it.

There was a tread on the stairs, and she turned to see Dr. Greitzer wiping his glasses.

Evelyn clutched a packet of shortbread to her chest. "How is he? His heart?"

"His heart is fine." Dr. Greitzer smiled. His eyes fell on the jumble of groceries on the counter.

"It's Marty's half day," Evelyn said, by way of explanation. "But I'd be happy to offer you something. We have plenty of fortifying, healthy foods: salt beef, or sardines? Or tongue?"

Dr. Greitzer sat down at the kitchen table with a sigh. "Thank you, but I don't take meat."

"Oh. Well." She nibbled the cuticle on her right index finger. "We have half a roast duck, is duck meat? Or there are some slices of cured ham, oh no, that's obviously meat, isn't it?" She started to laugh, nervously at first, then gathering speed like a motorcycle engine.

Dr. Greitzer lifted his palms. "Please, a slice of bread and butter would be perfect."

"Will I fetch Robert?"

The doctor shook his head. "I've sent him to bed with a couple of aspirin."

"I see."

Dr. Greitzer was smiling at her mildly. With his short neck, small, beady eyes, and tight cheeks, he reminded her somewhat of a penguin. She had the sudden, absurd image of herself throwing a kipper in the air to which he would rise, wings flapping, and gulp in one swoop.

Evelyn turned back to the counter and, pushing aside the barracks of preserves, concentrated on preparing the best, most delicious slice of bread and butter. She carved off the heel and put it aside for dripping, so the doctor could have the softest part of the loaf. She spread it with such a thick layer of yellow butter that he was bound to marvel at their careless affluence. Evelyn wiped her hands on her skirt. She'd have to light the fire in the dining room and there would be no way to wash afterwards without being seen. It was one thing to have no staff on the weekend; it was another to be witnessed covered in soot.

"Allow me to check that the dining room is prepared," she said, deciding she could run to the upstairs bathroom if she didn't touch the banister.

"No need." The doctor shrugged off his jacket, plucking at his bow tie so it unrolled. "Let's eat here. That's a beautiful gardenia you have." He tilted his head towards the plant by the window.

"Oh, yes. Thank you."

"I was given a gardenia as a wedding gift," he said. "Delightful flowers. I just couldn't keep it alive."

"What a shame," Evelyn said, nibbling her finger again. How could the doctor not know how to care for a gardenia? What did that say about his aptitude for healing?

"Please, take a seat," he said, gesturing to the table.

Evelyn obeyed, too numb to be insulted by being invited to her own table. The doctor unfastened his cuff links and rolled up his sleeves. Evelyn watched him take slow, small bites, following his chewing so carefully her head swayed with the movement of his jaw.

"So." The doctor wiped his hands on a napkin. "Bobby."

"Yes?"

"His heart is ticking along nicely. Temperature was a wee on the high side, but nothing to worry about." Something in his face indicated the pause of a person who has yet to finish their sentence.

Evelyn tucked her hair behind her ears, and then untucked it.

Dr. Greitzer dabbed his mouth with the napkin. "And, he's spoken to you, has he, about the, the visions?"

"Of course," Evelyn said, affronted.

"Yes, good. Well, he mentioned, some auditory, some visual, uh, disturbances."

"I know, yes." Evelyn shuffled to the front of her chair. "Do you think it could be scurvy?"

The doctor held her eye for a moment, and then laughed. "I'm sorry hen, I'm sorry for laughing. No. You have nothing to worry about on that front."

"What is your opinion, Doctor? As children, we had a neighbour; she started hearing voices, forgetting things. But she was an old woman. You don't think there's—" Evelyn stopped. She could see the doctor's expression was still fracturing with lingering amusement because of her scurvy comment. She pursed her lips and waited for him to compose himself.

Dr. Greitzer cleared his throat. "Lack of sleep often causes hallucinations," he said, his forehead wrinkling in a kindly way that Evelyn registered as theatrical, as if he were only performing kindliness. "That's the most likely cause. Otherwise—"

Evelyn took a deep breath. "That's good. Well, I can fix that," she said. She'd have Robert in bed by nine o'clock each evening. No more piano playing after dinner, in case it got him worked up. Tonight, she'd open the windows and get plenty of nice fresh air in there.

The doctor was pulling down his sleeves. Evelyn had to restrain herself from putting out a hand to pause his dressing. "Otherwise? Otherwise what?"

He put his jacket back on, straightening his lapels. "Well, for a sustained attack of this nature, I would propose only three alternative explanations."

Evelyn waited politely, but he showed no signs of finishing his diagnosis. "Yes?" She had an urge to shake him, to make his words roll loose like sherbets inside a penny dispensary.

"Well." Dr. Greitzer shot his cuffs. "The first possibility is that he is insane"—and as Evelyn began to babble, he interrupted her—"or, secondly, it is a falsehood." Evelyn shut her mouth with a snap. Her skin ran cold. That would be even a worse possibility than insanity.

"But—falsehood? To what end?"

Dr. Greitzer sighed. "Motives maketh the man," he said, cryptically. Evelyn imagined Robert, conducting an oratory from Parliament, bombastically declaring the strategic wisdom passed on to him by Napoleon's ghost as he winked roguishly at her from the podium.

Evelyn swallowed. "And the third?"

Dr. Greitzer gave her the hint of a smile. "The third option," he said, replacing his hat, "is that he's telling the truth."

2

THE ROOM WAS STILL DARK WHEN EVELYN WOKE THE
next day. A growl of freezing air swept across the blankets, scattering
hailstones across the end of the bed. She staggered onto the icy floor,
groping for the back of the chair, the corner of the table, to the window ledge. Leaning her whole weight onto the frame, she pushed
until it gave way with a sudden slam.

Robert rolled in the sheets. "Is it morning?"

Mornings were Robert's sole source of grumpiness, and Evelyn
spent a good half an hour before breakfast cajoling him out of bed,
massaging him into the day with soothing tones and gentle ministrations. She didn't begrudge him his disagreeable spells, but there
could be only one morning grumbler in the family, and it never left
her any space to grumble herself.

"No, darling, it's early, go back to sleep," Evelyn whispered. "Dr.
Greitzer said you need your rest."

"Who is that winking?" he said, in a thick voice.

"Winking? No, it's—Robert, go back to sleep."

Pulling the sheets aside, he stumbled out of bed. She raised her
arms hesitantly, thinking he was about to embrace her. But as he
drew closer, his expression was absent, his eyes unfocused and puffy.
Evelyn dropped her arms. "Robert?"

He tapped her on the shoulder, and she tried to catch his hand. He tapped her again. Confused, she stepped aside, anticipating that Robert was about to reopen the window. Licks of frost streaked the glass, reflecting shimmers from the lamps across the street. Instead, he pointed at the floorboard underneath her feet. "Winking, there."

Evelyn looked down. There, in between the floorboards, was one hazel eye, peering up at them. A whistle shot through her veins. Her eyes watered.

Robert was on his knees, prising up the floorboard.

"Don't!" she managed to gasp.

The board squeaked and Robert slipped his hand into the black space underneath. He pulled out his hand, revealing the eye in his palm. Not an eye. An earring. An earring that had caught the freckles of light on the window. Evelyn's skin tingled with relief.

Robert handed it to her and walked back across the room.

"Robert?" He climbed into bed. "Robert?" she whispered. But he tugged the blanket over his shoulders, nestling his face into the pillows. Evelyn looked down at the stud in her palm. This wasn't one of her earrings—amber, she'd never—and then her throat closed. It was Dolly's. It was one of Dolly's earrings. She dropped the earring into the pocket of her pajamas and, as quickly and calmly as she could, left the room and closed the door behind her.

Her heart was tumbling around in her chest. She sat on the chair in the hallway where no one ever sat, forcing herself to take long, deep breaths. She picked up a book from the shelf, replaced it, chewed her finger, picked up another book, put that down. Creeping back to the door, she put her eye to the keyhole. Robert was asleep, his face in the crook of his arm. Her blood was roaring in her ears. She took another deep breath. There was nothing in it. There was nothing in it.

A light snow was falling outside as Evelyn paced around the spare room. She smoothed the throw on the bed, nudged all the picture frames level. In the bathroom, she opened the cabinet, straightening her bottles of lotion. She went down to the parlour and stood, watching the peacock pattern in the curtains for any sign of motion. Back on the landing, she jostled the drawer in the card table until it was completely shut. Eventually, she took a seat at the top of the staircase, where a spider's web trailed softly from the banister. A feather from the mattress tick had got caught in the web. She reached to pull it out, and all at once, she was eighteen, in the bathing machine on the water at Whitby, unrolling her towel to find the bright flare of a jay feather. Black and blue, with a shimmer like oil on a hot road. His face appearing behind the bathing machine, his nose sunburnt above the gloss of the water. "It made me think of you," he said, bobbing under the waves in what she realised was a sudden fit of shyness. And it had hit her: he loved her. Standing at the door of the cabin, the lap of green against the steps, she jumped into the cold shock of water, swimming after him with all her strength.

The sound of Kitty knocking on the door broke her out of her reverie. Evelyn squeezed the feather until it was sodden into a little clump.

"Where's Marty?" Kitty said, when Evelyn opened the door. "She hasn't overslept again?" As Kitty rolled her perambulator into the corridor, baby Margaret hiccupped from within.

"I gave her a few days off," Evelyn said. What had she told the doctor, that it was Marty's half day? She would have to keep better track of both her real and fictitious housekeeping schedule.

Kitty's lips tightened. "She gets an awful lot of holiday, your Marty."

"Her mother's been ill," Evelyn added. "And anyway," she said, glancing upstairs, "I'm rather glad she wasn't here yesterday." She pictured Marty's dour, reproachful pout, her metonymic chains of misery that began at stubbing a toe, and meandered through electrocutions and accidental drowning.

Kitty's eyes swept over Evelyn's pajamas. "You're still in your nightclothes!"

Evelyn tugged on the bottom of her shirt, knocking against the shrapnel in her pocket. "I was a little preoccupied this morning," she said, weakly.

Kitty's face softened. "Try not to worry." She stepped past the pram and clutched Evelyn to her, patting her robustly on the back as if she were trying to dislodge something, rather than comfort her. Evelyn sighed into her sister's hair. She smelt like talcum powder and baby soap, a not completely pleasant nursery scent that evoked sick days and congealed rice pudding.

"Let's sit in the kitchen," Evelyn said. "I haven't had time . . ." She gestured at the parlour, where the silk throw lay rumpled on the chaise longue. The space felt somehow tarnished now; even looking at the throw made her stomach turn. She guided Kitty down into the kitchen, which was similarly dishevelled from the day before. The tins were still stacked on the counter and Dr. Greitzer's plate was lying on the table, flecked with hardened butter. Evelyn put another log on the fire, and Kitty pulled a chair away from the table and towards the grate. She brought Margaret out of the perambulator and passed her over to Evelyn. Evelyn reviewed the baby for a few seconds, before balancing her unsteadily on her knee.

"Tell me, what did the doctor say?" Kitty said, pouring them both cups of tea. "How is his heart?"

Evelyn decided that an appropriate amount of baby-handling time had elapsed and returned Margaret to the pram. "His heart is fine. He just needs some rest."

Kitty smiled. "There you go."

Evelyn nodded, blinking back tears. They sat in silence for a moment. The coals in the grate skittered, and Evelyn glanced nervously around the room. She took a sip of tea to steady herself.

"You know," Kitty said, jiggling the pram with her foot, "before we hired Abigail to take the baby in the night, I was half out of my mind with tiredness—imagining all kinds of nonsense."

"Such as?" This was the first Evelyn had heard of Kitty's weariness. Since Margaret's birth, Kitty had been nothing but a syrupy confection of bonneted delight.

Kitty shrugged. "That I could hear the baby crying when she wasn't. Or, have you ever had a dream where you think you've got up to do something? And it's so real that you can't believe you're still lying in bed?"

Evelyn nodded. But it was hardly the same thing—anticipating a baby's cries, and receiving messages from dead people. It was hardly the same thing at all.

"Has Dr. Greitzer been married long?" she said.

"Around five years?" Kitty said. "You must have seen his wife in Stockbridge, she's awfully tall, and handsome. Sort of hawkish."

"Really?" Evelyn pictured a penguin and a hawk, waddling side by side down a church aisle, their wings touching. Despite herself, she gave a little chortle.

"Why do you ask?" said Kitty, catching the smile from Evelyn.

Evelyn looked over at her gardenia plant. "He mentioned something about a wedding gift, and I didn't know he had a wife."

Kitty began describing her various encounters with Miriam Greitzer—the time she had seen her at the pharmacy, the time she had worn a darling black cap, the time she had stopped to admire Margaret. As Kitty talked, Evelyn drifted into a daydream. "Anyway," Kitty said at last. "She has beautiful curls. I'd die to have those curls."

"Hmm."

Kitty frowned. "What is it?"

"He, Dr. Greitzer, he said—" Evelyn cleared her throat. "No, never mind."

"What did he say?" Kitty put her teacup down.

Evelyn shook her head. "He mentioned in passing something—" She cleared her throat again. "Something more metaphysical than I expected. And I only wondered," Evelyn said, tugging on her sleeve, "if maybe his wife was . . ." She rolled her wrist in the air, searching for a suitable euphemism.

"Emotional," Kitty filled in diplomatically.

"Well, yes."

Kitty readjusted her shawl. "Dr. Greitzer is highly recommended," she said, eventually.

"I know that."

"He attended to Major MacArthur after his stroke."

"I know, I know."

"When Margaret's croup—"

Evelyn cut her off. "Look at this." She took Dolly's earring out of her pocket and put it on the table. "Robert found it."

Kitty picked it up, laughing. "I'd forgotten all about those earrings! Remember, she insisted they were a perfect match with that horrible resin brooch, the one with the dragonfly? Heavens, that was an ugly brooch. Whatever happened to that monster, did it end up in your pile? Oh!" Kitty gripped Evelyn's hand, and Evelyn's heart clenched. Here it was, she had seen it too, the possibility, the horror.

"We should have given that brooch to Heather Wormwood, and said it was a special remembrance gift—she would have been too embarrassed to refuse! Then she would've been forced to wear it whenever she saw us." Kitty leant back in her chair, chuckling to herself.

Evelyn watched her with a mixture of betrayal and envy. That she could pluck out memories of Dolores like that, sift through them to sample as if she were rooting about in a selection box of biscuits. Evelyn put the gem on the palm of her hand. It looked distinctly unmystical in the daylight, against the bread crumbs on the table. She stared down at her knees. Her pajamas were wearing a little thin, a single hair from her kneecap poking through the weave. She was overreacting to the earring. It meant more to her than it needed to. Everything of Dolly's meant more than it needed to. She now rather wanted Kitty to leave so she could be deflated and miserable in peace.

"Are you going to Heather's Christmas party?" Kitty was saying. "I'm surprised she thinks anyone will attend after last year's gannet."

Evelyn stood up. "I think that was Robert."

"It was? I didn't hear anything."

"I'll have to go see what he needs while he recovers—from his fever."

Kitty nodded, lifting her cup.

Evelyn felt herself growing desperate. "I'll call round later?"

Kitty gave her a brief, almost suspicious look before standing up. "Telephone if you need anything."

Evelyn hustled Kitty along the front passage, and then made a big show of stamping up the staircase. After the door closed, she watched through the narrow window at the top of the landing as Kitty ran her fingers around the brim of her hat, looked back at the door, then began pushing the perambulator down the path. Evelyn took a deep breath, and tapped on their bedroom door frame. "Robert?"

He groaned, rubbing his face. "Is it daytime already?" he said, as if it were a surprise insult, sent personally to slight him.

"It's half past ten." Evelyn crossed to the bed.

Robert struggled into a sitting position. "Half ten? Henry will be climbing the walls."

Evelyn scrutinised him. He seemed like his usual self, not the glassy-eyed stranger from the night before. Her nerves still felt cinched tight, as if it were somehow unsafe to loosen her vigilance against tragedy. It was a feeling that took her back to the bad days. At once, she had an odd smack of memory, the scent of that black dye boiling on the stove.

"I'll send Henry a note to explain about your fever." Evelyn put a hand on his forehead. His skin was cool to the touch. She stroked the side of his face, the crinkles next to his eyes, the freckles on his cheeks, the faint scar across his lips. "Are you feeling better? More like yourself?"

Robert kissed her hand. "I feel like a truant." He pulled back the bedclothes, patting the sheets beside him. "Come along," he said, smiling his lopsided smile.

Evelyn's heart squeezed. She kicked off her slippers and wriggled in beside him. He smelt of sweat, earthy and rich, like dirty chestnuts, but Evelyn let him embrace her, the crush of his body on hers, his damp undershirt against her silk pajamas.

"I'm tired," he said, finally.

"I'm not surprised." She hesitated, unsure if she should even mention it. "Do you remember waking up earlier?"

"I did? Was I snoring?"

"No." She shifted her weight onto her elbows. "You were walking around. You found an earring."

"An earring?"

"Yes. You got out of bed, pulled up the floorboard."

"Oh!" He smiled. "Yes, that. The earring. It was winking at me."

She stared at him. "And you didn't—you didn't—put it there yourself, did you?" Her cheeks were hot.

"Why would I do that?"

She faltered. The idea that he could be hoaxing her was impossible. "I don't know," she said.

Robert yawned. "The spirits must have told me it was there."

A lurch of vomit rose into her throat. His expression was calm, relaxed, as if he had been commenting on the football scores. Evelyn sat up, wrapping her arms around her waist. She wanted to cry. Robert was rummaging in his bedside drawer and pulled out a blue journal. "On that subject, I'd like to take you somewhere," he said, withdrawing a folded piece of paper from the journal and handing it to her. It was a poorly mimeographed pamphlet illustrated with a cheerful bunch of flowers: *Spiritualist Library and Psychical Research Centre.*

"What is this?" She tried to hold the leaflet steady in her hands.

"Exactly what it says! And it's only on Dundas Street." Robert gestured for her to unfold the leaflet. "What do you think?" he said.

Inside was a picture of a reading room equipped with sturdy chairs below shelves of hardback books. A menu on the right-hand side advertised the tea items on offer between the hours of noon and 4:00 PM. Evelyn tried to compose a response that would acknowledge Robert's interest, without committing any credence to it. After a moment, she said, "The price of currant buns is very reasonable."

Robert laughed, nuzzling her hair. "I should have known the tea cakes are all you care about, Evie." He pulled her to him, and she let him clasp her. Her eyes stung.

"How long have you been going there?"

"A few weeks, I suppose. It's been so useful. I've learned so much about the other side."

A bolt of terror ran through her. She clenched her buttocks together as if somehow it would clamp down the awfulness.

She tried to make her voice neutral. "Why didn't you mention it?"

Robert patted her. "You know how you get, Evie. I didn't want you to have the wrong idea."

"And what's the right idea?" she said, weakly.

"They have a spirit photographer coming next week to give a talk. You should see the pictures—in one of them, a white hand is coming right out of the table."

She had a flash of inspiration. "Somebody has been talking you into this, haven't they? Who gave you the idea, someone from the allotments?"

"No, no, I've been going on my own. But not anymore. You can come with me, now."

Evelyn stared at him.

"I'm so glad to be able to tell you all about this," Robert said, kissing the back of her hand. "Not being able to say anything, I felt awful. Creeping around. I didn't *want* to—"

"Lie to me," she filled in.

He had the decency to blush, the tips of his ears reddening. "I just left something out. I'd never deliberately lie to you, Evie. Leaving something out, it's not the same, is it, as lying?"

Evelyn's pulse picked up. "It's not the same, no." Her voice was level and straight; she congratulated herself on how normal she sounded. "Omission is not the same as a lie."

Robert let out a breath. "I knew you would understand. And now I can tell you everything, you can't imagine—it's such a relief not to be keeping anything from you."

Evelyn avoided his eye.

"All the things I've discovered, Evie, it's amazing! In one of the sessions, the planchette was spinning by itself on the table. It spelled out my own name, right there. But you can see for yourself."

A peppery, panicky horror tickled her stomach. "Robert, no, that's not—I don't—"

"There's demonstrations each week and each medium has their own speciality. Telling the future, or knowing your medical history."

"What if someone from work sees you there? Wouldn't they find that"—she hesitated—"questionable?"

Robert shrugged. "If someone from work is visiting the Spiritualist Library, they'll be doing their own questioning." Then he laughed. He stopped laughing, then began laughing again.

"But you're supposed to rest," Evelyn said.

Robert grinned. "What's more restful than a library?"

"Dr. Greitzer, yesterday, he gave me strict orders to keep you in bed." She paused. "He's worried about your heart."

"He is? But I feel fine. I feel better than I have in years, Evie. Years!"

"No, Robert, I can't allow it. Not with your heart. You need rest, not getting—getting—ideas. I won't allow it."

Robert looked up at her, his eyebrows drawn together. "You don't mean it? Oh, but, please, I . . ." His face was a very picture of piteousness, a trampled puppy, a wounded butterfly.

Evelyn's tongue felt thick, the inside of her mouth grainy. She pinched the skin on the back of her hand so she wouldn't cry. "Perhaps, when you've recovered. Some other day. Maybe."

Robert's face broke into a joyous smile, and a bitter sting pierced her chest. How happy she was to see his happiness. How much it was going to cost her.

"Yes, sir, Captain Evie," he said, saluting.

Evelyn closed the bedroom door and walked two steps down the stairs until she could catch the light from the hallway window. On the back of the leaflet, in Robert's neat handwriting: "Manifestachions in the mirror have bad intent?" he had written. "Hearing voices of the future dead." She almost tripped on the loose floorboard. Robert couldn't really believe in all that? In boards and candles, in conjuring apparitions? After Jock McClinnock died in the trenches at Vimy Ridge, old Mrs. McClinnock had gone a bit queer. Started visiting a medium in a horrible tenement near the Cowgate, dressing all in muslin, insisting that she was speaking to Jock each fortnight from heaven, where he gave her tips on the races that never came out right. She tried to remember, had Robert taken an unusual interest at the time? No—nobody had. They'd all just politely nodded when Mrs. McClinnock, spectrally swaddled, appeared at dinner parties, and stopped inviting her to funerals. As far as she could remember, Evelyn had never even seen Robert and Mrs. McClinnock speaking to each other. Evelyn paced around the hallway chair, laying all the tassels on the table sham until they lined up perfectly.

Dr. Greitzer's tripartite prognosis rang in her head: insane, fraud, truth. Surely there must be other possibilities? What if Robert was only pretending—but then, that would be fraud. What if he was imagining and—but who imagined *spirits*? Only prophets and maniacs! Evelyn chewed on her finger, running her tongue over the jagged end of her nail. She was seized with one of her sudden, mad impulses to telephone Dolores. Dolly would be halfway through a

Chelsea bun, smacking her lips into the receiver: "So divorce him. It's not so bad, like pulling out a splinter."

Evelyn's face burned. She put her hands to her cheeks to cool them, her right index finger wet against her skin. She wasn't going to divorce Robert. Was she? Was this the sort of thing one divorced over? She'd have to crop her hair, become one of those shingle and bingle girls, take up smoking cigars. Tears were prickling in her eyes, and she rubbed them with the back of her sleeve. No, she couldn't divorce him. It had been all very well for Dolores. Not even Mama and Papa had expected much from Dolores.

Evelyn felt in her pocket for the earring, twirling the gem between her fingers. She dug the stud into her fingertip. The snaky sense of dread lurking in her stomach slithered heavily through her insides. Dolores. If Robert really did have a gift—if it was even remotely possible, if there was even the smallest chance—what if he *could* talk to her? What if he spoke to her, and what if she told him everything?

3

ROBERT WAS WHISTLING AS HE LEFT THE HOUSE THE next day, and Evelyn waited until the refrain of "Dancing Time" had drifted down the street before following him. She pulled her hat low, wrapped a black scarf around her shoulders, and stepped onto the pavement. He was walking at a smart pace, and she struggled to keep up, pausing for breath behind postboxes and lampposts. When he rang the bell at the library's pale blue door on Dundas Street, Evelyn concealed herself at the tram stop until it had closed behind him. A thought struck her—suppose this was all some elaborate cover for an illicit liaison? Evelyn's own face leered at her, crooked and bulbous, in the library's metal door handle. It was better to know, wasn't it? Robert, smiling at a woman, a redhead with tumbling curls. A sentimental type, who recited poetry. But even as she tried to conjure this foe, the nightmare crumbled. Not her Robert. Although phantoms were hardly "her Robert" either. She took a deep breath, and rang the bell. A few moments later, the door was opened by a petite and ashy-coloured young woman with a sharp parting along the centre of her scalp. In her grey smock and scuffed brown oxfords, she looked so like a beleaguered governess that Evelyn's fears of seduction were assuaged.

"Are you visiting the library?" the woman said.

"I think I saw someone I know, a man. Mr. Hazard. He's here, is he?"

"That's right." The woman's face assumed a bland sort of cheerfulness. Evelyn inspected her for any evidence of tumbling curls or poetic sensibilities as the woman pulled back her sleeve to consult her wristwatch. "Yes, Mr. Hazard's attending the one o'clock demonstration. I'm afraid it's too late to join, but if it's urgent, I could put a slip under the door to let him know you're here?"

Evelyn squeaked. "No, don't do that!"

"You could come in, wait for him upstairs?"

Evelyn licked her lips. Surely the woman wouldn't be so guileless if she were hiding something. "Can I look around the—um, the library?"

"Absolutely." The woman smiled.

Evelyn nodded. Now that her pulse had settled, she felt distinctly unwell, limp and soft, like an old tulip. "Yes, I suppose I should."

"The tea shop will open in half an hour," the woman said. The corridor was so narrow, she had to climb back up the staircase to let Evelyn through the door. "I'm Miss Frelinski, the librarian. Geraldine."

Admitting, out loud, to a stranger, that she was spying on her own husband was so impossible that she hesitated for a moment. "Hawk," she said. "Mrs. Hawk."

Evelyn followed Geraldine up the stairs, pulling herself along the banister rail since the steps were too steep to be managed comfortably.

At the top of the stairs were two doors facing each other on a narrow landing. The left door was labelled "Meeting Room" with a brass plaque.

"Is that where the—session—is taking place? Where Mr. Hazard is?"

"Yes," Geraldine said.

Evelyn loitered. Through the door, she could hear Robert's voice. "And who is he talking to?" she said.

Geraldine blinked at her. "The spirits, I imagine."

Evelyn's throat squeezed. "Can you—do you hear them talking back?"

"I don't sit in on demonstrations during work hours, but the Spiritualist Hall regularly invites mediums on the weekends," Geraldine said. "I'd be happy to give you a leaflet, if you like?"

"Not necessary, thank you," Evelyn said. She shook herself. Talking back. What was she thinking!

With a bob of the head, Geraldine took a right through a door marked "Research Centre," which opened onto a suite of rooms. Immediately in front of them was a receptionist's desk and a tea station along the right-hand wall, with two circular tables either side. Geraldine took a seat behind the desk. To Evelyn's eye, it was reassuringly banal. A paperweight hewn out of flint secured a paper file labelled "December" and a brochure advertising a sale at a Princes Street milliners. A commemorative mug from the opening of the George Street Hotel held a bundle of sharpened pencils. With a start, Evelyn realised that Kitty owned the same mug. Geraldine opened a leather-bound ledger and retrieved one of the pencils.

"Is it H-A-W-K?" she said.

Evelyn stared at her.

"Like the bird?"

She nodded, and watched Geraldine write the time and date, and then "Mrs. Hawk" in neat capital letters. Geraldine nudged the book towards her and indicated where Evelyn should sign herself in. There, above her, was Robert's name. Evelyn improvised an illegible scribble.

Geraldine smiled, revealing white but crooked teeth. "Have you visited us before?"

"No, I have not."

"These are the tea rooms." Geraldine gestured to the gleaming trolley. "And the tea matron." She dropped in a little curtsy Evelyn supposed she was meant to find amusing.

"Ha," she said, instead of laughing.

"The research centre is next door." Geraldine walked Evelyn to the doorway. Rows of dun-coloured hardbacks lined the walls, and on the left was a recently whitewashed stucco fireplace, over which an oak school clock was ticking. There were two long tables by the window with mismatched pencils propped in the inkwells. Evelyn nodded along as Geraldine explained how to search through the catalogue cards, how to fill in a request slip. A matronly-looking woman in an oilskin raincoat was sitting at one of the tables by the window, reading a book entitled *A Discourse on Witchcraft*.

"I hope that won't be a problem?" Geraldine was saying.

"Pardon?"

"The rule forbidding ink."

"No, that's fine."

"Can I help you to locate some material? Is there a particular volume you're looking for today?"

"I'm not sure," Evelyn said, shifting her weight. "I'm not sure what I'm looking for." She wiped her face. Why *had* she come here? What had she been expecting to find?

"I'll leave you to peruse the catalogue." Geraldine flashed her a crooked smile. She turned back towards the receptionist's desk.

"Wait," Evelyn said. She leant forward and lowered her voice. "The material here," she said, fiddling with her collar, "what is it about, exactly?"

Geraldine's eyes grew vacant, and she stared into the middle distance. "Amathomancy, angels, astral bodies, auras, automatic writing, brownies." She took a wet, rattling breath, and continued. "Claircognizance, clairsentience, clairvoyance, demons, dowsing—"

"Ghosts," Evelyn interrupted.

"Pardon?"

"What about ghosts? People who think they talk to ghosts."

Geraldine gave her a knowing nod. "I see." She walked to the left of the doorway, and Evelyn thought for a moment she was about to be escorted away from the property. But Geraldine beckoned her over.

"Perhaps," Geraldine said, "you'd like to start here. This is our museum." She was pointing to a stained walnut cabinet with a glass door.

"Lovely," said Evelyn, since Geraldine seemed to be waiting for a reaction.

"We have a few rare items on display here you might find of interest. Many researchers visit the centre specially to see the Ouija board and planchette owned by Douglas Fenwick himself." Geraldine paused and watched Evelyn expectantly.

"Marvellous," Evelyn supplied.

"Here you will find a section of the table used during Madame Sousa's first performance in Edinburgh." Geraldine pointed at a piece of wood that had been clumsily sawn along the joist. "Field Marshal McWillis was in attendance at that particular meeting," she said.

"Is that so?" Evelyn said, mildly.

Geraldine sighed. "We used to have on display a box containing ectoplasm expressed by Madame Sousa here as well, but it's terribly fragile, and people *would* insist on trying to touch it." She shook her head. "We had to move it to the cellar."

"Ectoplasm," Evelyn repeated. The word squirmed in her stomach like a belly full of tadpoles. It evoked cold jellies and stained sheets and cottage cheese. "And that?" She pointed wildly into the corner of the lower shelf, simply to move the conversation forward.

Geraldine shot her a quizzical, evaluative look. "That is a dead moth."

"Thank you," Evelyn said. She turned towards the closest table. "I'll be fine for a minute."

"You don't need any further direction?"

"No thank you, thank you." Evelyn lowered herself into a chair. She heard Geraldine walk into the other room and, shortly, the rattle of teacups on wood. What was Robert *doing* when he came here? What was he doing, now? She pictured him through the wall, hunched over a table, a planchette on the table spinning, scrawling her name. She rubbed her forehead with the back of her hand.

"I know you." The woman in the raincoat leant over.

Instinctively, Evelyn shrank back. "I doubt it."

The woman peered at her over the top of her glasses. "We've spoken a few times at the suffragette rallies."

Evelyn shook her head, relieved that she decisively could rule out knowing anyone who might be discovered reading a book about witchcraft.

The woman pushed her glasses farther up her nose. "No, I *do* know you. You read that letter to the prime minister at the Grassmarket."

Evelyn's stomach flipped. "That was my older sister. Not me."

"Are you sure?" the woman said, frowning.

"Quite sure."

The woman's expression became annoyed, as if Evelyn were deliberately trying to trammel her. "Unfortunate."

Evelyn didn't know how to respond to that.

"Does your sister join you here ever? I'd love to talk to her about the society's new petition. I can't recall her name, Dorothy?"

Evelyn gave her a long look, trying to evaluate if it was worthwhile peeling off a layer of her heart to converse with this strange woman, in this strange place. The awkwardness, the pity. The surprise that Dolly had caught the flu so late, after the worst of it was supposed to be over. The list of other acquaintances who had also died from the flu that people felt compelled, for some reason, to provide, when she told them what had happened. Adding their own tragedies as if they were supposed to accompany her own. "No, she does not," Evelyn said, eventually. "She does not come here. Have a nice afternoon."

She sat back in the chair. Her ears were ringing, the room felt overheated, and she tugged at the stays of her bust bodice. The mention of Dolores in this place had jiggled her pulse in odd directions.

She grabbed a pencil from the inkwell and clasped it hard enough between her fingers that it dug into her skin. Satisfied that the woman had returned to her book, Evelyn stood and opened the drawer in the catalogue under "G–I." She located "Ghosts, apparitions of." There was a bewildering list of titles, and she selected one in the middle, written by Leonard, Jonathan, Sir. Surely, a book written by a "Sir" couldn't be too indelicate? She found the book on a low shelf beside the mantelpiece, and opened it at random. "The spirits know the darkest corners of our minds; they will confirm themselves by revealing information that is known only to the sitter . . ."

Evelyn closed the book with a snap. A drop of sweat dripped under her bust bodice. It wasn't true, it wasn't true it wasn't true. No one could read the thoughts of anyone else; nobody, dead or alive, could see into her mind or plunge into her thoughts. It was all make-believe, silliness. No one could find information out from the dead.

She crossed the room and snatched up her coat and hat.

Geraldine was adjusting a lace doily on one of the tea tables and glanced up at her, surprised. "Mrs. Hawk, are you leaving us?"

"I forgot," said Evelyn, hurrying herself into her coat. "I have an appointment. Sorry. Goodbye." Evelyn raced through the door, onto the narrow landing, and down the stairs.

"Will you sign yourself out?" Geraldine called.

"Sorry, thank you," Evelyn said, over her shoulder. "Thank you. Sorry. Goodbye." She wrenched open the front door and strode into the street. It was cold, gloriously cold, with peachy afternoon light stretching shadows across the cobbles. Seagulls wheeled through the rowan trees, and Evelyn picked up her pace until she was almost running. Halfway across the bridge home, she looked down and, with some surprise, discovered that she was still holding the book. With a flick of the wrist, she tossed it into the air, and it caught a flutter of sunlight before bubbling under the dark green Waters of Leith.

4

AS MARTY BEGAN HER MIDWEEK CLEANING ROUTINE, Evelyn supervised from the bottom of the staircase.

"Yes, that's the one," Evelyn said, as Marty leant over the banister and punctured the spider's web with her duster. "And would you mind checking between the floorboards later today?"

Marty frowned. "The floorboards, ma'am?"

"Yes." Evelyn was aware she was blinking a little too fast. "Yes, just a wee peek between the floorboards. Anything you find down there, put to one side and I'll look through it later." As Marty climbed the stairs, Evelyn called, "Will you take extra care to search the bedroom?"

Marty didn't reply, and Evelyn considered repeating her request, but Marty's silence had a deliberate quality to it, so she decided to say nothing.

In the parlour, Evelyn pinned the curtains back, poked the grate, and adjusted the clock on the mantelpiece. Pulling her shoulder blades together, she sat at her desk, laying out her pen and her letter opener. She drew a week's worth of unanswered post from her drawer and arranged it in a neat pile. With the sort of heralding throat-clear that announces a long task, she set herself to begin a reply to Marion Mackenzie, who had written from her motor tour of Belgian battlefields. But when Evelyn put her pen to the paper to formulate a polite response to Marion's laments about heavy sauces and crumbling soap, all she could think of was Robert, in a locked, dark room, whispering. Evelyn listened for Marty's footsteps upstairs before picking up the telephone in the corridor and requesting the extension for Robert's office.

It was Henry, Robert's partner, who answered. "Oh, good morning." Evelyn shuffled from foot to foot. "Is Robert not there?"

"He's here, with a client," Henry said.

"He arrived at work on time, he wasn't late?"

"No, he wasn't late. Everything OK, Evelyn?"

"All fabulous. Just fabulous. I was only calling because"—she thought wildly—"um, gosh, do you hear that?"

"Pardon?"

"The static on the line is terrible." Evelyn rustled her sleeve over the receiver.

The operator's voice cut in. "Would you like a new connection?"

"Evelyn? Are you still there?" Henry was saying.

Evelyn thrust the earpiece in the cradle, her face burning. She slunk back to her desk. Her reply to Marion had dried now; she'd have to start the whole thing again, or Marion would know from the ink that she'd taken a break in the middle. She put the letter aside. Next in the pile was an advertisement for a sale at Menzies bookstall. After that, an invitation to the baptism of Susan and Andrew Reid's baby, complete with an illustrated notecard of their rumpled and unattractive offspring. Evelyn scrutinised the picture. Imagine producing such homely progeny that even an *illustration* couldn't improve its appearance. There was a notice on their account from Jenners, which she set aside for Robert. And then a disgruntled postcard from Auntie Maude, who was on a tour of medieval architecture and, as far as Evelyn could tell, using the opportunity to object to the price of admission. Evelyn flipped the postcard over and her breath caught in her throat. Whitby Abbey glowered over a ripple of custard-coloured sand. Along the shoreline, day-trippers paddled in the water, and farther out, past the shallows, bathing machines had been rolled into the waves.

Her bathing machine was stippled with afternoon sun, the jay feather threaded through a pin on the curtain. His fingers were tracing her breasts, her skin a startling white against the gold of his hands. He brushed fine Whitby sand from the nape of her neck, kissing her ears, her shoulders, the hollow between her breasts where salt water had pooled. If only she had known then what those liaisons would lead to, she would never have unhooked one single button of her dress.

"Will you have your tea now, Mrs. Hazard?" Marty was standing behind her, carrying a tray. Evelyn yelped. Her pen had left a bubble of ink on the postcard. She threw the card back in her drawer and hastily relocated to an armchair by the fireplace. Marty put the cup down too hard; tea slopped over the rim and into the saucer. The aggrieved expression on her face let Evelyn know she must have been standing behind her for some moments without acknowledgement.

"Thank you, Marty," she said.

"Hmm," Marty replied. Evelyn summoned her most appreciative smile, nonetheless. Allowing Marty to bully her was part of a domestic synchronicity developed over many years. As Marty turned to leave the room, Evelyn suddenly didn't want to be alone.

"Tell me, how is your mother?" she called.

Marty paused at the doorway. "Not good, ma'am."

"I'm sorry to hear that. Come, sit with me." Evelyn gestured to the chaise longue. Marty glanced at it suspiciously. As a matter of principle, Marty snubbed padding, wadding, and cushioning of all kinds, deeming soft seating receptacles a papish sort of indulgence, befitting invalids and inbred European nobility of questionable morals. "I'd be happy to send Dr. Greitzer," Evelyn said. "On our account, naturally."

Marty sat on the chaise longue with the trace of a sneer, as if she were lowering her shoe slowly into manure. "The doctor won't help," she said.

"He won't?" A guilty zing of reprieve nipped through Evelyn's veins—she wouldn't have to face Dr. Greitzer again so soon.

Marty shook her head. "No, ma'am. It's rheumatism."

"Sounds terrible," Evelyn said. She had no idea what rheumatism really entailed, but solicitude to illness was a guaranteed means of camaraderie with Marty.

Marty's eyes lit up. "That it is, ma'am. It's awful painful. Your joints all swell in your hips and your knuckles. And especially when it's cold, or damp."

"Oh dear."

"And my mother suffers from it even more because of her gout."

Evelyn recalled a cruel caricature of Prime Minister Baldwin from a political magazine, dangling gout-stricken swollen toes into the Irish Sea. "I thought gout was a disease of sultans and child emperors," Evelyn said, before cursing herself.

Marty's eyes narrowed. "And decent, hardworking folk too. It's crystals in the blood, that's what people say."

Evelyn pictured the crystal chandelier at Mairibank, how it threw shimmering, rainbow-coloured bubbles onto the skirting board in the dining room. How often she and Dolly had spent Sunday afternoons trying to catch them in their palms.

"Anything else I can help you with, ma'am?" Marty's voice snapped Evelyn out of her daydream. She was now standing by the door, arms folded.

"No, thank you," Evelyn said timidly.

When the buff and scrape of Marty's scrub brush echoed along the corridor, Evelyn relaxed back into the armchair. She lifted her cup of tea, staring at a spot underneath their Japanese print where the wallpaper had blistered. There was a looping wind complaining against the windows, and the curtains stirred. Evelyn's heart jittered. She swallowed her tea in one scalding mouthful.

Robert.

There it was: a hard lump of horror in her stomach. And not even the familiar horror she had grown accustomed to over the last few years. This was a novel, grotesque horror. Robert, who called his chickens by nicknames, who could mend a bicycle and chop wood, and who ate blackberries right off the bush. Robert, who complained the cinema was too loud, who had knocked a tooth loose on cinder toffee. Robert, scrabbling between the floorboards in the dark.

Evelyn waited until she heard the pipes running in the scullery, then crossed the corridor and let herself into Robert's study. The new rug looked darling. Prussian blue, the woman had called it. It caught all the hues of aquamarine in the wallpaper. Then she came to herself and shut the door.

The room appeared normal. It hadn't, at least, transformed over-night into a den of horrors: a severed ram's head bleeding on the floor in a circle of candle stubs, crude pagan symbols chalked onto the mirror. There were no obvious signs of dementedness. Or maybe that was worse? Maybe the madness was all secreted away. There would be a box full of hair, a dried rose with a pin stuck through it. She shivered. Evelyn poked among the books on his shelf: field guides to wildflowers, semaphore signals, heraldry. All as usual. No runes or turbans or crystals. Nothing to indicate, at least, that he was trying to summon the dead in their home. She checked the mahogany cabinet in the corner that contained his boyhood relics: a cigar box of arrowheads, a pair of shattered binoculars he had won at a church raffle. His orphanage school photo was in its usual spot, discreetly obscured by a hatstand, Robert in the back row, his elbow poking out at an angle. The scar across his lips was a fresh mark then—a relic from a neighbourhood scuffle that Robert didn't like to talk about.

Evelyn sat in his armchair and dug behind the cushions. A penny. A lemon drop wrapped in wax paper. She took a long look at his desk. While searching for a tape measure last year, she had found in his bottom left-hand drawer a postcard book of women dressed, or rather, undressed, in a series of unconvincing costumes, as cowgirls and Dutch dairymaids. She pulled open this drawer now. Underneath a half-eaten packet of Valetta biscuits was a hardback library book, *Conferences with Angels*. Evelyn opened it, and yes, the flyleaf was stamped from the Spiritualist Library. Passages had been lightly underlined in grease pencil. An envelope in between the pages bore Robert's handwriting: "Angles protect and watch over innocents— children and babies. Are spirit guides a type of angle?" She put it down, a bayonet through her chest. Robert, wishing for guides, for angels? Evelyn rested her head on the cold wood of the desk.

As a young girl, ghosts were cloaked women that walked on moonlit nights through ruined bothies. Dukes who had strangled their mistresses. An echoing battle cry across Drumossie Moor on a frosty morning. But now, a ghost was something different. The scent of Dolly's soap on the tram. Shiny headstones on empty graves. Jimmy's fractured pocket watch in a box on Mrs. McLaren's mantelpiece. Beds dressed in stale linens in shut-up rooms. The blacked-out telephone numbers in her address book. Ghosts were in every corner of every room. That Robert would want to go hunting for spirit guides, for angels, for answers—it wasn't just insane, it was idiotic. He had misunderstood. He had fundamentally misunderstood death.

Evelyn was overcome with pity for him. Poor, lovely Robert, who wanted to be special enough to get answers from angels. She rubbed her forehead. She hadn't been giving him enough attention. She'd belittled him in some subtle way that men were sensitive to. And now he wanted to play wizard by searching out thin places and knocking on them. It crystallised before her like an icy puddle: wishing. Dr. Greitzer had missed that out of his prophecy. Robert wasn't insane, or a fraud. And he wasn't communicating with the dead. Robert was inventing angels because he wished to be special, to be powerful enough to get answers where there were none.

Evelyn looked again at the flyleaf of the book. Likely, the library had been encouraging him, putting ideas in his head, when there wasn't an awful lot of space in there to begin with. But it didn't matter. Evelyn snapped the book shut. Spirits weren't real, only a mixture of coincidence and suggestion. Robert just needed to be guided to understand that himself, and all the nonsense would go away.

5

AS THEY LEFT THE ZOO THAT SATURDAY, ROBERT PAUSED.
"We never saw the wallabies!"

"We can go back if you like?" Evelyn crossed her fingers in her
pockets. The soles of her feet were aching, and she dreaded the
thought of even more walking. But then the purpose of the visit had
been distraction, diversion, and redirection, and wallabies were as
good a tactic as any.

Robert looked her over, then held an experimental palm to the
sky. "No, it's starting to rain, isn't it? We can see them next time."
He kissed her on the cheek. "You know, I always wondered about
wallabies. Since they come from Australia, they must think *we're*
upside down."

"I suppose," Evelyn said distractedly. There was a column of
people crawling up the hill, a loose, poorly organised formation,
something more French than a line; a mélange, perhaps. Was there a
football match tonight?

"There was a boy in the orphanage who swore he was secretly the
prince of Australia," Robert said.

Evelyn looked at him. "Oh." She waited, in case he wanted to
say more.

"He insisted that one day they'd come and take him back in a
golden steamship." He laughed, ruefully.

She touched his hand.

"As if a golden steamship would make up for leaving him at St. Ternan's in the first place," Robert said. He kicked a loose pebble, and it bounced along the walkway and clattered against the gates. "Children want to forgive, that's the worst part. The hoping."

Evelyn turned away from him. She closed her eyes, focusing on the tap of rain on the path, the distant sound of animals chirruping from their darkening enclosures. She waited for the spasm to pass. It wasn't her fault. She was young, she had done the right thing; it wasn't her fault.

When she turned back, Robert was inspecting a handbill posted by the gates. She joined him, relieved for a change in subject. But her relief was short-lived. The poster was advertising "An Evening of Mystical Entertainment with Mistress Zaina" at the zoo caravanserai at 4:00 PM. In the image, "Mistress Zaina" was swathed in a scarlet gown, silver earrings dangling from her lobes. Beneath her, vaporous arms reached through a shattered coffin to caress her beturbaned head.

"Mistress Zaina is supposed to be amazing," Robert said, wiping a raindrop from the end of his nose. "She had a prophetic dream about Gretna, you know. And in the summer, she predicted the Redding pit disaster, she warned everyone about the flooding."

Evelyn tuned out. She lifted herself above her body and floated into the lights of the Pentland Hills, weaving between the knots of smoke tethered above the chimney pots.

"Of course, they all still died," Robert was saying.

"Hmm," Evelyn said. A thought struck her: the longer they lingered, the greater the danger that Robert would suggest joining the séance. "This rain is picking up, shall we go home?"

Robert nodded, shooting a regretful look at the poster.

Rain drummed on Evelyn's hat as she followed him through the crowd thronging up the hill. Toothless men with dirty, chapped hands were spitting tobacco juice into the gutter. Ex-servicemen wielded bottles of Drambuie. They had that grimy, temporary-housing look about them; likely they'd come from the Meadowbank hutments. There was a flash of a white apron underneath a woman's coat. Evelyn heard her mother's voice in her head: "Purse closer to your person." She raised her chin, trying to banish the whisper. A skinny teenage girl sheltering a stack of paper under an umbrella caught Evelyn's eye.

"Are you going to the show?" The girl looked Evelyn's beaver-fur coat up and down.

"No," Evelyn said, gratified that her outfit had put her attendance in question. Farther down the hill, the back of Robert's head disappeared into the crowd. "I must be on my way, good evening."

An odd expression crossed the girl's face, a sort of desperate resolve. "It's not too late," she said, thrusting a pamphlet into Evelyn's hand. A drop of water fell from the girl's umbrella onto the leaflet, where a macabre illustration depicted a turbaned woman grimacing in the fires of hell. In smudged type, it read: "Resist devilry, come to the Corstorphine New Parish Church and repent."

Evelyn looked from the paper to the girl's face. Her eyebrows were uneven, her lips had been nibbled. A hot spurt of shame bubbled inside Evelyn's stomach. "No thank you." She tried to give the paper back, but the girl stepped away.

"Please," she said. "Promise me you'll look at it. There's illustrations, everything all explained."

"I don't need pictures," Evelyn said, tersely. "I can read perfectly well, and I am not attending the show." She held out the leaflet.

The girl cocked her umbrella, leering close enough that Evelyn could see the bite marks on her lips. "Leviticus 20:6: 'The soul that turneth after mediums and spiritists, the soul who whores himself by following them, I will cut him off from his people,'" she said. Her voice was shrill in the air; people were turning to look.

With a violence that surprised even her, Evelyn threw the leaflet at the girl and fled through the crowd. She dodged vendors selling wooden fumsup dolls, children carrying footballs. The rain was slamming down on the pavement now, gathering detritus in grimy chutes that gurgled into the gutters. Robert's coat and hat appeared ahead through the veil of water. He was opening the door to a pub on the corner; he must be trying to shelter from the rain. Evelyn called after him, but he didn't seem to hear. She stumbled through the pub door into a warm fug of hops and cigarette smoke. When she smacked open the next door into the bar, a man who was not Robert blinked back at her in the reflection of the brass-trimmed mirror. The barman lowered his rag. "Do you need help, ma'am?"

Evelyn froze. "I'm sorry, I thought I saw someone else." She backed into the hallway, where an amber globe bulb overhead lay a medallion of light on the damp carpet. Her eyes stung, her mind whirling. The front door swung open, and Robert stepped into the vestibule.

"There you are," he said, with a bemused smile.

She knew she should be relieved to see him, but her body felt numb, as if she were wearing such a heavy cloak of shame that every other sensation was suppressed.

"One minute you were behind me, the next you were charging in here. Thirsty for a pint, are you?"

"I can't bear it. The séances." The words left her mouth before she had time to consider them.

Robert released a breath. "I had a feeling that was upsetting you."

"Of course it's upsetting me!"

He stepped closer, and under the circle of light, the tip of his nose was pink. "I know you don't like to talk about these things." He tucked a lock of hair behind her ear, and Evelyn wriggled away.

"Robert," she said.

He dropped his hand. "What is it that bothers you?"

Evelyn shook her head, unsure even how to begin. She gestured to the street outside. "For a start, it's so clearly a sham—taking ordinary people's hard-earned money!"

Robert shrugged. "What's a few pennies to speak to your loved ones again? You wouldn't care how much it cost if you got to talk to your sister."

"Don't." Evelyn put up her hand. This dingy hallway was not the place to invoke Dolores.

"But it might even be good for you, Evie. It's not healthy to carry grief."

Evelyn fixed him with a fierce look. He should know better. There were subjects that stayed unspoken between them; it was like violating a truce. She felt an urge to be cruel, to return the trespass. "Is this your way of trying to learn about your parents?"

Robert flinched. "Why would I care to know *anything* about those people?"

"If you want to find information on where you came from, I can help you do it properly. We can start with your family name, consult the archives—"

"Evelyn." Robert cut her off. "Hazard was the surname of the headmaster. Half the boys there were called Hazard."

Evelyn winced. She had never thought about that before.

"I know I came from people who threw me away like scrap," Robert said. His voice was even. "I don't need to learn any more."

Her shame tangled inside her in long snarls; she wished she could take it back. They stood in silence. A bead of rain dropped from the brim of Robert's hat. "Is it—is it angels?" she said, at last.

"Angels?"

"That you've been researching? Those trips to the library."

Robert thought for a moment. "In a way, it is."

"You know," she said, and swallowed. "I followed you there." What was she going to confess to next? She had a mad sense of liberty—maybe this terrible moment was no worse than any other.

"What do you mean, you followed me?"

"To the library. I wanted to see for myself the kind of place you were sneaking off to."

Robert's mouth fell open. Disappointment flickered over his face, and Evelyn's heart wobbled. He had never looked at her like that before. She couldn't bear it. She dug her fingernails into her palms, wanting to go back in time to yesterday, last week, back to when they'd first met. To start fresh from the beginning and make it right from the outset.

Robert rocked on his heels. "And did you find an answer?"

"I don't know," she said, weakly.

"You could have just asked me."

Evelyn pressed her palms into her eyes. "These angels, they visit you?"

"I suppose," Robert said. He was quiet, and Evelyn lowered her hands, her vision blurred with orange streaks from the sudden light.

"Tell me," she said.

Robert shifted his weight. "It's like, you know when you put your foot out for one more step, and it's not there?"

"Yes."

"It's like that, only the step isn't a step, it's a person."

Evelyn squinted at him. "On the floor?"

"No." He laughed, softly. "I mean, when your foot drops, you know for sure that the step is there, but then, all at once, it's gone. It's like that."

"But—" She faltered. "With dead people?"

"Yes, with spirits."

Evelyn shivered. "You hear them? The spirits?"

He reached out and gripped her hand. "They want to communicate with us, Evie, to give reassurance, to share messages." Robert's face was strangely blank, like he was wearing a mask of his own features. "I know it's the right thing to do."

"What is?" Evelyn's throat was tight.

His eyes focused on hers. "To help."

"Helping?" She almost choked on the word. "But it's just dredging up misery, reminding people of sad moments. How can *that* help anyone?"

Robert released her hand. His lip twitched. "Why shouldn't I help?"

Outside, Evelyn heard the shrill voice of that girl again, the echo of Leviticus over the rain. To any outside observer, Robert was indistinguishable from the gullible men in cheap boots paying in keepsakes to ward off bad luck. "Why can't you just be—serious?"

"I am serious." Robert was looking at her levelly. "I'm perfectly serious."

"I forbid you," she heard herself saying.

Robert looked as if he'd been slapped.

"I forbid you." Evelyn crossed her arms in front of her body. "From doing this, from talking about it, from any of it." She squeezed her arms tighter until her breath was bundled up tight and warm in her chest.

Robert looked down at the streaks of mud on the doormat.

"What will people say? You already know how—" She stopped herself, just. "Everyone will think you've lost your mind!"

"You forbid me?" Robert said, his eyes liquid.

Evelyn choked back a sob that pulsed in her gullet. "Find another way to help."

He hung his head, rubbing his mouth with his hand.

"The Salvation Army, or—a collection. Ghosts?" She struggled with the word. "No, I can't. I can't."

For a few moments all she could hear was the wet sound of his breathing. Evelyn clutched the fabric of her coat. Was this what divorce felt like? Slowly, Robert stepped towards her. Evelyn bit the inside of her cheek. Tears had gathered in Robert's eyelashes. He held out his arms.

"Evie," he said, in a croaking voice. He gestured for her to come into his embrace.

And although she didn't want to be touching him, she took a step forward and let him hold her.

His hands grasped the back of her head. "OK, my love, OK. It's all right." His voice reverberated through her skull, his cheek hot against her ear.

Evelyn relaxed herself into his body, her breath humid in the folds of Robert's overcoat.

"It's all right, my darling," Robert said. "The last thing I ever want to do is upset you. I won't say anything more. It's all forgotten about. Forget about the whole thing."

6

ON CHRISTMAS MORNING IT TOOK HALF AN HOUR TO coax Robert out of bed, and then another to entice him into his best suit for church. Since they were due to leave the house, it wasn't worth lighting the fire; instead, Evelyn tapped her feet along the corridor to keep warm while they waited for Alistair and Kitty.

"Shall we sing a song until they get here?" she said, checking her reflection again in the mirror. Her chamona suede coat had just come out of storage especially for the day and still smelt of camphor.

Robert shrugged. "If you like."

Evelyn gritted her teeth. It had been three weeks since their ill-fated trip to the zoo, and Robert had been nothing but glum and despondent since then. She was going to wrestle a normal, cheerful Christmas upon them with force, if necessary. "Yes, we must! What's your favourite carol?"

"I don't know," he said.

Evelyn ran through the options in her mind. "In the Bleak Midwinter" was a bit depressing, as was "God Rest Ye Merry Gentlemen." "What about 'Joy to the World'?"

Robert shrugged again.

"Joy to the world! The Lord is come, let earth receive her King," Evelyn began, and then hesitated. "What comes next?"

"Not sure," Robert said.

"Hmm. What about 'Silent Night'?" She looked at him, mustering her most jovial smile. "Or maybe you'd rather a silent morning?"

Robert was staring down the corridor. After a moment, he turned to her. "Sorry, what?"

Evelyn shook her head, trying to submerge her disappointment. What was she supposed to do? She felt a flutter of panic, a horrible sense of him standing on the other side of a faulty bridge. "We're still allies, aren't we?"

His face softened. "Always." He gave her a kiss on her forehead.

The sound of a pram rattled on the pavement, and they opened the door to join Kitty and Alistair. Baby Margaret was dressed in a new cap, and Evelyn admired, privately, how it disguised the unfortunate shape of her head. It was one of those strangely mild days; a wet, salty sea wind was tipping the afternoon over into a fool's thaw that would only fur hoary crusts on the branches by the next day. As they walked along the street, it started to rain with soft, dewy splashes, dissolving the ice in the roads to slush. Robert ducked back into the house to fetch an umbrella, and then, slowly, in deference to Alistair, they began to walk down past the playing fields. Church bells from all over the city startled blackbirds from their roosts; Evelyn followed their arc and chitter as they fluttered from one chimney to another.

"And there's apple cake," Kitty was saying.

"Sounds lovely."

Kitty froze, the wheels of the perambulator squeaking. "Oh no, goose makes you horribly ill! How could I have forgotten?"

Evelyn was admiring the effect of the parade of Christmas trees shining in front windows along the road. "What are you talking about? I had goose last Sunday."

"But—" Kitty's forehead crumpled. "That last year—at Mairibank."

A cold prickle ran over Evelyn's ears. She'd forgotten about that Christmas. None of them had known it was the last year at Mairibank, but they could feel it brewing, the "big move." Papa had been increasingly irritable since Van Schaik and Company collapsed, and Mama was sleeping off headaches more and more. That was the year the stables were sold, and Dolly and Papa argued for hours in his study about her taking up employment. Evelyn had spent the whole of Christmas afternoon being vigorously sick in the bathroom while Dolly patted her, quite ineffectually, on the back. Kitty, only seventeen, was emotionally overwrought since she was preparing for the season, and cried into the pudding, causing a row. Everyone went to bed early.

"Don't worry about that. I've recovered from my goose allergy," Evelyn said.

"Thank goodness!" Kitty kissed her on the cheek.

* * *

BY THE CORNER OF South Trinity Road, a man wearing a shredded army greatcoat was digging out a swollen gutter with his bare hands, his whistle and collection tin abandoned on a postbox. As the churchgoers passed him, he turned to wish them a happy Christmas with a jolly smile. His cheerfulness irked Evelyn, as if it were a deliberate means to illustrate his helpfulness and conviviality. The artifice of it unsettled her, and she had to look away as Robert crossed the street to give the man a crown.

The church was overheated, and a light, dank brume hovered above the pews, a miasma produced by sodden woollen overcoats and umbrellas dripping pools onto the flagstones. Evelyn flinched at each cough and wet sneeze, holding her handkerchief over her nose. She hated church on Christmas Day. It was always crowded and damp, a veritable incubator for influenza. Mrs. Wrigley in the pew in front kept nodding off, the brim of her hat tipping in sudden jolts.

After everyone had sung "Jerusalem" and shaken hands, Evelyn and Kitty stood outside under the umbrella while Robert and Alistair talked with Lieutenant General McGuinness. When the wind picked up, they gave up on the umbrella to shelter under a yew tree, taking turns to roll Margret's perambulator.

Kitty nudged her, pointing to where Mrs. Bridge was shaking a collection tin at the stream of people leaving the church. "Isn't that Mr. Rossi?"

Evelyn squinted. "Surely not. What would he be doing here? Italians are all Catholics, aren't they?"

Kitty shrugged. They were silent for a moment.

"Dolly loved that tobacco of his, the vanilla flavour. Remember, it used to come through the grate in her kitchen?" Kitty was smiling, but her eyes were misty.

Evelyn swallowed against the hard spot in her throat. When she looked over, Kitty was wiping her eyes.

"Don't, please," Evelyn said, her own eyes stinging. She patted Kitty, and over her shoulder, Kitty gave a little cough that was a mushy mixture of sob and laughter.

"Jeanie put her Christmas napkin ring out with the others this morning," Kitty said.

Evelyn hugged her tighter.

"I didn't know what to do with it, I just put it back in the box." With a sharp intake of breath, Kitty straightened up. "I keep thinking Christmas should get easier as time goes on, but . . ."

"I know." Evelyn squeezed her hand. "I know." She willed Kitty to stop, and yet she wanted her to keep talking about Dolly, to reminisce about everything that still felt too raw for Evelyn to volunteer. It was like yearning for a bitter kind of medicine, simultaneously awful and cleansing.

"And our first Christmas with the baby," Kitty glugged on through another bubble of tears. "I keep picturing her in that blue chair, fussing with her."

"She would have done nothing of the sort," Evelyn said, with some effort to get the words out normally. "You know how stiff she was about babies, like she was a field marshal giving them marching orders."

Kitty laughed, a fleck of spit on her lips that she wiped away. "True enough," she said. "Your Robert is the same, now I think of it."

Evelyn was relieved that the criticism had landed on Robert, rather than herself. "Yes, well, looking after children isn't really in Robert's domain."

With a sigh, Kitty blew her nose. She turned her face to Evelyn's for inspection. "Am I blotchy? I don't want Alistair to worry."

"You look like a peach," Evelyn said, taking off her glove to smudge where a tear had traced a line in Kitty's face powder.

❖ ❖ ❖

THEY TOOK THE LONGER route back to Kitty's house, through the grove of cedar trees that arched over the kirkyard. Melting snow trapped in the branches trickled upon their hats, and clementine peel lay discarded in the wet grass, evidence that someone had started their Christmas feast early. Robert was meek and affectionate, like a poorly animal that seeks doleful comfort in its keeper. He slipped his hand into her coat pocket, and she squeezed each of his fingers in turn. Evelyn snuck a look at him out of the corner of her eye. If there was ever a day to see ghosts, it was Christmas. All the people who would be looking at the extra chair around their tables, reflexively keeping the white meat aside for a person who was no longer there to savour it. Empty stocking pegs on the fireplace, doors closed on empty rooms.

Robert's breath was steamy in the cold air. "Penny for your thoughts?" he said.

She pictured Dolores, walking on the other side of Robert, sliding on the grass because she refused to have her boots resoled. Four Christmases now without her, like she was growing smaller in the rearview mirror of a motorcar. Evelyn bit the inside of her cheek. "No thoughts," she said.

"As usual then," Robert said. He gave her a feeble smile that somehow only made her feel sadder.

Kitty's house was ablaze with candles and rich with the scent of roasting goose and Orkney butter. It was fearsomely hot, and Jeanie had polished the floors so conscientiously that Evelyn's boots left tracks in the varnish.

Evelyn was sat next to Alistair at the lunch table, and she let him tell her all about the Halibut Treaty even though she'd read the exact article in the *Scotsman* that he was drawing his quotes from. All the while Alistair was talking, she was watching Robert at the opposite place. He cut his goose into precise cubes and then put his knife and fork back on the table. Kitty was explaining, at some length, the benefits of fresh air for babies, so Evelyn couldn't blame him for seeming uninterested, but he spent the whole meal staring out of the bay windows and wasn't even pretending to listen.

The doorbell rang as they were eating Christmas pudding, and Kitty tossed the silver sixpence she had excavated onto the tablecloth and ran to the door.

"Your feet are bare, Katherine," Papa said, embracing Kitty. She rolled her eyes over his shoulder as he turned to hug Evelyn.

Mama was wearing her Butterick coat with the antelope fur collar, so Evelyn knew she would be in an exhausted, tragic temper. And sure enough, she handed her hat to Jeanie with a dramatic flourish. "Bring me some brandy, will you, Jeanie? I need to be revived after this afternoon's ordeal." She turned to Evelyn and put her gloved hands either side of her face. "Evelyn, your hair."

Evelyn touched her hair self-consciously. "What about it?"

"It's different," Mama said, planting a kiss on her cheek. She kissed Kitty, before patting her aside and launching at baby Margaret, who was wriggling in Abigail's arms. "There she is, the wee princess!"

In the parlour, the baby was passed from nursemaid to knee while Mama fussed over the placement of the buttons on her smock. "Really, Katherine, you must tell that girl not to sew them on this side or she'll get a permanent mark. She'll be scarred for life."

Kitty was wearing an expression of stoic forbearance. "Yes, Mama," she said. Evelyn refilled her brandy glass.

"I can't tell you how awful it was," Mama was saying. "The McCull-ochs served us two potatoes each. Can you imagine? Two each."

"Ann, please can we stop talking about the potatoes?" Papa said, with a sigh.

"Did you *see* the size of that tree? They can certainly afford not to be rationing their potatoes. They had a nice goose, though, I'll say that for them. Of course *you* wouldn't have been able to manage it, Evelyn."

"She doesn't get ill from goose anymore, Mama," Kitty chimed in. "We had goose ourselves."

"Really? That last year at Mairibank—"

"How is Mr. McCulloch?" Evelyn said, in an attempt to move the conversation forward.

"Terrible." Mama shook her head. "He'll be dead by Hogmanay."

When the baby had been bounced and kissed, Abigail put her to bed, and the men retreated to the drawing room to smoke.

Kitty prised open the lid from a tin of candied hazelnuts. "Do you want one?" She shook the tin in Evelyn's direction.

"I'm suffering," Evelyn said, rubbing her stomach. "Yes."

"Don't eat too many," Mama said. "Tree nuts. They're full of poison."

Evelyn and Kitty raised their eyebrows at each other.

With some effort, Evelyn rolled off the couch and turned the lock in the parlour door. "Let's undo our sashes while the boys aren't here."

"Honestly," Mama said. "The girdle I had to wear when I was your age. You two don't know you're born."

Kitty pulled at her ribbon. "Thank heavens," she said, with a gasp. "My bodice has been a trial since Margaret, but today was a penance."

"You'll get used to it," Mama said.

"It's so difficult to nurse, though," Kitty said.

"Katherine, you're not still nursing, are you?"

Evelyn let her eyes unfocus. They should really swap out the fireguard in this room with the one in the drawing room; it was far too patterned against the wallpaper. Such a big, lovely house, and Kitty hardly cared to make the best of it.

"And you're still sleeping in your girdle, aren't you?" Mama was saying.

Evelyn broke out of her reverie. "Sleeping in your bust bodice?"

Mama and Kitty both turned to look at her, as if they'd forgotten she was in the room.

"You can't sleep in your bust bodice!" Evelyn said.

"It's perfectly usual. Puts things back in their place." Mama rustled for a gingerbread biscuit. "You'll see. Eventually."

Evelyn bit the inside of her mouth.

Kitty began coughing and Mama sat up. "I told you, poison, those tree nuts. Are you choking to death? Katherine? Am I watching you choke to death?"

"She's fine," Evelyn said. Relieved for the diversion, she poured her a glass of water from the decanter above the mantelpiece. As Kitty sipped her water, Evelyn moved the decanter and glasses from the mantelpiece to the marble console table, where the water would stay cold. After a moment, Mama picked up the decanter and glasses and put them instead at the far end of the room next to the poinsettia.

"And I don't care how important they are to your father's firm, I'm not going to the McCullochs' again next year," she continued, as if they had only just been talking about the subject.

"You can come here," Kitty said, smiling. "I'll make sure to serve you more than two potatoes. And we can *all* have goose, now."

Mama tutted. "No, I won't be doing that, either."

There was a horrible moment of silence. Kitty squeezed her eyes shut. The firelight drew a loop on Mama's face, throwing shadows in the hollows of her cheeks.

"To think, I used to look forward to Christmas," Mama said, quietly. "I'm not sitting around a family table without—you know I won't, Katherine."

Kitty reached out and put her hand on Mama's.

Mama looked at them both, her eyes watering. "Don't," she said, almost angrily. "No, don't. If I begin, I won't stop."

"Halibut stocks are lower than ever," Evelyn said, desperately.

Kitty laughed, wiping her eyes.

Mama turned to Evelyn. "Really, Evelyn, politics? On Christmas Day? I raised you better than that." Mama frowned. "And what's wrong with your Robert? No more hallucinations, I hope?"

Evelyn's mouth dropped open. "You told her?"

Kitty shifted in her seat. "I mentioned something in passing."

"I don't know why you didn't tell me yourself," Mama said. "He needs more fibre in his diet, that's all. And with his heart he should be especially careful."

"His heart has nothing to do with it," Evelyn said.

Mama and Kitty exchanged a glance that Evelyn pretended not to see.

Kitty gripped her hand. Her fingers were sticky. "Are you sure, Evie? Is everything all right?"

Mama was nodding. "He's looking awful wan. He must be sickening after something."

Evelyn licked her lips. She'd comforted herself by assuming Robert's dejected abstraction was the sort of melancholy obvious only to his wife, and not to anyone else. "He's fine."

Kitty started to speak, but Evelyn continued. "He's been busy at work."

Mama peered at her. "You look pale as well. I thought perhaps—"

Evelyn shook her head. "No."

"No?"

"No."

Kitty and Mama shared another look.

"Never mind," Kitty said, giving her a brave little smile. "It didn't exactly happen quickly for me and Alistair. There's plenty of time yet for wee Roberts."

Evelyn opened her mouth. She could tell them—she was going to tell them. She was going to say it. Detonate a fuse, watch her life combust. She snapped her mouth shut. She wasn't going to tell them. Her head swam and she sipped from her brandy glass. It happened every now and again. A strange flash of queasy power, knowing that just a few words would ruin everything. That last year at Mairibank, it wasn't the goose that had made Evelyn sick, though she hadn't admitted it to anyone; not even Dolly had known at the time. She had been pregnant.

"Oh," Mama was saying. "Wee Bobbies. Better hope they don't get your nose, Evelyn!"

"Anyway," Evelyn said. "Robert's right as rain now, so there is no need to worry." She held her hand out for Kitty's empty glass and slid it onto the bureau where it couldn't fall and be broken.

"Splendid," Kitty said. "That's very good indeed." Her tone, however, was forced. It was the sort of deliberate congratulations one gives to a dog that shakes one's hand with a muddy paw.

The men came back in to join them, bringing a gust of cigar and whisky. Robert was holding a book about Robert the Bruce, a gift from her father that Evelyn knew he would never read. He was doing a good job of pretending to be absorbed in it, turning the pages with an exaggerated frown of concentration that meant he was thinking about something else entirely.

"Evie's been asking about the new addition to your railroad," Kitty said to Alistair, batting her eyelashes.

"She's done nothing of the sort," Alistair said.

Evelyn was still feeling dazed from her bout of emotional vertigo, and it took a few seconds before she became alert to her role. "I have, yes, I'd love to see."

Alistair's expression softened. "Truly?"

"No. I mean, yes," Evelyn said. But she glanced over at Robert. What was the risk of leaving him unchaperoned? He was examining the flyleaf of the book, running his thumbs over the binding. He knew better than to mention ghosts on Christmas Day, didn't he? She gave Mama a good long look. "Mama, tell me, is Auntie Alice still letting that spaniel of hers eat off the china?"

Her mother's face darkened. She took a hissing inhale of breath. "A perfectly good piece of liver, she gave him, can you believe it? On a Wedgwood platter! My grandmother received that set from Mr. Wedgwood himself, and now . . ."

Evelyn followed Alistair along the corridor and down the stairs into the cellar. Alistair went ahead of her and she gritted her teeth as they arrived at the staircase, which was uncarpeted and uneven. Alistair thumped down slowly, his cane clacking against the wall, scoring the already well-scuffed skirting board. Though he was try-ing to cover for it with conversation about Margaret, his breath was laboured, and his speech punctuated by long pauses.

"You must get a proper light in here," Evelyn said at last, unable to help herself. "It's simply not safe on these stairs."

"Perhaps," Alistair said.

Evelyn and Robert's cellar was host to an odd assembly of excess furniture from Mairibank, but Kitty and Alistair had made much better use of their much better downstairs. Alistair had created a studio for himself in the left-hand room, while the right was used for wine storage. They manoeuvred around a worm-eaten champagne riddling rack to enter his workshop. At the far end was a desk lined with jam jars containing an indecipherable catalogue of screws and bolts. And in the centre of the room was a huge square table which held Alistair's recreation of Musselburgh, where he had grown up. Alistair had set the village for a winter scene, fir trees full and fluffy along the lanes, and barrels of plaster-cast Cox's Pippins apples sheltering under eaves. At the flick of a switch, an articulated train vaulted past the immobile villagers, fixed in the action of delivering minuscule parcels wrapped in wax paper. Evelyn clapped her hands as the train released a puff of white steam.

"Alistair, it's lovely!" She leant down to squeeze one of the trees between her fingers.

Alistair blushed. "Still a work in progress. You know, that's a Norwegian fir—I thought you'd appreciate them."

Evelyn stared at the tree. "Yes. Lovely." Suddenly, she felt exhausted; a wrung-out scrap of rag. She traced her fingertips over the rails. "Don't you wish we lived in miniature?"

"I suppose that everything would be proportionally the same, if we did," Alistair said.

Evelyn laughed, undeterred by his practicality. No one who spent time outfitting leaden villagers with knitted scarves was immune to sentimentality. "Nonsense," she said. "Everything would be so much cosier, if we were tiny." Her eyes settled on the model of a mallard duck, and a skewer of pain pierced her, like a forgotten pin in the stitching of a coat. She steadied herself on the table. He must have found it down here, jumbled with the other Mairibank detritus. He wouldn't have known it was Dolly's.

"Evie?"

"Yes?" She looked up to see him watching her. She tried to compose her face; it wasn't his fault, and she wasn't about to make him feel bad for no reason.

"I hope you don't mind me asking, but, Robert . . . is he quite all right?"

"What do you mean?"

"He mentioned something about"—Alistair squirmed—"elves."

Her body seized, a ripple of shame passing from her toes to her chin. "What did he say?"

He cleared his throat. "The specifics don't matter."

"I'm so sorry."

"Please, no need to apologise." Alistair looked shamefacedly at the corner of the table, fiddling with a little switch.

"Would you mind, maybe keep that between us?" Her voice was unsteady.

"Absolutely." He gave her a brave, encouraging nod. "Christmas is difficult for lots of people."

"Hmm," Evelyn said, looking again at Dolly's miniature duck. Still here while she was not. Out of everyone in the house, Robert had arguably the least right to find Christmas difficult. "Shall we rejoin the others?" she said in an artificially sunny tone.

Evelyn followed Alistair upstairs, watching the muscles in his shoulders tense before he took each step. Alistair, who had come back from the Somme without complaint and now had cause to squirm, because of Robert. As they approached the parlour, Alistair paused. "Oh, Katherine asked me for the sheet music, I left it in the drawing room."

"No, no, you go on in and sit down," Evelyn said. "I'll fetch it."

As she passed back down the corridor, she refurbished the house: they never used the garden room, it would be much better to bring Alistair's workshop in there and get him out of that damp cellar. And they should modernise the hallways while they were at it, the briar roses were far too busy; they should put in something fashionable. Stripes, perhaps. And that monstrosity of a carpet— Evelyn paused, hearing Robert's voice coming from the drawing room. Her heart gave an unquiet leap. What if he was now lecturing Papa about elves and ectoplasm? She would never recover from the humiliation. Holding her breath, she approached the threshold on tiptoe. The drawing room was dark, lit only by the candles on the Christmas tree, which cast gentle, flickering shadows across the wallpaper. Robert had dropped his voice now, but there was an edge of conciliation in his tone, as if he were advising a despairing friend. Evelyn put her eye to the hinge in the door.

Robert was alone. He was standing in the corner of the room, facing the wallpaper.

"No, there's never enough time, is there?" he was whispering. "There's never enough time."

7

USUALLY, EVELYN ENJOYED THE LOOSE, FUZZY DAYS between Christmas and Hogmanay. This year, though, she woke up on Boxing Day with an unnerving stomachache, a sort of crawling twitchiness, as if something scaly were hatching in her belly. She let Robert sleep late, and prepared cold duck sandwiches that they ate on their laps next to the fire. She left him reading the newspaper in the parlour, and rummaged in the guest room bookshelf for a biography of Brahms she'd never got round to reading. Locating it next to the window, she was cheered to find it also contained a forgotten birthday card with a one-pound note inside from Auntie Maude.

"Look at this." She fluttered the note as she came down the stairs. "We can—" And she stopped. Robert was sitting in a chair by the fire, staring fixedly into the hallway. He was leaning forward, his hands gripping the arms of the chair. It was a strange posture; anticipatory, poised. "Robert?"

His eyes met hers.

"Are you feeling all right?"

"I'm fine." His tone was annoyed.

Slowly, she came down to the bottom step. "Are you waiting for a call?"

"No. Are you?"

"No." She peered into the corridor, in the direction of where he had been staring. "Look." She raised the pound note. "I found it upstairs. Should we add it to the box for St. Ternan's?"

"If you like."

Evelyn took a breath, trying to rein in her irritation. They were supposed to be having fun. They were supposed to be listening to music, cracking walnuts, sipping cocktails, preparing for Hogmanay. But she couldn't risk taking him anywhere in this mood. "Are you sure you're feeling well?"

"I'm feeling fine, Evie," Robert said.

She lingered in the doorway, unconvinced. "Come on, let's finish the box, then." She gestured for him to follow her down to the kitchen. Marty had already begun preparing the package, but in a flurry of guilty agitation, Evelyn opened their cupboards and tumbled into the box anything that came to her hand, regardless of whether the orphans would make use of it. In went a bottle of coffee essence and a tin of baking powder and Oakey's knife polish and a light bulb, a half-eaten jar of cherries, another light bulb. She paused, hovering a bar of Fry's chocolate over the edge of the box, waiting for Robert to pretend to object, as he did every year. But he was looking over his shoulder into the hallway, staring at the cupboard under the stairs.

"Would you like me to do it without you?" she said, gently.

Robert frowned. "No, I like to do it."

She couldn't help herself. "You don't seem to be enjoying it."

"I am, Evie."

"Really? You look like you're rehearsing a eulogy!"

"Evie, please, don't fuss."

"I'm not fussing. All week you've—" She broke off. Robert's gaze had crept back to the cupboard. She tossed the bar of chocolate into the box and stamped into the corridor, where she threw open the cupboard door. In the light from the hallway, she could make out a pair of her galoshes, an umbrella that needed mending. She leant closer. In the shadows at the back, a zinc bucket containing a tablet of soap, a handkerchief from their picnic basket. Behind that, a round, hollow weight that had fallen from a sweep's brush and which they now used as a doorstop.

"There's nothing in here!"

Robert looked at her for a long moment.

"But what were you—not a mouse?"

"No. Not a mouse."

"What is it then?" Evelyn said, swinging the door even wider. "See, there's nothing there!"

Robert blinked at her. "Nothing I'm allowed to talk about."

The back of her neck prickled. "What do you mean?"

"I mean, I'm not allowed to tell you," Robert said. "If you could see it, you'd know."

She stepped away from the cupboard, her stomach writhing. There was nothing in there. Dust. Shadows. "I might go and have a lie-down, actually," she said, in a weak voice. At the top of the stairs, she paused. Robert was still staring at the open cupboard door.

✳ ✳ ✳

ON HOGMANAY, EVELYN WATCHED from the hallway window as Robert slid into the passenger seat of Henry's automobile. Henry squeezed the horn in greeting, raising his hand, and Evelyn jumped, dropping the net curtain. She returned to bed, pulling the blankets up to her chin. She tried reading the Brahms biography, but the words crossed over in diagonals until she gave up, resting the spine of the book across her brow.

Something was wrong with Robert.

With a twitch, Evelyn knocked the book off her forehead. She wanted to scream. Everything was supposed to be normal now. After everything. After the "big move." After the new calluses, the old clothes, the unreturned letters. After the zeppelin raids, the coal strikes, the black dye, the hungry evenings, the frosty mornings, the queuing, the queuing, the queuing. After the day they found out

Alistair was injured. The flu. The day Dolores died. Her funeral. After all the tedious small economies, the awful, grand sacrifices, the secret tears, the telephone ringing in the night. They were meant to be shipwrecked sailors, clinging together. Everything was supposed to be predictable, steady, survivable. Or what else was the point of loving Robert? As the thought crossed her mind, she felt a terrible sense of traitorousness, and snatched it back immediately. She buried her face in the pillow. This wasn't within her realm; she wasn't brave, like Dolly. Dolly would have known exactly how to handle this.

Evelyn heard the clatter of Margaret's pram and then a knock on the front door.

"Mrs. Hazard is unwell," Marty was saying.

"Not too unwell for me, surely," Kitty said, her voice haughty. Despite herself, Evelyn smiled into the sheets. After a moment, Kitty's tread came on the stairs. Quickly, Evelyn shut her eyes and produced her best imitation of sleep.

"Evie?" Kitty whispered, through a crack in the door. "Evelyn?"

Evelyn dropped her mouth open for good measure.

Kitty let herself in and sat on the edge of the bed. She smelt like lemon verbena eau de toilette, and her clothes radiated cold from coming in off the street. "You can't fool me, you know."

Evelyn sat up. "I surrender."

"What's wrong?" Kitty said, scanning Evelyn's face. "You've got good colour."

Evelyn looked to the door, and following her eyeline, Kitty leapt up and shut it. Evelyn motioned for her to shuffle closer. "It's Robert."

"He's not ill again, is he?" Kitty said.

"I don't know how to help him," Evelyn said. "I think it might be something to do with"—she broke off—"those *ideas*—you know, spiritualism."

Kitty grimaced. "Is he still talking about it?"

"No." Evelyn drew her silver locket to her lips and nibbled it until she could taste metal. "I forbade him."

"You *forbade* him?"

"I think giving it up has made him depressed. He's usually always so steady." Evelyn's throat was tight. She sat up straighter. She was not going to make another scene in front of Kitty.

"But it's nonsense," Kitty said. "Just like going to the theatre. Nothing to get so worked up about."

"That's what I've been telling him."

"No, *you*. Surely, Evie, it's not worth you getting worked up about."

Evelyn's mouth dropped open. "You're not saying I should encourage him? It's too… it's too…" She searched around for the right word, but couldn't find anything suitably outré and humiliating.

Kitty put her hand on Evelyn's knee. "It's important, to keep a home happy, to let men have their little fascinations. Mama agrees too."

"She does?" A sting flickered through her. She imagined the phone calls, Kitty and Mama whispering, their lips pursed. Was this what it had felt like for Dolly? It was horrible, like being shut in a draughty corridor. "What has Mama been saying?"

"Just that it might be good for him to have a restful pastime. With his heart—"

"Don't bring his heart into this."

"But Evie, I mean, you do think it's nonsense, don't you?"

"Of course I think it's nonsense!"

"Well, since it *is* nonsense, surely you could at least condone a little reading on the subject? It would be no different from those detective books Papa likes. And Robert's not a fanciful man."

"I didn't used to think so."

Kitty patted her knee. "Remember, that very first night you met him at that dance? He insisted on us taking that shortcut home along the river, even though we were scared there might be frogs. Remember how he laughed at us?"

"Gosh, how silly we were. Everything that was going on, and we were frightened of frogs."

"Exactly. He's a practical sort, he'll come around eventually."

Evelyn swallowed. "He doesn't usually like change."

Kitty smiled. "Who does?"

Evelyn looked at the blanket. She could feel that Kitty was thinking of Dolly. She willed her to speak of her, to say anything.

"Isn't it possible—and before you give me that look, let me finish—isn't it possible that Robert is trying, in his own way, to contribute?"

Evelyn balked. "Why would he need to contribute?"

"Well, you know . . ." Kitty trailed off.

"He didn't need to fight to contribute."

"I never said that! But perhaps he wants to find something he can be good at."

"Kitty, he runs a reputable accountancy business. He can fix an engine. Last summer he smoked out that wasps' nest, you were there. There's a hundred things he's good at."

"I meant more as something of his own he can feel proud of. You can be ever so hard on him."

"I'm not hard on him!" Evelyn felt a flutter of shame at being chided by her younger sister, and worse, that she was right.

"And you have some time yet, before you have a family," Kitty was saying.

"We are a family," Evelyn said, tersely. "The two of us."

"But I mean a *real* family. You won't believe how much it changes your priorities once you have a baby."

Evelyn gritted her teeth. "Neither Robert or me wants to change our priorities," she said. How didn't Kitty see it? How couldn't she understand, it wasn't going to happen. They didn't *want* it to happen!

"We've already had one divorce in the family," Kitty said, gently. "I don't think Mama will survive another one."

Evelyn bit her lip. She'd had a similar thought, about divorce; but Kitty saying the word out loud brought it painfully close, like cutting a nail down to the quick. She pictured herself watching from the upstairs hallway window as Robert lifted a suitcase into Henry's motorcar. Without Robert, she would be adrift in a big dark ocean, all alone. Her eyes stung. "I suppose him reading on the subject wouldn't be so bad. It might be good for his spelling."

"Exactly," Kitty said.

"But—but—it's not usual," and Evelyn began to laugh or cry, she wasn't sure which.

Kitty reached forward and wiped Evelyn's face with her thumb. "Nothing is usual anymore," she said.

They looked at each other and observed the moment of silence, the tired, sombre nod and half shrug that was obligatory when talking about the war.

❋ ❋ ❋

AFTER KITTY LEFT, EVELYN ran a bath. Soaping her legs, she watched the droplets of steam beading on the mirror. She leant back, closing her eyes. The warmth and lap of the water lulled her into a half doze. By the time the midwife came, the bathwater was cold, but she didn't care anymore. She didn't care anymore about the water or the sick floating in it, or the sounds she was making. By the time the midwife came, she was only saying, "I want it over over over over." And then it was time to push, and she drove the screams down into her body and she wasn't here, but she wasn't in the other place. She was in the middle, the middle place. And then out it came. The baby. A boy. Black hair, outraged, yelling. And she fell back, and waited for the brick of love to smash through her soul. But instead, she felt a sort of acquaintance. "Oh," she said, looking at his open mouth, his crumpled face. "It's you—I know you." And when the midwife took him away, she felt only relieved. And as the midwife pushed on her stomach, as she gathered the slithering meat of her insides into a pan, as her blood washed down the drain, as Dolly wiped her face, she didn't feel sad. She didn't feel anything. And in the night, when she woke with a start in the dark and thought, *Oh, the baby*, when she remembered it was done, when she remembered he was already with some other family by now, she only thought: *Thank God. Thank God, thank God.*

The door opened, and Evelyn sat up with a start, bubbles sloshing. Robert's face appeared around the doorway. "Knock knock," he said. When Evelyn didn't reply, he entered the room and perched on the edge of the bath. He smelt faintly of gravy. "Are you still not feeling well?"

"Not really." She avoided his eye, motioning for him to pass her a towel. He held it up like a shield, and as she climbed out of the bath, he wrapped the towel around her.

He wiped a froth of suds from her neck. "What's troubling my Evie?"

"Nothing."

Robert took another towel from the rail and draped it over her shoulders, mopping the wet ends of her hair. "Much better."

"Kitty was here today. She was talking about that first evening at the Lion's Club, when you made us take that shortcut," Evelyn said.

"Heavens, aye." Robert laughed, pulling the plug out of the bath. "You and Kitty both afraid of a few wee frogs. But it's twenty minutes shorter by that route! At least Alistair agreed with me."

Evelyn pulled the towel tighter around her. "You always were so practical. Remember when that bus broke down in Aberdeen?"

"The converter just needed draining," Robert said. "When the manifold . . ."

Evelyn watched him talk, the wrinkle in his forehead that meant he was concentrating.

"And if the sump isn't tight enough—" He stopped. "You're not listening, are you?"

Evelyn smiled. "Sorry."

He leant forward and kissed her on the bridge of her nose. "Why don't we do something cheerful? If you get dressed, I'll bring up the cards?"

Evelyn paused. She wanted to do something normal, somewhere normal. With other normal people, being normal. "We could go out for Hogmanay?"

"Would that help? Fireworks?"

She nodded.

He clapped his hands together. "Well, then, bliadhna mhath ùr!"

"Does that mean yes?"

"That means yes."

* * *

THAT EVENING THEY WALKED arm in arm along Princes Street. It had been shut off to traffic and had become a melee of revellers wrapped up against the cold. The snow hadn't settled, but a furious wind was blowing from the direction of the castle, and Evelyn pulled up her scarf until only her eyes were exposed. They wandered between rickety booths offering cocoa and slices of black bun and dips in a barrel of whisky. Robert lingered by a stall selling American crime novels that had drawn a gaggle of university students, flicking through the pages with tight elbows, careful not to crack the spines and incur the responsibility of paying for them. The cold swooped into her ears, and Evelyn ushered Robert into the centre of the crowd, where they would be more protected. There, she removed her scarf from her nose and took a deep breath of Hogmanay: roasting chestnuts, damp mud, spilled whisky evaporating from overcoats, leather gloves singed from lighting cigarettes. Three young women started up playing "A Guid New Year" on poorly tuned fiddles, and Evelyn gestured towards them. "Isn't it nice to be out, having fun?"

"Yes, very nice," Robert said, but his tone was subdued.

"Shall we have some spiced wine?" Evelyn said, pointing to a cart and waiting for him to begin his customary lecture about tuberculosis and shared drinking vessels. But he simply nodded and joined the queue for the glass tumblers.

Evelyn sat on the edge of the wall by Dickinson's and looked through the crowd for anyone she recognised. Mrs. Fairfeather from St. Serf's stopped to talk to her, until her son begged her for a ride on the donkey. Robert had been drawn into conversation with a man in a grubby army greatcoat who was trying to sell him a box of matches from a paper bag. From her place on the wall, Evelyn felt a gloom settle upon her. When everyone was out together, it was clear how thin the crowd was, even against last year. And it was harder to ignore how so many people were middle-aged, and so few young. The young men that she could see were missing arms, their faces sealed with scar tissue, patches of blistered scalp peeking out from underneath hat brims. She saw the looks lingering on Robert, assessing his clear complexion, his easy stride, his white hands. To overcompensate for her unease, she forced herself to meet the scarred faces, the punctured eyes, the pinned suit jackets. She forced herself to impose upon each veteran a cheerful smile. They seldom smiled back. And though she was aware her false cheer was one of pity, of guilt, of a simpering attempt to cover her guilt, she punished herself by allowing them to witness it. Her foolishness, her luck. Their shameful, shameful luck.

Robert approached with a tumbler of wine. "Here you go."

"Thank you," Evelyn said, but her good mood had dissolved. She stared into the cup of ruby liquid, letting it warm her hands.

A young boy in a cap approached them, selling mistletoe sprigs from an old cigar box. Robert bought one, holding it hopefully above his head until Evelyn placed a kiss on his cheek.

"You know," Robert said, twirling the mistletoe stem between his fingers. "I used to do that myself."

"To do what?"

"Sell flowers, sweeties. Pick fuller's teasels sometimes. Hogmanay was always a good night, Boer soldiers with holiday pay in their pocket."

"No one noticed you were gone?"

Robert gave a bitter laugh. He mimed drinking from a bottle. "No one noticed a thing after noon on Hogmanay." Evelyn put a hand on his arm. "There's no room to be a child, places like that," he said. "Shouldn't be legal."

Her stomach turned. She stared at the blackened end of a cigarette that had fallen between the cobbles. "But you turned out well, didn't you?"

She felt Robert looking at her.

"Even after"—she paused—"your upbringing. You've done so well. You're proof that it doesn't matter about your parents, that if you try hard enough you can make everything right." She turned to face him now. He was giving her a shy smile.

"I've tried my best."

"I know you have." Her throat was thick.

Robert covered her hand with his, and then leant forward, calling the boy back. "How many have you got in there, son? Twenty?" He handed over a half crown. "Why don't you take the night off, have some fun?"

The boy gawped at the coin, then shot one distrustful look at Robert before turning on his heels and running back through the market. Evelyn watched his cap vanish into the crowd. She chewed her lip. That boy was ten or eleven, about the age that hers would be now. But he wouldn't be in an orphanage, selling matches on the street. No, he was with a family. A kind family. Sleeping in bed with a warming pan, listening to his parents prepare for first footing downstairs. It wasn't the same. It wasn't remotely the same.

Evelyn tipped her now-cold wine into the gutter. "It's almost midnight. Let's get a better spot."

At the stroke of midnight, the clock bells at the station began, then St. Cuthbert's, joined finally by St. John's. And through the crowd, a tension wound, a tightening. The cannons at the castle shot in great booms over the gardens, and with a crackling hiss and pop, the fireworks began. Children cheered. A giant man on the corner of Hanover Street began playing "Auld Lang Syne" on the bagpipes. Everyone was strangely quiet, save for a carousel of drunken men jigging in a circle. Somewhere behind the wall, a young man in a smart navy coat broke out of the crowd with a scuffle. He took hold of his hat and let loose a bubbling shout that became a shriek. "Get down!" he was screaming. "Get down! Get down!" With some commotion, he was restrained by his friends, his pocket watch swinging against the cobbles. The fireworks glittered overhead, and everyone looked deliberately away.

8

THEY WALKED HOME DOWN THE HILL, PASSING PEOPLE coughing wetly through the railings into Queen Street gardens, swaying on doorsteps for first footing. Abandoned gloves lay crushed in the gutters; dogs whimpered under cars. The night had drawn in a milky mist that settled in the fine hairs on Evelyn's overcoat. On the corner of Heriot Row, a weeping woman in a green dress was being consoled by a young gentleman who looked extremely embarrassed. Now that the fireworks were over, a sense of anticlimax hung over Evelyn's head, a doom-laden feeling that she was somewhere she ought not to be.

Evelyn glanced over her shoulder as they passed the Spiritualist Library and Psychical Research Centre. The windows were shuttered, a rime of ice lined the windowsill. "I don't believe it."

"Pardon?"

"When people are gone, they're gone. You can't—you can't get them back."

"I never said that," Robert said, his expression sombre.

She stared at him, her insides squeezing. "I don't understand why you would want this," she said, in a whisper.

Robert's pupils were buttons under the streetlamp. "I just want to help."

They swerved past two men in derbies staggering on a doorstep, their arms full of coal.

"But, why don't you want things to be normal?" Evelyn said.

"Nothing is going back to normal, my love."

A claw raked through Evelyn's chest. "I know that. I know that as well as anyone. But we don't need to change anything."

He gripped her hand. "I can help, Evie. I can be useful."

"Isn't it enough, being useful to me?" Her voice was very small. "We're useful to each other. Isn't that the point?"

"Oh, Evie." Robert pressed her closer to him. "If I can do something, it's my duty to volunteer. I know you understand how hard it is, being left behind."

Evelyn pictured Dolores, on a rowboat ahead of her, disappearing into the mist.

"You still want to research?" She wanted to say more. That wishing for magic was childish and greedy. That it was embarrassing and silly, and grasping, like searching for pirate treasure, or hunting for the Holy Grail.

Robert glanced at her, a quick, darting look. "Research is close to getting real answers. Just last month, Madame Cixous helped the police find that communist. And scientists are on the verge of a breakthrough. Edison's valve—"

Evelyn interrupted him. "But you. Is this what you need?"

"If I can be useful, I need to be useful," Robert said.

There was a terrible sinking feeling inside her. Evelyn let go of his arm. Across the street, a dray horse tethered to a rag-and-bone cart sneezed, clacking its foreleg against the cobbles. A middle-aged woman in a flimsy hat dozing on a doorstep roused from her sleep with a screech, then looked around her, confused, for the source of the screech.

"I don't understand why you won't let me," Robert said, softly. "Don't you trust me?"

"Of course I trust you!"

"But then, why not let me give it a shot? I won't let you down, I promise. You'll be ever so proud."

Her throat was raw. "I'm already proud of you, you don't need to prove anything to me—to anyone."

"But my love, if you trust me, then what's the harm?"

Evelyn's eyes burned. Reflexively, she went to chew on her finger, then remembered she was wearing gloves. She wrapped her arms around her waist. There was nothing in it. "If you really need this, I suppose a few books on the subject would be harmless enough."

Robert rushed at her and bundled her in an embrace so tight she heard her shoulder joints cracking.

She wriggled out of his grip. "We will still go to church every Sunday."

Robert nodded eagerly.

"No discussions in public. No talking about Edison's valve or elves or ectoplasm or anything even in that *constituency*."

"No, I won't." Robert's eyes were bright.

"You can't tell Marty. Or Papa."

Robert tipped his head back and laughed. His breath formed a puff that hung like a pear drop in the air, before mingling with the mist.

"I mean it, you must not tell Papa."

Robert shook his head. "I promise."

"Then," Evelyn said, licking her lips, "I take back my forbidding—forbading."

Robert hugged her again, squeezing her until her vision blurred. He kissed her roughly on the side of her face, her chin, her nose, printing her with his bristles. "Do you mean it, Evie? Truly?"

Evelyn blinked away the tears in her eyes. "I mean it."

He stooped down and kissed her full on the mouth. An unwinding sort of surrender unfurled in her body. He reached for her hair, the small of her back. "Evie, my queen."

She nudged him aside, wiping her lips. "Robert, really. There are people everywhere."

"Let them look," he said, nuzzling her forehead.

Evelyn levered him away from her, readjusting her hat. She took a breath, intending to say something portentous, lawyerly, something that would bind him to his word. Instead, she said, "You are a good man."

* * *

THEY WERE HOME WITHIN half an hour, and after a brief, ceremonial opening of the parlour windows to welcome the New Year, it was time for bed.

As they climbed the stairs, Robert put his hand suggestively on her rump. Evelyn affected not to notice. The dark, misty mood of the evening was still clinging to her, and she wasn't sure if she was ready to succumb to his advances.

At the top of the stairs, he kissed her on the cheek. "I'll wash up and be through in a minute." His voice was full of meaning.

Evelyn searched herself for some animation. It was a good sign, she reminded herself, that he was feeling amorous. It was a good sign that he was cheerful. When Robert opened the bedroom door ten minutes later, she was under the blankets, pretending to read the biography of Brahms.

Robert sat on the bed, throwing his arm over her so heavily that he toppled her into the bedclothes. "You're a queen among women," he said, kissing her ear.

The threading in the sheets rubbed against Evelyn's cheeks. She shut her eyes. "You won't . . ." She trailed off.

Robert kissed her ear again, and then stopped. She felt the bed bounce as he righted himself. "My love, sit up."

Evelyn sat up.

He grabbed her arm, holding her wrist. His face was alarmed. "Is everything all right?"

Evelyn nodded, glumly.

"Whatever's wrong?" He reached out and tucked her hair behind her ears. The action was so gentle, so sweet, a pulse of tenderness for him surged into her chest. Robert pinched her chin and lifted it until she met his eyes. "My darling Evie, why on earth are you upset?"

Evelyn opened her mouth, her lips wobbling. She could tell him. She was going to tell him. He'd understand that she'd been young and scared. He would understand—wouldn't he?

"Evie?"

Evelyn had intended to confide in Dolores in a calm way. At a good moment. On a walk. Late at night, sharing a bed, their cold feet tucked under the same blanket. But in the end, they were in town for the afternoon, jostling for space under an umbrella and waiting to cross the road to the station. A tram was ringing its low bell to nudge a cyclist out of the way. Dolly stepped in a puddle. And it just burst out of her. Evelyn pictured her expression now. The dismay, the profound disappointment. Evelyn swallowed. If that's how even Dolly had reacted—she looked down at her knees.

"Evie?"

"You know that I don't believe in the spirits," Evelyn said.

Robert gave her a half smile. "Not yet."

She took a breath. "I don't like the idea of people . . . trying . . . thinking they can—I don't want you . . . anyone—please don't talk—"

"Dolores," Robert said.

"Yes."

Robert looked at her. "I wouldn't dream of it."

"Not at the library, not in your sessions. I don't want—" She paused, trying to control her breathing. "It's private." She sniffed. "It feels—" And she stopped, hearing her voice break.

"My love, you are the most precious thing in the world to me. My only family." Robert embraced her. "I'd never betray your confidence."

She nodded.

Robert was patting her head, mechanically. It was a clumsy gesture, and he was pulling her hair. "I've not lost my senses," he said.

Evelyn's lip twitched.

"Is that what your great fear is about? People talking?"

Gossip was nothing like her great fear. It barely trimmed the edges of her fear. But she nodded.

Robert leant forward and kissed her on the cheek. "I promise it's very respectable. We can go to the Spiritualist Hall together—no, it's not like that, it's called the *Christian* Spiritualist Hall, it's very neighbourly and normal. I'll be able to convince you."

Evelyn squinted at him. "What if I don't want to be convinced?"

"It gives people comfort, Evie. You'll see."

"You want me to come with you?"

"Of course you're coming with me," Robert said, his eyes wide. Acid bubbled in her stomach. "You *are* coming with me?"

There was nothing in it, there was nothing in it. "But . . ."

"You wouldn't leave me alone, would you, Evie?" Robert said, with something approaching panic in his expression. "We're allies, aren't we?"

She put her palm to his face, tracing her thumb over the faint scar across his lips, the line of whiskers that wandered up towards his left eye. "No, my love," she said, eventually. "I wouldn't leave you alone."

9

EVELYN DRESSED CAREFULLY FOR THEIR FIRST VISIT
to the Spiritualist Hall. She changed her outfit three times, growing
increasingly flustered and itchy, before finally deciding on a sober
navy dress that conferred restrained respectability. She and Robert
walked to the hall in silence. Evelyn hadn't been able to face eating any porridge at breakfast, and there was a hollow twang in her
stomach. Robert had scribbled a map on the back of an old envelope
and kept withdrawing it from his pocket to check the route. Evelyn
didn't ask him how he had procured the address, or from whom.

The hall proved to be an entirely nondescript two-storey
building behind an artist's gallery off Chalmers' Close. The close
blocked off any pedestrian thoroughfare, and the hall itself was
white pebbledash with a discreet wooden noticeboard. Nervous
that the crowd milling in the close might be decked in orange robes
and extravagant turbans, Evelyn allowed herself small, peripheral
glances, as if she were taking sips from a still-scalding cup of tea.
Young women in well-tailored coats carried the Chinese-style
umbrella that had become fashionable. Older women in Victorian
mourning dress sat upon the bench outside the venue, resting
their canes against the wall. There were university students in
shabby derby hats smoking unfiltered cigarettes. A portly woman
admonished a redheaded child who was chasing a pigeon. So far,

acceptable. The doors opened at noon exactly, the bells of St. Paul's Episcopal filling the passage as the crowd surged towards the hall. As they drew closer to the door, Evelyn set her teeth, girding herself for the coming fracas. One of the greeters at the doorway raised herself on tiptoes and caught Evelyn's eyes over the crowd. It was Geraldine, the librarian from the research centre. "Good afternoon!" she said, cheerfully, through the thicket of cloche hats.

"Afternoon."

"How nice to see you again," Geraldine said, as the crowd jostled Evelyn towards her. "Is it your first time visiting the hall?"

Evelyn nodded.

"I'd shake your hand, but I just spilt cocoa on myself," Geraldine said, with a grimace. She was dabbing her arm with her handkerchief. "Dear me, it's going to stain, isn't it?"

Evelyn concentrated on the liquid dripping from Geraldine's sleeve. This shuffling, umbrella-wielding, cocoa-spilling collection of eccentrics was hardly a menacing foe. She would be able to puncture their allure in no time.

✦ ✦ ✦

THE SERVICE BEGAN WITH a middle-aged brunette woman called Mrs. Downie, who came onto the stage and gave a reading from a poem entitled "Seeking Solace." It was poorly rhymed, and Mrs. Downie didn't look up once from her piece of paper. Then there was a prayer, that Evelyn was relieved to hear included reference to God, to King, and to country. Another speaker came on stage whose name Evelyn didn't catch. She was a grey-haired woman in ill-fitting tweed travelling from Ireland. She gave a meandering lecture about the "spiritual garden," the idea of populating one's life with art, poetry, music, in order to cultivate one's sensitivities. The congregation stood to sing "Nearer, My God, to Thee," and then after another prayer from Mrs. Downie, they were invited to depart.

As they stood, Evelyn chewed on her cuticle. It had all been superbly usual, which was both a comfort and a problem. It meant, at least, that Robert wasn't dabbling in anything elaborately scandalous. However, if the meeting *had* been a bacchanal of snake charmers and ectoplasm seeping from the walls, then she would have been justified in objecting. But the song, the reading, the prayer. It all felt, well, quite adolescent. It reminded Evelyn of the long summer afternoons when, as girls, she, Dolores, and Kitty had sat out on the grass lawn of Mairibank, imagining sprites and pixies, wizards, enchanted animals. The deep, drowsy afternoons when they had found themselves bewitched by their own acute in-betweenness. Charged with the knowledge of a potentiality, an almost-ness, they had stayed up late reading Christina Rossetti and snuck out to walk by the pool at the end of the garden, to sigh over the moonlight, the croaking frogs. Those summers, they had been convinced that there was something tantalisingly close, a transcendence shimmering on the edge of their abilities, that they alone had the special power to reach out, and capture. It was deluded, narcissistic, harmless.

As Evelyn and Robert queued to leave the room, he pinched her arm. "What did you think?"

Evelyn searched his face before answering. "Fine."

He grinned at her. "Isn't it?"

Robert tipped back and forth on his heels as they stood at the side of the hall, rubbing his hands together. Evelyn chewed her fingernail more vigorously. This was the part she had been most dreading: the séance. When Robert looked over, she gave him a game smile, but her stomach was tight. She took a deep breath. Nothing was going to happen. As Robert walked along the wall, examining pamphlets exhibited on the side table, Evelyn distracted herself by re-dressing the women as they passed. The young girl with the stern overcoat was far too formally attired—she'd look much more becoming in a cape, with a lower waistline to complement her figure. An auburn-haired woman piling up the hymnbooks was wearing a pink blouse that clashed abysmally with her hair, the two hues battling each other for a monstrous compromise. The woman turned and caught Evelyn's eye in the midst of its roving evaluation, and Evelyn was startled, ashamed that she'd been discovered. The woman approached Evelyn and leant in, plucking at her blouse. "Isn't it hideous?" she whispered, conspiratorially. "Christmas present." And she waved towards the crowd, pulling a face.

"It's not," Evelyn began, but the woman had turned back to the hymnbooks.

Mrs. Downie appeared behind Robert, looking harassed. The hem of her slip was hanging below her skirt, and she was clutching an open leather notebook. "Mr. and Mrs. Hazard?" she said, glancing between Robert and Evelyn.

Robert stepped forward and shook her hand.

"Is this your first time here?"

"Yes," Robert said. He looked over his shoulder at Evelyn with an impatient enthusiasm, like a spaniel does on a long country walk.

"I'll escort you to the room, then, if you'll kindly follow me." She led them through a chipped wooden door at the back of the hall and down a corridor that was stuffy with the playroom smell of tinned peaches and Lysol. They followed her up a narrow staircase and she stopped at the first door on the left, turning the handle for them. "If you could take a seat around the table, Madame Celeste will be with you shortly," she whispered.

Evelyn followed Robert into the room. The curtains were drawn, and it took a moment for her eyes to adjust. She pictured Mrs. Downie donning a beribboned bonnet in the corridor and reappearing behind them as "Madame Celeste."

The room was small, a round table in the middle, with heavy mahogany chairs that Evelyn had trouble pulling back on the carpet. Seated at the left of the table was a slim young Black man with a neat moustache, and a freckly middle-aged woman that Evelyn recognised as the proprietor of the grocer's on St. Andrew Square.

On the right side was a pale elderly woman dressed in old-fashioned widow's black bombazine.

Evelyn took a seat. Until this moment, she had not permitted the full reality of Robert's new obsession to settle upon her. These people were gathered, in this room, to contact the dead. She felt a hectic gurgle of laughter in her chest and swallowed down air until it subsided. Nothing was going to happen. It was childish, embarrassing. But then, wasn't there always a chance? She'd always had a misty concept of the afterlife. A sense that people's souls drifted up beyond the clouds, and one day all the souls would cheerfully mingle together, a lovely, sunshiny eschatological broth of eternity. After Dolly died, people said all sorts of well-meaning things: "She's watching over you," or "She's smiling down on you." But Evelyn never had the sense that she was being watched over or shepherded. Dolly was somewhere else, somewhere completely out of reach, along with her grandparents, and every last one of the boys she'd ever had on a dance card. But now she was in a room of people trying to dial directly into heaven. What if someone answered? This Madame Celeste could be about to provide proof that would forever shatter her sense of the universe. Evelyn squeezed her hands until the skin blanched.

"Do you meet with her often?" the freckled woman said to Evelyn.

"She's dead," Evelyn squeaked.

"I'm referring to Madame Celeste." The woman frowned.

Evelyn laughed, a little too wildly. "Of course. No. First time."

"I see her once a month," she said, with a certain haughtiness.

"This is my first audience also," the man said. His eyes were jittering, and he was dabbing at his forehead with a handkerchief. Evelyn detected in his face something of her own turmoil, and had an urge to grab him and run for the door.

"How did you hear about her?" Robert said to the man. "Mr. ... ?"

"Gough, Mr. Gough," the man said, shaking Robert's hand across the table. He didn't offer to shake Evelyn's hand and she was affronted, recanting the previous heroism that had compelled her to rescue Mr. Gough.

"Through a friend," Mr. Gough said. Then he stopped talking and began folding his handkerchief neatly on the table.

"I've known Celeste for many years," the elderly widow announced. Her voice was surprisingly deep. "What a great solace she has been through troubled waters."

Now Evelyn pictured Madame Celeste riding through the door on the crest of a wave, a wave of ectoplasm, tumbling with white jelly and curdled whey.

The single light overhead turned off, and the door on the far side of the room opened.

In came Madame Celeste.

Evelyn blinked. She was a short, ruddy woman in her fifties, wearing thick glasses, an unfashionable olive-green day dress, and a sensible purl-knit black cardigan. She had a sprinkle of dandruff on her shoulders and her cuffs were darned with thread that was a little too light. She was completely unremarkable.

"Good afternoon, ladies and gentlemen." She wrestled with the chair until Mr. Gough pulled it out for her. "Thank you," she said. "These ghastly chairs, so difficult to manoeuvre."

The freckled woman tittered politely.

Madame Celeste pushed her glasses farther up her nose, and when Evelyn met her eyes, she felt a great rush of relief. Myopic and unmagical was exactly what she wanted in a medium. She chided herself. What an idiot she had been for getting so carried away.

"Thank you for joining me today. I will shortly reach out to the beyond and make contact with your beloved souls." Madame Celeste rolled her cuffs higher on her wrists. "Now, shall we begin?" Without waiting for an answer, she continued, "Hold hands around the table. Do not break contact, no matter what."

Evelyn clasped Robert's hand on the left, and on the right, the hand of the widow, which was equipped with a ruby ring the size of a quail's egg.

"Close your eyes," the widow whispered.

Evelyn closed her eyes.

Dolores.

Dolly's voice coming out of that woman's mouth. Dolly's hand on her shoulder. Evelyn's throat felt like it was closing. She could talk to her again. Be sure that she was safe, out there, wherever she was. Her eyes prickled. What if Dolly had been waiting to talk to her? The anniversary of her death was coming up at the end of the month; the worst day of the whole year. Could that bring Dolly closer, somehow? What if she wanted to reach out so desperately that she shared their secrets, as validation? Evelyn snuck a look at Robert. Through the gloom, she could still make out the shape of his brow, scrunched in concentration. She should never have agreed to this, there was too much at risk.

Madame Celeste breathed heavily through her nose. "Between us and the shadow realm is nothing but a veil. And through the veil, the spirits watch our every movement."

Evelyn tried to control her pulse.

"Our hearts are enough," Madame Celeste said, "to summon forth our dearly departed souls. Your loved ones can hear your thoughts, calling to them, and in stillness, we will hear them calling back." Evelyn's hands were shaking so much now that her coral bracelet was clinking against the table.

Madame Celeste made a scraping noise at the back of her throat, and Evelyn clenched Robert's hand. "I'm receiving a connection to a name," Madame Celeste said. "A person with the name *C* or *C-H*."

Evelyn let out her breath.

Across the table the freckled woman was repeating, "*C* or *C-H*."

"It may be *S*, or *S-H*."

"Oh," Mr. Gough gasped. "Sean?"

Madame Celeste's eyelids fluttered. After a moment she said, "Yes. Sean. Sean is here with us now."

The back of Evelyn's neck tingled. She had the distinct impression that someone was standing behind her, and when she turned, a pale, moony face loomed out of the darkness. She dug her fingernails into Robert's hand, before realising it was only a mediocre cross-stitch of the King's face.

"Sean wishes to connect with us. He is reaching out through the veil. Sean, if you are present, make yourself known."

There was one hard knock on the table. It sounded as if it came from the centre. Evelyn yelped. The widow on her right patted her hand impatiently.

"Sean?" Mr. Gough whispered. "Is that—are you truly here?"

There was another knock.

She pictured a spectre appearing before them on the table. A vaporous ghoul. There was something *there*, something unhuman, sentient, otherworldly, right in the middle of the table. Was it crouching on top, watching her? Was it lurking, crawling along the carpet? What if it touched her on the ankle, a wintry, spectral hand, clasping her under her skirt? She drew her feet as far as she could underneath her, hooking them around the legs of the chair.

"Oh my God," Mr. Gough said, his forehead wrinkling. "Oh, heavens."

"Sean wishes you to know he is present," Madame Celeste said.

"Is he really with us?" Mr. Gough looked wildly around the room. Evelyn followed his gaze. There was a heavy Edwardian armoire in the corner of the room she hadn't noticed before. Something might creep out of it, towards her.

"Can I speak with him?"

"Speak out loud, he will be able to hear you."

"Sean, it's me, David. Do you—do you remember me?"

The table knocked.

"What does that mean?" he said, staring at Madame Celeste.

"He remembers you fondly."

Mr. Gough swallowed. "Are you—are you at, at peace?"

The knock came again.

Madame Celeste squinted. "He is at peace."

Mr. Gough stifled a sob. "Thank God."

"Sean crossed over before his time," Madame Celeste said.

"Yes," Mr. Gough said, his chin buried in his chest.

"His passing was not of his own doing. He's saying he wasn't at fault."

"That's right. We were in Belgium together. Mons."

Evelyn looked again at Mr. Gough. She'd taken him for a younger man, but he had to be at least as old as Alistair.

"He was wounded," Madame Celeste continued. "Gravely wounded."

"Yes."

Discreetly, Evelyn cleared her throat. If someone had died at Mons, then it was rather a safe guess that they had been wounded.

"But he wasn't alone when he died, someone was near," Madame Celeste said.

"That was me," Mr. Gough said, a hardness filtering over his eyes.

"Sean knows you were there, that you were with him at the end."

Mr. Gough groaned. His breath came in wet coughs.

"He thanks you for being there with him during his last moments. Your presence helped him cross over, to find peace."

Mr. Gough's lips were wobbling. "Does he have any messages?"

Madame Celeste's face crumpled and released. "He asks you to tell his family he is at peace on the other side, to send his love to them."

Evelyn wrinkled her nose. Not very specific. You'd think if you were going to break through the etheric barriers that contained the earthly plane, you'd at least have something interesting to say.

"I will, I'll tell them," Mr. Gough said.

"And he is showing me a clock, in his family home. Is there a clock, in their home?"

"Yes, yes, there's a clock."

"He is saying that his family are displaying something of his, near a clock."

"I don't know," Mr. Gough said, looking around the table, as if the rest of them might have the answer. Then he gasped. "Yes, his photograph is right next to the clock on the mantelpiece!"

Evelyn licked her lips. Where else does one keep a clock but with other items on display?

"He knows it is there. He knows when they look upon it and think of him."

Mr. Gough dropped his chin again. "Oh my God."

"Sean wants to thank you for being here. He invites you to come back and commune with him soon at another session. Perhaps next week?"

Mr. Gough nodded. "I will, I will, thank you."

Evelyn stared at Madame Celeste, her pulse settling, calm and steady. Maybe Robert had been right—maybe it *was* a way to help people feel better. But there wasn't anything miraculous happening here, no heavenly secrets were being unveiled. It was nothing more than cheap theatrical tricks melded to a guessing game. The spectacle was contrived to titillate the senses and to relieve existential remorse. She pulled her shoulders back. There was nothing to fear. She was safe. They were safe.

✦ ✦ ✦

AFTER THE MEETING, ROBERT and Evelyn took tea in a new teahouse on the corner of George and Frederick. It had become popular overnight after a write-up in *Pictorial*, and they'd been forced to queue in the drizzle, pressing their noses to the window to gauge the speed at which the diners within nibbled their tea cakes.

"Incredible session, wasn't it?" Robert said, draining the last of his cup.

Evelyn said nothing.

"Madame Celeste even knew his photograph was next to the clock!"

"Everybody keeps sentimental items near their clocks, don't they? Books or ornaments or photographs."

Robert looked at her.

"And it would be a bit strange if his family didn't have a picture of him out."

"What's that got to do with anything?"

Evelyn put a hand on Robert's, measuring her words. "Isn't there a chance, darling, that it was an educated guess?"

He shot her a pitying look. "Evie, Evie." He patted her on the wrist. "Have faith."

"But I don't want to have faith," she said, not able to help herself.

His jaw tightened.

"I mean, a real medium wouldn't need faith, would they? They would welcome a challenge, they'd want to give proof. Evidence."

Robert picked up his fork and toyed with the currants he had picked out of his scone. "I suppose. But it's not an exact science."

"It's not a science at all, is it?" Evelyn said.

Robert dropped his eyes to the tablecloth. "There's hundreds of scientists working in spiritualism," he said, tersely. "There's *geniuses* working in spiritualism. Edison? Conan Doyle?"

"Doesn't Conan Doyle also believe in fairies?"

Robert's face darkened. He pushed the plate away from him and clasped his hands on the tablecloth.

"More hot water?" A waitress appeared behind them and reached for the teapot.

Evelyn nodded. The silence between them was excruciating as the waitress filled up the pot. She was bound to know they were squabbling. Everyone in the café probably knew. Evelyn fixed her attention on an elderly woman at the tram stop across the road badgering her grandson to get under her umbrella. Evelyn chastised herself: she was pushing him too hard, she was never going to talk him down by being obstinate. He had to think it was his idea.

By the time they left the tearoom, a sharp sleet was needling through black clouds, and the lamplight threw gaunt shadows over the pavement. Robert opened the umbrella, and Evelyn slipped her arm through his. They walked to the bus stop in silence. A teenage boy in front of them fumbled in his pocket and dropped a bag of boilings that spilled out onto the pavement. He stopped, staring mournfully at the dissolving sweeties. Since it was bad manners to trample over his misadventure, Evelyn broke free of Robert's arm and darted into the sleet to avoid the site of the accident.

She dashed back under the umbrella and took a deep breath, taking Robert's arm. "I'm sorry. What I said before, I didn't mean to be dismissive."

She felt the weight of his shoulders drop. "I've as much right as anyone to research spiritualism."

"I know," she said. "I know that."

"I'm not stupid."

Evelyn stopped and stared at him. His expression was bashful; he wouldn't meet her eyes. "I never said that."

"I know I'm no professor."

Evelyn gripped his arm. "No, Robert, I would never even think that."

"Really?" He looked almost tearful now.

"Of course! You are cleverer than everybody I know!"

Robert turned his head and laughed, as if he didn't believe her.

"You've worked a lot harder and come a lot further than anyone I've ever met," Evelyn said.

Robert's lower lip twitched. "I don't understand why you won't give it a chance, Evie."

Evelyn tried to look earnest. "I am giving it a chance. I'm not objecting, am I? I came along today."

Robert broke into a smile, grabbing her into a damp hug. "I know. You're a good sport."

"I'm sorry if I offended you," she said into the lapels of his overcoat. His top button was loose; she'd need to set it aside for Marty.

"Thank you," Robert said, kissing her on the ear.

Evelyn waited for more, but nothing came. As they untangled themselves and crossed the road, she tucked her disappointment neatly inside her belly. She wanted more than a "thank you." She wanted a parade and a medal and a knighthood.

"And you'll do the reading too?" he said.

"Reading?"

They turned the corner to see a bus pulling away from the stop. Evelyn yanked Robert's arm back as the bus sprayed a fan of water over the pavement, but it was too late, and his trousers were swamped.

"It's like they've never driven in their lives." He shook his legs out one by one, water dripping from the toes of his shoes.

"Dear me, what a shame," Evelyn said, eager to get her sympathetic ministrations over with quickly.

Tutting, Robert backed up against the wall. He made a great show of pointing out to each passerby the puddle on the road and encouraging them to stay well away from the danger zone.

Evelyn put her hand into his pocket and squeezed his fingers. "So, what reading must I complete?" She tried to keep the prickliness out of her voice.

"Oh. The research. I can help you with it, if you like. It's awful complicated. There's amazing technological advances. Edison's building a device that would let us speak to spirits, like a telephone."

Evelyn frowned. "But how would"—she dropped her voice—"a ghost be able to lift the earpiece?"

"Not exactly like a telephone. More like a phonograph, with an electrode."

"Hmm," Evelyn said. Maybe she *would* need help with the reading.

Robert brought her hand to his mouth and rolled forward the leather of her glove until he could kiss her wrist. "I knew you'd be game, Evie. I knew you wouldn't be afraid of a challenge."

"Of course not. I'm not afraid of research." Yet Evelyn felt all the unsaid things she was afraid of swirling around in her stomach.

"If you join the library too, we can go there together."

Evelyn winced. But it was better to gather intelligence on the enemy. She could use the information to point out inconsistencies. "Yes, I can do that."

"That's fantastic!" He broke off, leaning forward and waving the elderly woman next to them away from the road. "Mind that puddle," he said. "It's like they've never driven in their lives, those bus drivers."

Robert pulled back. "So you won't mind if I recruit even more help?"

"Oh?" she said, sensing a trap.

"Aye, for a sort of mentor," he said, a flush rising to his cheeks. A bus ambled up the street and the elderly woman took a step towards the puddle, shooting Robert a nervous look. Evelyn fumbled in her purse for bus fare.

"What do you mean?"

"The hall has a development circle, and there's a medium— Clarence O'Grady, he's incredible, he'd help me. Except there's no other people waiting to get taught at the moment. I suppose not really a development circle, more like a development line." And Robert chuckled to himself.

"So, a tutor?"

"Exactly."

Evelyn pictured a drab man in tweed, moon spectacles slipping down his nose as he droned on about Epicurus. "That sounds fine."

The bus drew up beside them, but Robert just stood there, grinning at her. "This'll be such an adventure for us to go on together."

"Hmm, we'll see," she said, gesturing for him to board. She dug deep within her soul, striking the core of her reserves of jollity to produce a joke. Something to lighten the tone, shave down the edge of the strangeness. "Perhaps," she said, "perhaps you'll get insight into the winning horse at Ascot, and we can take a fabulous holiday."

Robert turned to her, one foot on the step of the bus. A wild expression of cheerful astonishment crossed his face. "That's a nice thought, Evie. Maybe I will!"

Evelyn stared at him until she was quite sure he wasn't being obtuse. No—he hadn't even known that she was joking. She followed him onto the bus with a queasy, flopping feeling in her stomach, like she had swallowed a live kipper.

10

AND SO, EACH SUNDAY, EVELYN AND ROBERT ATTENDED
St. Serf's in the morning with Kitty and Alistair, and the Spiritualist
Hall at noon. On Saturday afternoons, Robert took his tutoring at
the research centre, arranged through Mrs. Downie. Evelyn wondered if it was a voluntary service, or if they were paying for it, but
she daren't ask. His study accrued a series of flimsy pamphlets by
cloaked middle-aged women with European names: Madame Ther-
oux, Senora Da Rosa, Mrs. Van de Gees. Robert returned home
from his development sessions weary but glowing. "I've got to build
up the spiritual muscle," he said. "Like riding or hunting."

Evelyn didn't think it sounded anything like riding or hunting. More like panning for gold in a fishpond. For her part, Evelyn
subscribed to *Scientific American*, and gently probed Robert over
dinner about sham spirit photography. She underlined salient passages in articles about the Fox sisters and left them on his desk. And
then she waited for Robert to come to his senses. Meanwhile, she
dutifully sat through the Spiritualist Hall meetings, dozing through
speeches and readings given by the poorest speakers and readers.

Evelyn had not mentioned these visits to Kitty.

She thought of mentioning them to Kitty. She nearly mentioned
them to Kitty. On January 24th, the anniversary of Dolly's passing,
Evelyn forced herself from bed to telephone Kitty, with the precise

intention of telling her, only to lose her nerve at the first ring. She thought of telling her while they pushed Margaret's pram through the Botanics, while they queued for a matinee at the Palace Cinema, while they read, side-by-side, in Kitty's parlour. And yet, she said nothing. Kitty had suggested a book, a lecture series. But by the middle of February Robert was still spending each weekend playing wizard. Evelyn was waking in the middle of the night with a fearful tingling in her belly, scrunching her fists, chastising herself for leaving it so long. Her plan was to drop it into a sentence with a studied casualness, as if Kitty had been the one to forget that she and Robert had been attending what amounted to a second church, secretly, for weeks. And she was going along with it! How would Kitty be able to understand that going along with it was the only way to keep everything from collapsing? But letting Robert lead them somewhere, for once, was her gift to him, her show of trust. And it was the best way to keep things steady until she had time to correct.

By now, the other women at the meetings recognised her, welcomed her. Geraldine had laughed about her false name. Mrs. Downie always complimented Evelyn's dress. She'd befriended the auburn-haired woman she had stared at the first day in at the hall, Annie McCloud, who'd relocated from Aberdeen to live with an elderly aunt with poor health. Going to the Spiritualist Hall had begun to feel something not exactly close to normal, but certainly habitual. And it made Robert happy. He was elastic with enthusiasm, running up the stairs two at a time, whistling as he fed the chickens in the morning. He called Evelyn into his study to read her long paragraphs from journals about clootie wells and automatic writing and shadow boxes and cablegraphs while Evelyn fixed an interested expression on her face.

❖ ❖ ❖

ONE SATURDAY AFTERNOON ON the way home from shopping at Patrick Thomson's, she heard heavy footsteps behind her and turned to see Robert running towards the bridge, waving. He stopped at her side and leant against the wall, wheezing. "Saw you—from the top—didn't want to shout."

"You shouldn't be running!" Evelyn said, putting a hand on his shoulder as he wiped his sweaty face. "Your heart!"

"Yes, yes." Robert grabbed her hand. "If it's beating faster, it's just because I saw you."

Evelyn rolled her eyes, but she smiled, despite herself.

He took the package from under Evelyn's arm. "The session this afternoon was incredible, Evie."

"Glad to hear it." Her bladder was uncomfortably full, and she picked up her pace.

"The tutoring's really helping," he said, as they crossed the bridge.

"Lovely," Evelyn said. Waters of Leith were at high tide, and it was only magnifying her discomfort. "Do you mind if we hurry?"

"Clarence is a genius, of course. And I'm lucky he's even in town, his European circuit only finished last month."

"Is that so?" They paused at the edge of the road as John Douglas's motorcar passed. Evelyn crossed her fingers in her coat pocket that he wouldn't stop to talk to them, but he just honked the horn and waved.

"He thinks I show real talent," Robert was saying, stopping to pluck a snowdrop from a window box outside the public house and handing it to her with an extravagant bow.

"Yes, I'm sure," Evelyn said, dutifully tucking the flower into her buttonhole and marching at double speed.

"And he'll be demonstrating at the hall next week. You'll meet him, won't you, Evie?"

"Meet who?"

"Clarence. He'll be doing a special demonstration."

"Oh, the tutor, yes, I can meet him."

Back at home, Evelyn didn't even take off her coat but raced to the bathroom. When she emerged, she could smell Robert smoking a cigar in his study. Evelyn retrieved her book of word puzzles and sat in the parlour, propping her feet on the ottoman.

"Today was the best day I've had yet," Robert called from the study. Evelyn put her pen down, sighing. She stood and crossed to the doorway of his study. He had rolled up the sleeves of his shirt and there was ink on the cuffs.

"That's lovely, darling." Evelyn tucked the book under her arm and picked up his jacket from where it had fallen, or been thrown, onto the floor. "What's the capital city of Albania?" she said. "Don't tell me the whole thing, I'll get it, just the first letter."

Robert drummed his foot against the table. "I really connected, Evie."

Evelyn hung his jacket over the back of the door. She thought of the way bricklayers place down blocks so that they overlapped. "Connected?"

"To the other side," he said, widening his eyes.

Evelyn began to beat the jacket with the book, although it wasn't dusty.

"Don't mind that," he said, and pointed at the left armchair.

Evelyn perched on the arm. She decided to list all the capitals of Europe she could remember. She started with Paris and worked her way east.

"And Mrs. Jacobs was amazed. The message was so clear—the symbols suddenly made sense. Like decoding a cipher. You know what decoding means?"

Evelyn realised she was meant to supply a response. "Of course I do," she said, stiffly.

Robert sat back in his chair, his energy spent, although his eyes were bright. "And Mrs. Jacobs has asked me to read for her again, next week."

"Where is this to take place?" Evelyn said.

"At the library."

She chewed her lips. "I suppose that sounds all right."

✷ ✷ ✷

THE NEXT DAY, AS they queued up to enter the hall, Evelyn became aware of a sort of stirring in the crowd. Was she imagining it, or were people looking at Robert? There was a subtle nudging, a whispering. People were standing one step too far away from them, or else taking a step too close. They were shooting glances at Robert and then away, and then back again.

Mrs. Downie was standing at the door, and caught Evelyn's eye meaningfully through the crowd. She twisted her head to and fro, trying to signal something. Evelyn approached, and Mrs. Downie held out her hand.

"Mr. Hazard, Mrs. Hazard, good afternoon."

"Good afternoon."

"I must say," she gushed, gripping her leather notebook, "there has been tremendous excitement about your session with Mrs. Jacobs."

Robert grinned. "You're too kind."

"Not at all." Mrs. Downie gazed at Robert, starry-eyed. "The clarity of the message," she exhaled. "Such a blessing it's been for her. I've had enquiries all morning for your availability."

Robert chuckled, but his cheeks were pink. "Is that right?"

Mrs. Downie looked down at her notebook. "Perhaps, this afternoon, are you open to another session?"

"We're having tea with Kitty this afternoon," Evelyn said. Her voice came out alarmed, hoarse.

Robert smiled, generously. "I'm sure they won't mind."

Mrs. Downie was watching her, as if for authorisation. In turn, Evelyn stared at Robert. He was supposed to be their fourth for bridge. They wouldn't be able to play without him.

"Is there—do you have another appointment?" Mrs. Downie said, in a panicked voice.

"No, not at all." Robert bowed to her.

Evelyn nodded at Mrs. Downie, with a quick tilt of her head. Her cheeks were burning.

"Lovely," Mrs. Downie said. "I'll put you down for 4:00 PM."

Robert gripped Evelyn at the elbow as they walked into the hall. She could feel his posture straighten, as if he'd been pumped up with air. Evelyn cursed herself for not paying more attention. What had he said to Mrs. Jacobs? Something about ciphers? She couldn't focus on the reading, mouthed the words during "Scatter Seeds of Kindness." Next to her, Robert's voice rang out so loud she could feel the vibrations in her skeleton.

As everyone closed their hymnbooks, Evelyn leant over to whisper in his ear. "What was that about earlier, with Mrs. Jacobs?"

"Mrs. Jacobs? I'm reading her."

"Yes, but I thought you were talking about the library, before. When you say reading—"

"Channelling the spirits."

Evelyn's mouth fell open. "Oh, Robert."

"She's so grateful, you wouldn't believe it." He smiled.

Her stomach roiled. "I thought—I didn't realise you still wanted to—"

"I'm really helping her," Robert said, earnestly. "You'll be so proud of me, Evie."

Evelyn pressed her fingernails into her palms. This was all part of it. Letting him fail. It was all part of the plan.

❖ ❖ ❖

ON KITTY'S DOORSTEP THAT afternoon, Evelyn straightened her coat, then her hat, then her coat again. Jeanie opened the door, and Evelyn heard Kitty speaking to a man in the parlour. "Who's here?" Evelyn whispered to Jeanie, as she took off her coat.

"It's your father, ma'am," Jeanie said, blushing. It was silly of her to blush, but Evelyn looked away, not wanting to embarrass her by drawing attention to her silliness.

Evelyn loitered in the parlour doorway. Her shoulders began to itch with sweat. "Papa, I wasn't expecting to see you."

He motioned her over to the armchair, and she kissed his cheek. "I came back early from Dunfermline, the papers said snow," he said, pointing out the window as if he were accusing someone.

Evelyn lingered by the fire. Baby Margaret was lying on the rug, gnawing on a wine cork. Kitty saw her watching and said, "Before you say anything, I boiled it first."

Evelyn nodded without hearing her. She moved to stand behind the other armchair, so she could have something solid to lean on.

"Where's Robert?" Kitty said, looking pointedly into the corridor.

"He can't join us, I'm afraid." Evelyn gripped the chair. "And actually, I have something important to tell you both."

"Oh!" Kitty flew off the sofa, a great smile on her face.

Evelyn shook her head. "Not that."

Slowly, Kitty lowered herself back onto the sofa.

Papa turned to look at her, the newspaper tucked next to his arm rustling. "What is it? Are you ill? Not the flu?"

"No, no, I'm fine."

"Robert, then?"

"He's fine too."

Papa frowned at Kitty and then back at Evelyn. "Good grief, don't make me guess, Evelyn. What is the matter?"

Evelyn looked down at the armchair. There was a cigarette burn in the weave of the arm, and she pressed her thumb over the hole. "It's, he's, well—firstly, nothing's wrong." She took a deep breath. "But he's interested in becoming a member of a new society, and, well, they're a bit eccentric."

Papa's eyes blazed. "Not joining Glasgow Reds, is he?"

Evelyn almost laughed. "Oh, Papa, no, he's not a socialist." And then she stopped. *Was* he now a socialist? When she looked up again, her father was watching her.

"Politics, is it?"

Evelyn went to bite her fingernail and Papa's nostrils flared so fiercely she put her hand down. "No, it's not. It's the Spiritualist Library," she said, trying to ease the blow.

Papa wrinkled his nose. He shook out the newspaper and laid it over his knee. "A library? Is that it? For heaven's sake, Evelyn, you make it sound like he's running away to join the Black and Tans."

Evelyn chewed her lips. She didn't want to have to explain it further. "But—"

"But what?"

"Spiritualism," she said.

"Is that"—Papa squinted at Kitty—"the votes for women?"

"That's suffrage, Papa," Evelyn said, irritated.

"You know what suffrage is, remember Dolly and her societies?" Kitty said, in an encouraging tone. "Spiritualism is the one with—with spirits."

Papa scowled into the fire. "Conan Doyle and all that?"

Evelyn nodded.

Papa's eyes widened. "A sorry group of lunatics, aren't they? What's your Robert getting mixed up with those people for, doesn't he have enough to keep him occupied?"

Evelyn looked over his head at Kitty, pleading for help. "It's a pastime, Papa."

Kitty sat up on the sofa. "Like Alistair and his trains."

Papa scoffed. "Robert doesn't need to pass time. Why doesn't he do something useful if he has so much time on his hands? He should volunteer. Or he should work for me at the firm. Heaven knows I've suggested it often enough."

Evelyn gritted her teeth. "He has his own business, Papa. He doesn't want to work for you."

Papa thrust his newspaper between his knee and the arm of the chair. "Good Lord, Evelyn, people have enough to say as it is about your match with him, without involving spiritists. You'll have to tell him to stop, immediately. Or I will."

Evelyn stood up straighter. Everything that had happened—the "big move," the war, the flu, Dolly—and Papa was still fixated on Robert's humble background. Even though Robert was a good man, he still, apparently, wasn't good enough. "Robert's not doing any harm, going to a library," Evelyn said.

Kitty was nodding. "A library is a nice, restful place for him. With his hea—"

Evelyn cut her off. "Robert will fall out of interest with it eventually, but for now, well"—she took a breath—"that's what he wants to do. I thought I should mention it, out of respect, in case you heard anything."

"Respect?" Papa's lips tightened. "Respect! You girls haven't shown me and your mother anything *resembling* respect since we moved to Edinburgh."

"That's not fair," Kitty said. Her face was pale.

"Not you, Katherine," Papa said, offhandedly. He turned to Evelyn. "Elopement, divorce, suffragists, accountants, and now, what? Fortune tellers? Whatever will be next? It's been nothing but poor judgement chasing poor judgement."

"We wouldn't be living in Edinburgh at all if it weren't for your poor judgement," Evelyn snapped. She saw Kitty flinch in the corner of her vision, and she knew she had struck too hard. But even though it was cruel to say so, and even though she had made her own bad decisions, there was truth in it. Papa's poor judgement had wrested away the life she had known, and the war came for the rest of it.

Papa was blinking at her as if he had been doused in cold water.

"And since then, we've all had to make the best of things," Evelyn continued. Her hands were shaking; she had never challenged Papa before, and her nerves were flickering like a faulty light bulb. "Robert's choice of library is hardly a tragedy, given everything that has happened to us."

"To the world," Kitty added.

"Yes, quite. And you can disapprove all you like. But"—she swallowed—"it won't make any difference." She gathered her courage to divulge more. "There's a church, too."

Papa was shaking his head. The fire had drained out of him now, and he looked exhausted. Evelyn felt simultaneously victorious and sorry for him. "You'll break your mother's heart, Evelyn," he said.

"I'm sorry." Evelyn's lip wobbled. *But what about* my *heart?* she wanted to say. Mama and Kitty were allowed to have feelings in every direction, but nobody worried about her. Even Robert. Her job was to hold everything steady, for all of them, and they took it for granted she wasn't going to develop emotions and start demanding her own accommodations.

Kitty's cheeks were pink. "A church, too?"

"Yes," Evelyn said. "Well, it's not exactly a church. More like a meeting-place. But very respectable. And the library is respectable too. Robert has a tutor there. A very well-respected tutor."

"You've been going with him?" Kitty was buttoning the top of Margaret's pinafore.

"It's important to Robert," Evelyn said, "that I join him."

There was a moment of silence in the room. Evelyn looked between Papa, who was staring into the fire, and Kitty, who was repeatedly smoothing down the baby's tufty lock of hair.

"Don't use their towels," Papa said, eventually. "They probably all wash at the steamie."

Evelyn heard a gargling noise in her throat she realised was laughter. "OK, Papa." She released the back of the chair, where her fingers had made crescents in the upholstery, and ran to embrace him.

Papa put his hand up, stopping her before she reached him. She took a step back. "Evelyn. You understand I cannot approve of this." Papa's usual air of gruff abstraction was gone, and he was giving her a clear, analytical look. It was the kind of look delivered to a colleague.

"You recognise the harm this could do to the firm, don't you? I will not risk the security of this family for Bobby's foibles. I cannot be associated with scandal . . ." He trailed off, and Evelyn knew that the unfinished end of his sentence was "again."

She wrapped her arms around her waist. "I understand. I won't let that happen."

"It would be better for us not to associate in public," Papa said, rubbing his forehead. "Don't come to the party on the third, I'll have clients attending."

Evelyn nodded, her throat tight. She felt a surge of anger at Robert for putting her in this position. They had been managing just fine with Papa in a détente. Robert had no idea the sacrifices she was having to make for him.

"Your mother will need time. Don't call at the house until this has blown over."

Evelyn nodded again. She squeezed her hands into fists. She wasn't going to cry. She was a grown woman. It was silly to cry about your mother.

"Katherine." Papa turned to look at her. "You'll have to keep your mother calm. I hope there's one of you left I can trust not to lose your mind?"

"Yes, Papa," Kitty said.

Something in her tone was odd. Evelyn tried to catch Kitty's eye, but she was patting baby Margaret on the back with flustered little taps, her gaze fixed on the carpet.

II

ROBERT SPENT THE NEXT WEEK IN A STATE OF JITTERY excitement about Clarence's special session at the Spiritualist Hall. He marched up and down his study, nervous as a debutante. "We should get there early," he would say over dinner, and, "You don't think it will snow? Clog up the roads?" Evelyn provided him with bland reassurances, but her heart wasn't in it. Since Sunday, Kitty had been odd with her, maybe even avoiding her. She'd gone by Kitty's house on Wednesday afternoon, and even though Jeanie said she was out with the baby, Evelyn spotted the pram in the hallway. She'd returned home, nursing a hollow sadness that she couldn't bear to explain to Robert.

On Sunday, Robert cut himself shaving and was still dabbing at the graze while he put on his hat, sighing in the corridor while Evelyn tied her boots. "The earlier we go, the earlier we can leave," he said. Which had never been, in the history of all time, a feature of church. Kitty and Alistair arrived to walk with them to St. Serf's, and on the route down, Evelyn stuck close to Kitty's side.

"Did Jeanie tell you I came by on Wednesday?"

Kitty sniffed. "Yes, sorry I missed you. I went to the Colonies." She wiped her nose with a handkerchief.

Evelyn peered at her. "You're ill," she said. "You should be in bed. Not walking around the Colonies. Wait, why were you in that neighbourhood at all? You weren't swimming, were you? You mustn't get your hair wet if you're ill."

"It's just a cold," Kitty said. "And no, I wasn't swimming. I went for the collection, for that poor wee boy."

"Which boy?"

Kitty frowned at her. "Wee Charlie, of course."

"Who's wee Charlie?" Evelyn pulled off her gloves to feel Kitty's forehead. "Have you had a fever?"

Kitty batted her hand away. "No, stop fussing, it's just a chill. Don't tell me you've been too distracted to hear about wee Charlie?"

"I haven't been distracted."

Kitty's mouth flattened into a line.

"Do you think I've been distracted? I tried to come by."

"I know," Kitty said. "I mean, you've been busy with your new society."

Evelyn examined Kitty's expression, but Kitty was keeping her face blank. "I don't have much of a choice," she said. "It will take time to talk him out of it." She looked over her shoulder at Robert. "I didn't mention to him about Papa. I thought he might be sensitive to it."

"To what?"

Evelyn opened her mouth to untie the thought. She would never be able to tell Robert that her parents objected so vehemently to his spiritualism that Papa had told them to avoid contact. If Robert found out that the only parental figures in his life had been so quick to reject him, it would devastate him. Even once he snapped out of the spiritualism, it would colour all their future interactions, every Christmas and Burns Night, every party, every Saturday afternoon stroll through the Botanics. No, she could never tell him. It might even make Robert wounded enough to push him further into the arms of his new friends at the hall.

"It doesn't matter," Evelyn said, at last. She looked at Kitty, wondering if she should probe for her true feelings on the subject, and decided against it. There was only so much strife she could handle in a week. "So, you went for a collection?"

"Yes. Oh, it's terrible, everyone in the Colonies is worried sick about the poor wee boy."

"Is he ill?"

"No, he went missing, you really haven't heard? Doesn't your Marty's sister live that way?"

"That sounds right." Evelyn checked again that Robert and Alistair were far enough behind them not to overhear. "How was Papa after I left?" she said.

Kitty shrugged. "Mostly he just complained about all the unopened Christmas cards that came back from people who emigrated last year without telling him."

Evelyn had a sense Kitty was leaving something out, but her energy for confrontation had collapsed. "He'll save a fortune on stamps this year."

Kitty laughed, her shoulder brushing against Evelyn's. She put her arm around Kitty and squeezed her. "I'll have everything back to normal in no time, don't you worry. I've got this under control," she said, quietly.

Kitty nodded. "I know you do."

❖ ❖ ❖

AFTER THE SERVICE AT St. Serf's, Robert marched to the tram stop so fast that Evelyn could hardly keep up with him. "It's 11:30 already," he was saying. "11:35, now." Halfway up Jeffrey Street, a horse drawing a cart of apple crates paused on the tracks to defecate while its handler tugged uselessly on its reins. Tutting and puffing, Robert ushered her out of the tram and they walked the rest of the way up the hill. When they arrived at the mews in front of the hall, it was more crowded than usual. Teenage boys with downy moustaches jingled change in their pockets, and boisterous children ate cream buns from their handkerchiefs.

"Are you excited?" Annie leapt upon Evelyn so suddenly that her heel caught on a cobble and she had to grab Annie to right herself.

"About?"

"About Clarence." Annie flicked the brim of Evelyn's hat for emphasis.

"Oh yes, Robert's tutor. He seems popular, doesn't he?"

"Robert's tutor?" Annie squeaked.

"Yes," Evelyn said, looking for Robert for confirmation, but he was talking to an elderly gentleman wearing a pince-nez.

"I didn't know Clarence tutored." Annie stared at the side of Robert's head, greedily. "How lucky he is."

Evelyn followed Annie's line of sight. "Is that him?" She gestured at the man with the pince-nez.

Annie tipped her head back and laughed. "Dear me, no. You really don't know Clarence?"

"We've not met," Evelyn said, irritably.

Annie opened her purse and pressed a folded pamphlet into Evelyn's hand. "*That's* Clarence."

"This?" Evelyn swallowed. The pamphlet featured an etching of a small, ringleted doll-like figure with lustrous eyes, standing on a white cloud.

Robert snatched the pamphlet from her. "Where did you get that?"

"Auntie Agnes. But there's more at the front." Annie pointed towards the doors, where Geraldine and Mrs. Downie were holding great stacks of paper.

"What is it?" Evelyn squinted at the pamphlet. "Is it—an automaton?" Her voice was weak. She pictured Robert sitting in the library at one of the tables by the window, a terrible doll rolling in on oiled wheels, its porcelain face turning to him with stuttering tremors, its tiny hands icy.

Robert laughed. "Not at all. He's a genius. A child prodigy!"

"A child?" She grabbed Robert's arm as people began filing into the hall. "A child, Robert?"

"Yes." He was smiling.

"Why didn't you mention it?"

"Didn't I? I'm sure I did."

Acid rose into Evelyn's throat. "I would remember if you told me that you have a child tutor, Robert!"

Robert patted her hand. "Just wait until you see him, he's a genius. Like Mozart."

"Mozart didn't summon the dead," Evelyn hissed.

Robert squeezed past two elderly ladies and pointed to the middle of the second row. He put his face close to Evelyn's, until she could feel his stubble tickle her ears. "I promise, my love, it's not as odd as it sounds. See for yourself."

Stiffly, Evelyn took a seat. She gripped her handbag on her lap, her jaw tight. Everyone must have known about Robert and his infant tutor. Mrs. Downie, Geraldine. Everyone must have been laughing about it for weeks. God, Papa would have a seizure if he found out! It was beyond careless for Robert not to have told her. Suspicious, even. She shot him an inquisitorial look. Would he have kept that from her, deliberately, just to get his way? But that kind of deception was beyond him. Wasn't it?

The room swished with rustling as people behind them unwrapped cough lozenges and straightened hats and wiped spectacles. Mrs. Downie came on the stage, and the crowd sat up in their seats.

"Good afternoon, ladies and gentlemen," Mrs. Downie said. "What a pleasure to see such a lot of new faces here. If it's your first time at the Spiritualist Hall today, please come and speak to me or Miss Frelinski after the service." She clapped her hands. "Well, we have a slightly different schedule today, allowing for our honoured guest who has recently returned from his European circuit." She beamed into the wings. "Please join me in welcoming Clarence O'Grady."

Evelyn gritted her teeth.

On came the child. He was perhaps ten years old, dressed in a neat blue uniform like he was the mascot for an elite sailing academy.

Evelyn wanted to cry. Robert was clapping loudly, whistling through his teeth, and she couldn't even bear to look at him. Clarence was a wee child! He had bouncy, golden-blond waves and freckles across his nose. He took a seat on a stool in the centre of the stage and slipped his hands underneath him.

"Good day," he said.

The audience laughed. The woman next to her was saying, "Isn't he darling?"

Someone called out, "Hello, Clarence."

The boy waved into the crowd.

Evelyn shuddered. Where was this boy's mother? Who was permitting this? It was like leasing your baby to a circus, to be fed biscuits through the bars.

Clarence began kicking the stool, and reached for a tumbler of milk on the table. He took too large a drink and it slopped onto his uniform. "Oh dear," he said. "Don't tell Mama."

The crowd roared with laughter.

"Who is Albert?" Clarence said, suddenly, staring into the audience with one hand against his brow. "Albert," he said again.

At the back of the hall, a young brunette woman stood, staggering. "Albert—Albert was my husband's name," she said.

"Then you must join me," Clarence said.

"Oh, oh," the woman was saying as she picked her way through the aisle. Mrs. Downie helped her climb the steps onto the stage, even though she didn't need helping.

"Nice to meet you," said Clarence, holding out his hand.

The woman was perhaps twenty, long-limbed and thin, with a fashionably cropped haircut. She broke into tears as she approached Clarence. "I'm sorry," she said, wiping her eyes with a handkerchief. "I'm sorry, already making a fool of myself."

"There is nothing foolish about grief," Clarence said.

Evelyn took a breath. An unexpected wave of emotion bubbled over her and she blinked it back.

Clarence held the woman's hand. She was shaking, her hand almost eclipsing the boy's tiny paw.

"Albert says you look lovely," Clarence said.

The woman laughed, a confused laugh that was soft with tears. Self-consciously, she touched her hat.

"Did you dress with him in mind, today?" Clarence said.

"I did, yes, I did."

"Albert apologises for not taking more notice of the care which you always took with your dress."

She sobbed, pressing her handkerchief into her eyes.

"And you talk to him."

She nodded.

"Albert says that he hears you," Clarence said, with a radiant smile. "When you speak to him, you confide in him your concerns. He may not be able to reply, but he hears you."

"I miss him every single day," the woman said, so simply that it struck Evelyn in the chest like a blow.

"But you must know that he watches over you, that he is always by your side, especially when you walk—" He paused for a second, as if listening to an external voice. "Do you walk somewhere beside a great cliff? Red cliffs. With many birds?"

The woman flinched. "Yes."

"Is it—" Clarence squinted. "Is it St. Abb's Head?"

"Yes! My goodness."

The audience began to laugh, some to clap. Others were shaking their heads, glancing at each other in disbelief.

"Albert," Clarence said and paused, looking shyly down at the floor. "He had a special nickname for you, did he not?"

The woman laughed through her tears. "Yes."

"He's embarrassed, he doesn't want me to say it out loud in front of all of these people, because he was a private person, wasn't he?"

"Yes, he was, he was."

"Well, he's repeating his special pet name for you," Clarence said. "He watches over you when you're at your deepest sleep, and he calls you by that special name—" Clarence broke off, listening to the air, before tilting his head back towards the woman. "He says you recently redecorated your bedroom, is that right?"

"My goodness!" The woman was shaking so much, Evelyn could hear the pins in her boots tap against the wooden stage.

"New bedspread, and a new paint colour. Is that so?"

"It is!"

"Albert says it is very pretty. And if you feel his presence there at night, it's because he visits you. He is saying, 'I never let you go to sleep without touching you.'"

A prickle of goose bumps rose on Evelyn's arms. The woman on stage, however, broke into a huge smile. "Thank you, yes," she said.

"Do you ever feel him? When he comes, it will be like a cold breeze over your body, or perhaps a weight next to you on the bed."

"I've felt it, yes," the woman said, smiling.

Evelyn shivered. She thought of Dolores's earring, glowing under the floorboards. What was it Robert had said, in the beginning? One of the ways spirits communicate is in lost items. She shifted her weight in her seat.

"He knows something, a secret you've been keeping," Clarence said, in a low voice.

Evelyn squeezed her fingernails into her palms.

"A secret? I don't know what that could be."

"It's about a birthday present," Clarence said, with a conspiratorial grin. "You're hiding it away for his niece, aren't you? An expensive present, too. He's laughing about it, saying he would have never let you buy such an expensive present."

The woman covered her face with her hands before releasing them. "It's true! How true!"

"Albert has to leave us now, but he wants to share with you so much love," Clarence said. "May I embrace you?"

The woman gathered Clarence in her arms, tears rolling down her cheeks. She pushed her face into the boy's shoulder and whispered something. Clarence nodded.

Evelyn's mouth was dry. How had the child known all that? St. Abb's Head, the new paint colour? The birthday gift? He couldn't possibly have made idle guesses. A cold trickle of sweat gathered underneath her bust bodice.

The audience began to filter out of the hall, and Evelyn followed Robert as he nudged past people collecting their bags and umbrellas. She was now quite damp with sweat, her slip sticking to her stockings.

"Quickly, Evie," Robert said, motioning to her with his head.

"Yes, I am being quick," she said, but her slip was bunching uncomfortably. "Wait." She stopped shuffling. "What are we being quick for?"

Robert stared at her, aghast. "I want to introduce you."

A thrill of horror crept up her neck. "I'd forgotten. No thank you."

Robert's face fell. "You promised you would."

Evelyn opened her mouth and closed it again.

"Please?" He looked over at the doorway. "If we don't hurry now—"

"Fine, but only quickly," Evelyn said, following as he almost pushed poor old Mrs. McTavish out of his way.

In the room off the hall, women were lining up in an orderly queue behind Mrs. Downie. Some had pamphlets in their hands, waiting to be autographed. Others had brought the child bunches of daffodils or straw dolls. The boy himself was sitting on a stool, eating a slice of fruitcake.

Robert lined up behind Mrs. Lees, and they began a conversation about the reading.

Evelyn watched Clarence methodically picking the cherries out of the cake and eating them first. She had performed the same operations on her own fruitcake, when their governess wasn't watching. The boy caught her eye and she looked away.

"Bobby! Please, come." Clarence waved to Robert and gestured for him to approach. The others in the queue turned to shoot malevolent looks at them as they stepped out of line. Robert ushered Evelyn to the front, her hands clenched into fists.

Clarence shook Robert's hand. "Thank you so much for coming."

"This is my wife, Evelyn." Robert pushed Evelyn forward, and she crossed her arms, giving Clarence a stiff tip of the head.

"How do you do?"

Up close, Evelyn saw to her horror that the boy was wearing rouge and a face of powder, that his freckles had been drawn on with cosmetic pencil. Clarence must have noticed her expression, because he grimaced.

"I know," he said. "It looks strange off stage. Mama?"

A woman stood up from a chair behind Clarence's. She was a short, plump teapot of a woman, wearing a dress so profoundly drab that Evelyn hadn't even noticed her.

"Mama, when may I wash off all this powder?"

The woman glanced at her wristwatch. "In an hour, perhaps. After the photographs."

He sighed, exaggeratedly.

Clarence's mother extended a stubby, trembling hand. "You're Mrs. Hazard? I've been desperate to meet you. I'm Mrs. O'Grady. Bernice." Evelyn felt a pulse of empathy for her; she didn't seem like the kind of woman to chain her child to a barrel organ. Perhaps Clarence was much like Robert—stubborn, idealistic. Imagine how ghoulish it must be to have strange adults crowding your child, harassing him about dead husbands.

"Would you like anything to sign? I have some pamphlets and also some leaflets and some memorial cards if you prefer. Or perhaps you have brought your own items?" Bernice said.

"Robert, please, you are the true audience," Evelyn said, stepping to the side.

"Sorry," said Bernice, "I thought you hadn't brought anything with you to sign, and I was going to offer you something to sign, but I suppose you don't want anything signed?"

"No thank you." Evelyn tried, as discreetly as possible, to edge away from Clarence. She didn't want to get too close to him, as if he might be able to see through her skin.

Robert beamed at Clarence. "You were ever so good today."

Clarence shrugged. "Thank you."

"Do you mind?" Robert searched around for a chair. "I have a question about clairsentience."

Evelyn loitered next to Bernice while Robert and Clarence began talking. After a moment of silence, she cleared her throat, politely. "You must do a great deal of travelling," she said, to Bernice.

"We do. Travelling to and fro," and Bernice dissolved into a twittery, over-exhausted laugh.

"That sounds tiring," Evelyn said.

"Yes, a rest would be nice. No rest for the wicked!" Bernice said, and blushed. Evelyn saw right away she hadn't meant to imply they were wicked. She searched for a way to ease Bernice out of her embarrassment.

"Do you often come to the hall?"

"Now and then. Have you come from far?" Bernice said, swivelling the ring on her finger. It was an onyx band, like one a man might wear.

"No, we live next to the Botanics."

"That's not far. Many people travel far, to see Clarence at work."

"I imagine."

"But it wasn't far for you, was it?"

"No," said Evelyn, trying to get a grasp on the conversation. Should she have said they'd travelled far? What had the woman expected her to say?

"And has it yet begun to rain?" Bernice said.

"Not at the moment."

"It did look like rain, earlier. Although the paper hasn't printed it."

"Yes, it does look like rain," Evelyn said, searching for Robert as he questioned Clarence. It was a funny sight, like watching a gendarme interrogate a rabbit.

"But I suppose it may still rain, later," Bernice said. She was standing too close to Evelyn; her breath was bitter. Evelyn took a step back.

Bernice took a step forward.

Evelyn looked over at Robert again.

"Mrs. Downie mentioned a European tour?" Evelyn said, a faint headache beginning at the back of her eyes.

"Yes, we were in London, and Cardiff, and Manchester. Also Birmingham."

"Oh," said Evelyn. She was almost disappointed. She'd imagined the child holding forth at a Parisian salon, raised on a dais before Venetian courtiers wearing sumptuous masks.

"And Abergavenny," said Bernice.

"Lovely," supplied Evelyn. "And were the events well received?"

"Ever so well received. You never know, do you, if they will be well received or ill received?"

"Yes. Or no, rather," Evelyn said, flustered. The conversation was spinning around her. Had she not had enough porridge at breakfast? They stood in silence while Robert and Clarence conversed.

"And we'll shortly begin our Edinburgh circuit. But of course, you know about that," Bernice said, twisting her ring.

"Of course." Evelyn smiled politely. "And—" She wondered how to begin. "May I ask, what exactly does Clarence's tutoring—"

She was interrupted by a young man walking towards them. He was slight with a pretty face and large green eyes; the sort of anodyne beauty that one might find minted onto a coin.

"This is Walter, my son. My other son, that is," Bernice said. "Walter began attending a spiritualist church after the war," she went on, with a doting smile. "It's thanks to Walter that I had the opportunity to discover Clarence's gift at all."

"Nice to meet you," Walter said, his eyes focused on Evelyn's.

She shook his hand, feeling the answer slot into place for a question she had not asked. Of course this nervous woman and her spectral child couldn't have been travelling around Europe unaccompanied. No doubt he was the architect behind their tours.

"How do you do," Evelyn said.

"I should've known Bobby would have a lot of questions," he said, with an almost imperceptible roll of his eyes.

Evelyn started. "You know my husband?"

Walter chuckled. "It's a small circle," he said. "Us gentlemen have to help each other."

"I'm sure," Evelyn said. "In that case, maybe you can tell me how your brother has been helping Robert?"

Walter turned his eyes on her. They were the colour of expensive cologne. "I'm not sure Bobby needs Clarence's help, actually." Relieved, Evelyn began to speak, but Walter cut her off, "You see, your husband's kind of talent can't be taught."

Evelyn frowned at him. "It can't?"

"Oh no, Mrs. Hazard, it's a gift. A gift from beyond."

Evelyn looked at Robert. He was tipping his chair back and forth, his hands in his pockets. The top of his handkerchief had fallen out of his waistcoat and was bobbing with each movement. Evelyn bit down on her tongue, the sharp taste of metal filling her mouth.

12

WEDNESDAY WAS THE FIFTH OF MARCH, AND ALSO
their fifth wedding anniversary. To celebrate the occasion, Robert and Evelyn had made a reservation at Le Terroir restaurant on
George Street. It was the venue in which they had celebrated Evelyn's birthday in October, and in the taxicab on the way there, she
suffered a paroxysm of embarrassment to realise she was wearing the
exact same outfit, down to her jade earrings. Only when the waitress
was revealed to be a young Indian woman that Evelyn didn't recognise did she give herself permission to enjoy the evening.

They were seated in the middle of the room, underneath a lamp
that threw a fierce, theatrical glow upon them, and Evelyn could see
a new speckled rash on her cheeks in the reflection in the window.
As soon as the waitress turned away, Evelyn gave her cheeks a good
hard pinch in the hopes she might be able to pass it off as rosiness.
As she administered the pinch, she became aware that beyond her
reflection, someone was standing in the street.

Watching her.

She dropped her hand, trying to see past the fractures of light
on the glass. A man, dressed all in black, holding a black umbrella.
He was completely still, staring directly at her. The hairs on her
arms stood on end. She looked at the brass lamps in the restaurant,
and then back. He was still there. He had come for her. He knew

something. An icy shudder slunk over her skin. The man wasn't moving. A ghost. She reached out for Robert's hand, making a squeaking noise.

"Yes?" Robert followed her gaze.

The man was still staring into the restaurant, but she now saw movement near his knees. A dog. He was waiting for his dog to finish urinating against the restaurant fence. He wasn't watching Evelyn at all. She rubbed her face, reaching out for a wineglass that hadn't yet been delivered.

"I must say, you look beautiful tonight, Evie," Robert said, putting his hand on hers.

Evelyn nodded. Over Robert's head, she motioned to the waitress for their drinks. Her hands were shaking.

"What terrible manners you have."

Evelyn focused on him. "Sorry?"

Robert batted his eyelashes, coquettishly.

She laughed, despite herself. "Thank you. And you look very handsome as well."

"Quite right."

Two glasses of wine were placed in front of them, and Robert raised his glass. "To my beautiful Evie." He opened his mouth wide, drawing breath in such a way that Evelyn knew, with a certain inevitable panic, that he was about to sing.

She put her hand on his arm. "Not here, Robert, please."

He shot her a wounded expression. "Very well. A toast to your good health, and all the blessings you bring me." They clinked glasses. "It hardly seems like five years, does it, my love?" Robert said, starry-eyed.

"We've been married more than one war," she heard herself saying.

Robert blinked at her. "Right you are."

"I didn't mean, I don't mean—"

"I know." Robert patted her hand.

"It's just that *that* felt like ten years, and so these five years . . ."

Robert stroked the back of her wrist. "We're very lucky."

"Yes, we are." Evelyn felt a lump in her throat that she tried to assuage with a sip of wine. She pictured the ugly brown dress with the blouson bodice that Dolly had worn to their wedding. How she had found the dress, later, amongst Dolly's belongings, with a daffodil from her bouquet dried in the pocket. She pretended to be looking at the menu to give her time to compose herself. What was it about anniversaries that made life seem so bittersweet? It was the tender pull of all that was to come and all that had been, jumbled up together.

The waitress approached them. "Would you like to order?"

Evelyn propped up her menu, knowing she would have the same meal she always did.

"We also have lemon sole today," the waitress said, tapping her pencil against her pad. "Lovely and fresh, caught yesterday in Whitby."

Evelyn's pulse raced to her head, her ears popping.

"Lovely," Robert said. "Are you ready, Evie?"

Evelyn stared at him blankly.

"We might need a moment," he said.

Evelyn fanned herself with the menu. The strange man, Dolly's dress, Whitby, it was too much. "No, it's fine," she said, ordering for them both: scallops with cream, chicken à la rose, orange and brandy cake.

As the waitress left the table, Robert tipped back in his chair. "The lemon sole sounded nice, next time we should try that. Never been to Whitby. Have you?"

Evelyn's chest tightened. "When I was younger."

"Summer holiday?"

She nodded.

"Nice swimming they've got there."

"Yes."

"Who is it we know from Whitby?"

"Nobody."

"What's that?"

"We don't know anybody," Evelyn said.

"Your mother talks about a family from near there, doesn't she?"

Evelyn forced a smile. "You know better than to listen to Mama, Robert."

"Maybe it was Whithorn. No, I could swear it was Whitby."

Evelyn took a large swig of wine. A drop rolled down her chin and she caught it with her finger. "You're thinking of the Gaskells. They moved to America before the war."

"That's the one." Robert smiled. "How is it that you always know what I'm thinking? I wish I could do the same!"

Evelyn placed her hands on the tablecloth. The drop of red wine bloomed into the lace.

The first day of the regatta, the crowd was so thick along Pier Road that it was hard to see the water. Rowers in white outfits were cheering at the edge of the water, unfamiliar flags fluttering in the air. When Mama stopped to talk to the Gaskells, at first, Evelyn was distracted by a seagull that had got its head stuck in an ice cream cone. Only after the seagull had freed itself did her eyes snap to the young man standing next to Mrs. Gaskell. He was in his early twenties, his skin golden from the sun, his wavy black hair a little too long. He was watching her.

"Oscar is here all summer," Mrs. Gaskell was saying, "and Emmeline, of course. She's with her governess at the moment."

"How nice." Mama smiled. "Emmeline must come by the hotel and have tea with Dolores."

Dolly was examining her shoe. "I stepped in fudge," she said.

"What a lovely idea." Oscar bowed to Mama. With a pointed kind of swivel, he turned towards Evelyn. "And will the young ladies also be making the most of the English seaside?"

"I expect so," Mama said. "Evelyn's not a strong swimmer, though—"

"I've been bird-watching," Evelyn almost shouted. Her face burned. Why had she volunteered that? But Oscar was smiling at her.

"Yes," Mama said, giving Evelyn a perplexed pat on the shoulder. "Yes, darling, congratulations."

"Perhaps I will see you both on the beach," Oscar said, with a dip of his head. "I would be happy to volunteer my skills as lifeguard."

Robert was still tipping his chair back and forth. "Did you hear me, Evie?"

"Sorry?" Evelyn stared at the crimson stain in the tablecloth. Sensing Robert's eyes on her, she turned to him.

"You thought he was good, didn't you? Clarence?"

She licked her lips.

"Did you know last month he contacted one of the victims of the Stockbridge Strangler?" Robert said, cheerily. "She said her bones will never be recovered!"

Evelyn felt a rush of boldness, fostered by the restaurant, by Robert's good mood. "You really should have warned me about Clarence. I'm not comfortable with your being tutored by"—she lowered her voice—"a child. And to find out in front of everyone!"

Robert dropped his chin. "I'm sorry."

Evelyn waited; she wanted an exact diagram of his apology. But nothing more came. "He's certainly"—she paused—"effective. But just think how it must seem, Robert!"

Robert twirled the stem of his wineglass between his fingers. She wasn't convinced that he was listening to her. Just then, the waitress put down their scallops. There was a heavy kind of silence, and Evelyn tucked her napkin across her lap.

Robert picked up his knife and fork. "I understand," he said, after a moment.

Evelyn sliced her scallop; it was perfectly cooked—like cutting through summer butter. "You do?"

"While you were with Annie, I had a good chat with Walter."

She remembered in a flash she had wanted to tell Robert about Annie's new romance with Edward Parsons, but swatted away the urge to interrupt him while he was apologising. Instead, she said, "Yes?"

"We both agreed Clarence won't be acting as my mentor from here out."

Evelyn took a deep breath. It felt like the air was reaching a place in her chest that had been locked up since the weekend. "I do think that's a good idea."

Robert nodded, pushing his plate to one side so he could take Evelyn's hand. But she hadn't finished eating her scallop, and mournfully watched the rest of it growing cold as Robert clamped her hand to the tablecloth. "I realise how it might look."

She nodded. "Darling, thank you." Here it was, the beginning of the end. She had been right to keep her calm, let him burn himself out.

The waitress came to take their plates, and at the last moment before it was whisked away, Evelyn speared the scallop and ate it, even though it was now cool and rubbery.

"And there's something else I wanted to talk to you about," Robert said. He was sitting oddly on his chair, his weight all on the side nearest her.

"Yes?"

"It's sort of a proposition," Robert said.

"For what? Is there something new you're interested in?" Over his shoulder, she saw that the waitress was approaching with their chicken, and snapped her mouth shut. The meal was a thing of beauty, golden brown with a scattering of crimson petals. Gratefully, Evelyn picked up her fork. "Eat up, quickly," she said. "It won't be nice when it's cold."

Robert touched his knife and fork, but didn't make any gesture towards eating. "Now, at least hear me out, Evie, it's only three weekends."

She stopped cutting her chicken. "What's only three weekends?"

"The circuit. It's only three weekends."

"What circuit?"

"Clarence's tour," Robert said. "Walter's asked me to go with them." Evelyn wiped her mouth with her napkin. "Does he need an accountant?"

Robert laughed. "No, you silly goose. Not as his accountant. As his colleague."

"Colleague?"

"As a sort of partner."

She stared at him.

"Walter wants to trial a 'master and mister' act," he said.

Evelyn pictured Robert outfitted in a navy sailor suit, his face powdered and rouged. "What?"

"He thinks it might help draw in a different crowd, reach more people."

Evelyn leant over and took Robert's wineglass, helping herself to a long sip.

"Henry's already let me take Fridays off," Robert said, watching her.

"You told Henry?"

"No, no, I said I had a family issue to deal with."

"You said it wouldn't interfere with business."

Robert's ears were pink. "It hasn't."

"You didn't take any time from work when Aunt Emily died."

Robert's eyelids twitched.

"I had to go to Dundee on my own, remember?"

"I remember," Robert said, sighing.

Evelyn began chewing on her finger, and gently, Robert took her hand away from her mouth. "It's only a few sessions. And it's my chance to see if I really have it in me."

Her nerves jangled, bright and sharp, like a set of keys knocking together. How would she be able to tell her parents? Kitty? And then there was Clarence. That uncanny child, prying into places he shouldn't have access to. His knowingness, his accuracy. "I can't allow it."

He blinked. "Pardon?"

"No, Robert, I can't allow it. This is too much." Papa, at the door of the Spiritualist Hall, and Robert, on stage, freckles pencilled onto his cheeks. "It's out of the question."

Robert looked down at the floor. "Evie." He drew a breath. "I'm sorry, but I'm going. You took back your foreboding, you can't reinstate it now."

"I can't change my mind?" Her eyes were prickling from a mixture of surprise and humiliation. He had never rejected her appeals, before.

"You can. But so can I," he said, softly.

"What do you mean?" She had a horrible sense of a rope, sliding through her grip.

"I mean, I intend to go, Evie."

"But—but I don't want you to."

"Aye, I realise that," Robert said. "But this is too important to me to miss out."

Evelyn wiped her eyes. "I don't understand—what it is that's so important that you would risk . . ." She waved her hand. The list was too long. His reputation, her family, their social capital, her peace of mind.

"This is the sort of opportunity that will never come round again," Robert said. "And there's so much to learn from Clarence."

Evelyn swallowed. "You can't."

"Evie." He gave her an almost apologetic smile. "I can."

A shameful thought sputtered around her insides. "You're not doing this for money, are you?"

"There's a fee," he said, straightening his knife and fork on the tablecloth, "but I thought I'd donate it, any earnings. To the Belgian Refugee Fund, maybe. Doesn't seem right, does it? To take people's money when I'm supposed to be helping them."

"But—" She faltered. "You'd go, even"—she paused—"even without me?"

Robert looked pained. "I don't want to. I want you by my side, as my ally." He squeezed her hand.

"I can't . . ." She trailed off. If she mentioned Papa's disapproval now, it might only push him further into the decision. And

Clarence—how could she explain it? She didn't want to get too close to Clarence. The things he had known—

"Evie." Robert held her eyes. "Don't force me to make the decision without you."

Evelyn opened her mouth. She would be left behind, clinging to splinters in a huge ocean. She would walk the empty rooms of the empty house; she would sleep alone in the dark in a cold bed.

The rose petals on her chicken had wilted into sad, wet little scraps. "Fine," she said. "I'll come."

13

THE TOUR OPENED AT PALTERN HALL. IT WAS JUST outside Edinburgh at the end of a winding pine tree avenue. The trees were fringed dark and thick, the needles so deep on the ground that the air sweeping through the motorcar windows smelt mentholated, like cough drops.

Evelyn had never been to the building itself, although she had long admired the Teutonic efficiency of its panelling, and had once bought a tin of barley mints just because it pictured the building snuggled merrily under a trim of snow. So it was strange, now, to be loitering in the entrance of the hall with such a burbling sense of dread. Walter had snatched Robert away for some private preparations with Clarence in advance of the séance, and Evelyn was skittering around the hallway, twisting her gloves and pretending to examine the beeswax candles on sale in the lobby. After a while, she forgot she was merely pretending to admire them, since they were rather fine, and bought one from the moustachioed man at the front door. It was only a penny!

But then the audience began to trickle in. Robert's audience. Engineering students, with the sharp, indoor look of people who spend time chewing on pencils. A group of flushed men with dirty earlobes who were unsteady on their feet. Women in antelope and leopard. Unchaperoned young boys who could only have been from the same family since they all were wearing shirts made from an identical bolt of cloth. A scruffy man carrying a spade. Another scruffy man with another spade. Three scruffy men with spades. A peculiar-looking fellow wearing—yes—an ermine-trimmed cape. This assortment box of people were now taking seats, lighting their pipes, admiring the beeswax candles. The hall was already half-full. There was the distinct, anticipatory sense of a theatre before the curtains opened. Evelyn started to sweat into her bust bodice. At the front of the room, Bernice was standing with a woman in an ugly orange hat. Bernice was bright-eyed and smiling, fidgeting with her ugly ring and standing far too close to her ugly-hatted friend. Bernice—even Bernice—was comfortable here! Evelyn joined the queue for the ladies' washroom, waves of heat rushing over her in that horrible green way that happens before one is sick. When a stall was vacated, she dashed in and stood there. There was a sprinkle of urine on the toilet seat. She turned to face the door and forced herself to take a deep breath.

Robert. On stage. In front of all those people. A bubble of hysteria tickled her throat, and she gulped it back into her stomach where it whinnied. He was going to humiliate himself, and the worst part was, he wouldn't even realise. Evelyn put her hands to her forehead and said a prayer. Let it be just bad enough. Just bad enough that he would go home disheartened, and she would never, ever, ever mention it again.

Too much time had passed; she'd been in the stall too long. She turned around to the lavatory. It was so unfair when people insisted on urinating on the seat. She tossed a piece of paper on the seat and, with her shoe, nudged it over the stain and into the bowl. Then she tugged on the flush, leaping back so no water might spritz her with its foul miasma. At the sink, her lips were pale. She ran cold water over her wrists.

"It's not easy, is it?" the woman next to her said. It was the lady with the ugly orange hat who had been talking to Bernice.

"Excuse me?"

"I always try not to get my hopes up for the demonstrations, but it's hard, isn't it, love, to keep yourself from hoping?"

"Yes." Evelyn watched the water running down into the sink drain.

"I'm Mrs. Young." The woman adjusted her hat in the mirror. "Nice to meet you."

Evelyn nodded, politely.

"I'm hoping to hear from my Harry," Mrs. Young said, turning to her. "Jutland."

"Oh," Evelyn said. "I'm sorry." And she stammered, jittered, backed out of the bathroom, nearly knocking aside a woman in a tram conductor's uniform. A fresh horror had come over her. All these people, paying out of their pockets, for Robert. To try and reach the ones they loved. To go back to their dark rooms that night and lie on their pillows with some ease in their hearts.

Evelyn stumbled down the corridor towards the door at the back. She knocked on it once, then opened it without waiting. Robert and Clarence were seated at a sticky-looking table, making notes on a large piece of paper. Walter frowned at her. "Do you need something?"

"Robert? A moment?"

She ushered him into the corridor, and then, in a panic, through an unmarked door into a closet containing a sour-smelling mop. It was so cramped, they were forced to stand almost nose to nose.

"Are you all right, my love?" Robert said.

"You know, you don't have to do this. If you feel unwell, we can leave. We can just go home right now, and no one will mind. No one will even think of it at all. Or, or, I can be unwell. I could have a seizure or something horrible. Cholera?"

Robert's smile twinkled in the gloom. "Evie, you are so sweet. I'm doing just grand. Don't worry on my account."

"There are so many people in there!"

He rubbed his hands together. "I know, isn't it exciting?"

"But—your heart!"

Robert took her clammy hand in his cool one and pressed it to his chest. "It's ticking along very nicely, see?"

The beat was steady against her palm, but her hands were shaking. "What if—but you know, you've proven you can do this—you know, I think it's enough," Evelyn said.

"I've not even started proving myself," Robert said, and kissed her on the forehead. It was a prompt, dismissive kiss; a kiss that is distributed as someone is about to leave a room, and indeed, there he was, out the door.

＊ ＊ ＊

WHEN THE LIGHTS WERE raised, the audience politely applauded as Robert walked onto the stage. "Welcome all," he said. "Thank you for coming. Before I start, let me introduce myself. My name is Robert Hazard, and until a few months ago, I was just an accountant. Nowhere in my calculations did I predict that I'd become a spirit medium."

A cough broke out at the back of the hall, and a door squeaked open as the cougher let themselves out to cough on the steps. On stage, Robert shifted his weight. Evelyn's face was burning. How would she be able to watch this? What had she done—she should have fought harder to prevent this folly!

"Right, so let's get on with it, shall we? I've got someone's grandmother in spirit." He looked around the hall. "Her name begins with an *S*. Sarah or Siobhan, Sophie. Or it might end in an *S* sound, like Agnes."

Someone near the window cried out, "Sarah, did you say?"

Robert's face relaxed so clearly it struck Evelyn in the chest.

"Aye, Sarah it was," he said.

"That'll be me, then." A group of men shuffled aside until the speaker could be seen, a man with grey sideburns.

"That'll be you, then," Robert said, opening his arms. "Do you want to come up?"

The man hesitated, and one of his friends pushed him roughly forward. Slowly, he made his way up onto the stage.

Robert smiled. "Welcome. And what's your name?"

The man crossed his arms. "Thought you'd be able to tell me that."

"It doesn't work like that I'm afraid, or I'd be a rich man."

"That's Arthur," one of the men yelled from the crowd. He was drinking from a tumbler that Evelyn suspected was not filled with water.

"Hello, Arthur," Robert said. "Arthur, do you mind if I hold your hand? It'll make it easier to connect to the spirits."

It took so long for Arthur to extend his hand that Evelyn's skin crawled. The discomfort on his face was almost contagious. "It won't shock me or anything?"

"Oh no, Arthur, you won't feel anything. Unless you're a medium too," and he laughed.

Robert stared down at Arthur's hand. He ran his tongue over his top lip.

"Nothing's happening," Arthur said.

"Aye, well, give me a moment, Arthur," Robert said. "Spirit's come a long way, I don't want to make a mess at the last moment." His face was pink, his eyes watery with concentration. "Sarah, that's your grandmother?"

Arthur nodded. "Yes."

"She passed into spirit recently, am I right?"

"That she did."

"She was old, over seventy, when she passed?"

Arthur made a whistling noise through his teeth. "I'm no spring chicken, am I?"

Robert cuffed him around the shoulder. "Plenty of life in you yet."

A flush ran over Evelyn's body. She couldn't watch it. She couldn't. It was too much, somehow, too intimate, like catching someone rehearsing an acceptance speech for an imaginary prize. Her eardrums felt like they were shrinking in her head. She rose from her seat and let herself out the side door. By the entrance, she rolled pine needles under her boots, thinking of the "Great Lafay-ette" fire at the Palace Empire Theatre. If this building were to go up in flames now, Robert would be one of the named entertainers. They might call it the "Robert Hazard" fire. She cringed to think of her obituary circling at St. Serf's, how people would raise their eyebrows at the mortifying circumstances of her demise.

At six thirty, Clarence was due to take over, and with a deep breath, Evelyn let herself back in the building. But when she opened the door to the hall, Robert was still on stage. He was holding the hand of a white-haired woman in a green woollen shawl.

"And they were laid to rest in strangers' graves?" he was saying.

"That's right," the woman said. "They were so wee, and we didn't have the money—"

"But they weren't alone," Robert said. "Your babies want to make sure you know this. 'We weren't alone,' that's what they say."

What was he *doing*? Dragging old ladies up to air their trage-dies. Talking about dead children. It was macabre, it was disgraceful. How would she look him in the eye?

"And you'll always be their mamie," Robert said. "That's what they're saying now: 'It's my mamie! It's my mamie!' They are so happy to see you."

The woman nodded, but didn't reply.

"And you know, when your time comes, they'll be there to meet you. They're waiting for you, on the other side."

Evelyn's throat tightened.

"And—" Robert paused. "They weren't the only twins in the family, were they?" he said.

"No, that's right." The woman said.

Evelyn took a seat, adjusting her purse on her lap. How had he known that?

"There'll be another set of twins in the family before long," he said. "That's what they're telling me: 'We won't be the only ones.'"

The woman gasped, putting her hand to her collar. "My grand-daughter is expecting."

A thrilled whisper echoed around the room.

"There you go, then," Robert said.

Evelyn's skin was tingling in strange waves.

"Your babies, oh, they love their mamie so much, they do," Robert said. "And they'll be watching over the new wains from the other side." He tapped the old lady's hand, gently, before releasing her. He turned to address the audience. "Well, that's it from me. We have Clarence O'Grady now, thank you very much."

He gave a bow, and as he and the old lady left the stage, the crowd broke into applause. Real, actual applause! Evelyn wrapped her arms around her waist. What did that mean? Did everyone here consider him a success? How had he known that, about the twins? Her ears were roaring. As Clarence took the stage, she tried to locate Robert at the front of the room, as if she would understand better, somehow, if she could catch his eye, if she could just look directly at him. But a group of people were crowding around him, their heads bent towards his. Evelyn sat back in her seat again, releasing the top button on her blouse.

Clarence was on stage now, and he had already called up a young brunette woman in a cheap cloche hat. Evelyn tried to focus on him, to distract herself from the tumble of emotions in her stomach. The woman holding Clarence's hand looked to Evelyn to be in her early thirties, but was of such diminutive stature that she was barely any taller than Clarence.

"Before the war, I have the sense that your husband worked on the water, perhaps as a fisherman?"

The young woman nodded. "He was, yes!"

"But his fish, they were special, weren't they?"

"Yes."

"He was very proud of his catch. He took great pride in his trade," Clarence said.

She smiled, knowingly. "Exactly, very proud."

"He sold them for a special purpose." Clarence furrowed his brow. "To be smoked, is that right?"

"That's it!" The woman laughed, slapping her hand on her raincoat.

"But he's telling me, they weren't just any smoked fish—he's particular about that. He's saying Arbroath smokies," Clarence said.

She gasped. "Yes, that's right!" The crowd began clapping, and Clarence tipped his head towards them in a modest bow.

The hairs on the back of Evelyn's neck tingled. It could hardly be a lucky guess. But still, spirits? Evelyn scrutinised him. His blond curls and his tiny white hands. There was something unmistakably eerie about him, something knowing, numinous.

"He is telling me that his boat had an extremely special name."

The woman nodded, pursing her lips as if she were trying to suppress a smile.

"It was named after you, wasn't it?" Clarence said, gently. "He named it after you."

"He did!" The woman looked into the audience, beaming at an older lady who was shaking her head in amazement. "I told you," she said, from the stage. "Didn't I tell you?"

A reverent hum of appreciation rumbled around the room as Clarence embraced the young woman. An icy flicker was travelling up and down Evelyn's spine. She would have to do everything she could to avoid being alone with Clarence. Or worse, picked out of a crowd by Clarence.

❖ ❖ ❖

AT THE INTERVAL, EVELYN squeezed through the aisle to reach Robert. She still wasn't sure what she was going to say to him about the reading. As she nudged her way to the front of the room, she could see that Robert had been surrounded by audience members. The man in the cape was nodding along with whatever Robert was saying. Robert gestured, a bit too theatrically. Everyone laughed. Evelyn lingered by the doorway, flicking through a stand of pamphlets for tea leaf readings, until Robert was left with just one middle-aged woman with a cloud of hair of such suspiciously uniform blackness that it could only have been dyed.

"And what a blessing to be able to connect to the common man," she was saying, a hand on Robert's shoulder. She had a European accent and the husky voice of a cigar smoker. "There's such a danger when gentlemen forget to help those less fortunate."

"Well, the spirit world knows no privilege," Robert said.

Evelyn blinked at him. It was a surprisingly adroit thought, for Robert. He caught her eye and ushered her forward. "Evie, this is Countess Margrit Lugosi. This is my wife, Evelyn Hazard."

"Please call me Margrit," she said. "How beautiful you are—you are a very lucky man," she said, to Robert.

A countess! Beautiful! A countess!

"Mrs. Montford was right about you." Margrit clasped her hands together. "Where is your next reception?"

Robert opened his mouth, but Evelyn got there first. "His next reading is at Stanton Abbey. Will you be attending?"

"Nothing could keep me away," Margrit said. "It's so rare to meet someone with the true gift."

Evelyn stared at Robert.

The true gift?

14

STANTON ABBEY WAS JUST OUTSIDE THE WHIMSI-
cally named suburb of Georgina's Leap. Robert had spent a summer
working in Frill before the war, and as they drove their rented automobile down winding roads, dodging pheasants that fluttered over
the hedges, Robert hung his head out the window and pointed out
grisly local landmarks. "Look," he said, pointing to the dark, collapsed lung of an old well, "that's where wee Bobby Reilly drowned."
Later, at a rocky outcrop: "That's where the preacher hung himself."

The redbrick facade of Stanton Abbey loomed high over a wall
of pear trees in full blossom. In one of the windows, a maid was
shaking out a duster, and drew back quickly as their car approached.
In the hour before the meeting, Evelyn strolled around the garden,
which had been converted to allotments during the war. Flowering
sweet cicely poured from terra-cotta pots, and a white butterfly
landed on her hat. The merry sound of a reel came from the building, and a dance master counting out steps. Impulsively, Evelyn
picked a fluffy head of Good King Henry and then was forced to
stash it in her pocket when she noticed a gardener peering fiercely at
her from the cucumber patch on the other side of the wall.

The summer before Evelyn turned eleven, the gardeners spent
weeks preparing for the outdoor ceilidh. It was a whim of her mother,

not usually whimsical, to hold the dance on the lawns, and every shrub
had to be trimmed to perfection. When the afternoon of the ceilidh
finally arrived, Kitty was still recovering from an ear infection and,
with much protest, was sent to bed early. Their governess distracted
by Kitty's complaints, Evelyn and Dolores had been free to watch
from the window over the back staircase as the guests arrived for
the dance. Mama's outrageously large hat sailed over the buffet, her
gloved hand pointing out plating offences to their butler. Underneath
the oak tree, a wooden bandstand had been set up, and as the music
floated through the open windows, Evelyn and Dolly followed the
caller's instructions on the landing; Evelyn was the lady, Dolly the
gentleman. Evelyn was wearing one of Dolly's old dresses, and after
one especially acrobatic interpretation of Strip the Willow—difficult
with only two partners—she tumbled, and ripped right through the
seat of the dress. "Well-dressed children have ill-bred parents," Dolly
said, in her best imitation of Mama. The Dashing White Sergeant was
Evelyn's favourite dance, but Dolly liked the Gay Gordons. Evelyn ran
her hand over the flower in her pocket. No, that wasn't right. Dolly's
favourite was the St. Bernard's Waltz. She squeezed the flower. She
didn't remember. How couldn't she remember?

Back in the building, she took a seat at the far end of the Blue
Room. People trickled in: teenage girls with matching headbands, a
couple in tennis whites carrying their rackets, a weather-lined man
in his sixties with what looked like a border collie puppy snuggled
inside his jacket. At twenty to six, Margrit appeared wearing a white
capelet over a grey voile dress. Evelyn stood to wave, but Margrit
was talking to a short Indian man—maybe he was the count? Evelyn
diverted the wave, pretending to scratch the back of her head. It was
surely gauche to introduce oneself to a count; she would have to wait
for an appropriate moment to cultivate an introduction. As Margrit
and her companion took seats in the front row, Evelyn was granted
full view of her darling feather-trimmed hat. The room was filling

up with men wearing ill-fitting jackets, women with wheezing, bon-neted babies. A pallid brunette woman dressed in a spectacular gold tuxedo swanned into the room and kissed Margrit on both cheeks before lighting what looked like a glass pipe. From downstairs, the thumping sound of a jig was audible through the floorboards. A girl in a kilt holding a flute took the seat next to Evelyn for a few moments before looking around in confusion and slipping out of the chair.

At five minutes to five, Bernice flittered into the room and grabbed Evelyn by the wrist. "Where's Bobby?"

Evelyn fought against the instinct to shake Bernice off. There was a special unpleasantness about being handled by Bernice, like touching something brittle; a moth casing or a dead tooth. "I thought Robert was with you?"

"Perhaps he's in the bathroom? I looked in the Rose Room, but he wasn't there, so maybe he's in the bathroom?"

Evelyn took a breath. "What do you need him for?"

"There are some horrible men making trouble downstairs."

"And you want Robert to do what, exactly?" She knew she was being cruel, but she couldn't help it. It was so hard to resist the urge to be cruel to Bernice.

"Could you let him know Walter needs his help?"

One eye on the countess, Evelyn left the room and loitered out-side the first-floor gentlemen's bathroom.

"Darling? Are you in there?"

"Evie?" came Robert's muffled reply. Evelyn squirmed. It was unbearable, holding a conversation with someone when they were in the bathroom.

"When you're"—she cleared her throat—"ready, would you mind coming downstairs? Walter needs help with something."

A few minutes later, Robert emerged. "Shall we?" he said. His eyes were glossy. He was in a good mood. A great mood. Evelyn crossed her fingers in her pocket as they went to the ground floor. He had managed it once, but now that she knew the countess was here, maybe the count too, there was pressure for him to do well. It *mattered* now that he do well. At the front of the building, six men were standing in the driveway. They were a little shabby looking, with dusty boots and pencils tucked behind their ears. They were in their twenties and thirties, and Evelyn surveyed them. They all had that look about them. That frozen look.

"You've got no right," a dark-haired man at the back was saying. "No right."

Walter was standing, pink-nosed, on the doorstep. "I have every right."

Robert opened the door. "Hello, lads, what's the trouble?"

"This one," the dark-haired man said. "He says it's ties only."

"The venue has a dress code," Walter said. "These aren't my regulations. It's at the discretion of the management."

"He's the management, isn't he?" another man shouted, pointing at the doorman, a freckled youth who was standing to attention behind Walter.

"It's threepence to rent a tie," the doorman said, his face puce.

"I already paid ten for the ticket!" said a blond man with a scarred left cheek.

"It clearly expresses the dress code on the ticket," Walter said. "Or can't you read?"

There was a horrible moment of silence.

"Now look here, we already paid once. Now we have to pay again. That makes it thirteen pence a ticket!" someone shouted.

Robert bent towards the young doorman. "Can't you waive the rules, as a favour?"

"I need this work, sir," the boy said, in a quiet voice.

"All right." Robert sighed. "I'll cover it myself. How much did you say?"

"I don't want no tie now, if I'm not right enough for you as I am," the dark-haired man was shouting. "Come on, let's go."

"Hold up." Robert put his hand out to the men. "Hold up, lads, please." He turned to Walter. "Why don't you check on Clarence? I'll get this straightened out."

Walter gave him a long, cool look, then pushed past Evelyn back into the building.

"Look here." Robert gripped the boy's shoulder. "What's your name, son?"

"Robin," he said.

"Robin here couldn't have known, but we put aside ten ties for anyone who'd need them for the evening. No fee required. I've got one on, myself." He winked at the boy. "I forgot to tell you, Robin, I'm very sorry."

"It's all right, sir." Robin nodded.

"It's part of the philosophy of spiritualism," Robert said, his voice louder now. "It's for anyone."

"That's right," the blond man said, grumpily. "All for anyone."

"Robin, pal, why don't you fetch those ties for the gentlemen." Robin scampered away, and Robert put his hands in his pockets. "Poor lad. His hearing gone in the Somme."

The child couldn't have been a day over seventeen, but the men nodded.

"So," Robert said. "Travelled from far?"

"Frill."

"Oh? I spent a summer picking fruit in Frill. Andrew Blithe, did you know him?"

"Aye, Andrew Blithe, nice man, he was."

"That he was. Of course, he's dead now. Is that pub still there? Great kidney pie they used to do."

"No," a man with one eye tutted. "Burnt down last year. Awful shame. Whole family up in flames. All the whisky too."

Robert whistled through his teeth.

Evelyn watched him through the doorway. He did have it, that knack for talking to people. Being normal. After everything, that was a special gift, all of its own.

When Robert finally came out into the Blue Room, it was ten minutes past five, and Bernice was looking again and again at her watch, practically choking with anxiety.

Robert walked along the stage, paused at the chairs towards the left. He smiled into the audience, caught Evelyn's eye, and smiled even more broadly. Evelyn's heart gave a little lift. He looked so happy.

"Hello, my name is Robert Hazard. I'll be passing on messages from the spirit world this afternoon."

"Hello!" a girl's voice called from the middle, and the crowd tittered. There was a different feeling in the room than the last time, an amiable sense of expectation, like a street-side audience waiting for the Prince of Wales.

Robert smiled. He put his hands in his pockets and Evelyn tensed. She heard her mother's voice in her mind, clucking about vulgarity. But she shook her head, and the voice disappeared. On stage, the posture made Robert look relaxed, confident. "Messages from the spirits—it's not easy making sense of them, but I'll do my best," he said.

Robert pulled his hands out of his pockets and clapped. "So. I have someone here who was in an accident at work," he said. "Somewhere cramped. A barn, maybe, or an old building, somewhere dark. Maybe even a trench, a dark trench, or a mine."

There was a muttering amongst the audience. People turned to look at their neighbours, frowning, as they reviewed their own personal tragedies.

"That's us," a deep voice called from the right-hand side of the room. Two men stood from their chairs. Both were in their forties, pale, with deeply lined faces. They were standing elbow to elbow, huddled like they were anticipating a loud noise.

Robert nodded at them. "Afternoon. You knew someone who was in an accident?"

"Yes," the shorter man said. His voice was unsteady, and he already had tears in his eyes. He wiped them away with the back of his hand. Evelyn's heart pinched. She would never get used to the sight of men crying.

"Johnny. He was in a mine with us."

Robert shook his head. "I'm awful sorry. It was a terrible accident."

The men nodded.

"Johnny is happy you came today," Robert said. "He says, 'I'm happy to see you lads.' The way he crossed into spirit, the accident, it wasn't his fault, was it? Johnny just didn't have enough time to react."

The two men looked at each other. "That's it. That's exactly right," the taller man said. "It happened so quick."

Evelyn rubbed her face. There was no way Robert could have met these men before. So how was he doing this? He was so at ease, so assured, as if it were perfectly natural to get on stage and talk about ghosts.

"Johnny's spirit is very brave. He was brave, wasn't he?" Robert said.

"He was and all." The taller man gripped his friend tighter.

"Johnny wants you to know something really important," Robert said. "Johnny is saying, 'There's nothing you could've done that would've made any bit of difference.'"

Both men were weeping now.

"It's dark in there. There isn't enough time. It goes black so quick, and the smoke," the taller man was saying. "You can't see anything. But we can hear it, though—the sounds."

Robert shook his head sympathetically. "Johnny says, 'It was my time. You were lucky to get out yourselves,' that's what he says."

"I told you, didn't I tell you?" the taller man said to his friend.

"Johnny says he was glad to know you in life. He says, 'You did good by me, you always did good by me.'"

"Is he—" the shorter man said, in a broken voice. "Is his dad with him?"

Robert paused. "Yes," he said. "Yes, his dad is there with him. They are sticking together, in the afterlife." He smiled at the men. "Johnny's so glad you came here today, and he says goodbye to you both."

"Wait," the shorter man said. "We want to say—we want to say we're sorry."

Robert looked at him for a long moment. "You've got nothing to be sorry for. It'd be a disgrace to his memory if you live the rest of your life being sorry. You have to live as he'd want you to. Remember him as he was. Can you do that?"

The man nodded.

"Then may God bless you both," Robert said. As the men sat back down, the audience applauded. Evelyn's throat was tight. In his own way, Robert *had* found a way to be helpful. She worried at the cuticle of her thumb. Maybe this was exactly what he needed.

Robert walked along the stage and took a sip from a glass of water on a low table. His face assumed a serious, professional expression. She had never seen him look like that. At once, he was a stranger to her.

Robert let out a breath. "Does anyone know a woman who had something to do with horses? Maybe she was a good rider, or maybe she lived near some fields?"

A woman in the middle of the room raised her hand. She had unfashionably long, greying hair, and was wearing a wool velour coat. "That's for me," she said. "Our dad was a stable hand. We grew up next to stables."

Robert invited her to join him, and she came up onto the stage. "What's your name, hen?"

"I'm Mary. Nellie was my sister."

"Mary, Nellie is saying you were nervous about coming here today."

She gave a sort of half shrug. "Yes, I was."

"Nellie wants me to mention that you've got something quirky with your kitchen, Mary."

Mary frowned.

"Nellie's saying, 'You've got to sort your kitchen out,' that's what she says. 'Tell her to fix her kitchen.'"

Mary gave an abrupt laugh, her face relaxing. "The sink keeps blocking. I don't know how many times I've had to keep fixing it."

Robert smiled. "She has many happy memories in the kitchen. You spent lots of time together in the kitchen, is that right?"

"Yes, that's right," Mary said, "lots of happy memories." Suddenly, she wrung her hands. "I don't know what to say, I don't know what to say to her."

Robert squeezed her shoulder. "Nellie already knows what's in your heart, Mary, you don't have to say anything. You don't have to be talking about her every day, she knows you think about her all the time. That you miss her."

Evelyn shifted her weight in her seat.

Robert looked closer at Mary. "Is that right? You don't like to speak about her too much?"

Mary shook her head. "I didn't see her much in the end."

"Nellie's got a strong personality," Robert said, smiling. "Once you got to know her, she was a strong person, wasn't she?"

Mary nodded.

"She's saying, 'Don't you be worrying on my account,' that's what she says. 'You get on and worry about yourself, not about me.'"

Laughing, Mary dabbed her eyes with a handkerchief. "That sounds like her."

"It doesn't matter how far apart you were, you have a special bond, linked by love. That doesn't go away in death," Robert said.

Evelyn swallowed.

"And, she's in heaven?" Mary said, her voice wavering.

"She's safe and sound," Robert said, gently. "And she's with someone, on the other side. A motherly sort of person."

Mary twisted her handkerchief. "Auntie—Auntie Joan. She went a week after. I thought, I always wondered—" She broke off.

"They've got each other, Nellie and Joan."

"She's not alone?"

"She's not alone."

Evelyn's eyes burned; she gripped the undersides of her knees. In the early days, she'd had dreams of Dolores at the threshold of their front door in Mairibank. They would be chatting by the umbrella stand, and then Dolores would embrace her, saying, "I have to go now," and the dream would turn. Evelyn would beg her not to leave, catch her arm; she'd say, "I'll come with you," and Dolly would smile and shake her off. She would open the door, and step out, away, forever. Evelyn hadn't had the dream in a year. But the feeling of that dream was always with her. It was its own dark room in her heart. When Dolores left, she'd had to go alone. No one could help her. No one could escort her safely to the other side. In her last moments, it didn't matter who was in the room. She was all by herself. Evelyn let out her breath in a measured whistle. It was a way she'd trained herself to cry as quietly as possible in public. But the woman next to her turned, seeming to recognise the sound. She was in her late fifties, wearing a dusty pinafore. Her own face was mottled, and her tears matched Evelyn's. She held her broad, callused hand to Evelyn, who, after a pause, took it.

"Mary, Nellie says, 'I'm free here, there's no pain,' that's what she says. 'I'm free,'" Robert said.

Mary leant forward. She stood, hunched like that, for a few long seconds. When she stood upright, her lips were white. "Thank you," she said.

"She loves you and she wants you to rest, now," Robert said. "Nellie says, 'I'll always be looking over you.' She says to keep a lookout for her messages."

"Messages?"

"Signs—reminders. She says, 'I'll send you buttons,' that's what she says. Whenever you see a loose button, it'll be from Nellie, a gift."

Mary gasped, turning to her husband. "Didn't I say—didn't I say about those buttons?"

"Look out for them," Robert said. "Whenever you find one, it means she's close, that she's watching over you."

Mary put the handkerchief to her face. "I'll look for them. I'll look for her. Thank you."

* * *

AS SOON AS ROBERT left the stage, Evelyn stood from her seat and made her way to a tiny bathroom on the ground floor that she calculated no one else had spotted. She locked the door and examined her reflection in the mirror. Her nose was swollen, and her eyes were red: in no way presentable to approach a countess. She ran a hand towel under the tap, then pressed the cold cloth under her eyes. The room had been papered in green velvet, and the walls were marked with water stains around the basins. A terrible choice of wallpaper for a bathroom. Evelyn took a deep breath. That woman's sister: it felt so true in the moment. Her stomach turned and she met her eyes in the mirror. It still felt true, even out of the moment.

She let herself back into the garden instead of attending Clarence's session. It was important to let her face calm down before she spoke to Margrit, and she wasn't prepared to risk any more spontaneous outbursts. She sat on a wooden bench, listening to the music of the dance lesson and allowing the weak, late afternoon light to warm her cheeks. Over the sound of the reel, she became aware of a whispering noise, a rustle, and faint clucking. Evelyn opened her eyes. On the far side of the garden, a magpie was sailing in loops over the radishes, its tail fanned, a collar of white. Evelyn smiled, watching as the bird dove in sudden twists. With each swoop, it got closer. Evelyn looked around in case she had sat by a nest without realising. She shifted down to the other end of the bench, adjusting her hat. The bird got closer and closer, its wings arched. Evelyn stood, steeling herself to go back in the room—but Clarence. She didn't want to be anywhere near Clarence. She turned, indecisive, and with a click, the bird plunged down on her. Evelyn yelped, putting out her hand, reflexively. It struck, horribly, against the animal. A brush of feathers. An oily, fluttery warmth. A little heart, beating. She lowered her hand. The bird lay half on the path, its head in the soil. Evelyn stepped back, gripping her hand where it had touched the bird. A gurgle rose from her throat.

"Help!" she said. "Somebody!"

The gardener's face reappeared over the wall. "Ma'am?"

"I didn't mean to." She pointed at where the feathers, crooked, twitched in the earth. "I didn't mean to."

The man squinted at where she was pointing. "That'll be Jack," he said, with a sigh. "Nest's over by the wall. Doesn't like strangers."

Evelyn wrapped her arms around her waist. It was a bad omen, a sign. Dolly. Dolores was trying to reach her. To warn her. "I killed it."

"No, hen." The gardener unlocked the gate at the door. "Just a tumble, that's all."

"I didn't mean to."

The man looked her in the eye. "Go on, I'll see to him. Why don't you go back in now."

Applause and squeaking chairs drifted from the upstairs window.

"Go on, hen," the gardener said.

Back in the green-wallpapered bathroom, Evelyn washed her hands until her skin stung from the hot water. She stared again at her reflection, measuring her breaths. There was nothing to be afraid of. Just a silly accident. The bird was hardly injured, the gardener had said so himself. Robert's session had gone well, there were important people here, she had to get a hold of herself.

As she jostled upstream of the crowd, Evelyn tried to quiet the skittery dread inside her chest. This was her opportunity to make a good impression on the count and countess. She needed to be delightful. Flawless. Spotting Margrit from the top of the stairs, Evelyn elbowed her way towards her. Margrit's male companion was nowhere to be seen, but she was chatting to the woman in the golden tuxedo.

"Didn't I tell you?" Margrit was saying. "Such a raw talent."

"And there was a different crowd here tonight," the woman in the tuxedo said. "It's good to see such a range of faces." She was fair, with blonde-brown hair that was so thin that Evelyn could see her scalp shining through. She had a large forehead and wide-set eyes with a dramatic, pointed chin. Evelyn inspected her: she looked vaguely familiar. But then lots of English debutante girls had that undernourished look—all teeth and cheekbones. Up close, though, her outfit was spectacular. It was clearly a man's suit that had been tailored to fit her.

"This is Mrs. Hazard," Margrit said, noticing her lurking behind them. "Let me introduce Lily Penhaligon-Beaumont."

"Call me Evelyn," she said, laughing in a high-pitched, witless way.

"Lily," the tuxedoed woman said. She held out her hand, and it was surprisingly callused around the fingers.

"What an impressive session that was," Margrit said. "And so affecting, how Clarence talked to that poor seamstress."

"Yes," Evelyn said. "Poor, poor seamstress."

"Now." Margrit adjusted her handbag onto the crook of her arm. "I'd like to invite you and Robert to my next salon in May, I hope you'll be in the city?"

"Yes please, yes," Evelyn said. A salon!

"Fabulous." Margrit clasped her hands. "Lily is abandoning us for the highlands, so she won't be able to join in the fun."

"It's for work," Lily said, patting Margrit's shoulder affection-ately. "Otherwise I'd be there in a heartbeat."

Evelyn couldn't help herself. "Are you an actress?" she said.

Lily laughed. "No, but I do a bit of posing here and there. I have to keep the castle from crumbling somehow."

Evelyn laughed politely, although she wasn't sure if that was a figure of speech, or if Lily really did live in a castle.

"Your husband is awfully good," Lily said. "Of course, I knew he would be, if he was working with Clarence."

"Have you been to many of Clarence's readings?" Evelyn asked.

"Hundreds. Vikram has him over at weekends all the time," Lily said, raising her arms. All of a sudden, her face snapped into context.

"You're the Cleaneen girl!" Evelyn heard herself squeak.

Lily smiled. "Oh, that, yes."

Margrit frowned. "What is that?"

"The soap, darling, the advertisements."

"I don't read advertisements," Margrit sniffed.

Lily beamed at Evelyn. "Bless you for even knowing that. Yes, that's me. Or a version of me."

Evelyn recalled, with a start, that emblazoned on a tablet of soap in her own scullery was Lily's pink and glowing visage, swimming out of a frothy veil of bubbles.

"And do you use Cleaneen?"

"What? No, no. It makes my eczema much worse." Lily showed her palms, which were blistered. Behind her back, Evelyn squeezed her own hands together. The twitch of the bird against her skin, the quivering thump—

"Aleppo soap is the best kind of soap for skin complaints," Margrit began, then paused. Evelyn turned around to see that Robert had appeared behind her.

As Margrit and Lily exclaimed over his performance, Evelyn willed him away. There were plenty of men with printer's ink on their clothes for him to talk to—couldn't he leave her with the ladies for five minutes? She set her teeth and waited for the exchange of pleasantries to be terminated.

"Lily is the Cleaneen model!" she said, finally. "Don't you recognise her?"

Lily smiled. "It was that, or take up hatting."

"Millinery, my dear," Margrit said. "Poor Lily knows nothing about hats."

"Your hat is divine," Evelyn said, gesturing to Margrit's feather-trimmed cloche. "I was admiring it the moment you came in. The tone of the feathers, it's perfect for your colouring. People think you can't wear ostrich in spring, but they don't understand it just has to be balanced . . ." She became aware they were staring at her, and shut her mouth.

Lily raised her eyebrows, amused. "You're a darling, aren't you? Quite an unusual pair, you and your husband. Like the princess and the pea." She laughed.

Evelyn laughed too, although the expression was all wrong. She was glad that Robert was too busy talking to Margrit to have overheard. Being compared to a pea didn't sound like much of a compliment.

"Well, Evelyn, I hope very much to see you at Usher Hall one of these days. Or at Vikram's estate."

"Yes, thank you," Evelyn said. Usher Hall! Vikram's estate! Who was Vikram?

"And where were you during the war? France?" Margrit was saying to Robert. Evelyn immediately forgot all about Usher Hall.

"To my great disappointment, a health complaint stole my military career," Robert said.

Evelyn relaxed. A perfect delivery.

"Ah." Margrit nodded. "I understand all about that. I have suffered on account of my health for my whole life. It brings one a greater understanding of the other side, don't you think?"

"I entirely agree," Robert said.

Evelyn looked at him. She knew that was untrue; he didn't believe his weak heart brought him any special knowledge about death. Or did he? Maybe that was exactly the sort of frailty one could admit to a perfect stranger, but not to a wife. She looked over his face, the way he was standing. He was himself, but calibrated differently. All this time, he'd been keeping this aptitude tucked away. She pictured the bird, plunging towards her, a flash of white, of warning.

15

THE MURRAY HOTEL BY EAGLE ROCK OVERLOOKED the ocean from a grove of young chestnut trees planted for acetone during the war. It was dark as they drove up, the wind high. Shredded chestnut leaves collected in the windscreen wiper, and Robert had to stick his arm out to pick them away. The entrance hall was windowless and dingy, panelled in smoke-smudged mahogany, although there was a merry little fire in the grate. Dangling from every corner of the room were pennants embroidered with the buxom figure of the selkie. Evelyn tried not to look directly at it, which was difficult, since the selkie and her generous seashell brassiere also adorned the doormat, the antimacassars, the fountain pens and fireguard.

As they signed the visitors' book, Robert picked up a collection tin on the front desk and examined the note attached. "Who's wee Charlie?"

Evelyn paused, a dash of ink under their address. "He's a boy from the Colonies. Went missing." She hesitated, wondering if she should say that she had heard about it from Kitty. But she didn't want to prompt any conversation of her family.

"They've still not found him," the clerk volunteered, leaning farther over the desk. Evelyn turned to acknowledge him. He had a patch of blistered skin over his chin and forehead, but in the context of the hotel, she wasn't sure if his eye patch was thematic rather than functional. "Poor lad. Only ten, out on his own. And it's supposed to get cold again this week."

Evelyn didn't want to think about the idea too closely. "Awful," she said, looking down into the fire.

Robert tutted, searching in his pocket for change to add to the tin.

"Thank you, sir," the clerk said. "And can I interest you in our selkie boat trip? We have outings daily at 10:00 AM."

"What do you say?" Robert turned to her, with a hopeful twinkle in his eye.

"Absolutely not."

Robert's face fell.

"We also have tours of the caves if you don't wish to take a boat."

"No, thank you," Evelyn said stiffly. "We're not here for the selkie. Mr. Hazard is conducting the session on Saturday evening."

The clerk gawped at him. "You're the reader. We've heard so much about you."

"You have?" Robert grinned.

"Absolutely, we've had telephone calls all day. Do you think you'll be able to reach her?"

"Reach who?"

He pointed to the statuette of the selkie on the desk. "Her!"

Robert looked at Evelyn. She raised her eyebrows.

"My wife doesn't approve of me speaking to showgirls," he said.

The clerk laughed, then stopped laughing, then began laughing again. Evelyn rolled her eyes.

A housemaid with a pug nose took them up to their room on the second floor. The room was large, with windows on two sides facing the sea, and in the centre was a monstrous four-poster bed in a threadbare bird-pattern brocade.

Robert launched himself onto the bed and thumped the bedspread. "Look, Evie, like being in a castle!" he said. Evelyn watched for any telltale puffs of dust, but it was reassuringly clean.

Robert lay back, stretching his arms behind his head. "Oh, here she is again."

Evelyn peered under the canopy to see the creature herself winking down at them. "That's indecent!" she said.

Robert chuckled. "Maybe you should put some stockings on her. A nice winter mackintosh? A Norwegian fur coat, perhaps. You'd know just how to tuck her in for a sleigh ride, wouldn't you, Evie?" He reached out to tickle her, and Evelyn squirmed away. She crossed the room to the basin and splashed water on her face.

By the time she was standing in front of Mama and Papa, the postcard was crumpled and soft from being handled.

Her parents looked at each other. "Norway?"

"The Ladies Service League is in desperate need," Dolly was saying.

Papa wrinkled his nose. "But I've never seen you read the Bible yourself, Evelyn! How much help could you possibly be?"

"I'd like to be of service," Evelyn said, weakly.

"We'll be tutoring together, Papa," Dolores said. "And it's only three months." She looked at Evelyn. "Maybe four. Some girls volunteer for years at a time. The least we can do is help for a little while."

Papa looked again at the postcard. "But this would mean you'd be away in Norway for the big move, doesn't it?" Papa said, and Mama leant over, putting a hand on his wrist.

"That might be better," she said, softly. "All things considered."

Papa's shoulders fell. "Let me discuss it with your mother."

As the drawing room door closed, Evelyn turned to Dolly. "What will we do if they don't agree?" She gestured to her midriff.

"I'll *make* them agree." Dolores motioned for Evelyn to follow her along the corridor to the library. She poured Evelyn a glass of water from the cabinet at the back of the room. "The boarding house is all ready."

Evelyn nodded.

"Don't you want to know anything about it?"

Evelyn looked at her blankly. Since telling Dolly, she felt like a kite that was being held by a string. "What should I ask?"

Dolores frowned at her. "Nothing," she said, with a sigh. "It's outside Troon. My friend will drive us, it should only take a couple of hours from here."

Evelyn nodded. "But what will the Ladies Service League say when we don't arrive?" She sipped her glass of water. "Won't they get suspicious? What if they write to Mama and Papa?"

An expression of profound exhaustion washed over Dolores's face. "Evelyn, there is no Ladies Service League."

"Are you becoming a mermaid yourself?" Robert said, as Evelyn splashed herself again.

She forced a cheerful tone into her voice. "Only trying to wake up."

It had begun to rain outside, and specks of water appeared on the windowpanes. Evelyn took off her travelling dress, her arms and legs pink from the cold.

"Hullo there," Robert said, turning over on the bedspread.

"Don't get any ideas," she said, snatching up her tweed dress. "I'm too hungry for nonsense."

Robert got off the bed and came up behind her, rubbing her shoulders, kissing the back of her neck. "You can rip off my head like a Serengeti lioness."

Evelyn laughed, pushing him away and climbing into her dress. "Maybe later," she said, knowing that she would never feel amorous later, with that fishy strumpet as an audience for their marital union.

At six thirty they went in search of the dining room, first getting lost in a corridor lined with mounted antlers. When they finally found the right room, Clarence, Walter, and Bernice were already seated at a circular table near the window. At the neighbouring table were two young men bent over a picture book of the selkie in various poses of aquatic temptation. Evelyn shot them a disapproving look.

"Good evening," Bernice said, as Robert and Evelyn joined their table. "I see it's started raining." She motioned towards the window frames overlooking the seafront. "And it's windy, isn't it? They said it might be windy, but I just wasn't sure. You never know if it's going to be windy this time of year, do you?"

"No," said Evelyn.

A maid carried over bowls on a tray and placed them on the table. Evelyn peered into the soup. It was orange-coloured—carrot, she supposed—with overcooked, swollen pearls of barley disintegrating into mush. They picked up their spoons, but Clarence was staring mournfully into his dish. "Are you feeling well, Clarence?" Evelyn said.

"He's sulking because he has a sty," Walter said, far too loud. Evelyn snuck a glance at Clarence's face. His right eye was a little inflamed.

Clarence tapped his spoon against the rim of the bowl. "Not sulking," he said.

Evelyn felt a rush of sympathy for him. A memory came back to her: lying in her bed in the nursery at Mairibank, and overhearing their governess tell Dolly that Evelyn couldn't come out to play hopscotch because she'd been vomiting. How degrading it was to have adults discuss your body like the weather. "I used to get them all the time, Clarence. Have you tried a cold tea bag?"

Clarence ignored her, clinking his spoon against the bowl.

Walter pushed his chair back from the table and lit a cigarette. Evelyn glared at him. Ex-soldiers and their table-manners.

"All the people who will be coming here for respite, and you're sulking because of your eye?" Walter said.

Evelyn began eating the soup as quickly as possible.

"You've got a long day of talking to actual, suffering people ahead of you tomorrow," Walter said. "So you'd better get a hold of yourself, sharp."

Clarence slumped over the table, resting his head on his hand.

"Elbows," Bernice said, nudging Clarence. He sighed, putting his hands in his lap.

"Can I go up now?" he said to Bernice. "I'm tired."

Bernice looked around the table. "Go up now? But you haven't finished your soup."

"Not hungry."

"Just one more bite, darling."

Clarence put the spoon in his mouth and licked it. "There. Now may I go?"

"Don't be a child," Walter said, tipping his ash carelessly over his shoulder.

"He *is* a child," Bernice said, her voice wobbling. "Off you go, darling, and get into bed nice and quick."

Clarence left the table without another word.

In silence, they ate the rest of the soup. The maid took their bowls and gave Evelyn an accusatory look. "Not hungry was he, the bairn?"

Evelyn was discomfited to realise that the maid had mistaken her for Clarence's mother. She looked pointedly at Bernice. "I don't know. He's not mine."

The maid carried the plates away. She returned with new plates, turbot with boiled potatoes. Evelyn was still embarrassed about being associated with Clarence's wastefulness and said, "My, how lovely it looks," but she could tell immediately it had been over-cooked; the flesh was white as soap.

"You shouldn't baby him," Walter said to Bernice. He stabbed out his cigarette in the ashtray.

"He's exhausted, Walter." Bernice put down her fork and swivelled her ring. "And tomorrow will be a hard day for him."

"It's no harder on him than it is on Bobby," Walter said, cutting his fish with such delicacy that Evelyn felt he was trying to make an obscure kind of point.

"Are the caves far from here?" Evelyn said, forcing herself to eat a mouthful of fish.

"Not so far," Robert said. "Although those boats might not get out tomorrow. The wind is supposed to pick up in the night."

"Yes," Bernice said, lifting her glass of water to her lips. "You never know when it's going to be windy, and when it won't be windy."

✦ ✦ ✦

AS ROBERT UNDRESSED, EVELYN stretched out on the bed. She felt herself jolting off to sleep and reluctantly struggled awake to brush her hair and get into her pajamas. As she rolled over, she noticed that midway up the wall next to the bed was a miniature door, the size of an envelope, with an ivory knob. Evelyn opened it and found to her surprise that it was not a cabinet but a sort of chute that turned right and travelled inside the cavity of the wall. She put her head to the wall, close enough to smell the mildew in the wallpaper, but the tunnel simply vanished into the darkness. A slow, fluttery terror crept over her. What was meant to go through this macabre tiny door? Or worse, come out of it?

"Robert, look." She stood back from the door, holding her shoulders.

"Odd," he said, putting his face to the hatch. "Like something from 'The Speckled Band.'"

Evelyn shuddered. After a moment, she began dragging the bureau over the floorboards, clattering the metal tray upon it. Sweating, she nudged it along the wall until it pressed against the door.

"What on earth are you doing?" Robert said, plumping his pillow.

She turned to him, open-mouthed. Wasn't he the expert in all things uncanny? There it was, a ghastly miniature tunnel hovering mere inches from their faces. "What do you *think* I'm doing?" she said, in a strangled way. Suddenly she felt she was sitting very high up, on a ledge, away from him. How could he possibly have so little imagination?

"Careful of your cologne," Robert said, frowning at the bottle that had fallen on its side. Evelyn righted the bottle. But her irritation had formed something hard in her stomach. Robert was allowed to have feelings and notions and intuitions, but the moment she was sensitive, it was absurd? She busied herself tidying the room, allowing the anger to settle somewhere quiet. By the time she joined Robert in bed, he was asleep in his still, silent way. But sleep was now impossible for her. Wind swooped and wailed through the building, ruffling the drapes of the four-poster bed. She wasn't sure if it was worse with the uncertain terror of them being closed and thrashing open, or if it was better to have leave them open and therefore have a direct view of any horrors that might loom out of the murk. Doors slammed in the building, and the ivory handle of the gruesome little door knocked against the back of the bureau. She lay alert to each creak, slam, creak, slam, for what seemed like hours. Evelyn tried to seek solace from Robert, but he was so asleep and so still that it was hard even to embrace him. She tried unsuccessfully to prise comfort from him, resting a foot and then an arm on him, trying to absorb some consolation from his body.

With a shudder of wind and a swell of rain, the windows bounced in their frames, shooting jabs of icy air across the room and down the collar of her pajamas. Rain thrummed against the glass, and the windows shook again. Evelyn took a breath, and bracing herself against the cold, slipped from under the blanket and crossed to the windows. Seizing the curtain by the hem, she began stuffing it into the gap in the frame. Frigid air was still pouring into the room, but the fabric buffered the worst of the rattling. As she tugged at the curtain on the far window, the ocean came into view. The moonlight was soft, a pretty peach colour illuminating the sprays of foam blasting over the water. She continued stuffing the frame, and then stopped. Something was moving, out in the ocean. Evelyn put her nose to the glass. Of course something was moving out there, the waves were tossing every which way! She tutted to herself and slipped the corner of the curtain hem into a crack in the sill. Something squirmed in her vision again. A lick of fear ran over her body.

There *was* something moving in the water. Moving backward. Out by the flat rock a few yards from shore. There was something slithering, slithering out of the waves and under again.

Evelyn's eyes tingled; her nose stung. Something was trying to climb out of the ocean.

Someone.

A woman.

A smooth limb slid from the waves and clasped the rock; the crown of a head appeared above the froth, shoulders, another limb. Acid shot into her throat. She was out there, creeping. Evelyn staggered back from the window. "Robert!" she gasped. "Robert! Robert!"

He snuffled from under the blanket. "What is it?"

"Robert!" She couldn't move. Her breath had fogged the glass, but she could still see the shape of it, crouching.

"What're you doing? Close the curtains, it's freezing."

"There's a person in the water," Evelyn hissed.

"What?"

Evelyn ran to the bed and tugged on Robert's elbow. "There's someone out there."

"Seal," Robert said.

Evelyn sniffed. Her eyes were watering. "It's not a seal."

"Come on." Robert pulled her towards the bed. He was musty and warm; his breath smelt like carrots. "Nightmare. Come on, Evie."

"No." Evelyn wiped her eyes. "I thought—it's—she's—there's someone."

With an exaggerated groan, Robert swept back the sheets and crossed to the window. "Evie, come look. There's nothing there. Not even a madman'd be out in that. There's not even any boats. It must've been an otter, or a bit of wood."

Evelyn shivered by the bed. "No, no."

"Evie, come." Robert gripped her by the hand and, not unkindly, ushered her towards the window. "See?"

Sure enough, there was only ocean and rock. No slithering limbs, no monstrous figure writhing out of the surf. No woman. She wasn't there.

Robert kissed the side of her head, accidentally tugging at her hair. "No mermaids for us tonight."

"There was something," Evelyn said, though now she was less certain.

"Come along." Robert patted her on the behind towards the bed. "Come on, get in, that's right." He steered her under the blanket, nuzzled his cheek into the back of her neck, and clamped his heavy arm over her waist. Within moments, Robert was asleep, but Evelyn lay awake until the sun rose, listening to the sound of footsteps creaking up and down the stairs.

16

THE NEXT MORNING AT BREAKFAST, THE WIND WAS still roaring down the chimneys, skittering soft ashes over the carpet. Evelyn toyed with the plate of kippers in front of her. They were lukewarm, fleshy.

"Feeling better this morning?" Robert refilled her teacup.

Evelyn shook her head. In the daylight, her nighttime panic seemed risible, but she wasn't ready to be teased about it.

"Not seen any mermaids up and about?" Robert grinned at her, his eyes twinkling.

"Amusing." Evelyn sipped her tea.

A housemaid approached the table with a letter on a tray and, bending down, handed Robert the letter and murmured into his ear. She crossed to the freckled young man sitting at the neighbouring table and whispered something in his ear as well.

"What was that?" Evelyn said, as the maid retreated.

"Apparently we're due for a spot of high wind."

"Worse than this?" The other side of the seawall was still roaring great fans of white water into the air, and the chestnut trees around the hotel creaked with menacing squeals.

"Looks like it. They'll be boarding the windows."

Evelyn swallowed. "But we'll be safe here, won't we?"

"Of course."

The hotel clerk with the eye patch entered the dining room carrying a sandbag over his shoulder. With a groan, he knelt and propped it against the glass doors overlooking the sea, returning a few minutes later with another bag. As the clerk loaded more sandbags against the doors, the young man at the next table lost the colour in his face. With a polite nod at Evelyn, he pushed his chair back and left the room. He hadn't eaten his kippers either.

"With the weather so bad, what will happen to the reading today?" Evelyn said.

"We'll have to call it off, there'll be trees down on the road." Robert sighed. "I'll find Clarence after breakfast."

Evelyn pushed the plate of kippers away from her and peered out of the windows. Strange debris had been tossed over the seawall by the surf: crispy crab shells, an old paintbrush, a cracked porcelain sausage dog. On the sloping lawn at the back of the hotel was the cage of a polio brace that rolled to and fro, clattering against the heavy stone pots at the edge of the patio. Every time it struck against the urns, she suppressed a twitch of horror—what tragedy had surrendered a leg brace to the water in the first place?

Robert turned the letter over and held it towards her. "This is for you."

"For me?" Evelyn squinted at the envelope. She didn't recognise the writing, or the monogram stamped on the back. She opened it carefully and gripped Robert's arm. "It's an invitation."

"That's nice," Robert said, pulling her abandoned plate of kippers towards him.

"No, Robert, it's a *real* invitation."

"It's not imaginary?" He grinned, pleased with himself. She batted him away.

"It's from Corporal Singh!"

"Who's that?"

Evelyn's mouth dropped open. "Corporal Vikram Singh? The Hero of the Highlands, Robert!"

"Oh, aye, Vikram. Nice chap." He tossed salt from the shaker over the kippers.

Evelyn gawped at him. "You've met him before?"

Robert reached for the saltshaker again and Evelyn intercepted it. "They're plenty salty already. Why didn't you say you knew the Hero of the Highlands?"

Robert shrugged. "I met him at the library. I can't remember everyone I meet, Evie."

Evelyn clutched the envelope to her chest. "He's invited us to a weekend at his house next Saturday." She flipped the envelope over and gazed at the address. "I wonder why he sent it to me?"

"I told him you're in charge of our socials," Robert said. He scraped the last of the fish from the plate and, depositing a kippery kiss on her forehead, stood from the table. "I'll let Clarence know about the storm."

Evelyn nodded, barely hearing him. She slipped the invitation into her book and searched out the downstairs reading room for some hotel stationery to post an RSVP. Even as she passed through the narrow antlered corridor, the shadowy terror of the night before melted away. The Hero of the Highlands! What would Kitty say?

The reading room was at the front of the hotel. It would usually have looked out onto the chestnut grove, but a wooden board emblazoned with the selkie had been slotted over the window, and Evelyn glared at her resentfully. Walter was sitting in an armchair, holding a book, and Evelyn nodded to him, flicking through the box of headed paper for a perfect piece with crisp edges.

"Robert was looking for you. I think the reading might be cancelled today, on account of the wind," she said.

Walter rolled his eyes. "How tiresome."

As she took a seat near the fire, Evelyn took in the gingery stubble on Walter's cheeks, his collar hanging loose around his jaw. His particular kind of prettiness didn't suit dishevelment. It made him look seedy, untrustworthy. "Did you sleep well?" Evelyn said.

"No." Walter steepled his hands, and sighed.

"Me neither," she said. "They won't be doing the boat trips while it's like this, will they?" She pictured the boat keeling wildly, thundering iron sheets of water smashing against its sides.

Walter turned his whole head to look at her. "No."

"Well. Probably for the best." She set the paper on the side table, giving it a good hard stare. She would have to compose a perfect, delightful reply, but one that sounded effortless, as if they were always invited to countryside weekends. Perhaps she should have chosen a wrinkled piece of paper; that would add an insouciant flair to her response. Evelyn cleared her throat. "Do you know Corporal Vikram Singh?"

Walter leant back, pulling a tin of Capstan Navy Cut tobacco from his pocket. He glanced at Evelyn and seemed to change his mind, laying the tin on the table. "Yes, I know Vikram. Why?"

"I received a letter from him this morning," Evelyn said, as casually as she could manage. "Robert mentioned he frequents the library."

"Yes, I put him and Robert together. Vikram is a great patron of spiritualism."

"He's invited us for a weekend."

"Yes, next Saturday? Vikram is always collecting people." Walter raised his eyebrows. "That's bohemians for you."

Evelyn frowned. Could an army man be a bohemian? Somehow, she associated the word with shaggy-haired dogs, and pale women drowning in pools filled with water lilies. "Anyway," she said, after a moment. "Thank you for making the introduction."

Walter blinked, slowly. "It's important for business to keep Vikram happy."

"I'm sure," she said, startled. "We'll be perfect guests, I promise."

Walter gave her a minute shrug. An impudent, rude shrug. Evelyn wondered for the first time if she hated Walter. A drop of water fell down the chimney and sizzled on the grate. She searched for a way to change the subject. "And what novel is that you're reading?"

Walter turned his head towards her. "Fiction is entirely a waste of time," he said, so loudly it was as if he were pronouncing a declaration on stage.

Perhaps she did hate Walter.

"You're probably right," she said, forcing a smile. "So, what book has captured your attention?"

"I can't focus on it at all," Walter said, tossing it now onto the floor, and sitting forward, rubbing his fingers into his forehead.

"It was a rough evening," Evelyn said, eventually, in the most confidential tone she could muster. She was hoping he might begin to complain. Of an unsettled night. Of a poor rest. It would be rude if she were to begin the complaint, but she might join in. "Tell me. Did your room, yours and Clarence's, did it have a tunnel?"

"A tunnel?"

"Yes," Evelyn said, faltering under the disdain in his expression.

"No, our room did not have a tunnel," he said, finally.

"Oh."

Walter was scrutinising her. His eyes were a clear, luminous green. His body was absolutely still, but his gaze was evaluative. Evelyn had a sudden, mad thought he might reach over and kiss her. As he stared at her, Evelyn realised it was the predatory watchfulness of his look that had given her the strange pang of sexual intimacy. But it wasn't tender, or even romantic; it was as if he were the judge of a firing squad, trying to make a last-minute decision to reprieve only one prisoner. Evelyn squirmed in the seat and pretended to be absorbed by the fire.

"Your husband," he said.

"Robert," Evelyn supplied, then cursed herself. He hadn't been prompting her for his name.

"I intend to ask him to join the next circuit."

"I see." She sat back in the chair. On one hand, there was Clarence, his perceptiveness, his precision. On the other, there was the countess, the salon, Corporal Singh. Papa and Mama still weren't taking her calls. But surely even *they* couldn't disapprove of the Hero of the Highlands!

"Are you likely to object?"

Evelyn chewed her lip. "I suppose it's good to be helpful," she said.

After a beat, Walter said, in his declarative way, "That's a very naive sentiment."

Yes, Evelyn decided, yes, she did hate Walter.

"But perhaps the sentiment of someone who has not yet found a real opportunity to be of use to society," he continued.

Evelyn felt a flush of mortification and anger shooting into her stomach.

"I recognise it," he said. "I recognise that in myself." He stared into the fire.

Evelyn closed her mouth. Was Walter really trying to help people? To do good? She felt ashamed of herself. His behaviour was odd, that was all. He had that constipated, supercilious sort of temperament, a common affliction in men who spend too much time with other men. It wasn't his fault he was so difficult to talk to.

A scream of wind shook the chimney, and another wet, mushy spot of ash fell onto the wood. Evelyn unscrewed one of the hotel fountain pens and tested it on the back of Vikram's envelope. Black ink. Shame, a bit sombre, to send an RSVP in black ink.

"He's seeing things."

"Pardon?"

"Clarence. He's seeing things, you know."

Evelyn's neck prickled. "Do you mean here? In the hotel? Or . . . outside?"

"He says that he sees turbulence. Ahead."

"In the water?" she whispered. "Someone coming out of the water?"

"No, Evelyn," he said, his voice sharp. "Turbulence in the future."

The chintzy shepherdess clock on the mantelpiece struck quarter to ten. "And"—she hesitated—"you believe him?"

He examined her for a moment, then turned away, apparently disappointed by what he had discovered. "Of course I believe him."

"I mean, you believe—" She paused. "All of his, insights, you—" She cleared her throat. "Children often have vivid imaginations, don't they?"

Walter reached for the tin of tobacco and began to roll a cigarette. "Did you know, it was a pure accident of fate that Clarence discovered his gift?"

"No, I didn't."

"My mother was resistant to join me at the spiritualist church—I had been asking her for months. But after only two weeks as a visitor at my church, she revealed to me that Clarence had come to her, in private, and brought forth her own mother in spirit. If she hadn't attended my church, she never would have believed the miracle of his gift. We might never have known about it. He's a marvel. One would be a fool to doubt Clarence's insight."

Evelyn stuttered, unsure whether she was being insulted.

"He's never been wrong yet, you know." Walter's expression was a little wild, the threads in his eyeballs the colour of cherries. "It's an art, you see, deciphering spirit. Most mediums, they deliver the odd message that doesn't fit, or they get their wires crossed, read for someone else by accident. Clarence—" He produced a lighter from his jacket pocket and lit his cigarette. "Clarence has never been wrong. Not a single mistake. He's—we're lucky to have him."

Evelyn fiddled with the cap of the hotel fountain pen. It was the most she had ever heard Walter speak, and the passion in his voice was unnerving. "Absolutely," she said, with a croak. "Yes, of course."

She sat back in the chair as Walter smoked in silence. She hadn't understood, until now, that he truly believed in Clarence's gift. Walter had the pompous deportment of a businessman, the tumid humourlessness of the pragmatist. She had considered his investment in the family business to be one of administration, rather than sentiment. The unexpected expansion of Walter's inner life made Evelyn feel small and strangely alone.

She thought, now, of the early days of marriage, when she and Robert had lived in a flat near Dumbiedykes. It was only for a few months, before they'd found an affordable house at the more humble end of Kitty's street. The flat was outfitted in odd pieces of Mairibank furniture that crowded the rooms, and a squeaky bed from an old guest chamber that caused her no end of mortification in the honeymoon stage of their union. The back windows of the flat looked onto Holyrood Park, and on a lucky day, if it wasn't too overcast, the Salisbury Crags would light up a buttery yellow, just before sunset. In that dingy flat with the low ceilings and the smoky fireplace, it was Evelyn's favourite moment of the day. And yet, each afternoon, Robert would come home from work, march straight to the window, and draw the curtain across the rail. Eventually, frustrated, she'd pounced on him in the act of blocking the view.

"Darling, it's the only nice thing about this flat. Can't you just let me enjoy it for half an hour? I can move the armchair if the light is bothering you."

Robert went very quiet. He looked at her, chewed his lips, and then after a moment, motioned for her to come closer. She stood by the window, nestled underneath his chin.

"Do you see that?" He pointed to the top of an old water pump on the other side of the wall. "It's hidden in the other window because of the trees. You can only see it from here."

"Yes, I see it."

"I don't want to . . ." He trailed off. She heard the sound of him swallowing, and turned. In those days, she wasn't as sensitive to his ellipses; she couldn't sense when was appropriate to push.

"You don't want to see it? But it's just an old pump!"

Robert opened his mouth and shut it again.

"But why don't you want to see it? Did something happen there? Is it to do with the orphanage?" She reached up to touch his face. "You can tell me, I promise I won't be shocked."

Robert took her hand. "Evie, there are some things about that time I can't tell you. If you knew them, I wouldn't be able to forget them while I was with you, either."

Evelyn withdrew her hand as if it were scalded. She knew exactly what he meant. And yet, there were parts of Robert's history she would never reach. That he never wanted her to reach. It felt like an arcane form of abandonment, of loneliness, to be shut off from so much of his past.

But from then on, when she saw the curtain closed, she left it, just as it was.

17

AGAINST ALL PREDICTIONS, THE WIND HAD DIED down by noon the next day, and Evelyn wrapped her hair in a scarf and forced herself to go for a walk. The grounds were littered with felled trees, shattered boughs rattling in the breeze. The carpet of chestnut leaves concealed mushy puddles and cracked shards of roof shingles, so Evelyn changed route and went past the back of the hotel, down towards the oceanfront. The water was still flecked with whitecaps, waltzing in the distance. She kept her eyes on the flat rock near the shore, getting as near to it as she dared. She paused at the edge of the beach. Standing there made her uneasy, somehow exposed. She glanced over her shoulder towards the hotel, but all the ground-floor windows were boarded.

By the waterline, a sparkle caught her eye. Pebbles rolling under the soles of her shoes, she strolled down the beach towards the waves. More detritus had been washed up overnight by the storm: an empty jar of Lemco meat extract, the tarnished lid from a teakettle. Swollen, liver-coloured polyps of seaweed lay tangled between wine corks and broken and glass. The flash glimmered again, and this time she was able to locate it. It was moving, slowly, along the beach. A crab! A crab was scuttling across the stones. In its right claw, it was holding a woman's pearl hairpin. Evelyn's stomach roiled. Under other circumstances, it might have been absurd, even amusing, but instead, the image burrowed somewhere awful. The creeping, insectile creature, picking over the remnants of what had been, nibbling away with its grasping claws. She thought of what Robert had said about the signs, the reminders. She looked closer at the hairpin. It wasn't Dolly's, was it? She shook herself, picking up her pace and walking back up the beach, square against the oncoming wind. Fishing boats had been pulled up beyond the reach of the waves, and the shrill chime of their rigging clinked in the wind. She wound between their hulls, coated in slippery algae and garlands of milky barnacles. Higher up the beach, a young boy and his mother were raking sea coal into mounds, and Evelyn passed them without acknowledgement.

What could it mean for Robert to be right? For everything he said to be true? If Robert was right, then she had only ever known half the world. There was so much more, so many more unimaginable things, separated from her only by a veil. If Robert was right, then spirits were close. They were here, everywhere. They watched, followed, stood, silently, behind mirrors, behind birthday cakes. In the early days, it seemed impossible that Dolly would be gone forever. That she would keep being gone. It felt as if at any moment, she was due to come back and tell her what it was like being dead, as if she'd taken some exotic walking holiday. Evelyn closed her eyes. She tried to lean her very soul forward, up, out of her body. In her mind she said, *Dolores*. There was no answer, no prickle or pinch. If Dolly were close, she would know, she would feel it in her soul. Wouldn't she? But Evelyn hadn't *wanted* her to come. What if she'd been trying to talk to her, to Robert, and Evelyn had blocked her? What if she was lonely, on the other side? What if she needed something? Evelyn's eyes burned. But then, if she reached out—if Robert knew—the pebbles were unsteady under her feet; she swayed with each step. She couldn't risk it. No matter how tempting, she couldn't risk it.

The wind picked up even more, ramming into her ears, blowing her overcoat into a parachute, chucking up grit that she crunched between her teeth. After all this time—maybe Robert was telling the truth. Maybe he did have a gift, a gift of genuine magic. But then, that would mean he was someone she didn't know, someone she had never known. Someone unknowable.

That afternoon, Evelyn was restless. She lay on the bed, she sat in the chair in the corner of their room, she sat in the reading room, she sat in the dining room. Never before had she spent so much time indoors at a hotel, and it was horrible to be so aware of her intrusion on the mechanics of the business. When the housemaid came to clean the bedroom, Evelyn stepped out into the hallway, where yet another maid was sweeping the corridor. In the reading room, a young boy was sweeping the grate, the front desk clerk mopping the dining room. Eventually she stood in the telephone vestibule and, whenever she heard a person approaching, picked up the phone and held it clamped in her hand as if she were waiting for the operator to connect her. After the third time she was passed by the young boy hauling a bucket of coal, he called, "I wouldn't waste your time, Miss, the line's been down all day and not likely to go back until next week."

Mortified, Evelyn nodded at him, and affected a frowning, thwarted expression, as if the urgency of her call was such that she had failed to notice the lack of service.

By the evening, the hot water had gone off, and Evelyn rinsed herself before dinner with numb fingers. Someone in the hotel had developed a cough, and it was racketing through the floorboards. Evelyn felt existentially soiled. It was a grubby, abrasive kind of discomfort, as if there were crumbs inside her underclothes.

When she was dressed for dinner, she left Robert searching for his cuff links, and took the staircase up to Clarence's room. He was housed in a nicer part of the hotel; the carpet was scarlet, here, instead of brown, the speaking tube in the corridor adorned with a gold cap.

Evelyn took a breath before knocking on Clarence's door.

"Come in."

Clarence was lying across a four-poster bed even bigger than the one in their room. He was tapping his heels against the bedspread, dangling a yo-yo over the side of the bed. Bernice was sitting in an armchair by the window, reading a society magazine with her feet propped on an ottoman.

"Sorry to intrude. Can I talk to you for a minute?"

"Certainly," Bernice said. "Do you want to talk here, or downstairs? I suppose if you came up here, you'd rather talk here?"

"I meant talk to Clarence," Evelyn said. She licked her lips. "Alone, if you don't mind."

Bernice shot a glance at Clarence, and he shrugged.

"I'll leave you to it then, but I'll be in the reading room if you need me. Just come and get me downstairs if you like. You know where the reading room is, don't you? Just down the stairs?"

Evelyn gave Bernice a frozen smile as she passed, and closed the door firmly behind her. After a moment of hesitation, she moved a pile of newspapers from the chair by the bureau and took a seat. She twisted her shawl between her hands. "I wanted to ask you a question," she said. Her voice was scratchy, and she cleared her throat.

Clarence raised his eyebrows, looking a lot like his brother as he did so.

Evelyn waited for a response, but none seemed to be forthcoming. "My question. It's about spirits."

"Yes?"

"When someone . . ." She rolled her wrist.

"Dies," Clarence said.

"Yes. When someone dies, they, can they hear us on the other side?"

Clarence put his yo-yo down on the bedspread. "Seems like it."

"OK, well." Evelyn rubbed her face. Why was it so difficult? "Would they know what we are thinking? Could they know our minds?"

"Evelyn," Clarence said, and she started. A child calling her by her first name felt indecent, almost impudent. "Evelyn, is there something you want to ask specifically?"

"Yes. I want to ask, there's someone I don't want to—" She paused. A scurfy rush of emotion surged up in her, bristly, stifling, like radio static. "There's someone I don't want to come through. I don't ever want them to come through. Maybe if I'm alone, but never, not ever in the presence of other people. Is that—can I—prevent—" She stopped. It felt as if there were granules of salt on the roof of her mouth.

Clarence was watching her. "You have to be open to the message, to want it. It's like a telephone line."

"Edison's valve?" Evelyn said.

Clarence smiled, not unkindly. "I mean, you have to pick up the other end. Otherwise it will keep ringing."

Evelyn sat back in the chair. Her eyes filled with tears; she didn't trust herself to speak. After a moment she said. "OK."

"OK?"

"So I'm safe?"

Clarence gave her a wary look.

"Safe from the séances?" she said.

He shrugged. "Apparently." He rolled onto his back. "Anything else?" he said, picking up his yo-yo.

"No." She stood, tugging her shawl tighter around her. She paused at the door handle. "Thank you, Clarence."

"You're welcome, Mrs. Hazard," he said, in a singsong tone she wasn't sure was genuine.

As she left the room, she caught her reflection shimmering in the gilt-framed mirror in the corridor. There was a hectic energy darting across her face; her lips were pale, her eyes bright. She felt as if she had suddenly been sprinkled with sugar.

She was safe.

They were safe.

She wanted to jump on the stair, bounce and touch the cornice in the ceiling. She wanted to fly. Everything was going to be fine. Better than fine.

＊ ＊ ＊

DINNER THAT EVENING WAS tinned potatoes and corned beef. A totally bland and reasonable meal that Evelyn felt much better for afterwards. She went up to her room to collect her book, but when she came down to the reading room, Bernice, Clarence, Walter, and Robert were all sitting at a round table at the back of the room, as if they were having a committee meeting.

"There she is!" Robert smiled at her. "Since we had to cancel the reading, Walter thought we'd have a session of our own. Will you join us?"

She hesitated. Even with her new reprieve, the idea of sitting in a darkened room with Clarence made her skin crawl. She was skittish enough already, without introducing new phantoms to her nighttime terrors. "Join you? I'd rather not, thank you."

"Please, Evie?"

"Um, sorry, I feel a cold coming on."

Walter made a breathy sound that she realised was a scoff. She stared at him, the blood rushing to her cheeks.

"A cold is hardly enough to prevent you, is it?" There was a hint of a sneer on his face.

"Not at all," she said. She wanted to reach out and tweak his stupid, perfect nose. With a thump, she sat at the table and tucked her skirt under her knees.

Bernice stood up. "I'll turn the lights out, shall I? Or would you prefer with just the light overhead? Or maybe I can shut the drapes? The evenings are light for so long now, it's lovely, but perhaps it's better—"

"Please, just turn the lights off," Evelyn snapped. Robert flashed her a smile, but she wasn't in the mood to smile back at him. She reached out and grabbed his hand. "Let's start, shall we?"

Walter blinked at her, coolly, but she could detect a certain smugness buzzing off him. She seized his hand. It was callused, a ridge of scar tissue running between his thumb and finger.

"Don't break hands until I have said so," Clarence said. He was looking at Evelyn, and she realised, of course, the instruction was for her benefit. "And you may find it helps if you keep your eyes closed."

She squeezed her eyes shut. After a moment Clarence said, "It's so cold."

Evelyn opened her eyes, thinking to offer him her shawl, and then shut them again. He wasn't talking about the here and now. Her stomach clenched.

"There's someone trying to make contact." Clarence paused. "I can hear the voice of a young man calling out to us. He's been trying to reach out for days."

Evelyn straightened her shoulders.

"He's young, and he knows someone here very well."

She tried to stop her mind from sifting through all the dead young men in her life. There was a long list. "He is showing me images of pheasants. He used to hunt pheasants? I think he's here for you, Walter?"

Next to her, Walter made a sound in the back of his throat, a sort of squeak. Evelyn looked at him.

"Is he here for you?" Clarence said.

Walter's lip twitched. "Yes."

"He's trying to say something." Clarence wrinkled his brow. "He wants to tell you something important but . . . I'm having trouble hearing him." Clarence was silent for several moments. "I'm trying to bring him back, but he's hard to understand. You must concentrate very hard on your memory of him."

"I am," Walter said. His hand was sweaty in hers.

"Oh dear," Clarence said. "I'm afraid it was too hard, he didn't have enough will drawing him through on this side. He's pulling away, I'm sorry."

Walter was breathing heavily through his nose. Evelyn looked at Clarence. Was he trying to get revenge on Walter for embarrassing him at dinner the other night? Or was there truly someone in the room, slipping back into their own private darkness? Clarence's face was blank, innocent as a milkmaid.

Robert leant forward, his eyes closed, a line of concentration on his brow. "Let me see, let me see. A young man. Yes. Young, and brave, is that right?"

Walter nodded. "Yes."

"Young and brave, that's him. I have him, don't worry, I have him. He didn't pass from—he wasn't on the *Iolaire*, was he?"

"No."

Robert's forehead relaxed. "But it was a boat? His passing had something to do with a boat, with being at sea?"

"Yes, that's right."

Robert paused. "Was he in the navy?"

"He was."

A trickly, treacly horror was creeping along Evelyn's body. How did Robert know that? How could he possibly know? Perhaps Clarence had coached him in advance? But that would be irredeemably cruel. Robert had his faults; cruelty was not one of them.

"I can see the letters *A* and *J*. I think they may be initials. Was his Christian name Angus? Andrew?"

Walter was making a coughing sound. "Yes. Angus."

"He's important to you. You think of him often, almost every day."

Walter sniffed. "Yes, yes."

"He's saying, 'I went much too soon,' that's what he says. He says, 'You don't need to miss me, because I'm always here with you.'"

Walter's lips were trembling. Evelyn looked down at her knees. It now felt uncomfortably intimate to be holding his hand, and she wished she could pull away.

"There's something to do with bells?" Robert said. "I can't understand it, but it seems to be important. Bells, does that mean anything to you?"

Walter laughed. "Yes, yes, I know exactly what that is. Yes, of course."

The hairs on Evelyn's arms were standing up.

"That's all I can get, I'm afraid," Robert said.

"Thank you." Walter's voice was uncharacteristically soft. "Thank you, it's enough."

✦ ✦ ✦

THAT NIGHT, EVELYN LAY awake long into the wee hours. Robert beside her was perfectly still, so still that she rolled over and watched to make sure he was breathing. All this time she had spent doubting him. Underestimating him. She would have to get to know him all over again, like he was a new person. His eyelids twitched, and Evelyn swallowed. She had disbelieved Robert for so long, misunderstood him, trivialised his gift, wouldn't she be punished by the heavens, somehow? She turned in the bedclothes, inching her toes down into the icy part of the sheets. The rain had died down, yet wind swept around the room, shuffling the bed curtains, rattling the handle of the tiny door. She blinked into the darkness, alert to every squeak of the floorboards, every crack of the window frame. There was a flutter of air, a squeal, and a stir by the window, and for one second, just one second, Dolores, sitting in the chair in the corner of the room.

18

THE FOLLOWING SATURDAY MORNING, EVELYN DRESSED in her tweed and waited for Robert in the parlour. She pulled the curtains back, then wiped her breath from the glass. There came the sound of an automobile horn, and Evelyn jumped up and down, clapping. She ran out to the pavement, where Robert again beeped the horn of Henry's brand new Oxford bullnose.

"Please thank Henry for the loan. Papa's still isn't fixed, or else I could have asked him to lend it to us," she said, as casually as she could manage.

"This motorcar is more fun anyway," he said with a wink, which Evelyn decided not to comment on.

Marty stood by the front gate, crossing her arms. "It has brakes, does it?"

Evelyn laughed. "Of course it does."

Marty disappeared and then reappeared with two scratchy angora blankets which she handed to Evelyn, frowning. "Mind you don't let the windows down or the wind'll get in your ears and freeze your brain."

Evelyn smiled. "We won't." And overcome with sudden affection, she clutched Marty to her. Marty's fingers were stiff on her shoulders.

"Drive careful, now," she said.

"We will."

Evelyn settled next to Robert, he tucked the blanket around her knees, and then they set off. As Robert pulled into the street, Evelyn immediately abandoned her pledge not to roll down the window, and leant out to wave until Marty became a pearly streak in her rear-view mirror.

The drive was supposed to take two hours, but hindered by a late-season snow and a few wrong turns, it took closer to three. They passed out of Edinburgh, winding through Danderhall and Dalkeith and then out into the fields. They drove through spindly pine forests, along narrow roads hedged with hawthorn. Feathery little chips of snow melted on the bonnet where the engine rumbled. Evelyn pulled the blanket to her chin and surrendered to the glorious grogginess of being driven somewhere.

"Evie, don't you fall asleep on me," Robert said, reaching over and rocking her knee.

"I'm not," she said crossly, starting awake.

"Good. I need my navigator."

Evelyn pulled out the map. Reading while driving made her queasy, and she blamed Robert a little bit for not having planned out their route in advance. After a false turn at Swintonmill, they finally arrived at Colbreck, the village closest to Vikram's house. Robert slowed to admire the new war memorial in the village, then took a narrow road left at a sheep croft and over the River Tweed. Evelyn rolled down her window and leant out as they crossed the water. It looked deceivingly warm, glossy and agate against the white-tipped trees. They had to turn back on themselves and cross another bridge to reach Vikram's house, Robert beeping the horn at each twist in the road. Eventually they approached the gates for Halworth. A muddy, rutted path swerved through sparkling rowans and opened at the house. It was a magnificent Georgian affair with a wide, imposing facade and a strange turret from the middle, as if it had once been a boarding school.

"It's a mansion," Evelyn said, with a gasp. At once she reviewed her outfits. Why had she not brought her silk? And her brushes! Oh Lord, the maids would see her old brushes!

"Of course it's a mansion." Robert turned to look at her. "It's the McGreaths' old estate."

"But—"

"Death duties, Evie," Robert said, parking the car between two urns filled with purple heather. "He snapped it up for a penny."

Evelyn nibbled her finger. "Why didn't you say so?"

Robert gave her a quizzical expression. "I'm saying so now."

"But my walking boots are all muddy," Evelyn squeaked. "I packed grey brocade for the evening. Brocade!" She covered her face with her hands. "And I brought him some of Marty's marmalade as a gift."

"What's wrong with that?"

Evelyn pointed to the house. "I can't give a man who lives in Lord McGreath's estate Marty's homemade marmalade."

The front door swung open, and Vikram appeared on the steps. He was in his thirties, with dark brown skin, heavily lashed eyes, and a nose that was a little too long for his face. He was wearing a cable-knit green jumper that was snug around the middle.

He crossed to Evelyn's side of the car. "Mrs. Hazard, a pleasure to meet you."

Evelyn hastily checked her face in the rearview mirror. "What a beautiful home," she said, accepting his arm.

He shook Robert's hand. "Do you have bags?"

Evelyn nodded. "Yes," she said, with a flash of inspiration. "But I think I may have left one of my cases behind. Forgotten it. So you must forgive my outfits."

Vikram motioned towards the house. "Don't worry about that. I'm sure one of the girls can lend you something, if you need. Let's go in, shall we? Matthew will take the cases to your room."

Behind Vikram's shoulder, Evelyn raised her eyebrows at Robert. A *male* servant? How wealthy was he?

They followed Vikram into the entrance. It was outfitted in the usual, sombre, country house grandeur: russet wallpaper, a monstrous golden chandelier, dark, heavy furniture, a series of military pennants of some kind hanging over the fireplace. There was the sound of clinking and sweeping from the left. A mahogany staircase led up to a balcony where a young scullery maid hurried past. Hanging over a Jacobean chest to the left of the room was an odd painting, a canvas filled with spindly black whirls and splashes of yellow paint. Here and there amongst the chaos, tiny words had been inscribed in grease pencil.

Vikram noticed Evelyn's eyes lingering on the painting. "Isn't it mesmerising? It's a Manet."

Evelyn squinted. It didn't *look* like a Manet, but then she didn't know much about art.

"It's via Greg Bailish, of course," Vikram said. "Are you familiar with his work?"

Evelyn considered lying before shaking her head.

Vikram's eyes brightened. "Really? He's an automatic painter; spirit channels him to produce the pieces. See here?" He gestured to a yellow arc, obscuring the word "potatoes." "See how the brushstrokes have the brief, directional quality that made Manet such a genius?"

"What a talent!" Robert said, with apparently genuine enthusiasm.

"Would you like to meet him?" Vikram said. "I can introduce you at his next session. He'll be trying to channel wee Charlie."

"Wee Charlie?" Robert frowned. "I'm not familiar with his work."

Vikram paused. "The missing boy?"

"Yes, of course," Evelyn said, a little too loud. "We've been following the case. Awful." She looked at a black smear of paint that dribbled down the middle of the canvas, searching for an opportunity to change the subject. She thought of a pale young boy, locked inside a dark cupboard, pleading for his mother.

"Greg's parties are always popular." Vikram crossed the corridor. "And his atelier is a sight to behold."

Evelyn beamed at him. That was better. Atelier!

Vikram opened the library door, which, from the doorway, appeared to be reassuringly free of spirit drawings. Instead, the wall was lined with lugubrious oil paintings of horses, bloodshot eyes peering through the gloom. A marble bust of a bewigged figure that Evelyn didn't recognise stood on the mantelpiece. Displayed in a case along the back wall was a collection of pretty Turkish jars. A fire was burning in a small grate, where four velvet chairs had been pulled in front of a table set with a pot in a knitted cosy and heavy-looking bannocks.

"I thought we'd have some tea, and then I can give you a tour before the rest of the guests arrive."

"We're not the first here, are we?" Evelyn said.

"No." Vikram pointed upstairs. "The others, I'm afraid, are still resting off their endeavours."

Evelyn laughed, although she wasn't sure what he meant.

They sat by the fire, and Robert and Vikram talked politely of their drive up to the house, the route taken, the route best avoided, the war memorial in Colbreck, the stray dog that had been scaring the local sheep.

While they traded tedious niceties, Evelyn searched the bookshelves. The shelves were staffed with one of those bought-in libraries, with the important works of classics and history and literature and philosophy all bound in identical red leather.

"It came with the house, you know," Vikram said, noticing her gaze. "I've never even opened a single one." He gestured to a matching set of Gibbons in a case next to the Turkish jars. "Goodness knows how expensive they must have been. Poor old McGreath."

Evelyn nodded, not able to meet his eyes. She pictured some young ex-officer, putting his muddy boots on the ottoman in the Mairibank library, casually tipping his cigar ash into her mother's Wedgwood teacup.

"Good luck for you, though," Robert said, jovially, and Evelyn shot him a look. "I mean—" Robert faltered. "Not lucky, but . . ." He waved his teaspoon.

"Let me give you the tour." Vikram stood up and brushed the crumbs from his lap. He accompanied them out of the library and into a small, formal front room. The room was cold, the fireplace swept and spotless. A white sheet was draped over a stiff Edwardian sofa. Vikram pointed out a portrait of Lord McGreath hanging on the far wall. Other than the portrait and the sofa, the room was unfurnished but for a china bust of a Pekingese dog. "I don't use this room much," Vikram said. "We open it for the summer when people come visiting to reminisce about the house."

Robert wrinkled his nose. "Really? Perfect strangers?"

Vikram shrugged. "All the time. I've started to think I should charge for admission."

Evelyn imagined standing in line at the Mairibank doors, searching in her purse for enough pennies to buy a ticket to view her own childhood bedroom.

The "drawing room" behind the formal front room was the size of a banquet hall, with heavy beams across the low ceiling. There was a large oval table in the centre of the room, the kind with panels that could be raised up to allow for more guests. Lining the walls were a collection of odd chairs: studded ottomans, mahogany dining chairs, high-backed affairs with horsehair leaking from holes in the antimacassars. Evelyn walked through to the windows on the other side, where at the back right was a deep recess that seemed to serve no purpose except to display a chestnut bureau that contained a collection of mudlarked clay pipes. She looked out of the window and caught the eye of a robin pecking at a berry in the yew hedge. If this were her house, she would throw out all these horrible chairs and have sofas against the back wall. And she'd turn that silly little recess into a cupboard by putting up some doors.

Behind her, Vikram was pointing out a collection of Indian miniatures on the left of the fireplace.

"Quite exquisite," Robert was saying, examining a portrait of a young woman sitting underneath a pink-blossoming tree.

Evelyn frowned at him. He'd never used the word "exquisite" before, and this was not the venue in which to start.

Vikram handed him a heavy, ivory-handled magnifying glass. "Aren't they? I have a dealer in Edinburgh who puts them aside the second they come in."

"Ladies first," Robert said, handing her the glass.

Evelyn bent down and inspected the pearlescent buttons on the woman's gown. With some irritation, the word "exquisite" leapt into her mind. "Beautiful," she said, instead.

Just then, there was a snuffle in the corner and Evelyn jumped, catching the magnifying glass before it dropped to the floor.

A woman sat up from a stiff-backed armchair in the corner where she had clearly been sleeping. She wiped her lips and eyes. "I'm sorry," she said, "I didn't mean to frighten you—must have dozed off." Vikram was laughing.

It was Lily, from Robert's meeting in Stanton Abbey. This time she was wearing a handsome pair of cigarette trousers and a silk blouse. Vikram crossed the room and put his hand on Lily's shoulder. Evelyn's interest in her sharpened.

Lily rubbed her eyes. "I wasn't snoring, was I?"

"No, my dear," Vikram said.

"It's so deliciously warm in here." Lily yawned, stretching. A tasselled onyx necklace clicked against the buttons of her blouse. "Wait." She stood, and put her hand out for Robert's. "You're the fortune teller!"

Robert cleared his throat. "Spirit medium."

Lily shrugged. "All the same."

A circle of blush appeared on the bridge of Robert's nose. "Not exactly."

Lily grinned at him. "Your reading at Stanton Abbey was amazing. I was sorry not to get out to the Murray Hotel, but trees were down on the road. Did you have to cancel in the end?"

"Yes, ma'am."

Evelyn flinched. She nudged him, hard, in the side.

"I mean, just yes," Robert said.

Lily sat back in the chair, even though everyone else was standing. "Do you read palms as well?"

Robert twitched. "No."

"I had my palms read once in Manhattan," Lily said, dreamily. "I was told I'd find true love," and she burst out in a shriek of laughter.

Evelyn and Robert shared an alarmed glance. Vikram laughed along.

"Well, Bobby will give you a much more accurate reading than that," Vikram said. "You'll just have to wait for tonight."

Evelyn looked at Robert, who was staring at the carpet. She felt her stomach squirm with a rustle of unease. It was one thing for Robert to comfort miners and housemaids, but they were in real company now. "And do you have a dining room?" she said, even though that was a stupid question—anything to give them something else to focus on.

"Yes, of course," Vikram said. "Although first let me show you my favourite part of the house." He led them away from Lily, out of the room, then right and along the corridor to a large, bolted door at the back of the house. "I added this after I bought the place." He opened the door, and they stepped not into the garden, as she had expected, but into a humid, warm conservatory. Glass windows made up the walls and the ceiling, and the room was filled with wilted-looking ferns shedding leafy scraps onto the tiles.

Vikram made a clicking sound with his tongue, and a canary flew to his shoulder. He opened the front pocket of his shirt and the bird nipped in and reappeared with a seed in its beak.

Robert's face broke into a smile. "What a beautiful little chap! Can I hold him?"

Carefully, Vikram handed the bird to Robert, and the expression of tender concentration on Robert's face as he held the creature cupped in his hands was somehow so heartbreaking that Evelyn had to look away.

"What's his name?" Robert said, releasing one finger to stroke the fluff on the bird's head.

"He doesn't have a name," Vikram said, settling down into one of the wicker chairs. "I just call him Bird."

"Hello, Bird," Robert said, rubbing it under the chin.

She watched the canary pecking at Robert's fingers, strangely unsettled. Who wouldn't give their pet a name? It would be like if she began calling Robert "Husband."

"Would you like to hold him, Evie?" Robert gestured to her.

Evelyn's throat squeezed. She thought of the magpie's black feathers, twitching, in the dirt. She shook her head.

"Please, make yourself comfortable," Vikram said. Evelyn took a look at the wicker chairs, pearly with condensation and flecked with bird droppings. The beautiful tiles, that Persian rug—covered in seed and feathers and rotted fern leaves. She refurnished the space in her mind. First, the bird would be given a lovely big cage. And flowers, she would grow orchids in every colour. And she'd reupholster the love seat in the corner. What a crime, to let such a beautiful love seat get frayed like that.

"I always wanted a glasshouse," Vikram said, as Robert released the bird. "My aunt had one, in Fife, and she grew cherries in there."

He and Robert began to talk about netting for cherries and netting for apples and netting for nettles, and Evelyn found herself yawning.

"I'm sorry," Vikram said. "I'll ask Matthew to take you up to your room."

Matthew proved to be a tall blond man in his thirties and a very handsome butler indeed. He led them up the mahogany staircase and to the west wing of the house, where they were shown to a simple bedroom. It had a small double bed and a fireplace, which Evelyn was grateful to see had already been lit. Robert excused himself to the bathroom down the hall, and Evelyn rifled through the books on the shelf under the window. They were the sort of tattered collection abandoned by previous guests: a few cheap adventure novels, a *Farmers' Almanac* from 1919, a riddle book that had been half completed with crude words pencilled giddily into the answer boxes. Her clothes had already been unpacked; her brushes were laid out on the dresser. Why on earth hadn't she thought to pack her wedding brushes? And the housemaids, in their bonnets and starched uniform! How much should they leave as a tip? It would almost be worse to leave too much—like peasants unaccustomed to splendour. Or worse, like middle-class people out of their depths. She chewed her fingernail, watching the drizzle wash away the mantle of snow on the hedges in the driveway.

When Robert reappeared, he looked sheepishly around the door. "Funny, for such a grand house they've tied the nailbrush to the sink. As if Vikram's guests would steal it!" He walked over to peer at the painting of a birlinn over the fireplace.

"Oh Robert, that's so one-armed men can still scrub their nails," she said, impatiently.

"Ah." Robert was kicking out a pleat in the carpet where it had buckled. He had the air of waiting to get told off.

Evelyn folded her arms. "I wish you'd warned me it was going to be so grand."

"I thought you knew," he said, churlishly. "He is the Hero of the Highlands."

"But—" Evelyn said. She'd been about to say, "But he's a foreigner," and she caught herself. The rules were all different now. Young men living in old men's castles. Debutantes with day jobs.

There was money and there was *money*. But she could hardly expect Robert to understand—he was so wilfully ignorant about the subtleties of wealth.

"I want to make a good impression. For *us* to make a good impression."

Robert sat heavily on the bed next to her and took her hand. "You'll always make a good impression. You're a queen among women."

"Hmm," Evelyn said. "Does he seem a bit eccentric?"

"Maybe? Letting your pets use the furniture as a cludgie—" His body seized with a sudden tension, and Evelyn looked at him, alarmed. "A budgie cludgie!" he finally pronounced, with something like a yelp of victory.

"It's a canary, Robert, not a budgie," Evelyn said, tutting. She wasn't in the mood to be distracted from worrying. "But how will I talk to his guests? I won't know what to say—I'm not eccentric."

"No, my love, you're perfectly normal."

"I know," Evelyn said. She licked her lips, aching to be able to return the compliment. But she couldn't. Maybe this was Robert's station now—peculiar foreigners and girls in gold tuxedos. It was better than Clarence and Bernice, at least. How odd it was, after everything, that it was Robert who'd brought her back to society. Mama and Papa's disapproval, their denunciation, might end up helping her return to where she belonged, albeit under unconventional circumstances.

A motorcar roared up the drive, and Evelyn leapt up to catch a glimpse of the guests. A woman in a cerise capelet got out of the passenger seat, shielding her white-blonde hair from the rain with a newspaper. The driver was a chubby man who looked vaguely Middle Eastern, with a full beard and a teal pochette sticking out of his jacket pocket. The front door was opened, and the corresponding draught pulled at the door to their bedroom. Footsteps on the stairs, the corridor; a loud voice in the adjoining room, "It's warmer than hell in here. Open a window, will you?"

Evelyn took a seat back on the bed and appraised her husband. Strange, silly man. How inscrutable he was now, when she had married someone so very easy to scrute. She let out a long breath, putting her hand to his cheek. "You'll be able to do it? To give them the messages?"

"Of course." Robert nuzzled his face into her hand, his whiskers tickling her palm.

"And remember not to waste any messages on me," she said.

"It would never be a waste," Robert began.

"I don't require healing, remember," she interrupted. "I don't require it and I don't want it. I've told Clarence the same thing." Her voice was even and steady. She felt calm, impenetrable, as if she were made of obsidian.

"You'll see though, Evie." Robert smiled. "You'll get the reassurances you need, even if you resist. Spirit will find a way to reach you."

"I don't need reassurances, my love," she said, gently. "The others do, though. Vikram, Margrit, *they* need you."

Robert kissed her fingers. "Oh Evie, I'm so glad you understand how much I can help. It means so much to me, the world to me, that you support me, you know that."

"I do."

"I know it hasn't been easy for you."

Evelyn leant forward and kissed his cheek. "It's OK, darling. I'm glad to be here, I truly am." She looked around the room at the Louis Philippe violin table, at the amaranth inlay on the dresser, the zebra-skin cushion on the divan. When she looked back at Robert, he was smiling at her, almost bashfully. "We've spent such a long time only trying to survive, haven't we?" Evelyn said. "It's so nice to just live."

19

WHEN THEY REENTERED THE DRAWING ROOM, IT HAD transformed into a riot of blue taffeta, Sudanese brooches, diamond earrings, raven feathers, Cartier comb bandeaus. A woman dressed in picot-trimmed Chanel was talking to a young man of such effervescent good looks that Evelyn felt quite woozy. Two pale teenage girls in paint-splattered dungarees were smoking by the window. The white-blonde woman from the driveway was now in a black Patou ball gown with a monkey-hair collar, laughing with a pretty red-haired man wearing a monocle. A tall, thin woman in a sleeveless Callot Soeurs was pulling a galuchat cigarette box out of her bag. Amongst the swans were an improbable miscellany of creatures: a stooped, elderly vicar was dribbling sherry into his beard, and an ugly, beet-faced baby was bawling, unattended in one of the upholstered armchairs. And standing far too close to an owlish-looking young man was Bernice. She was flushed, fiddling with her ring, and the poor young man was trying to back away from her without knocking into the Indian miniatures. Evelyn took a breath. She should probably go and rescue him; Bernice was the only person she recognised in the room, anyway.

She felt a cold, chapped hand on hers. "Darling, there you are," Lily said. "Come and sit with me, I'm dying to know everything about you." Lily was wearing an African-style Myrbor jacket over a silk chemise, pearls the size of gooseberries hanging down to her navel.

"There's not much to know," Evelyn said, with a tinkly little laugh. But she was relieved she wouldn't have to talk to Bernice.

Lily wiped her nose carelessly on her sleeve. "Tosh." She motioned her into an armchair next to the fire. "Tell me, did you grow up in Edinburgh?"

"Near Byrne."

Lily's eyes widened. "At Locklear Manor?"

"No, it's called Mairibank."

"Charming," Lily said. "And are there stables out there?"

"There were, yes."

"Do you ride?"

"I haven't been near a horse since I was a child," Evelyn said, not wanting to be drawn into a conversation about horses. Conversations about horses were even more tedious than conversations about babies.

A maid approached them with a tray of glasses.

"What is it?" Lily frowned.

"Champagne, ma'am."

Lily coughed, dramatically. "No, thank you. Be a dear and fix me a gin and lime, will you?"

"Certainly." The maid gave her a little bob.

Evelyn took her glass of champagne and tried to sip from it. Her nose never quite fit inside champagne flutes and it was always embarrassing to have people watch her try to drink from one.

"Champagne makes me sick," Lily said, with a sneer. "I drank so much of it during the war that the very taste takes me back to all those bad years."

Evelyn opened her mouth and closed it again.

"Tell me, who are you sitting with at Usher next week?" Lily asked.

"Next week?"

"It is next week, isn't it? I always get these Usher parties confused. Don't tell me I've got the date wrong?"

"Um, I'll have to check my appointment book," Evelyn said.

Lily's face relaxed. "Yes, do, and telephone me, so we can make sure we sit together. Vikram said something about the chancellor, but it would be much more fun—oh, hold on!" Lily spun, and grabbed the arm of the good-looking man Evelyn had spotted earlier. Up close, he was almost offensively handsome: brown skin, shiny black curls that tumbled over thick eyelashes, a reticent, flickering dimple that seemed to be flirting with his own cheek.

"This is Pups Janssen."

"How do you do?" Evelyn reached for a handshake and then panicked. Was that the right way to greet him? He was so polished, she felt as if she should drop to her knee and kiss the hilt of his sword.

"Pups is part of our Malacca duplet," Lily said.

"The worst half," Pups said, affecting a bow. Evelyn fumbled for something witty to say. His accent was vaguely English, with an unplaceable lilt. That twinkle in his eye! She felt a flutter of nervous laughter bubble into her throat.

"I'm sure you're not," she said, weakly. A wave of self-hatred roared over her. Was that the best she could manage?

"Evelyn here is married to the fortune teller!" Lily said, pointing, quite rudely, across the room at Robert.

"Are you really?" Pups said.

Evelyn chewed her lips. "Yes." At that moment, being married to Robert seemed a terrible disadvantage.

"Wait, don't say another word. I'll get Flossie," Pups said. He charged across the room towards a homely brunette in a chestnut-coloured day dress.

"That's the other one—his twin," Lily said, breathing into Evelyn's ear a sweet and bitter smell, like sugared coffee. "Whatever you do, don't ask her about Hegel, or you'll never hear the end of it."

Evelyn, who was not in the habit of spontaneously asking people about Hegel, merely nodded. As Pups tugged the girl across the room towards them, the maid reappeared with a glass of gin and lime, and Lily took it from the tray without even looking at her.

"This is my sister, Florence. But you can call her Flossie," Pups announced. Flossie looked startled, but Pups continued, "Evelyn is married to a fortune teller."

Flossie stared at Evelyn. Her hair was lank and parted severely down the middle. She had heavy eyebrows, and no eyelashes to speak of. Her glasses were expensive, though, with mother-of-pearl handles. "A fortune teller?"

"Medium."

"Medium what?" Flossie squinted.

"He's a medium."

Lily shrieked with laughter. Flossie said, with a serious expression, "Yes, funny."

"Flo has all kinds of theories about mediums." Pups threw his arms around her shoulder, leaning on her heavily. "Go on."

Flossie gave him a stern look, one that Evelyn recognised to mean "shut up."

"Tell us," Lily said.

"I'd rather not." Flossie tugged on a lock of her flat hair. Poor girl, Evelyn thought. Imagine having to look at this reflection of oneself. It was like a cruel mirror at a seaside carnival. At least, with Kitty, they were about the same level of prettiness. Well, maybe that wasn't exactly true. Maybe Kitty was a bit prettier. But she was younger, so it was hardly a fair comparison.

"Go on." Pups poked Flossie in the ribs. "What was that book you were reading?"

Flossie twitched away from Pups's jostling. "Houdini." She turned to Evelyn. "Have you heard of him?"

"Of course," Evelyn said, affronted.

"It's just, well, he says it's all a sham. Mediumship. And I'm inclined to believe him."

Lily rolled her eyes. "Don't listen to her. She's such a bluestocking."

Evelyn shot a surreptitious glance at Flossie's stockings. They were black.

"I'm sorry," Flossie said, although she didn't appear to be sorry. "I don't want to offend you. I just, I ascribe more to the Freudian theories. Psychosexual repression, and so forth."

Evelyn's ears went hot. Being called upon to defend Robert's psychosexual liberty in front of strangers was not what she had anticipated from the evening. "Have you ever been to a séance?"

"Yes," said Pups.

"No," said Flossie.

They looked at each other. "You have?" Flossie said.

"Yeah, at Boxer's house." Pups took a lacquer case from inside his jacket and lit a cigarette. "You had a headache."

"You could've told me," Flossie said.

"I know how you feel about it," Pups said, flashing Evelyn a raffish smile, a smile so gilded and glittery that her blood surged. But as soon as her pulse bubbled down from her head, Evelyn felt a pang of pity for Flossie. Her own brother, smiling rakishly at a perfect stranger so she'd take his side. Evelyn narrowed her eyes at Pups.

"This evening Robert and Clarence will be giving a reading, so you can have a chance to see one firsthand," she said.

"Tonight?" Flossie grimaced. "I suppose." She looked around the room. "Which one is your husband, Robert or Clarence?"

"Robert." Evelyn laughed. She gestured to the corner of the room where Clarence was sitting on the floor, flicking through a book of maps. "Clarence is a child."

"A child?" Flossie gasped.

Evelyn cleared her throat. "He's very mature for his age, it's not as odd as it sounds." In truth, Clarence looked a little uncanny. He was dressed in evening wear, and his hair was brilliantined back from his head with so much pomade that she could see teeth marks from the comb. He looked like a whimsical lawn ornament.

"But where are his parents?"

"His mother is the woman over there in the brown dress. Bernice. She goes everywhere with him. And he has a brother too, as his manager. I'm not sure about the father." It suddenly occurred to Evelyn that she had never even asked about Clarence's father—it always seemed obvious that Bernice had the drab, nervous aspect of a widow. But now she thought about it, there was a chance that faced with the responsibility of such unnerving offspring, Mr. O'Grady had deserted his familial duties. Evelyn pictured Papa's expression in Kitty's parlour, how easily he had sliced them out of his circle.

"He's so young, though." Flossie began biting her nails, and Pups swatted her hand away.

"Nonsense," Lily said. "They send children up chimneys."

Flossie stared at her. "But that doesn't make it any *better*."

"You'll see, tonight," Lily said, taking a sip of her gin and lime. "He's read for me tens of times, you won't believe how spooky he is!"

The bell rang for dinner. As they passed into the dining room, Evelyn loitered by the door to be delivered to her place, but people were mingling with abandon, nudging chairs out of the way, calling, "Come sit next to me!" over the table.

With a flash of recognition and gratitude, Evelyn scrambled for a seat next to Margrit.

"Darling Evelyn," Margrit said. "How lovely to see you."

"Your hat is divine," Evelyn said. She cleared her throat. "Is your husband here this evening?"

"He had a bad case of gout this weekend," Margrit said. "But he can't wait to be read by Robert. Vikram has been talking about him relentlessly."

"He has?" A flush of pride tickled Evelyn's belly.

"Day and night." Margrit turned her wineglass upside down on the tablecloth, and for a wild second, Evelyn thought Margrit was about to begin a conjuring trick. Margrit caught her expression.

"Wine makes me bilious," she said, rubbing her stomach.

"I see."

"Young sir." Margrit turned and wiggled her fingers at a footman. "Will you mix me half a glass of tonic water with one teaspoon of bromide salts."

The footman looked nervously around him and then gave her a shallow bow.

"I'll be awake all night otherwise, tossing around. As it is, I have to sleep quite upright."

"Oh dear," said Evelyn, relinquishing control of the conversation to Margrit's nervous stomach. After all, there was nothing that people with nervous stomachs loved to talk about more than their nervous stomachs. "You must have to avoid a great deal of foods."

Margrit's eyes brightened. "I do!"

As the first course of watercress soup was delivered, Margrit began to catalogue all the various foodstuffs that she had been forced to avoid. Evelyn nodded along politely.

"This haddock, for example," Margrit was saying, as their fish course arrived. "If it were to have been cooked with the skin, I couldn't eat it at all."

"Ah."

"But since it *hasn't* been cooked with the skin, then I may eat it." Margrit addressed the footman. "Young man, run and ask the cook if this was seared in its skin, will you?"

Evelyn ate her fish in silence. Directly across the table, Flossie reached out and, with a practised, choreographed gesture, poured Pups's wineglass into her own, refilling his with water.

"Ma'am." The footman reappeared, looking flustered. "The cook says it were prepared special, just for you."

Margrit nodded.

"And," Evelyn said, steeling herself, "desserts? Do they aggravate your digestion?"

"Most terribly. Apples, oranges, red currants, black currants, raspberries . . ."

Evelyn began to drift off.

". . . most ingenious with oats. At my next salon, you'll have to tell me which you prefer."

"Excuse me?"

"You will be joining your husband, won't you? My guests are bound to take up all your husband's attention, so we can have plenty of time to ourselves. You'll *love* my rose garden," Margrit said, with surprising confidence for someone that had not, to any degree, ascertained what Evelyn loved.

"Of course, I'd be honoured," Evelyn said, her voice squeaky. This was her moment to quiz Margrit about the salon. Would she be expected to speak French? A frantic series of images ran through her head: Persian settees with studded cushions, fiddle-leaf figs, peacocks, velvet berets, glass bowls piled with marron glacé. Would she have to wear slippers of some kind? Would she have to sit on the floor? Surely a count wouldn't be sitting on the floor? But then, a salon sounded decidedly bohemian. As she reviewed the sort of slippers that might be appropriate for sitting on the floor, she became aware that Flossie was watching her across the table.

Flossie cleared her throat. "I hope I didn't offend you before," she said.

"Not at all," Evelyn said.

"Are you familiar with Sigmund Freud? The new theories about the unconscious?"

"Yes."

"And yet, you don't believe spiritualism is part of a repression, working itself out?"

"I don't," Evelyn said. She didn't much like the word "repression." It sounded like a kind of brassiere that was stretched at its seams.

"And you haven't read Houdini's book?"

"Not yet." She wished Flossie would stop talking so she could probe Margrit about the salon. She turned back to Margrit, but she was now in conversation with the woman in the Chanel.

"If potatoes are boiled, then I may eat them," Margrit was saying.

"Don't you think it's hurtful? Giving people false hope?" Flossie's voice was loud, far too loud, and Evelyn glanced at Robert, but he didn't appear to have heard.

"I think it gives people comfort," Evelyn said.

"But it's not proven."

Evelyn's ears were burning. She looked around the table, hoping for assistance.

"Houdini is trying to prove it," Flossie continued. "You know, surely, that in *Scientific American* he promised $5,000 to anyone that can demonstrate mediumship is real."

"I'm aware. Rather an expensive pastime," Evelyn said, tersely.

"Not so far, since no one has provided any evidence," Flossie said.

Evelyn ached for her to be quiet. How could she not be embarrassed to say such things in present company? With Robert a yard away, and their host himself a committed spiritualist? It was just the kind of boldness you'd expect from a bohemian.

Flossie cut into her steak Florentine. "Have you read the work of Mansworth? He has some interesting insights into mediumship. Sexual terror, and all that."

"No. I did, however, read the biography of Amersly, who has disproved that theory," Evelyn said, as sweetly as she could.

Something flickered in Flossie's eyes, a spark of hungry amusement. "Amersly is a tedious bore who mistranslates his Latin."

Evelyn touched her napkin to her lips. "And his French."

Flossie raised her eyebrows. "Quite. Well, at least we agree on something."

* * *

AFTER DINNER, AS EVERYONE scraped back their chairs and lit cigars, Evelyn hurried Robert away from the dinner table, down the corridor, and through the door into the conservatory. It was now dark outside, and a white mist was creeping up from the river, folding itself around the hawthorn maze at the bottom of the garden.

"How do you feel?" she said, taking his hand. There were no lights in the conservatory, and his face was deep in shadow.

"About?"

"About tonight," she said, irritably. "The reading."

"Looking forward to it," Robert said, although his voice was studiously cheerful.

"Can I help in any way?" Now that the moment had come, it would be so much worse if it wasn't perfect. If one *had* to perform, one might at least perform well. If he didn't do well, would the invitation to the salon still be forthcoming? Would they still be able to go to Usher Hall?

"No, my love." Robert chuckled. "You can't be of help, but bless you." He came close to her, and she could smell the haddock on his breath.

She switched her weight from foot to foot. "Can you tell, ahead of time, if a reading is going to be a success?" It felt horribly strange to be asking about his process. It was like inquiring about the health of someone in a hospital bed: generalities were fine, but volumes of liquids, numbers of pills—well, those sorts of quantifiable intimacies were better left private.

"Sometimes I can tell," Robert said, quietly. "In advance, I get a sort of feeling."

"And tonight? Do you have any feelings about tonight?"

Robert put his arms around her waist. "You're so precious to worry."

Evelyn resisted the urge to squirm away. How could she explain it—she wasn't worried about *him*, as much as *them*.

"Clarence has read for people here before, so I'm sure we'll do just fine." Robert reached down to kiss her, and in the crush of their bodies, the darkness of the glasshouse, a kind of intensity in his kiss alerted her to his rising excitement.

"Darling, don't get distracted," she said, wrestling away from him.

Robert grimaced, running his fingers through his hair. "Aye, right you are."

Back in the drawing room, Robert was beckoned into a corner by Vikram. The table in the centre of the room had been set up with all its leaves, and the various chairs and ottomans drawn haphazardly around the edges. People were dawdling at the back of the room, sipping champagne, speaking in hushed, anticipatory tones. Evelyn's stomach was tight. Maybe the wine had made *her* bilious?

"Such a nice house, isn't it?" Bernice had crept up on her. Evelyn turned her eyes without turning her head, to avoid the full gale of Bernice's stale breath upon her face.

"Vikram always puts me in such a nice room, but it is warm. Is your room warm?"

"It's fine."

"My room here is always so warm, and I was just wondering if your room was warm as well."

"No," Evelyn said. She looked desperately over Bernice's shoulder and gestured to Lily until she approached.

"Have you two met?" she said.

Lily smiled. "Yes. Bernadette, isn't it? Now, I must ask you all about your son."

"Clarence will be down any second," Bernice said. "He always likes to rest before a reading."

"I meant your other son. The handsome one." Lily smiled, coquettishly. Evelyn stared at her, struggling with a strange pang of territorial annoyance. Where had that come from? She rather hated Walter; why should she mind if Lily wanted to engage in a spot of flirtation? But somehow, the comment made Evelyn feel acutely lonely. On the other side of a closed door. It was a reminder that all these young people were starting their lives, having adventures. And Evelyn was part of the fusty older set, the married ladies. The boring ones, whom you dreaded being stuck next to at dinner. She shook her head. Why, she'd just been invited to a salon! How silly to begrudge other people their fun.

"Walter is next door in the library," Bernice said. "I think it's cooler there than in our rooms. Is your room warm?"

"Yes, boiling. Now, did Walter bring his wife with him?" Lily batted her eyelashes.

"He's not married," Bernice said. "He nearly was, once."

Lily clinked her fingernails against her glass of gin. "Weren't we all?" she said, raising an eyebrow at Evelyn. Her expression of ironic complicity made Evelyn laugh; it was something Dolores might have said.

Vikram was rapping his wineglass with a knife, and everyone fell silent. "Thank you for joining me this evening. As you know, we have arranged a special reading from two genius spiritualist mediums. Master Clarence O'Grady"—he pointed to Clarence, who performed a stiff little bow; the women laughed and clapped—"and Mr. Robert Hazard." Robert gave a self-conscious salute.

They all took places around the table. Evelyn tried to slip towards Lily, but a large-eared English man who introduced himself as "Boxer" pulled a chair out for Evelyn and bowed over it, obsequiously.

"Thank you," she said, taking a seat. She wasn't looking forward to holding Boxer's hand. He was pale but with a pinkish tinge, the shade of an unwholesome variety of mushroom. She had a feeling his hand would be soft and clammy, like squeezing a hunk of undercooked gammon. On her left was Bernice, who was on a low-seated wicker chair and who had to, with some considerable fuss, source cushions so she could be at Clarence's eyeline, "for moral support."

Vikram turned off the electric lights until only the firelight and the sideboard candles remained.

Clarence took a deep breath. "I'm sorry if not all of you get messages tonight. The spirits decide who comes through, and sometimes this means that only one or two messages can be delivered. But if you wish, you can always arrange to speak to us privately. I think we will begin, if you could all hold hands."

Evelyn held Bernice's hand, and then Boxer's. With a perverse vindication she was satisfied that his hand *was* both clammy and soft.

"I can feel the presence of the spirits joining us in the room," Clarence said. "There is a great deal of magnetism in this arrangement of people, many strong personalities."

Next to her, Boxer laughed softly.

Clarence dropped his voice to a whisper. "Out of the darkness, two souls are stepping forward. Two young men."

Evelyn opened her eyes, peering into the corner of the room where the firelight danced against the wooden panelling. It was an old house, a historical house, even. What if the McGreath sons were unhappy in the afterlife, angry that the estate had been sold out of the family? They would be sure to take revenge on the guests merry-making in their ancestral home. She would do the same, if she were snatched away from the afterlife to entertain bohemians drinking champagne in the Mairibank drawing room.

"These two young men look very similar to each other," Clarence said. "They are brothers."

Evelyn swallowed. What if the spirits of the McGreath boys roamed the corridors at night, twisting the door handles, throwing shapes in the mirrors? She had a sudden, awful thought. A thought so sudden and awful she couldn't believe she'd never had it before. What if Dolly was trapped, somehow, at Mairibank? Wouldn't she go back there, if she were to go anywhere? She pictured a child watching Dolly's spectral figure flickering on the library staircase.

"The two young men, they aren't twins, but they look so similar that even their friends would be confused, sometimes. They passed six years ago, in Europe, they say. Belgium."

"That's me," Lily said. Her voice was steady. "My brothers."

Clarence paused. "They are speaking together, in perfect unison, as if they were the best of friends."

"Yes." Lily gave a sad, hollow laugh. "They were like that, tight as thieves."

"In the afterlife, they are with each other at every moment," Clarence said. "Never parted."

Lily nodded. "I know, I can feel it."

"They are telling me about a birthday in the family."

"A birthday?"

"Yes, a birthday. One that has just passed, perhaps, or one that is coming up."

Lily gasped. "Uncle Douglas, it was his birthday last month."

Around the table, people were mumbling. Evelyn heard the sound of Robert clearing his throat.

"I've got the image of a pudding of some kind? A cake?" Robert said.

"Yes!" Lily said. "Yes, we had a currant cake, it's Uncle Douglas's favourite."

"When you cut the cake, they were standing with you, at that exact moment," Robert said.

Lily nodded. "Do they—do they have any messages?"

Clarence hesitated. "They want you only to know that they love you, and they keep repeating, 'The duchess, the duchess.'"

She gave a strangled kind of laugh. "Mother."

"They miss the duchess very much," Robert said.

"Well, she's not actually a duchess, they just used to call her that to tease her," Lily said, frowning.

Evelyn's heart flared. Had Robert got something wrong? Had he committed some terrible faux pas? A bolt of panic darted over her skin.

"Aye, right, so they send all their love to your mother. They miss her," Robert said.

Lily was silent. She was wearing a strange expression, as if she were trying to gulp down a lozenge she had swallowed by accident. "They should miss me *more*."

"They do," Robert said. "They're laughing, 'She'll be thinking, forget about old Mother, what about me?' that's what they're saying. They say, 'You were always our favourite.'"

She nodded, as if reassured.

Robert paused. "And is there something about a pet rabbit?"

Lily chewed her lips. "I don't know, *did* we have a pet rabbit? There was a fox terrier that went into pup. Oh, and these wretched white mice they used to keep in a cage. Always escaping. Mother had to ban them in the end, the maids were screaming the house down every ten minutes."

Robert squinted. "Maybe it's not a pet rabbit, maybe it's a rabbit's foot? Like a lucky charm?"

"Oh!" Lily sat up straighter. "Yes!"

"Did one of them carry a lucky charm?" Robert said. "Or did you give them a lucky charm when they went off to fight?"

"Yes." Lily leant back in her chair. "Yes, God, I'd forgotten all about that."

Evelyn let out a long breath. He had got it! Of course he'd got it! A pulse of affection went out to him. What a marvel he was.

"Yes, of course," Lily was saying. "I gave them both a four-leaf clover. From the long field behind the stables. Took me *weeks* to find two." She stared off into the dark corners of the room. "Much good it did them."

Robert was shaking his head. "They say, 'You did bring us luck, Lils. We went over to spirit without even knowing. Like the blink of an eye.' They seem full of mischief, these two. Were they always getting in trouble?"

Lily smiled. "Oh yes, they were a terrible handful."

"'Don't forget to have some fun,' that's what they say," Robert said. "'Don't get too serious.'"

She laughed. "I'll try."

"They have to go now," Robert said, "but they send you love."

"I send them love as well," Lily said. She closed her eyes, letting out a breath. "God, it's lonely, being left behind."

There was a moment of silence around the table.

A slight line appeared on Clarence's brow. "There is another woman here who wishes to come through. She looks very glamorous, she is wearing a gold dress. Sparkling, with, what do you call it? Embroidery. And a fur coat."

People looked expectantly at each other, but nobody claimed the woman.

"She spent many a happy evening here, in this house. She says her initials are D. T. Her first name is Dorothy, I think. And for some reason, she is showing me a river, a big river."

Everyone gasped.

"Dorothy Tay!" Margrit said. "It must be her!"

Clarence looked confused.

"Bless you." Lily turned, laughing, to the rest of the table. "He's too young to know who she is!"

"Who is she?" Clarence asked.

Margrit leant forward. "She was quite a sensation in her day. A theatre actress. My, she had a tragic death."

Clarence held up one small white hand. "No, don't tell me, let me see what I can get from spirit."

Evelyn was impressed by his self-possession. A child, silencing a countess. His cool could only have been forged in response to Bernice's particular kind of nervous twittering. In a way, perhaps, she had done Clarence and Walter a favour, being so agitated and fluttery all the time.

"Was it a lovers' quarrel of some kind that caused her passing?" Clarence said.

"Yes, that's right." Margrit shook her head. "It was awful."

"But who here knows Dorothy Tay?" Lily said, craning her neck around.

Vikram leant forward in his seat so abruptly that the leather squeaked. "Wait, she stayed here! I remember, now, seeing it in the guest book. She stayed here for a week during the war!"

"Oh my goodness," people were whispering.

Robert licked his lips. "She's saying, 'I hope you enjoy the house as much as I did.' And that she left something behind in one of the rooms."

Everyone looked at each other. "Is it still there?" Lily asked, wrinkling her nose.

"She says that it is!" Robert said, with some surprise.

"Say goodbye to spirit," Vikram said, giddily. "Say goodbye, and let's go up and look."

"We'll let you go now, Miss Tay," Robert said. "Thank you for joining us, and sharing the happy memories of the house."

Vikram stood up and clapped his hands. "Right, let's go, shall we? See what kind of message Dorothy Tay could have left here!" He dashed to the sideboard and seized a rose-spray porcelain candelabra that must once have belonged in a morning room. "Who else is coming?"

There was a clamour as people knocked into each other, shoving aside chairs, stepping on each other's shoes. "Wait," Vikram cried, over the rabble, "Robert, Clarence, you should lead the way." He ushered Robert and Clarence to the doorway, and handed Robert a mirrored candlestick.

"But I don't know where I'm going," Robert laughed.

"Let spirit guide you," Vikram said, throwing open the door.

Evelyn joined the crush, somewhere between Lily and a short Asian woman wearing grey silk Lanvin to whom she hadn't been introduced. People snatched candlesticks from around the room, and Boxer flicked his lighter. He drew close, wielding the flame at waist height, and Evelyn surreptitiously brushed the Lanvin out of harm's way. As they crowded into the hallway, Evelyn nibbled on her finger. What if Robert had misunderstood, somehow, and there was nothing left behind? The evening would end on a sour note, everyone disappointed and restless. Would Vikram ever invite them back?

Robert went first up the stairs, Clarence following at his elbow, like an illustration out of a macabre storybook. The convoy of guests trailed behind them, whispering.

"What could it be? Do you think she left some sheet music?"

"Probably a piece of jewellery."

"Maybe a note? She hid something in a book in the library!"

The jabs of candlelight stretched between the banisters, catching on a cigarette mark on the carpet, a staple winking in the wallpaper.

As they approached the landing, Vikram called, "To the left or the right?"

Robert and Clarence conferred. Robert pointed into the west wing of the building. "To the left, we think."

As they turned down the corridor, Lily began giggling. "If they go in my room they'll get a shock," she said, into Evelyn's ear. "I left my garters to soak in the basin."

Evelyn hiccupped. What if Robert and Clarence stopped at their room? Her old brushes would be exposed! And Robert's battered suitcase. And the jar of Marty's homemade marmalade, what would they make of that? But as Robert passed their room, she exhaled in relief.

"I think," Robert said, stopping by an oak door at the end of the corridor. "I think we're to go upstairs."

"Wait, wait." Vikram held up a hand. "The door will be locked by now, the servants only use it in the daytime, as a sort of shortcut. Wait a moment." He rustled back past them, taking the steps two at a time. As they waited for him to reappear, people began nervously cracking their knuckles, chewing their lips, fiddling with buttons and handkerchiefs.

"Did you hear that?" Margrit whispered. "It sounded like a footstep. From upstairs."

Everyone hushed each other, straining to hear the faint sounds stirring within the house. The tap of a latch bolt against a doorjamb, the whirr of the dumbwaiter, a pipe, glugging softly behind the wallpaper. Overhead, a floorboard creaked, and everyone gasped, fumbling with their candles and throwing elbows of light across the ceiling panels. Evelyn pictured a hunched figure, crouching at the top of the dark staircase, waiting for them.

"Here we go!" Vikram reappeared on the landing, leading a housemaid. Her bonnet was squashed, her apron strings untied, and Evelyn had the sense she had been summoned from her bed-chamber. "But we only use it to get across the house, sir," she was whispering, as she fumbled with a set of keys strung on a brass hoop. "We could have the rooms all opened for you by morning?"

"No, no, it's better this way," Vikram said, grinning. "It'll be more obvious what we're looking for."

The maid slid a key into the lock, and with a click, the door opened. She withdrew and scurried down the corridor to where another maid, pale-faced and capless, was peeping from around a green baize curtain.

Robert stepped forward, holding the candlestick aloft. In its mirrored surface, the smudge of Clarence's white face glimmered. With a surge, the guests followed Robert and Clarence through the doorway. Evelyn had been expecting a butler's staircase, but it had clearly once been a part of the main house. The railing was moulded into curlicues, and corkscrewed beneath a daisy-chain stained glass window. As they ascended, however, it was evident that no guests had used the stairs in some time. Dust had collected in the dimples in the glass panels, and a wicker basket of grease-stained linens had been abandoned on the landing.

The top of the staircase opened directly onto a dark corridor, where slices of dim moonlight cut underneath doors and across threadbare carpet. "Somewhere here," Robert said.

With a rush, Lily leapt past Robert and Clarence, and darted into the first room on the left. And then everyone followed. Racing from room to room, tearing white sheets from dressers, raising clouds of dust, dripping candle wax onto the rugs. The chase generated a sort of frenzy. Lamps were being turned over, floorboards prised up, curtains yanked apart and shutters thrown open. Evelyn hung back, the nape of her neck damp. What would happen once every room had been searched, and nothing was found? Robert was strolling the length of the corridor, his expression measured. Why wasn't he worried? She tucked her hands under her elbows, trying to control her pulse.

"How could we know which room she was in?" Boxer was shouting, as he opened the creaking doors of a walnut escritoire.

"There would have been a hostess record, I suppose," Margrit said, her voice echoing from inside a Queen Anne sideboard. "A log of menus, and room allocations."

"I've never found anything like that," Vikram said, "but the single ladies were often put up here, out of the way of any mischief makers."

Evelyn followed the woman in Lanvin to a room on the right, which had been decorated in fern-coloured wallpaper. She stood with her back against the wall, away from the melee. At her knee was a stool, embroidered with green hairstreak butterflies, and as Pups approached to peer inside a rosewood chest at the end of the bed, she nudged it aside.

Pups took a sharp inhale of breath. He bounded over and gripped Evelyn by the shoulder. "Evelyn, you genius."

She looked at him, blinking.

"You found it!" He knelt and held his candle to the wall. She turned, following the arc of light. And there, carved into the skirting board, was a single small letter:

D

Evelyn's breath caught in her throat.

"My God, will you look at that?" Lily shrieked, taking the candlestick from Pups and leaning over the stool.

Flossie appeared behind her, frowning. "That could easily be a circle. Anyone might have done it."

"What are you talking about?" Pups said, open-mouthed. "It's clearly a capital *D*."

Evelyn knelt on the carpet. Her mouth was dry.

D

Dolores.

She had left it there, for Evelyn to find. Evelyn traced the shape with her finger, rubbing the wood warm. It wasn't for the others. It was for her.

"Everyone! Everyone, come see!" Pups was shouting now. "Evelyn's found it, it's in here!"

People flooded into the room. Vikram and Margrit and the woman in Chanel and the man with the monocle and Boxer and Walter and the woman in the ball gown and Bernice and the pale teenage girls. And then Clarence, and then Robert.

"Evelyn, how incredible!" Margrit was saying, standing precariously on the four-poster bed. Vikram was shouting down the hall for the electricity to be turned on at the switch. Pups called for champagne. Lily was asking Walter about sourcing a camera.

Evelyn caught Robert's eye at the doorway, giving him a long look as she followed the shape of the carving again with her finger. Robert smiled at her, and she understood what he'd been trying to tell her before. The spirits had found a way to give her what she needed: reassurance. She wasn't going to come through the readings, so she'd sent a sign instead, a gift.

It was a gift, from Dolores.

20

EVELYN WAS LOOKING AGAIN AT THE PHOTOGRAPH after lunch on Tuesday. The picture was smudged from where her finger had followed the line of the *D*, but she couldn't stop staring at it. Vikram had had copies made for everyone at the weekend from the makeshift studio in his stillroom, and it was odd to think that all these other people now possessed the same image, without knowing what it truly meant. That it was a symbol of safety, trust, protection.

The afternoon post rattled through their letterbox and Evelyn jumped, flipping the photo, and using the edge to underline a recipe for "Pike in Cream," while Marty set the letters down on her tray.

Marty came running back into the parlour at her squeal. "Ma'am?"

"Look, Marty, the opera!" Evelyn said, thrusting the invitation at her. "The opera, the opera!"

Marty put her hand to her chest. "I thought you'd cut yourself, ma'am."

Evelyn clutched the invitation. "What will I wear?"

Marty frowned. "Something warm?" She leant on the back of the chair. "I heard one of those young girls was cold enough to get close to the lights and she was burned to a crisp."

"Hmm, fantastic," Evelyn said. The opera! She and Robert were going to the opera and they were going to drink champagne and they were going to sit in a box with the Hero of the Highlands!

Maybe Mrs. Wrigley would be there. "Oh, hello," Evelyn would say, a diamond bracelet dangling carelessly off her wrist, "I hadn't noticed you."

"And then his nephew choked on one of his own teeth," Marty was saying.

Evelyn put the invitation in her pocket and slipped past Marty. "I'm just going out to Kitty's for a minute," she said, grabbing an umbrella.

* * *

THE LAMP IN KITTY'S parlour was on, so she knocked on the front door.

"Afternoon, Mrs. Hazard," Jeanie said, opening the door.

"Kitty?"

"Mrs. Fraser is in the nursery," Jeanie said.

"Really?" Evelyn wrinkled her nose. "What's she doing up there?"

Jeanie stuttered. "Putting the baby down, ma'am."

"Oh." Evelyn laughed, handing her coat to Jeanie. She climbed the stairs and let herself into the nursery.

Kitty was sitting by the crib, absently flicking the paper mobile.

"Hello," Evelyn whispered.

"You needn't whisper," Kitty said, rubbing her left eye. "She's just lying there staring at me, not even remotely sleeping."

Evelyn dragged a stool closer to the crib and kissed Kitty on the cheek. She peered over to see baby Margaret chewing on her own foot. Kitty sighed and pulled the baby out, settling her on her shoulder. "I'll bounce her for a bit," Kitty said. "That sometimes helps." She stood up and began swaying side to side.

"Why are you doing this? Where's Abigail?"

"I put her down, sometimes," Kitty said.

"But why?" Kitty was always tutting over Marty's schedule. What was the point in having a nursemaid if you didn't use her?

"A child needs her mother," Kitty said, rather grandly.

Evelyn let out her breath instead of saying anything. "Look what I just received." She thrust the invitation towards Kitty.

Kitty squinted at it. "What's that?"

"An invitation to the opera! And guess who from?"

"Who?"

"Vikram Singh!" Evelyn said. "The Hero of the Highlands!"

"Hmm."

"We spent the weekend at his estate near Colbreck, and Robert made such a good impression. And remember I wrote you about the countess?"

Kitty readjusted the baby. "I think so?"

"Of course you do," Evelyn said, tugging down baby Margaret's dress where it had ridden up. "She's invited us to a salon! Lily says that she always serves horrible food, but I don't mind about that. Do you think I should wear my brown silk charmeuse?"

"For?"

"For the salon! I have a feeling that reclining might be involved somehow. I don't want anything that will crush, so my green satin is out."

Kitty licked her lips. "What is a salon, exactly?"

"I'm not sure," Evelyn said. "But doesn't it sound so European? Margrit is from Hungary, after all."

"Lots of foreigners amongst your new friends," Kitty said, tersely.

Evelyn paused. "I suppose. Well, at first I didn't understand that Vikram is Scottish, either, but he was born in Inverness. And Lily is English, but you can't blame her for that."

"Your letter said something about Malayan millionaires?"

"Oh, yes, the twins. I'm not sure they are really my friends. At least not yet."

"Hmm." Kitty jiggled the baby.

Evelyn looked down at the invitation. "Anyhow, I had to run over here when this arrived. Could I borrow your blue taffeta, do you think? He has his own box, so I'll have to make a good impression!"

"In public?"

"I don't think it's a public box. They usually aren't, are they?"

"I mean—" Kitty paced over to the window. "People will see you."

Evelyn opened her mouth and shut it again. She put the invitation back in her pocket. "Kitty, what is it?"

Kitty gave an insincere laugh. "Sorry?"

Evelyn watched her. "Is something wrong?"

"Really, Evie, now's not the time," Kitty said. "I'm busy with Midge, I don't want to get her agitated."

"Midge?" Evelyn repeated. "When did you begin calling her that?"

Kitty's cheeks coloured. "Mama came up with it, and it sort of stuck."

Inside her pocket, Evelyn ran her finger over the edge of the invitation card. "Is Mama here often?"

"Almost every day. You should see them rolling around on the floor together."

"Mama sits on the floor?"

"She'd do anything for Midge," Kitty said, nuzzling the baby. "She'd do anything for you, wee Midgey, wouldn't she?"

"You should have called me, I would have come over too," Evelyn said, trying to swallow the plaintiveness in her voice.

"I didn't want to bother you," Kitty said. "You're always so busy these days."

Evelyn stared at the floorboards. Her irritation had gone now, and she felt cold, as if she were standing in an icy stream. "Have I done or said something?"

"Not at all," Kitty said, in an artificially bright tone.

"Did I forget something?" It was April 8th. Evelyn tried to think— Kitty's birthday was July 15th, her wedding anniversary May 31st.

Kitty touched her top lip with her tongue. "No. It's just—it's just—" She shifted her weight, lowering her voice. "All the superstitions."

"Superstition?" Evelyn said, at a normal volume. Kitty shushed her. "Superstition? Do you mean Robert's spiritualism?"

Kitty gave her a one-shouldered shrug. "If that's what you want to call it."

Evelyn blinked at her. "But—but you can't be angry at me about Robert."

Kitty's eyes flicked to the wall behind Evelyn. "I told you, I'm not angry."

"Well, you're something," Evelyn said. "Disappointed or disapproving or judging."

Kitty began to pat baby Margaret. "Do you blame me?" she said. A lock of hair fell into her eyes, and she blew it out. "Do you blame me for judging?"

Evelyn flinched.

"A *child* cabaret act?" Kitty hissed.

"It's not a cabaret act," Evelyn said, but her ears were hot.

Kitty scoffed, a sound so frustratingly like Papa that a pulse of anger throbbed through Evelyn. She measured her breaths until it had abated. "I know how strange it seems. It was strange to me too, at first. But it's not what you think."

Kitty said nothing, swaying from side to side.

"It's something . . ." Evelyn cast around for the right word, and thought about using "magical," but it was too much. "It's something different," she said, in the end.

Kitty's eyes were heavy, and baby Margaret squirmed on her shoulder.

Evelyn gripped the underside of the stool. "While we were on the tour, Robert—I don't know how to explain it. He connected to something." She thought of Walter's face during the reading, his trembling hands. "Robert's helping. He truly is helping."

Kitty's head twitched. "So, you believe it now, do you?"

Evelyn looked down into the lap of her skirt. She pictured the carved D, growing warm under her fingertips. Would she be able to explain it to Kitty? How could she capture the sense of profound truth and calm she had felt at that moment, knowing Dolly was protecting her? "I think I do." She looked up at her, carefully. "I've been given reason to believe it. Special reason."

Kitty turned to face the window.

"I was sceptical at first as well, but the messages—it isn't like you'd expect." She took a breath. "Last weekend I found something extraordinary—" Evelyn broke off. Kitty was making a burbling noise, and she realised she was crying.

"Kitty, please don't cry." She stood up, her own eyes stinging.

Kitty shook her head, wiping her eyes on the back of her wrist. "It's too strange." Her voice was thick.

From behind, Evelyn could see baby Margaret chewing enthusiastically on her fist. "There's no reason to be upset, I promise you."

Kitty spun around. "My only sister and she's hunting phantoms," she spat. "Of course I'm upset."

Evelyn stifled an inappropriate urge to laugh. "Come now, it's not *that* bad."

"It's absolutely that bad," Kitty said, raising her voice. Her face turned puce, and Evelyn realised how truly angry Kitty was. There was no way she would be open to hearing about Dolly's sign, now.

"It really isn't," Evelyn said. "Robert's helping people."

Kitty laughed, horribly. "You can't even *see* it!" she said. "It's one thing for Robert to have a quirky pastime at home, in private. But to parade it around like this—after everything this family has done to accept him! It's no better than a circus act!"

Evelyn set her teeth. "Don't be like that."

"Like what?" Kitty's eyes widened. "Truthful?"

Evelyn's pulse quickened, a mixture of anger and hurt. It was bad enough for Papa to be dismissive, rejecting. But Kitty was supposed to be on her side. She gestured around the nursery. "You hardly even go out in the world! What does it matter to you what society I keep?"

Kitty shook her head. "You're making a fool out of yourself, Evelyn. A fool of this family—for nothing more than a silly fad. It's a disgrace! Don't you care what people think?"

"I'm surprised you care! All that seems to interest you these days are hiccups and ribbons. And you have the nerve to judge me for wanting more than that?" As she spoke, she knew she was being cruel. But oh, what a bitter relief to say the words.

Kitty bounced the baby, mechanically. "I don't know who you are anymore." Her face was blank. "I don't even recognise you."

Evelyn took a step backward towards the door. Her ears were prickling but her blood was cool. "Since Dolly—I've gone out of my way to look after you. And for once, for *once* I'm not lavishing attention on you. Finally, I'm free to enjoy myself. And maybe it won't last forever! Maybe it won't, but you know what? Nothing lasts forever. So for once, I'm concentrating on what *I* want. That's why you don't recognise me."

With a last look at Kitty, she turned and left the room, hearing the door close behind her.

21

IT SEEMED AS THOUGH EACH MORNING, ANOTHER invitation was balanced on Evelyn's tea tray: galas at the Cadogan Club, high tea at the King's Inn, matinees at Theatre Royal, soirées at Usher Hall, lunch at the Elgin Chambers. Evelyn RSVP'd "yes" to all of them. And as she replied to the invitation cards, she did so with a vicious flourish of pleasure. Let her family criticise, let them judge. There was nothing shameful about her new social circle; if anything, it was closer to how they would have been living if the "big move" had never happened. To keep up with the demands of her new social calendar, Evelyn visited a seamstress on Princes Street and had four new gowns made: a gold silk, an embroidered black dress with a dropped waist, a sleeveless emerald-green gown, and a white tennis-style affair with a pleated skirt. They retained Marty for weekends again, with a new uniform and cap. They were invited to go roller-skating at the Industrial Hall, where a lady instructor helped Evelyn stumble around the rink, avoiding errant shuttle-cocks that had sailed over from the lawn. Margrit's salon proved to be rather a sober evening, dominated by a discussion of the site of the upcoming Paris world's fair. Still, Evelyn was gratified that she was, indeed, required to sit upon cushions on the floor. They attended a dance party at the Beauchamp Rooms, where professional ballroom dancers led a waltz, and a young, mustachioed man picked Evelyn to dance in the centre of the hall. She sailed from corner to corner, her emerald silk sweeping around her, enjoying Robert's awestruck stare from the crowd.

At the opera, Evelyn walked on Robert's arm through the lobby, past young women greeting each other with kisses, fluffing up their furs, the feathers in their hats trembling as they bent to light cigarettes. Young women dressed in velvet capelets, beaded chiffon, jade bracelets slipping down their wrists as they sipped champagne. And young men too—pretty young men, with clear skin and sparkling eyes. Young men with silk cravats and bouncy hair, young men with full smiles and a jaunty lilt in their step. As Vikram hailed them from beside the cloakroom, Evelyn caught sight of herself in the dark reflection of the window. Anyone would have thought that she belonged there. That she was one of these people. That she was young, pretty, carefree, fun. She held herself taller, remembering the disapproving expression on Kitty's face. Kitty had disapproved of Dolly's interests too. And after everything that had happened in the last ten years, she was owed a bit of fun. Now the chance had come to snatch it—snatch it she would.

✦ ✦ ✦

GREG BAILISH'S ATELIER WAS located on the top floor of a towering apartment block on Canongate. Arriving late for the party, Evelyn and Robert stood doubtfully for some moments as their taxi-cab drove away. It was still light out, but the street had an unkempt look—wooden crates were piled by the side of the road, and stray cats rustled within for scraps. Abandoned on the pavement outside the building was a single man's shoe. Evelyn stared at it. Who loses *one* shoe?

"Are you sure this is the address?" Evelyn said, retying her silk wrapper. They were so close to the station that the sound of train doors slamming echoed under the bridge.

Robert squinted at the invitation. "Aye, quite sure," he said, over the sound of the conductor's whistle. "He is an artist, after all."

As the train chattered past, lights flickering on the bridge, they climbed the building's shadowy stairwell, dodging a viscous liquid that was dripping from the steps. Evelyn shuddered at each turn, expecting to see a man with a dagger concealed behind his cloak. Arriving breathlessly at the top floor, they found that the door of the atelier was propped open with a sack of flour, and the crush of bodies within had steamed up the windows. In the left-hand corner of the room Evelyn was surprised to see a wooden swing nailed into the ceiling, and the young, owlish man she recognised from Vikram's house gamely being pushed back and forth. Robert was immediately hailed by a middle-aged Black man with a receding hairline, and they began to discuss spirit photography. After a few moments of hovering, Evelyn decided to explore. She'd never been in an atelier before, and she wanted to inspect the bathroom *before* she needed to use it, in case it was indeed some kind of bohemian lark to expect her to go down the stairs to an outhouse in the dark courtyard, where, no doubt, the daggered assassin would be lurking. She opened a door into a room with an army-style cot and an overflowing ashtray. There was an incongruous marble bookcase, and she flicked through the titles, most of which were in German.

"Hello," came a voice from the corner of the room, and Evelyn yelped. Flossie was sitting on a wicker chair next to the unmade bed, holding a book in her hands.

"Sorry," Evelyn said, stepping back.

"Evelyn? You don't need to go just because I'm here."

Evelyn lingered by the doorway. She looked more closely at the book in Flossie's hand. "Is that McGilvary's biography of Disraeli?"

"Yes," said Flossie. "Do you know it?"

"It's better than Owen's."

Flossie rested the book on her lap. A moment of silence passed between them. "Evelyn." Flossie straightened her glasses. "I hope we can be friends, even if we don't share the same beliefs."

Evelyn's ears grew hot. It sounded almost immature, childlish, coming from Flossie's mouth. It wasn't as if she could *refuse*, and Flossie would know that. What an awkward trap. But then again, it had been a long time since someone had courted her friendship. "Of course," she said, eventually.

Flossie smiled. It was a nice smile; it lifted up her whole face. "The Belgian Refugee Society is having a fundraiser tomorrow afternoon. Perhaps, if you're not busy, would you like to join me?"

Evelyn blinked at her, searching for a subtle way to ask how much it would cost.

"It's a tea-and-cake afternoon," Flossie added. "Or, if you're busy tomorrow, then next week the Abolition of Slum Tenements Society is marching in Glasgow to protest evictions?"

"Tea and cake sounds lovely," Evelyn said, quickly.

Flossie tapped the cover of the book. "I'm glad. It's so nice to have a new friend."

Evelyn nodded. A new friend. She would make a new friend. Dolores would never meet her. She stared at her feet. After a moment, she looked up. "So, what exactly is automatic painting? I've never been to an event like this."

Flossie replaced the book on the shelf. She turned to Evelyn, her expression almost pained. "Greg claims that he channels famous artists and that they 'inhabit' his arm." She looked seriously at Evelyn. "But obviously, I have my doubts. Why do all the artists want to draw spirals? And Michelangelo was left-handed, so I'm not sure how much of that series one could attribute to Michelangelo, rather than Greg."

"Vikram seems to like his art," Evelyn said, churlishly.

"Oh, the whole crowd loves him," Flossie said, waving her arm around the apartment. "But I don't see how—"

"Do you know where the bathroom is?" Evelyn said, keen to avoid a disagreement so soon after their détente.

Flossie pointed to the door down the hallway.

"Thank you, I won't be a moment."

Evelyn jiggled the handle of the bathroom and someone called out, "Occupied!" Embarrassed, she took a few steps back from the door so it wouldn't seem like she was unduly urgent in need. A sleepy-eyed woman in her sixties, wearing a shawl, appeared behind Evelyn and joined the queue. The water ran and a man emerged, bowing demurely to her.

Evelyn stepped past him, and stared at herself in the mirror. A new friend. Along with Lily, that was two new friends. Well, with Vikram, that was perhaps three—it was so hard to know if one was truly friends with a man. And Flossie wasn't so bad. Respectable, even. She could put Flossie and Kitty in the same room. Thinking of Kitty now, she felt a sort of petulant resolve. Yes. Flossie would be her friend. To add to her new acquaintances. Counts, debutantes, soldiers, Englishmen. Evelyn washed her hands, noticing as she did so a dark hair wound around the soap. Reluctantly, she scraped the hair out of the tablet: she didn't want the sleepy-eyed woman to think it was *her* hair.

As she made her way back to the party, Evelyn found Flossie standing at the edge of a group of people jostling in the doorway of a room she had taken to be a linen cupboard. The crush inside the tiny chamber was even worse. People had crammed themselves inside in a series of uncomfortable-looking configurations: elbow to ear, knee to shoulder. At the back of the room was a thick Burmese curtain, and on a window seat a man was sitting, cross-legged, with a board in his lap.

"What's happening?" Evelyn whispered.

"That's Greg. He's started"—Flossie winced—"channelling."

Greg Bailish was a thin, pale man, with small eyes that sat close together, giving the impression that he was wearing goggles. "Of course this will, in its nature and intent, be rather different from my usual work," he was saying.

The board on his lap was equipped with a small lead bell. He picked it up and began ringing the bell, back and forth. In the adjoining room, someone was laughing, and a heavy piece of furniture was being scraped along wooden floorboards.

"He's beginning," Robert's voice breathed into her hair. He smelt like sherry. He gripped Evelyn in an embrace around her waist and she looked around them. No one was going to judge them, here. She relaxed into his arms.

Greg finally silenced the bell. From a wooden box at the edge of the window seat, he removed a large, feathered headdress, with a beaded band. Using both hands, he lowered it onto his brow. "I will now ask my spirit guide, Running River, to help me draw the location of wee Charlie. Running River will surely help us establish the path."

"How 'wee' is wee Charlie?" Robert whispered.

"Ten. That's what the man at the Murray Hotel said."

"Hmm. That's not so wee," Robert said. "There's young ones that age working."

"It is, Robert." She squeezed his arm. "It's far too young for a boy to be out on his own."

"Oh, Running River," Greg said, holding a pen in the air. "Assist me to find the whereabouts of this poor little chap."

With an atonal hum, he began drawing on a piece of paper taped to the board. From the next room came the sound of someone hiccupping and a crash of glass. Robert nuzzled into her ear.

"Yes, yes, yes," Greg was muttering.

Flossie turned and rolled her eyes at Evelyn.

Evelyn felt a flush of annoyance at Flossie. She didn't want to be judged, or else she could have invited Kitty. Why come to a party if you only wanted to disapprove of everyone else there?

After several more minutes, Greg sat back, triumphant. "It is finished," he said, wiping his face with his sleeve. He rang the bell, before sombrely peeling back the tape and lifting the paper to show his audience. Everyone around the room whispered with awe. To Evelyn, it looked, very much, like a series of squiggles.

"It's a church," someone said.

"No, look, it's a well, and a hill."

Greg examined the painting. "We may need to consult an atlas."

A young man wearing a beret scurried into the bedroom and returned with an atlas that proved to be both prewar, and in Japanese.

"I can't believe the poor little thing still hasn't been found," Flossie said. "Imagine trying to sleep at night, not knowing where your own—"

"Why must we keep talking about this boy instead of just solving the problem?" Evelyn said, cutting her off. Her cheeks were stinging. "Aren't the police involved?"

"They should be checking steamships, that's where I would have been at ten, given a chance," Robert said, as the young man dashed from person to person, searching for a Japanese speaker.

Flossie rubbed a fingerprint from her glasses. "The police *are* involved. And pursuing this kind of nonsense is hardly the best use of the collective resources—"

From the other room came a splintery crash, and a yell. Flossie froze, her eyes wide, before turning and running towards the noise. Evelyn shrugged out of Robert's embrace and followed. Pups was kneeling on the floor in front of the broken swing, cradling his arm. A group of people had gathered around him and were looking awkwardly at each other.

"What happened? Are you hurt?" Flossie said, pushing through the crowd to reach Pups.

"No," he said, but his face was shining with sweat.

"All right there, let's have a look," Lily's voice called from by the window. Evelyn hadn't even realised she was at the party. Lily plucked her cigarette from her mouth and tucked it, still smoking, behind her ear, and climbed over the arm of a chaise longue to reach

Pups. She knelt next to him, and her eyes sharpened in the professional manner of a jeweller appraising a ring through a magnifying glass. She sat back on her heels. "Looks like a break, I'm afraid. Not an especially bad one, but you'll need to get it set."

"Can't you do it?" Pups said, through his teeth.

Lily withdrew the cigarette from her hair and puffed on it. "You should go to a doctor."

Flossie said something to Pups in a language Evelyn didn't understand. Was that what Malay sounded like? Her tone was sharp, and she was pointing at the door.

Pups ignored her. "Lils, please, bind it up now, and I'll go in the morning."

"Stephen!" Flossie said. Her eyes were blazing. "You can't be serious."

Evelyn looked around, confused, and then realised that she meant Pups. She felt suddenly embarrassed; of course Pups wasn't his Christian name.

"Back off," Pups said. "I'll go in the morning."

Flossie's lips wobbled. She blinked at him, and then across the room, catching Evelyn's eye. There was something in the expression, some kind of plea for help. Evelyn shot her a grimace.

"Come on, Lils. Patch me up."

Lily drew on her cigarette and then shrugged. There was a scurry of activity. Greg Bailish provided a wooden ruler and a ream of calico, and Lily squatted on her haunches, tying up Pups's left arm until it was in a bundle. Someone passed Pups a glass of whisky and he sipped on it, casually. A girl Evelyn had never seen before sat by his side, passing a cigarette to his lips, even though his right hand was working just fine.

"That was amazing," said Robert, as Lily retreated. People were patting her on the back, cheering. "How'd you learn how to do that?"

"France," Lily said, dismissively waving her hand.

Robert laughed. "What kind of parties do you go to in France?"

"She means in the VAD," Evelyn said, sharply. Then she doubted herself. "That is what you mean, isn't it?"

"Huh?" Lily wrinkled her nose. "Oh, yes. You know, doing my part, blah blah."

Evelyn reviewed her again. There was still a glint of steel in Lily's expression. Lily lit another cigarette and went to the baccarat table, where she draped herself across Boxer's lap. "I'll be your lucky charm," she said, tugging on one of his oversized ears.

Evelyn nudged past Robert to approach Flossie. "Are you OK? Can I help?"

Flossie shook her head. Her hands were trembling. She shook a cigarette out of a packet of Woodbines that was lying on a side table. "He's so difficult. And it forces me to be so . . ." She lit her cigarette.

Evelyn gave her a sympathetic smile. "Siblings can be hard work."

Flossie sighed. "And I'm the youngest! By three minutes, but still." She flicked her cigarette ash. Then she focused on Evelyn. "You have siblings, then? How many?"

"Two," Evelyn said, then caught herself. "I mean, there's two of us, now." She took a breath. "Sorry, I mean, yes, I have one sister."

"Is she a handful?" Flossie waved her cigarette in Pups's direction.

"No," Evelyn said, with a tight smile. "I think, actually, at the moment, that I'm the handful."

22

THE NEXT SATURDAY, THEY PILED INTO THREE
motorcars for a picnic in Pentland Hills Park, where Boxer and
Pups, with his bandaged arm, took turns clay pigeon shooting.
The following day, Cynthia arranged a treasure hunt on her estate,
issuing bone-inlay trowels, and maps aged with tea. Guests spent
the long, May afternoon crawling in the rhododendron bushes,
trampling over bluebells, gouging ugly divots in the lawn. Shouts
of triumph and disappointment echoed over Cynthia's ornamental
koi pond, and at dinner that evening, everyone had compresses
wrapped around their knees. At a ceilidh on Vikram's birthday,
Lily's hat caught fire, and instead of removing the flickering wreath
from her head, she doused herself with a half-empty bottle of
Chablis. A rabbit race at Stirling Manor; rabbit pie served at dinner.
Robert and Clarence held a séance in the dining hall of Leighburn
Castle, and everybody in attendance swore that the door opened
and closed of its own accord. Margrit motored Lily and Evelyn to
a radium cream treatment in the basement of a Glasgow beauty
parlour. At the full moon, Vikram boated a quartet of Spanish
troubadours along the stream at the bottom of his estate. Flossie
and Evelyn spent an afternoon sampling pastries at the Kardomah
Café. Boxer demanded a "Siberian winter" party for his birthday,
and blocks of ice were delivered by special trucks to create igloos

on the patio of the Mulberry Hotel. At a jazz evening at the Edinburgh Zoo, Pups drank eleven scofflaw cocktails and liberated a penguin that defecated all over his shoes and then got into the tray of smoked salmon. A midnight picnic on the grounds of Lees Castle, where the liveried staff dug a pit in which a whole pig was smoked. On Lily's instruction, Evelyn had her hair darkened to a rich mahogany colour at Maison Tensfeldt on Princes Street. High tea in Vikram's orchard, cherry-coloured blossoms floating in the butter, drowsy bees struggling in the marmalade. Golf near Haggs Castle, where, despite the mild weather, Robert got such a bad sunburn he had to be put to bed with a towel full of ice on his neck. A *1,001 Arabian Nights* party, with a sword juggler and a merry-go-round. A party themed on the *Rubaiyat of Omar Khayyam*, which was indistinguishable from the *Arabian Nights* party. Lemonade at Mackie's Roof Garden, watching a thunderstorm roll in over the castle. An afternoon at the vicar's croft, where Lily got bored and wandered off, only to be discovered hours later, asleep in the stables. A Japanese chef who took the wrong train from King's Cross and had to be motored down from Fort William. A morning of trying on polar bear fur hats at Russ and Winkler's. A trip to visit Vikram's whisky barrels maturing at the distillery in St. Andrews, and afterwards, merry and unsteady, they ate fresh crab omelettes at a café overlooking the ocean, salt air in Evelyn's lungs, seagulls overhead. The spring days were long, the light gold and sweet, like brandy. The nights, when they came, were swift and giddy, full of laughter, starlit.

23

ON MAY 31st, EVELYN WAS FLICKING THROUGH THE *Scotsman* in the parlour after breakfast when she noticed the date printed on the paper. Kitty and Alistair's wedding anniversary. She folded the paper on her lap. Ten years was a long time. Evelyn pulled her etiquette book from her desk drawer: the gift for ten years of marriage was tin. She wrinkled her nose; there wasn't much romance in tin. A new addition for Alistair's railway, perhaps? Two figurines to represent them both—three, with a little baby. She stood up, tucking the paper under her arm, and then stopped. No. If Kitty couldn't celebrate her life, she wasn't going to celebrate Kitty's either.

She sat back down, turning the pages of the newspaper. A glass and china sale at Maule's, the first Southern Rhodesian parliament, a fall in the price of milk. She stopped on page three. "Concern Grows for Missing Boy." Ten-year-old Charles McBride, now missing since February, was last seen chasing a dog in the Colonies. His father, a greengrocer, described him as a sensible lad who would never be a night away from home, and yet another search of the area had found no trace of his whereabouts. In the accompanying picture, the boy was standing next to an elderly woman on Leith Walk, the scrummage of tram passengers behind them only a smudgy blur that gave it an eerie, ethereal quality. His black hair was combed neatly to the side, his socks pulled up over legs so skinny that his knees looked like doorknobs. Ten years old. Evelyn's stomach twisted. There was no way—of course there was no way. She wiped her face with the back of her hand, shutting the paper.

The telephone in the corridor rang before cutting off. It rang again, and then again, in short little bleats, as if someone was trying not to incur the cost of connection. The fourth time, Evelyn was standing to attention, ready to seize the handpiece.

"Darling." It was Lily. Evelyn could hear her puffing on a cigarette. "What's your costume for the Egyptian soirée?"

Evelyn chewed her finger. She had thought she wouldn't go in costume at all, but in a sort of vaguely Eastern-style dress, with embroidery. There was one in the catalogue at Jenners, but it was black, and that wasn't nearly festive enough. "I haven't decided."

"I was going to dress as a pharaoh, but it's so overdone, isn't it?" Lily said.

"Is it?"

"And I thought, Evie will be game for something different."

"I will?"

"I'll be Lord Carnarvon, and you'll be Howard Carter."

Evelyn laughed. "I will?"

"Come over so I can see how it looks on you."

"Come over?"

"Yes, darling."

"To your house?"

"Yes."

"Now?"

"Yes, Evie, yes. Hurry up."

And she hung up the phone. Evelyn scampered to her address book and turned in a perfect circle of consternation before running back and asking the operator to reconnect them.

"Darling?"

"How did you know it was me?"

"Was who? Who is this?"

Evelyn frowned into the receiver. "It's Evelyn. I don't have your address."

"Forty-three Evergreen Terrace. No, sorry. Forty-four. No, no, it is forty-three. Darling, is it forty-three?" she said to someone in the background, and Evelyn heard a woman's voice say, "Forty-three."

"Forty-three. Byeee."

Evelyn put her face through Robert's study door. He was sitting in the armchair, throwing a cricket ball up in the air and catching it again. "I'm going to Lily's for the afternoon," Evelyn said.

"How jolly!"

"Marty will see to your lunch—make sure and don't let her boil those scallops. It should be punishable by law."

"Yes, quite illegal. Scotland Yard will catch him," Robert said, distractedly, throwing the ball in the air again.

Evelyn rolled her eyes and charged upstairs to change her dress before calling a taxicab to Evergreen Terrace.

* * *

LILY ANSWERED THE DOOR herself, wrapped in a lime-green kimono with cigarette burns in the sleeves. The walls of her house were papered in peach Liberty print, and the hall furniture was distinctly French, chestnut and gleaming.

"We're in the back," Lily said, gesturing Evelyn down the hallway, kicking aside a hollowed-out tortoise shell that was filled with lipsticked cigar butts. They went up a narrow set of carpeted stairs and left at a bookcase occupied by coffee-table books of horses. On the ceiling, the laundry hanger was displaying an incongruous arrangement of practical black cotton undergarments and diaphanous, jewelled stockings. Evelyn averted her eyes.

Lily opened the door to her bedroom, where Flossie was sitting on a modest white pine bed, eating a sleeve of cream crackers. Evelyn was surprised to see her there; she hadn't thought Flossie and Lily even liked each other.

"Are you dressing with us?" Evelyn said, looking around for somewhere to sit. A red velvet chair in the corner of the room was piled with clothes, and a framed Cleaneen poster of Lily's bubbled décolletage was lying, shattered, behind an umbrella clearly stolen from the George Street Hotel.

Flossie shook her head. "No, I already arranged a costume for Pups."

"She doesn't want to wear a costume." Lily's voice came from a deep wardrobe at the back of the room. "Don't bother trying to convince her, I've had no luck." After some rustling and cursing, Lily emerged, holding a garment bag. "This is for you."

Evelyn unzipped the bag. It was a camphorous-smelling tweed suit, with a grey silk lining. Stitched into the inside pocket was a curlicued monogram: "JVPB."

"J. V.?"

"John Vere. My youngest brother."

"But—" Evelyn's throat was tight.

"Darling, he's not coming back for it. We may as well put it to some good use." Lily rubbed the sleeve of the suit. "Poor thing deserves to have some fun, don't you think?"

Evelyn nodded, weakly.

Lily clapped her hands. "He was slight, Johnny. I think it will fit—go on."

Evelyn stepped out of her dress and into the suit. It was vaguely itchy, and unyielding in the way of a freshly starched garment that hasn't been worn in some time. The buttons barely met across her bosom, revealing her bust bodice through the gaps. "I think it's too small," she said.

"Nonsense." Lily helped her off with the jacket and then ambushed her from behind with a bolt of fabric that she winched around Evelyn's chest. "Just needs a little flattening out, that's all."

Evelyn coughed. "Can't breathe."

Lily tutted. "You can so. Now look," she said, as she helped Evelyn put on the jacket again. "Isn't that fabulous?"

Flossie sat up on the bed. "It looks well on you, Evie. You should wear a suit all the time." Her face was very serious.

"There." Lily swung open a closet door and pointed the full-length mirror at her. In the glass, the figure of a svelte young thing shimmered. Evelyn's stomach gave a funny little burble. She put her hands in her pockets as she had seen Robert do.

"See?" Flossie said, standing behind her. "You need a whole wardrobe of suits."

Lily tossed her a derby hat, and Evelyn caught it. Despite the constriction around her ribs, she felt almost buoyant. Was this what men felt like all the time? How easy it was! Their ankles must never be cold. And to run and catch an omnibus, or stretch out in an ostentatious yawn in church. She felt newly athletic, ready to supply opinions about trade unions and their role in promoting anarchy. Evelyn tucked her hair into the hat and admired herself.

"Now wait and see mine!" Lily squealed. She disappeared into the closet and reappeared wearing a tweed suit, a silk bow tie, and a monocle. "Good evening, sir," she said, spluttering.

Evelyn laughed. "You look fantastic!"

"The final touch." Lily snapped open a spectacles case and Evelyn recoiled. It looked like two caterpillars in there, nesting. "One for you." Lily picked up a hairy strip and held it against Evelyn's lip. "With paste. Won't we look quite the picture?"

Evelyn held it to her face. It suited her perfectly. What a shame she couldn't always wear a moustache. If they'd had a brother, this was maybe what he would have looked like.

"Let's break into some tombs, shall we, old chap?" Lily said, frowning seriously.

Evelyn turned to Flossie. "Can't we tempt you? There was a third gentleman, wasn't there? The other one that got cursed."

"No thank you," Flossie said.

"Flossie is meeting her beau there," Lily said, raising her eyebrows. "She won't want her young man to remember her with whiskers, will you, Flo?" Lily pressed the moustache onto her face and leapt onto the bed, pretending to bestow kisses on Flossie, who pushed her off.

"A beau?" Evelyn said. "Will Lord Carnarvon and Mr. Carter have an opportunity to ask this young gentleman about his intentions?"

Flossie flushed. "There is no young gentleman."

Lily turned to Evelyn with a roguish wink, and Evelyn felt a rush of happiness for Flossie. She pictured him perfectly, a sober Latin master, perhaps, with slender white hands. Or maybe an older man, a genteel widower seeking a sharp, bookish wife with her own fortune to manage his highland estate.

"Well, I look forward to meeting this nobody," Evelyn said.

✦ ✦ ✦

THE FOLLOWING SATURDAY, EVELYN and Robert arrived at Birkenhill Manor at 7:00 PM, the time indicated on the invitation, but it was clear that they had made a terrible etiquette error. Drawing up outside the house, they saw no cars in the driveway. In the lobby were four abashed-looking sheikhs speaking in hushed tones to avoid drawing the echo from the empty room. Robert went off to check his reading chamber for later, and Evelyn peeked around the doors into the ballroom. The floors were inlaid with jade and the tiles dazzled jewelled light onto the ceiling. Real palm trees in Qing dynasty pots towered to the ceiling, and smouldering braziers were affixed to the walls. Gold statuettes of mummies flickered in the shadows, and a samovar of incense in the centre of the room burned eucalyptus leaves. When Robert reappeared, he handed her a cocktail glass, putting one hand on her back. Evelyn looked up at him, her eyes liquid.

"Whatever is wrong?" Robert said, alarmed.

"Nothing," Evelyn said, and sipped her drink. It was the colour of a sunset, with a slice of real orange peel at the bottom of the glass. "Everything is perfect."

The guests began arriving after eight. Robert and Evelyn stood in a dark recess under one of the staircases and, from their vantage point, watched the parade of pharaohs and harem dancers, women in embroidered Hathor wrap dresses, women with kohl-lined eyes, carrying Folies Bergère ostrich-feather fans. The two teenage sisters from Vikram's house were dressed again in matching outfits, as black cats with real ruby collars, which Evelyn thought was a darling idea. One man in a kilt had clearly not read the invitation and was hastily having his head wrapped in a turban fashioned out of a pair of women's stockings. A lute player strummed on the balcony above. Waiters circulated with silver boxes of Turkish delight and trays of iced cocktails. Boxer appeared in a camel costume that had him bumping into the braziers and sending swinging spots of light on the walls. The cocktails swam amber and sweet in her veins.

Just after eight thirty, Robert spotted Vikram in the crowd, dressed in a white galabia. As Robert started towards him, Evelyn held him back. "Wait," she said. "Let me, first."

She dodged a man bandaged up like a mummy, and patted Vikram robustly on the shoulder. "Old man," she said, affecting a deep voice.

Vikram turned and his eyes darted over her outfit. "Evening," he said. His voice was warm, but uncertain.

"Lovely to see you again," Evelyn said.

"Indeed, and your costume is very—is it Mr. Carter?"

"It is! How was your drive? Did you come from Colbreck, or were you in the city?"

Vikram licked his lips. "I was in the city for the weekend. How about yourself—were you—have you been in the city?"

Evelyn couldn't keep going. "It's me!" she squealed in her own voice. "Evelyn! Robert's Evelyn."

Vikram's face relaxed. "Evie!" He roared with laughter. "My goodness, I had no idea, you had me terrified of offending. How well it suits you!" He kissed her on both cheeks. "Really, it's marvellous. How clever you are."

Evelyn was giddy with cocktails and eucalyptus smoke. "Robert's just here," she said, pulling him by the arm.

Vikram clapped him around the shoulder. "Everyone is so excited about your session. It's all anyone has been talking about tonight!"

"I think we've got competition, with that boy," Robert said.

"What boy?" Evelyn frowned at him. "Not another child medium?"

Robert laughed. "No, no, wee Charlie, the one who went missing, it was in the papers again today. A false sighting, apparently, got everyone's hopes up."

"Oh." Evelyn's stomach fluttered as she remembered his bare knees in the photograph. She didn't want the fun of the evening to be punctured with dark thoughts about missing little boys. She took a long drink from her glass. "But people are still excited for your session, aren't they? They're not getting distracted?"

Vikram put a reassuring hand on her arm. "The chance to speak to a pharaoh is much more diverting, I promise you."

Evelyn nodded, mollified. The invitation itself had Robert and Clarence's séance printed at the bottom in gilt letters: "Spirit Mediums Relay Ancient Wisdom, RSVP to reserve a private session." She scrutinised Robert. Even if he were wearing a costume for the readings, he'd be able to remove it later, take a tour of the room. "And you won't forget to come out afterwards so we can meet everyone properly together?" Evelyn said.

"No, of course," Robert said, pulling back the sleeve of his robe. "We've got our first booking in ten minutes. Sorry, Evie."

Evelyn took his arm and followed him to the room that had been allocated as his reading chamber. It was usually a drawing room, but it had been decorated like a tomb for the occasion. Gold paper streamers hung from the ceiling, and a circular table in the middle of the room was laid with yellow pillar candles. A list of the guests who had reserved sessions was lying perilously near to the flames, and Evelyn moved it away so it wouldn't start a fire and kill everyone in their flammable costumes. Leaning against the back wall was a six-foot sarcophagus painted with the figure of a bedizened young man.

"Where's Clarence?" Evelyn said, inspecting the sarcophagus. It looked suspiciously realistic.

Robert took a seat on the right side of the table. "His mother is helping him get into his costume. Speaking of which—" He opened a cigar box on the floor and withdrew a pharaonic papier-mâché mask, which he fastened in front of his face with an elastic string. "Does it make me look monstrous?"

The mask was supposed to resemble Tutankhamun, with a shiny golden face and a turquoise headdress. The eyes and mouth had been cut out so that Robert's own face peered through. Against the mask's jewelled torpor, the quick, liquid movement of his eyes, the twitching of his lips, looked grotesque, almost insectile. "It is a bit monstrous," Evelyn said. "But it sets the mood nicely, I suppose."

Robert slid it to the top of his head. "I wish they'd measured me for it. Whoever sat for this thing has a very wee mouth. It keeps steaming up."

"You'll be all right, though, won't you, darling?" Evelyn said. "You'll be able to give the messages without any problems?"

"I will," he said, kissing her hand. "Now, go on and have yourself some fun. Squeeze back in for the group session and maybe we can introduce you to some real pharaohs."

She kissed him on the cheek, and he gave her an odd look.

"What is it?"

"Your moustache." He rubbed his cheek. "Does mine always tickle like that?"

"Yes."

Robert grimaced. He pulled the mask over his face. "You do put up with a lot, don't you, Evie?"

✦ ✦ ✦

LILY DESCENDED ON EVELYN as soon as she went back into the ballroom. She was already drunk, her eyes red-veined. She scooped Evelyn through the arm. "Let's circulate together," she said, "so people can get the full effect of our costume."

Evelyn and Lily twirled around the room. More people crowded into the ballroom, and the windows fogged with pearly steam. Margrit and the count arrived, dressed in matching gold tunics. Abdulla cigarettes were passed around in boxes decorated to look like sarcophagi. A real python had been procured, but was locked in the library after it was discovered that the handler had drunk too many gin rickeys. Lily conducted a long conversation in French with a dumpy young man wearing a Bakelite scarab-beetle necklace, later revealed to be a prince of Monaco.

As the young man bowed and turned away, Lily rolled her eyes. "What a crashing bore."

"Shhh," Evelyn hissed at her. "He'll hear."

Lily tossed her hand. With a yelp, she flew across the room and leapt upon Pups, who was dressed all in black, even his bandaged arm. Tied at his waist was a sharp-looking scimitar that Evelyn privately decided to remove from his person before he got too drunk. Arms locked at the elbows, Lily swerved her and Pups behind one of the potted palm trees. "Let's play a game," she said.

Pups drained his glass and dropped it carelessly on the floor. "Excellent."

"Swapsie turvy," Lily said, peeking through the fronds of the palm.

"All right." Pups pressed his hands together.

"I don't know that game," Evelyn said, a little irritated that Pups had monopolised Lily's attention.

"Well, pick three people at the party you'd replace with someone better who died in the war," Lily said.

Evelyn coughed on a mouthful of her drink. "What?"

Lily clapped Pups on the shoulder, pointing at a middle-aged man polishing his glasses on his robe. "Him! Ugh, Chester something, he is always trying to *tickle* me, it's awful. I'll knock him out and add in Martin McLower. You didn't know him, did you?" Lily turned to Pups, who shook his head. "No, I didn't think so. He played the trumpet beautifully. So much fun at parties."

"My turn," Pups said. "Let me see, I'll knock off—"

The sound of a gong striking echoed from above their heads, and the room hushed.

"Ladies and gentlemen, please join in the excavation, and uncover the treasure within," a butler announced from the balcony.

Waiters circulated through the room with trays piled with dainty pick hammers. Cheering, guests flocked to the plaster panel at the far end of the room that had been painted with hieroglyphics. With much crashing, bashing, and splintering, they hammered upon the wall, breaking the panel in unwieldy chunks to reveal a spectacular buffet laid on the other side. Salmon mousse, oysters on ice, baked ham, solan goose, crab legs, cucumber sandwiches, black olives, asparagus terrine, lemon fancies, petticoat cake, sliced pineapple.

Lily bolted through a gash in the wall and began tearing into a glistening slice of gannet. "Everyone's been talking about the missing boy," she said, wiping her mouth with her sleeve. "Have you heard about him? Wee Callum." Lily was even drunker than Evelyn had realised and was almost shouting.

"Of course I've heard of him," Evelyn said, stiffly. "We were both at Greg Bailish's party, don't you remember?"

"Greg had a party?"

Evelyn stared at her. "Pups broke his arm, you bandaged it up."

"Doesn't sound like me," Lily said.

"Greg was trying to find him, channelling the spirits—you really don't remember?"

"Don't you start on about that boy," Lily yelled. "It's all anyone's been talking about all evening."

Evelyn bristled. She didn't want to spend the evening talking about him either. "How morbid," she sniffed, knowing that she had no right to sniff at the glamorous tragedy of morbidity.

"Flossie was so upset," Lily said, lifting the Waldorf salad from her plate with her fingers and dropping it into her open mouth.

"Flossie? Why?"

"Oh, you know, someone called her from one of those charities she's always going on about. The Society for the Promotion of Poverty or something."

Evelyn frowned at her. "That doesn't sound right."

"Anyway, they were having some kind of search party and she was almost going to go to that instead. I had to force her," Lily said, chasing a slice of apple around her plate with a dirty spoon she'd seized from the table, "force her to get dressed and come for that young man of hers." Lily leant over her and grabbed a satsuma jelly set into an exquisite crystal glass. "Want one?" She jiggled it in Evelyn's face.

"No thank you." Evelyn flinched. "I might wait for you out there." She pointed into the ballroom, but Lily wasn't listening. She picked up a tumbler of whisky from the table and tipped the jelly into it, giving it a good mix until it formed a glistening slurry. Evelyn was almost certain it wasn't even her whisky glass.

She squeezed back through the crowd into the ballroom where one of the glass doors out to the lawn was opened and followed the delicious slice of cool air. Nudging past a Black woman wearing a fez, Evelyn leant in the doorway. On the lawn a pair of pale women dressed as mummies were trying to do cartwheels, scattering scraps of bandages in their wake. There was a tap on her shoulder, and she turned.

"It *is* you."

Evelyn's mouth dropped open. "Malcolm?"

Malcolm licked his lips. "Hello, Evelyn." He was wearing an ambiguously Middle Eastern headpiece, with strange hanging flaps that dangled over his cheeks. The tips of his ears poked behind the tassels.

Her cheeks began to burn. She searched over his shoulder for Lily, but couldn't see past the scrum of people crowding around the buffet.

"I'm surprised to see you here."

Evelyn swallowed. "Yes. Me too."

"I was invited by my friend Bastien Cromwell. Do you know him?"

"No, I don't."

They stared at each other.

"I haven't seen you since the funeral," Malcolm said.

Evelyn put her fingers to her face and pulled off her false moustache. She held it in her palm where it was sticky and limp. "No."

"How have you been?"

Evelyn rubbed her top lip. "Fine. And you?"

Malcolm gave her a small shrug. "As well as you'd expect."

"Good."

Evelyn surveyed him. He had put on a bit of weight, but he still had that oddly cool colouring, like an underwater animal. Yes, he had those curls, those cheekbones. But his skin was translucent. It made him look bloodless, somehow anachronistic, as if he were a portrait of an Edwardian tuberculosis patient that had come to life for one last cough. Evelyn had never understood how anyone could find him handsome. "I'm afraid I have to go. My friend—" Evelyn gestured to where the back of Vikram's head bobbed behind a palm tree. As he turned, Evelyn waved, wildly, until Vikram caught her eye.

"I've been meaning to say—" Malcolm grabbed her arm. Evelyn looked down at it. At his pallid hand on her wrist. She shook him off.

"I must go. Have a lovely evening."

Vikram came a few steps towards her, shooting a look at Malcolm. "All well? Not being bothered, I hope?"

Evelyn's cheeks were hot. "No." And like an idiot, she began to cry.

Vikram produced a handkerchief from his top pocket and offered it to her. "Oh dear. Let's get you some water, shall we?" He steered her past the lute player and into an alcove where a plaster-cast baboon peeked out from behind a towering fern.

"I'm so sorry." Evelyn gulped. "I'm fine now, I'm sorry. I must look deranged."

"Not at all." Gently, Vikram took the handkerchief and wiped under her eye, where the cloth came away black from her makeup. Evelyn swelled up with a strange feeling, it was so intimate, so kind. Another sob hurtled into her throat.

"I'm so sorry, please ignore me."

"Did he say something to you? That man? Should I interrupt Robert's session?"

"No." Evelyn made an effort to smile. "No, not at all. He was—he used to be married to my sister, that's all."

Vikram frowned. "And now he's jealous?"

"Nothing like that. She divorced him."

"A bad type, is he?"

Evelyn shook her head. "It was one of those khaki-fever weddings. She walked straight past him at Edinburgh Waverley when he was out of his uniform."

"And now he wants you to fix up a reunion?"

"No, she's dead. She died. I don't suppose he wants anything from her."

Vikram grimaced. "Ah. I'm sorry."

"I wasn't expecting to see him here. It gave me a shock, that's all."

Vikram sighed. He filled her glass with water and then stood beside her, his back against the wall. He was close enough that Evelyn could smell his scent, a lovely lavender smell, like fresh laundry. He opened his cigarette case and offered one to her, but she declined.

"You know, my best friend in the Thirty-Third, he had this one white lock of hair. He said it appeared overnight after getting a tooth pulled." He shrugged. "It was terribly strange. Just this one circle of white hair on his head."

Evelyn nodded.

"I was waiting in line at the cinema two months ago, and I saw him."

Evelyn glanced up at Vikram, but his eyes were fixed absently in front of them.

"The back of his head. That white spot. It was him. It was Richard. I ran over and grabbed him by the shoulder and"—he took a pull on the cigarette—"and it wasn't him."

"Oh."

"Of course it wasn't him. But . . ." He trailed off.

They were silent for a moment. A man wearing a gold toga was on his hands and knees, searching for his spectacles. "It's a land of ghosts, now. For the rest of us."

Evelyn looked at him. She felt almost guilty for even mentioning Dolores. Vikram, who had been at the front. Who had gone out with fifty-four men, and come back alone.

"I'm sorry," she said. "I shouldn't have made such a fuss. Here you're having a nice time. Please ignore me, I'm quite all right now."

"It's like that plaster wall," Vikram said. His gaze was on the man cleaning his fractured spectacles, but his stare was blank. "The dead are coming closer now. Don't you think?" He turned to look at her.

Evelyn felt a chill under her tweed suit. "I don't know."

"I think they are. I *feel* they are. Robert feels it too. They're so close. Close enough that we can hear their voices through the bricks."

Evelyn's neck was tingling.

Vikram seemed to break out of his reverie. "Champagne?" he said, focusing his eyes on her. He snatched two glasses from a side table and raised his. "To the dearly and nearly," he said.

"Cheers." Evelyn clinked his glass. She drank the whole thing, right to the bottom.

"Let me walk you to Robert's chamber," Vikram said. "No one will mind if we jump the line for a minute."

"I'm fine now, really. I don't want to skip ahead of anyone."

He held out his arm. "At least let me escort you."

Evelyn took his arm, and as they manoeuvred through the ball-room, she tried to quiet the spasm in her throat. It wasn't right, to be sad at such a beautiful party. To ruin it for Vikram, or Robert, by blub-bering like a big child. Over what? Nothing had even happened. A few minutes in a quiet room with Robert and another glass of champagne. That was all she needed. Vikram left her at the back of the queue for "readings from the pharaohs" with a brotherly kiss on the forehead. There were three people ahead of her, and Evelyn fanned herself with her bowler hat. She took another glass of champagne from a passing waiter and balanced it on the sideboard. The doors opened, and the woman in front of Evelyn jostled forward expectantly. Out of the room came Malcolm. Evelyn quickly dropped to one knee, as if her shoelace had become untied. Malcolm looked around him, rubbing his face, apparently oblivious to the man in line who was trying to get into the room. Shaking his head slightly, Malcolm ambled into the ballroom, and Evelyn stood back up. She fanned herself again with the bowler hat. This was ridiculous. Was she going to spend the whole evening ducking and hiding from him? Malcolm was standing half behind a pillar now, his body obscured by the ferns. He was smiling; she could see that funny sharp tooth of his at the side of his mouth. And suddenly, he reached forward and kissed his companion, his hands around her waist. Evelyn balked. So tacky of him. A divorcé! Kissing in public! She switched her weight from foot to foot. Kitty would have a seizure. And his companion—all she could see of her was a black wig. A Cleopatra, no doubt. How unimaginative.

And then Cleopatra turned.

It was Flossie.

Evelyn's heart seized in a wild pump. The air around her head swam and pulsed, in and out with the music. She turned to face the wallpaper, so close that the brim of her bowler hat left a mark. Flossie. Flossie and Malcolm? Malcolm and Flossie? It couldn't be. She snuck another look over her shoulder. There was no mistaking it. Malcolm was murmuring something into Flossie's wrist, and she was flushed with pleasure. Her face was almost beautiful. Evelyn spun back around, the tips of her ears burning. Malcolm was Flossie's young man? Malcolm, at Vikram's house. Malcolm, his hand on Flossie's knee. "Poor Mal, his ex-wife never let him smoke in the house," Flossie would say. Malcolm, at every picnic, every dinner, squeezed next to her in the back of a motorcar, raising his champagne glass, laughing, happy.

And then an acid taste flooded her throat.

What if he knew?

Evelyn almost dropped her glass. Dolores always swore it would be their secret. She swore it. But Malcolm had been her husband. A moment of passion, of panic. The confidences they could have exchanged, worried they might never see each other again. Evelyn's stomach heaved. A crawling, quivering-mandible feeling skittered over her scalp. Malcolm could already have told Flossie. Flossie, who was so righteous. Or Pups, who was so loose. Her top lip prickled with sweat.

The man behind her gave her a nudge, and Evelyn jumped.

"Please," he said, motioning towards Robert's chamber.

Evelyn stumbled through the doors.

"Robert."

Robert pulled off his mask. "Hello, darling."

Evelyn gripped the champagne glass. Robert's face was pink, the hair at his hairline lank and sweaty. He was smiling. Cheerfully, normally.

"Is that for me?"

Evelyn looked blankly down at the champagne glass in her hand.

"Pass it over then, my love." Robert laughed.

Woodenly, Evelyn held out the glass.

"It's like a furnace in here." He wiped his brow with his sleeve.

"She didn't say?" Her voice was weak.

Robert held the glass to his forehead. "That's better. Who didn't say?"

"Is Mama bringing any milk?" Clarence said.

Evelyn had forgotten he was even in the room. He was wearing a sphinx mask, and a fluffy sort of suit with gloves shaped like paws. "Could you leave?" Evelyn said.

Clarence pulled off the mask. He was rosy-cheeked, his nose running. "I'm thirsty anyway," he said, petulantly.

Evelyn gripped the back of the chair until the door closed behind Clarence. "What happened? With Malcolm."

Robert wrinkled his nose. "Malcolm? Who's Malcolm?"

Evelyn stared at him. "Dolly's ex-husband."

"Oh. Oh! That was him before? With the hat with those flaps?"

Evelyn sat heavily in the chair. The cushion was still warm from the last sitter. "You didn't know?"

"I thought he looked familiar. Wonder why he didn't say anything?"

Wordlessly, Evelyn gestured to Robert's mask.

Robert sipped from the champagne glass. "Goodness, that is sweet. Won't it give you a headache?"

"Robert, please. Did you have a session with him?"

"Aye, of course."

She clenched her hands into fists. "What was—did—"

"Oh." Robert shuffled his chair closer to her. He put a hot hand on her wrist. "My love, I'm so sorry, I didn't think."

Evelyn looked up at him. "Nothing—she didn't?"

"No, I'm sorry." Robert rubbed her arm. "I'm so sorry, my love. She didn't come through. I didn't get anything."

Evelyn fell back in her chair. The room spun around her. There was a leap; a horrible, wet, froggy leap inside her chest. She had been wrong to doubt her. Of course she wouldn't come through. She was protecting her, still. Evelyn put her elbows on the table and put her head in her hands. Robert patted her on the back.

Evelyn controlled her breathing until the ache in her throat lessened. "But he did have a reading?"

"Yes."

Evelyn focused her pulse. She raised her head. "So what did come through for him?"

Robert grimaced. "Evie, I can't share that."

She stared at him.

"You know if I had a choice, but—I can't." He licked his lips.

"I am your wife."

Robert's mouth twitched. "My love, you've had an awful fright. Don't let's get carried away. Clarence can work alone for a bit. Why don't we take a break, get some air? I heard there's a wishing well in the grounds."

"I need you to tell me." Evelyn's tongue felt heavy.

"I . . . there . . ."

"Please," she whispered. "I'm begging you."

Robert looked almost wounded. He wiped his face. After a moment, he said, "I didn't get anything for him. I tried, but nothing came through. But Clarence . . ."

"Clarence? What did he say?"

Robert took a deep breath. "Money troubles. Gambling debts."

"Debts?"

"Cards, he said."

"Gambling debts," Evelyn said to herself. Her face felt numb. Her head was very far away from her body. "Money troubles. I understand completely."

24

AS THEY PASSED HOLYROOD ABBEY, A PIGEON FLEW from one of the arched windows, and Flossie shrieked, leaping back. Her hat almost toppled from her head, and Evelyn reached out to grab it before it tumbled into the grass.

"It's only a pigeon," Evelyn said, shooing it away.

Flossie shivered. "I don't like birds."

"Birds? What's not to like about birds? Birds are lovely! Birds are—" The image of the poor broken little magpie came into her head, and Evelyn crossed her arms.

Flossie shuddered, reaffixing her hat. "They're flappy. Unpredictable, swooping, ugh."

Evelyn produced a spare hatpin from her purse and helped to secure it at the back. "I shouldn't have brought you up here, if you have a problem with birds."

Flossie tested her hat. "No, I'm glad. It's terrible, isn't it, that I've never been up here before?"

"A bit, yes."

Flossie smiled. Activity looked well on her; it ruffled her hair into some animation. What was it that Malcolm liked about her? She was so serious. Was there anything Dolorish about her? Something in the nose, perhaps? Dolly hadn't been a beautiful woman either, objectively speaking, but she had that sober kind of calmness that inspired authority. Flossie had it too. You listened when she spoke.

"Where else haven't you been?" Evelyn said, closing her jacket around her. The breeze was cool and saline, and she wished she had worn a scarf. "Have you been to St. Mary's Passage?"

"I enjoyed that." Flossie brightened. "I've visited all the usual places. Just not anywhere too high up, you know, where there might be nests or anything." She looked around them, suspiciously, as if a battalion of pigeons might be poised, ready to attack. "Maybe you can be my touring guide."

"Maybe." Evelyn felt glum. Her stomach was tight and acidy. It was often like that when she was anticipating something. She told herself, *when we get to the next bench, then I'll mention it*. But then they passed the bench, and she told herself, at that rock, that discarded beer bottle.

"You know, Margrit's related to Houdini," Flossie said.

"Excuse me?"

"She'll deny it if you ask her about it." Flossie put her hands into her pockets, chuckling to herself. "She really does not like to be asked about it. But it's true."

"You know that's not his real name, don't you?" Evelyn said, churlishly.

"Yes—originally he was Mr. Weisz."

"If he's lying about his name, who knows what else he is lying about."

Flossie fixed her with a sharp look. "He's a magician. He knows all the tricks that make spiritualism seem convincing. Take slate writing, for example—he explains how easily it can be accomplished. One only has to make a small hole in the floor and—"

"Slate writers are well known to be frauds," Evelyn said, cutting her off. It was Robert's voice, though, coming out of her mouth, and as soon as she said the words, she regretted how pompous she sounded.

"Perhaps so, but doesn't that prove Houdini's point?"

Evelyn pretended to be absorbed by a seagull feather tangled in the grass.

"Have I offended you?"

Evelyn sighed. "I just feel as if you're trying to start a debate."

Flossie turned to her. A lock of her lank hair blew across her face and snagged on her chapped lips. "You're an intelligent woman, Evelyn. It's beyond me how you could believe in all this hokum."

Evelyn bristled. "Do you often go about sniffing at people's beliefs?"

"But this is different."

"That young gentleman of yours," Evelyn said, suddenly.

"What?"

Evelyn could see that she had startled her, and was strangely glad for it. Let Flossie be startled for once. She was always so quick to know everything. "I saw you with him, at the party."

Flossie looked at the ground. A blush rose from her cheeks to the shells of her ears.

"Malcolm Holmes," Evelyn said. Her voice wavered, and she cleared her throat.

Flossie blinked. "Mal. Do you know him?"

Evelyn ignored the question. "Shall we sit?" She gestured to a bench below them. Flossie took out her handkerchief to wipe her nose and dropped it into the grass. Evelyn sat on the bench, waiting for her to retrieve it.

Flossie approached, anxiously gripping her handkerchief.

"Is it serious?" Evelyn said.

"I don't understand. Do you know him?"

Evelyn's queer moment of victory had bubbled down to a simmer. "How well do *you* know him?"

Flossie looked out at where three young men were climbing down from Arthur's Seat, windblown and rosy-cheeked. One of them was holding a broken kite. "I met him through Bastien, at a fishing weekend."

"I didn't know you liked to fish," Evelyn said, tersely. "I would have thought there'd be too many birds, near a river."

"I wasn't at the river, just the weekend. Pups enjoys it. We always had fresh fish, when we were growing up. Anyhow, Malcolm and I, we got sat together at dinner, and, well . . ." Flossie squinted myopically ahead of her.

"Are you in love?" Evelyn said. As she said it, she heard the old woman in her voice, the judgemental dowager, the stuffy, fussy, miserable spoilsport.

"It's not, I don't—" Flossie peered at her, earnestly. "How does one *know*?"

Evelyn started. "I think you're just supposed to know."

"I don't feel dizzy, or anything," Flossie said.

"Dizzy?"

"Isn't it supposed to feel dizzy?"

"That sounds horrible. No," Evelyn said, watching the hikers climbing the hill. A Jack Russell terrier was bounding through the grass with an overlarge branch in its mouth, pleased with itself. "Married love," she began, then trailed off. How ridiculous! Love! Like she was a schoolgirl. "It's a form of habituation, and fondness, I think. And resolution."

"Resolution."

"Yes." Evelyn crossed her legs. "You know, you resolve to forge love. It needn't be roses and poetry."

"I know that."

"I know you do, you're a sensible girl, but—it's beside the point. I meant, how entangled are you with him?"

"As a matter of fact, he's asked me to marry him."

Evelyn heard herself make a sound that was halfway between a gulp and a snort. "What answer did you give?"

"I haven't given any answer, yet." Flossie looked down at her handkerchief. "Pups doesn't much like him, and I suppose it would mean staying here, which, I don't know. We were only supposed to be here until Papa finishes up with North British."

Evelyn stared ahead at nothing. Malcolm. Throwing sugared almonds at Flossie and Malcolm's wedding, as if she hadn't thrown them at his first wedding. Dolores's name tossed casually across the dinner table. "My second marriage, actually," he would say, smiling, as if it had been a minor inconvenience. Dolly's life, just a puddle on the road to his destination. Malcolm, who got to keep on living, breathing, who got to keep on being happy. The pin sticking through her heart at the sight of his pallid face. The pin sticking straight through her new life. "I have to tell you something," Evelyn said, swallowing.

Flossie turned to her.

"Malcolm has gambling debts," she said. "Terrible debts. His motives, his interest—I don't think you should trust him."

Flossie's eyes were wide; a pulse underneath her temple was ticking hard enough that it throbbed in the sunlight. "What?"

Evelyn reached forward and took her hand. "He's terribly in debt. I'm very sorry, Florence, I think it's important for you to know. His interest in marriage—it may be motivated by finances."

Flossie's hand was limp on her own. "I don't understand."

"I'm sorry. I didn't want to tell you. He's not trustworthy."

"But you can't be serious. You're joking, aren't you?"

Evelyn shook her head. "I'm not joking. I'm completely serious."

The tears that had been growing in Flossie's eyes rolled down her cheeks and over her lips. She made no move to wipe them away, as if she hadn't even noticed. "But—how could you know?"

Evelyn hesitated. Flossie didn't believe in Robert's gift. She wouldn't take it seriously, if that were the source. She took a deep breath. It would be worth the risk, to volunteer a little of the truth. "I've known Malcolm for a long time. My sister was his first wife."

Flossie stared into the middle distance. Another tear ran down her face. "Can I, could I talk to her?"

"She's dead," Evelyn said gently.

"Oh."

"You can't trust him," Evelyn said. "I'm sorry."

Flossie gave a sudden sob. "I didn't know." She wiped her face with the back of her wrist. "God, what a fool I've made out of myself."

Evelyn's heart pulsed. "No, not at all."

Flossie put her hands to her head. "What an idiot I am." She sobbed. One of the hikers walking past shot them a compassionate look.

Evelyn patted her back. "Come now, it's not your fault."

"It is my fault." Flossie gulped. "I let him, I didn't question it. I thought—" Her voice wavered. "I thought, oh, it's finally happening."

Evelyn's eyes began to sting, and she rubbed them, hastily.

"I thought—I thought, maybe I could have some fun now."

Evelyn stroked her back. "I'm sorry."

Over Flossie's shoulder, she looked out past the abbey ruins, over the hillocks of stubbly grass. From here she could just about make out, in the distance, their old Dumbiedykes flat. She pictured the curtain, being slowly pulled over the window.

"How stupid I am," Flossie said. "I thought the time for happiness was coming to me. But it's over, isn't it?"

"Not at all," Evelyn said, patting her methodically. "You're young, plenty of happiness is headed your way." But even as she said it, she knew she was lying. Happiness would never come to someone who didn't know you had to fight for it.

25

EVELYN WAS PREPARING FOR ANOTHER SATURDAY TO Monday at Vikram's estate. She packed into her case a blue chiffon dress for the evening, her emerald necklace, a new pair of gloves, a tasselled shawl, her new underclothes, and her wedding brushes. Robert was sitting on the bed, staring into the distance.

"Are you feeling all right, darling?"

Robert sighed. "Tired."

"I'm sorry." She went over and kissed his forehead. "You've been very in demand recently. It's no wonder you're exhausted."

Robert lay back on the bed and she tried not to mind about his shoes on the bedspread. He closed his eyes. Evelyn was alarmed now. Flossie still hadn't returned her calls. She needed to see her, face-to-face, to make sure. "Darling, don't nap, we'll have to leave in an hour."

Robert grunted. Within the minute, he was asleep.

Evelyn looked at her watch. If she let him rest for half an hour, that would be enough to rouse him with some tea, and they could still leave in time. She put the kettle to boil and flicked through a copy of the *Daily Express*. On page sixteen, they had published a picture of the Egyptian party, and she'd saved it from Marty's eyes to enjoy when she was alone. There she was, between two palm trees, a glass of champagne in her hand. A pang of regret ran through her. Dolly would have loved this picture. She would have made fun of

Evelyn in the moment; made a quippy remark about temperance. But later she would frame it on her writing desk, force visitors to admire it. Evelyn took a deep breath. This was not a crying occasion. She looked closer at the image. "Gala Brings Out the Young Set" was the headline. Was she young enough to be part of the young set? Certainly, Vikram wasn't especially young. But it was hard to tell people's ages, these days. Evelyn nibbled her finger. Goodness knows her own youth hadn't been especially youthful; it was a stroke of fortune to have another shot at it.

It was now six and swallows were swooping over the garden in whispery clouds. She went upstairs, banging heavily on each step in the hopes of waking Robert. But when she opened the door, he was still lying there, his arm over his face.

She nudged his elbow, and he grumbled and rolled away.

"Come along, darling, it's time to get up now."

"Sleeping," Robert said.

Evelyn gritted her teeth. "Once we get going you can sleep there, but we don't want to leave too late. We'll miss dinner otherwise."

Robert groaned.

"Please, darling. I'll make you some tea, shall I?" She turned on the light, and then began ostentatiously checking her case, humming out loud. In the mirror she saw Robert sitting up on the bed and rubbing his eyes.

* * *

BY THE TIME THEY set off for Vikram's estate it was ten past seven, and a soft June mist was rolling in over the roads. Cows chewed amiably in the fields, and the sky was a bruised-peach colour. Robert was taciturn and grumpy, and Evelyn felt compelled to compensate by chattering about the *Daily Express* article. Somewhere outside Swintonmill, she gave up and simply sat, her hands clenched underneath her as they drove.

They arrived at Vikram's estate just before nine. Evelyn slumped with relief in the car seat when they pulled up outside the house, utterly exhausted, as if she'd been the one driving. There was no one to meet them at the steps, and Robert pushed open the front door, calling, "Hello?" into the entrance hall. The sound of laughter and the clinking of glasses came from the drawing room and Matthew the butler appeared, wearing a harried expression.

"Mr. and Mrs. Hazard, we didn't hear you." He shot an icy glance at a footman, who grabbed their bags with indecent haste and whisked them up the stairs. "I'm afraid dinner has already been served, but I'll ensure the cook prepares you a meal. Would you like to take it in your room?"

"Yes, thank you," Evelyn said, at the same time that Robert said, "No need."

They looked at each other.

"We'll miss out on all the fun," Robert said, pointing to the drawing room.

"But I need to change my dress anyway," Evelyn whispered, aware that Matthew had discreetly averted his eyes.

"Don't be silly, Evie, no one's going to care what you're wearing."

Evelyn smiled at him, tensely. "Perhaps we could just have something small in the drawing room," she said, to Matthew. He nodded and retreated into the dining room, where she could see through the doors that maids were clearing the table.

"Why don't you go ahead?" she said to Robert. "I'll be down in a moment." She took the stairs two at a time, and entered their room to pounce upon a housemaid in the process of unpacking her trunk.

The maid froze, her hands full of Evelyn's undergarments.

"I'm so sorry." Evelyn took a step back and then one forward. "Please, don't worry about that for now. I'll need to change for dinner. I won't be a moment."

"Of course." The maid blushed to her ears, looking around for somewhere to put the undergarments. Evelyn stepped forward and took them from her. "Thank you."

When the door shut, she raced out of her dress and into her blue chiffon. In the mirror the marks from her bust bodice were still visible, and she gave them a frustrated pat. There was a knock at the door.

"A couple more moments!" Evelyn shrieked.

"It's me." It was Flossie's voice.

Evelyn's heart gibbered in her chest. "Just a second." She surveyed the mess on the bed. They were new undergarments, so Flossie wouldn't be able to judge her on the quality, but still, she wasn't about to have her life blown up in front of an exhibition of her intimates. But then Flossie had seen her *wearing* only her undergarments, at Lily's house. Why were they so much more indecent, somehow, now that they were not on her person? She threw her day dress over the case to conceal the contents.

She cleared her throat. "Come in."

"I'm so glad you're here." Flossie opened the door and crossed to sit on the edge of the bed. Her nose was pink and the skin around her mouth was chapped. "I broke it off with Malcolm," she said.

Evelyn's head swam. She sat heavily on the bed, her case bouncing. "I'm sorry." She tried to look sorry.

Flossie sniffed.

Evelyn fiddled with the catch on her earring. "Did you—did you have a long talk?"

"Not really," Flossie said. "He stormed off pretty quickly."

Evelyn nodded, controlling her breath.

"He was horribly unfair about the whole thing."

"Really?" Evelyn frowned. Even when Dolores had asked for a divorce, he'd just whistled through his front teeth, and gone along with it without complaint. Dolly used to do an uncanny mime of that whistle.

"He denied everything. The debts, the gambling. There was a horrible scene."

Evelyn tried to think of a polite way to respond. "That sounds difficult."

"It was awful," Flossie said, picking at a thread in her skirt. "But at least Stephen was pleased."

"Stephen?"

"Pups."

"Oh, of course."

"He never liked him. Says he looks like a bird."

"A moth," Evelyn said, unable to help herself.

Flossie stared at her, unblinking, for a moment before bursting into laughter.

"I'm sorry."

Flossie was wiping her eyes. "No, no, I need to hear it."

"Well, in that case, yes, he looks like a moth. One of those spindly, big pale ones you get at the end of the summer. Sometimes I'd see one knocking against the glass and think, oh, Malcolm has cut his hair."

Flossie was wheezing. "Thank you, Evie." She reached out and gripped her hand.

❖ ❖ ❖

ARM IN ARM, THEY went down to rejoin the others. Even from the top of the staircase it was clear that the party had become rowdy. A young man with a wispy moustache was picking out "Clair de Lune" on the untuned piano in the hallway, and someone in the library was squealing in either pain or mirth, it wasn't clear. In the drawing room, Vikram was conducting a session of chemin de fer, wearing a feathered necklace, and Robert was gamely allowing a young man to wrap a bow tie around his forehead. Behind him were several wet-eyed men with similarly bow-tied foreheads crouching over a complicated arrangement of wineglasses balanced on the floor.

"There aren't any ladies here," Evelyn said, stopping at the doorway.

"Lily's here." Flossie pointed to the back of a white tennis dress. Lily turned and looked in their direction for some moments before giving them a slow wave. Her eyes were glassy, and she looked distinctly wobbly.

"Is she all right?"

"She started having fun yesterday and hasn't yet taken a break," Flossie said.

Behind them, Matthew cleared his throat, and Evelyn turned. "Mrs. Hazard. I have set your tray in the nook." He bowed in the direction of the recess at the back of the room, where a card table had been set up with a tray. Laid on it were silver cutlery, a lace napkin, and a single candle.

Evelyn felt mortified. "Thank you so much."

"Can I help you with anything else?"

"No, thank you." Evelyn wished he would go away. There were all these rowdy young men toasting each other and cheering, and her in the corner with her silver tea tray and lace napkin.

Matthew hesitated.

"Is everything all right?" Evelyn said.

"The staff will be dismissed at ten this evening, so please ring promptly if you change your mind."

Evelyn nodded. As soon as Matthew turned away, she elbowed Flossie. "Why did Vikram dismiss all the staff?"

"Sometimes Vikram gives them the night off if it gets a bit . . ." She raised her eyebrows at the bow-tied collective, where a man in an Aztec jacket was administering a kiss to one of Vikram's Indian miniatures.

"Ah." Evelyn pictured Marty, in the corner, tight-lipped and tutting. She took a chair in the recess, and Flossie pulled a stool to join her on the other side, helping herself to a meringue on the edge of Evelyn's tray.

"There you are." Pups came over and put a hand on Flossie's shoulder. "A word?" he said.

"I'm busy," Flossie said.

"For heaven's sake." He slouched off into a corner towards the owlish young man.

Flossie and Evelyn exchanged a look. "He's so pleased with himself about Malcolm. I'm not ready for him to gloat," Flossie said, brushing meringue crumbs from her lap.

Evelyn made an internal note, not to say anything that could be too conceivably gloaty. "Has Pups ever been married?" She began to cut her watercress sandwich.

Flossie shook her head. "My parents tried to match him with this girl, Vivien, but she was a bit silly. Giggly, you know."

"Oh dear." Evelyn shook her head.

"Not that there's anything wrong with being giggly," Flossie added.

"Of course not."

"It's just—" Flossie grimaced. "I never understood what was so funny all the time."

"I often feel like that," Evelyn said, watching the group of men roaring in the corner.

Flossie took another meringue and sat back in the chair. "Do you think—I mean, should he *be* here? It's getting too boisterous for a child, isn't it?"

Evelyn followed her gesture and spotted Clarence, cowering below a man who was waving a glass of Sauternes over his head in rococo loops.

"Is Bernice here?"

"No, she didn't come this time. Just the brother."

"Where is he, then?"

Flossie shrugged.

Evelyn slipped out from behind the tea tray and, as politely as she could, nudged the Sauternes-brandisher aside. "Clarence, how are you?"

"I'm well."

"Is there a reading tonight?"

Clarence took a piece of string out of his pocket and knotted it. "There was supposed to be, but everyone seems drunk now."

"Yes, they do rather. Where's your brother?"

Clarence looked around the room. "I don't know."

"Well." Evelyn realised she was still holding her napkin. "Maybe I should fetch him. It's quite loud in here. Maybe you'd prefer to be in the library?"

"He's fine," Vikram said, walking over. His walk was not entirely steady. "You're fine, aren't you, Clarence?"

Clarence nodded.

"Whisky?" He held a glass out to him.

"He's a bit young for whisky," Evelyn said, trying, and failing, not to sound too prim.

"Nonsense," Vikram said. "A wee dram—puts hair on your chest. Come on, Clarence, what do you say?"

"No thank you," Clarence said, unknotting his piece of string. "I don't like alcohol."

"What about brandy? Brandy hardly counts."

"I'll see if I can find your brother, shall I?" Evelyn said, her voice sounding sharp, even to her.

She let herself out of the drawing room and glanced around the dining room. The table was now cleared. Lying on the floor was a trampled black wig. She put her head into the library. It was a chilly evening, and the fire had been lit, but the room was empty. As she closed the door, she heard voices, so she opened the door again. She walked in and recognised Walter's knee sticking out from the armchair closest to the fire. As she came closer, she saw he was pink-cheeked and tousled. His shirtsleeves were rolled up, and on his right arm, she was surprised to see a tattoo of an anchor, with a little bell, and a string of initials. A tattoo? Walter? Then she remembered—he'd been in the navy, after all. There was a funny little laugh, a kitteny giggle, and there, kneeling on the floor, was

Lily, her chin resting on the arm of the chair. Evelyn pulled out of the room as quickly as she had ever moved in her life.

"He's busy right now," Evelyn said, returning to Clarence. Her voice sounded shrill. "Why don't you have a little rest though, in our room? I can have some shortbread sent up before the staff leave."

Clarence shot her a fierce look. "I have my own room. And I don't like shortbread."

"Clarence, I really must insist." Evelyn felt a flush creeping up her face.

"Mrs. Hazard," Clarence said, coolly, "I can look after myself."

Churlishly, Evelyn returned to her tea tray. Her cheeks were prickling. There was a special kind of humiliation in being an adult that couldn't control a child.

Flossie had now taken Evelyn's place in the armchair and was polishing off the watercress sandwiches. "That was excellent. I wish I'd thought to have a second dinner," she said.

"That was my first dinner," Evelyn muttered under her breath.

Flossie opened a drawer in a side table with lavish ease. Evelyn would have been too shy to open drawers in someone else's house. Inside was a pack of long-stemmed matches and a marble coaster. Flossie rummaged in the back and pulled out a pack of cards. They moved the tray onto a side table and Flossie dealt them a hand of whist. Every now and then there was a cheer from the room, and Evelyn strained her head around the corner to see the vicar and Boxer pouring champagne into their shoes and drinking from them.

Pups circled again. "Flo, let's go outside for a chat—just you and me."

"Maybe we should go up to my room?" Flossie said, to Evelyn.

Pups said something in Malay, and Flossie snapped back at him.

"Let me check on Robert," Evelyn said, desperate for an excuse to step away.

Flossie nodded. "See you up in my room."

Evelyn gently inserted herself between Robert and a man with a monocle who was unsteadily trying to light a pipe, dropping flickering matches onto the carpet while missing the bowl entirely. "It's getting a bit raucous here, I think Flossie and I are going to retire."

"Good idea," Robert said. He took a step forward and stamped out one of the smouldering matches.

"Will you keep an eye on Clarence?" Clarence was sitting cross-legged on the floor while the owlish young man talked about Nietzsche at some volume. "It doesn't seem wholesome, somehow, for a boy."

Robert nodded, seriously. "Evie, you're a queen for worrying about him." He embraced her, too hard, and Evelyn coughed.

"Yes, darling, well, have a nice evening. And mind the boy."

❈ ❈ ❈

FLOSSIE'S ROOM WAS SMALL and more personal than Evelyn and Robert's room, with coral-coloured wallpaper. It had obviously once been a woman's room; cherubs were carved into the headboard and there was a dusty statuette of an angel on the windowsill. It looked out over the top of the glasshouse and the garden. The mist had crept up from the river and taken on an orange glow around the blinking lights of Vikram's generator.

Flossie slipped off her shoes and unzipped the top of her dress. "It's so tiring when they get like this," she said, twisting her neck until it cracked.

"It was perfectly civilised last weekend we were here," Evelyn said.

Flossie laughed. "I think they build up enough civilised days and then trade them for a barbaric day."

Evelyn sat on the bed. "Does Pups sleep in here with you?" She gestured to the second bed, which had been unceremoniously wedged under the window.

Flossie stared at her. "Heavens, no. He's next door."

Evelyn felt the blood in her cheeks. "I don't have a brother, you see, so I don't know what's usual," she said, as Flossie laughed again.

"It's a sister you have, isn't it?" Flossie leant back against the pillows. "I mean another sister."

"Yes. Katherine." Evelyn felt a lump in her throat as she said it. She was suddenly desperate not to talk about Kitty. "How did you meet Vikram?"

"You know, I can't remember. This crowd just runs together so we got thrown together somehow. It was when he was in his painter phase."

"Vikram paints?"

"No, he collected painters for a while. Lindsworth? Do you know him, the one who only paints rotten fruit?"

Evelyn shook her head.

"Well, as Lily says, he's a crashing bore. He keeps talking about memento mori, but I don't think he knows what it means."

"I think I saw Lily," Evelyn said, blushing, "in the library."

"Oh?"

"She seemed a bit odd."

Flossie frowned. "She wasn't *reading*, was she?"

"No, she was with Walter."

"Who?"

"Walter, Clarence's brother."

"Oh?" Flossie's eyes grew wide. "Oh."

Evelyn felt embarrassed, like she'd been tattling. "Anyway, it doesn't matter. I just thought, you know, well."

Flossie stretched out on the bed and shuffled the playing cards. "Lily's very modern. I could stand to learn from her example," and Flossie gave Evelyn a grin that might have been roguish. For a moment, she looked a lot like Pups. "I'm surprised she's interested in Walter, though. He's pretty, but strange."

Evelyn's ears tingled. Now they had begun gossiping, she was ready to pick up speed. "Do you think so?" she said, casually.

"Like one of those drugged animals at the circus."

Evelyn thought about this. He did have a certain sedation about him, a certain flatness. It wasn't an opiate languor, though; more a detachment, a superiority. She caught herself biting her fingernail and stopped herself.

"Him and Clarence, they're both so moony."

"I suppose."

"But then, what do you expect?" Flossie dealt them a hand of cards.

Evelyn hesitated. "What do you mean?"

"Well, you've heard him. The readings." Flossie shrugged.

Evelyn felt they were drifting back into dangerous territory. From downstairs came the sound of a glass smashing, and people cheering. "I think Clarence is extremely talented," Evelyn said, stiffly. "And very mature for his age."

Flossie gave her a long, serious look. A look that was so long and so serious that Evelyn ran her tongue around the inside of her mouth, searching for an offending piece of food in her teeth.

"I tell you what." Flossie put the pack of cards down and crossed her legs. "What if I gave you a spiritualist reading now?"

Evelyn almost laughed. "You?"

"Yes, me." Flossie tucked her hair behind her ears. "I'll do a reading for you."

"But—" Evelyn frowned. "But you don't believe in it."

"Exactly," Flossie said. Her eyes were bright. "I don't believe a word of it. But if even I can do it, then you have to at least concede it's possible for other people to do the same."

Evelyn shook her head. It felt like she was being laughed at somehow, a baroque kind of joke that was too subtle for her to understand. "I don't think so."

"Come on, please, Evie." Flossie leant forward. "Give me a chance, and then I promise I will shut up about it."

Evelyn felt half a smile on her face. "For how long?"

Flossie grinned. "For the rest of the weekend."

"A month," Evelyn said, crossing her arms. "If you do this . . . experiment, then you can't make any comments about spiritualism for one month."

Flossie clapped her hands. "Deal."

"All right then, I agree."

Flossie leapt up and turned the lights off. For a moment it was too dark to see anything, and Evelyn felt the bed lurch as Flossie returned. "Let's hold hands."

Evelyn took Flossie's cold hands in hers. Flossie took a deep breath, then another.

"Dearly beloved," she said, and they both laughed. "No, really. Close your eyes. Reach out to your loved ones."

Evelyn closed her eyes. Downstairs someone wandered into the corridor, singing "Mairi's Wedding."

"I feel someone coming through who died before their time."

Evelyn rolled her eyes underneath her lids.

"It is someone who died young. A young woman."

Evelyn cleared her throat.

"She is very funny."

Evelyn's blood tickled her eardrums. She shifted on the bed.

"She had the flu and it seemed like she was going to be fine, and then she wasn't."

Evelyn pulled her hands away. In the dark she stared at Flossie.

"What is it?" Flossie said.

"What do you know?" Evelyn said, her voice tight.

Flossie jumped up and turned on the lamp. "Oh, Evelyn, I'm sorry."

"Did Malcolm say something to you?" Evelyn's heart was leaping in her chest.

Flossie stood by the edge of the bed, her lips pale. "God, Evelyn, I was only playing about. No one told me anything about anyone."

Evelyn put her fingers to the top of her breastbone. Her pulse was scuttering in quick darts.

"I swear, I was just fooling around. I wasn't thinking." She sat back on the bed and tried to catch Evelyn's eye. "That's the way it works, see? I was just saying general things."

"But—"

"Everyone in the world knows a woman that died from the flu. It was a wild guess."

"You said she was funny," Evelyn said, weakly.

Flossie put her hand on her arm. "Evie, we always think the people we love are funny. I'm such an idiot." She reached forward and hugged Evelyn.

Evelyn pressed her knees together. "Please don't do that again."

"Never, I swear it." Flossie held on to her, hard. They were silent for a moment. "I'm sorry, Evelyn. I shouldn't have been so stupid."

"He's not a fraud," Evelyn said. "I've heard him say things—things no one could know."

"I'm sure it seems like that."

"Vikram believes him. Very intelligent people believe in him. You don't know something they don't."

"Don't you think," Flossie said, softly, "that people believe what they want to?"

"Robert is not a fraud."

Flossie held her gaze for a moment too long.

"He's not. He would never hurt anyone, ever. He can barely bring himself to kill fruit flies."

Flossie opened her mouth and closed it again.

"He's a very kind man. Too kind. He would have to be the worst kind of ghoul to defraud people. I'm married to him. I know he's not a ghoul."

Flossie's lips were twitching. "I'm sure he's not."

"He's a good man. The best." Evelyn gulped. Her face was throbbing. "I think—would you mind if I call it a night? I've tired myself out."

"By all means." Flossie's eyes followed her as she stood to open the door. She could tell Flossie was alarmed but that she didn't want to stop her. Evelyn went back into her room, and changed into her nightdress. Her sinuses were aching, as if they had been filled with mashed potato. She pressed her fingers down on the bridge of her nose. Downstairs, people were moving furniture about. There was the sound of another glass smashing, followed by a roaring cheer.

* * *

THAT FIRST NIGHT IN the Lion's Club, the band was clear through the wall of the cloakroom. One of her stool's legs was shorter than the others and Evelyn kept losing her balance, jolting on the flagstones. She was running her fingers appreciatively through the pelt of a fox-fur coat when, from the back of the room, someone sneezed. She yelped, grabbing an umbrella.

A sandy-haired, long-limbed young man stood up in the corner, holding his hands aloft. "I'm unarmed."

Evelyn smiled, despite herself. "What are you doing in here?"

He gestured to his left shoe, where the sole was flapping. "What's your excuse?"

Evelyn lowered the umbrella. She was embarrassed now to admit that she hadn't been asked for a dance all evening. "So why not just go home?"

He grinned. There was a faint trace of a scar across his lips. "I could ask you the same question."

"I'm waiting for my sister, Katherine," Evelyn began. "Her husband is on leave."

The opening of "The Thistledown Waltz" started up from the band next door, and the man held his hand out. "If you lose the weapon, would you like to dance?"

Evelyn crossed her arms. "Me?"

"Only you and me around, isn't there?" he said, with a smile. "Don't make me waltz with the umbrella."

Evelyn hesitated. He looked clean enough, nice-looking, even. His jacket had been poorly darned, and there was the flapping shoe. But there was something unusual about his posture. It took a moment before she realised what it was: a kind of relaxedness, a slouchy easiness that bore none of the rigid apprehension that had seized every man under fifty. After a moment, she approached him. "Just this dance."

"Nice to meet you, I'm Robert." His grip was firm on her waist.

"Evelyn Grant."

He was a competent dancer, given that they were forced to box-step between the rows of overcoats. He didn't breathe on her, or hold her too tight, and only once stumbled on his shoe. As the waltz finished, his fingers grazed her shoulder, and she looked up, startled. Robert was brushing a fox-fur hair from the shoulder of her dress. His eyes were crinkled with a sort of tender concentration. Evelyn stared up at him. An unfamiliar warmth charged up inside her, like a heated brick had been fired in her belly.

❖ ❖ ❖

EVELYN WOKE TO THE sound of a gunshot. She sat up, the skin on her arms and legs tingling. Robert wasn't in the bed next to her. There was commotion downstairs, footsteps, the kind of humid breeze that was possible only if the front door had been left open. Someone was playing a penny whistle, badly. Evelyn ran to the window and pulled back the curtain. It was too dark to see anything outside except for the shapes of light from the front of the house on the gravel. She swung open the bedroom door. The corridor was empty. Her head was ringing. Had she imagined it? Flossie appeared from a door farther down the hallway. She was wearing a pair of gold silk pajamas, and her hair was pinned and wrapped in a scarf.

"Flossie?"

"Did you hear that? It sounded like a gunshot."

"Robert's not here," Evelyn said, her throat tightening.

"Pups neither."

"You don't think—" Evelyn broke off. She saw it perfectly, Robert giving a message at the table, a young man, eyes wild with absinthe, picking up a shotgun and firing it at him.

Flossie looked over the banister into the hallway.

"Don't!" Evelyn cried.

"There's no one down there," Flossie said. "It's empty. Come on." She ran to the stairs and went down them two at a time. Evelyn followed behind, her legs stiff with fright. They checked the library, where a black-and-white cat was napping in front of the embers. The drawing room was empty as they passed. A man's oxford was lying on the floor.

The door to the glasshouse was open and Evelyn followed Flossie through. It was cold, the doors wide onto the night. And there, down at the far end of the garden, were the guests.

"It must be a mistake. A firework," Evelyn said. The figures were crowded near the end of the hawthorn maze by the river, the sound of the penny whistle louder now.

Flossie looked at her and grimaced. "What are they doing out there? What time is it?"

"Just past three."

Flossie shook her head, reaching to close the door.

"Wait." Evelyn looked around for Vikram's bird. "There was a bird in here, do you think it got out? Maybe it won't be able to come back in."

Another gunshot cracked across the lawn. Flossie started running across the garden and Evelyn followed, the grass wet under her feet, the mist thick and woolly around her. There was a shriek. Evelyn heard someone laughing, someone behind her. She turned and no one was there. Flossie's golden pajamas flickered, a sickle in the mist. Her heart was in her eyeballs. The back of Vikram's head appeared; he was knee-deep in long grass. He turned at the sound of their footsteps, swinging to Flossie, a rifle in his hands. Evelyn screamed. Vikram lowered his gun.

"It's me!" Flossie was yelling. "Put that down!"

There was a group of men standing behind Vikram. "Where is Robert?" She grabbed Boxer by his jacket.

"Joining us?" he said, leering. His teeth were stained with red wine.

"What's happening?" Flossie was patting Pups down. "Are you hurt? What are you doing?"

"Relax, Florence," Vikram said, hoisting the rifle onto his shoulder. "We're having a little hunting party."

"It's the middle of the night!" Flossie gripped his elbow. "I thought someone was being murdered."

Vikram laughed. He was unsteady on his feet. "Robert said he'd never tried any hunting, and we thought this would be as good a time as any."

Evelyn pushed past him, wading into the rushes. Water squelched between her toes, dragging the bottom of her nightdress. "Robert?" She stepped onto a snail shell and felt it crack, felt the slither of the snail under the arch of her foot.

"Evie?"

Evelyn stumbled towards the voice. Robert was standing on the edge of the river, aiming a rifle into the water.

She stood completely still. "What are you doing?"

"Evelyn." He blinked at her. "Want to give it a try?" He was still holding the gun.

"Don't point that at me," she said.

"Come on." He waved the rifle at her. "It's awful good fun."

Her stomach lurched up against her ribs and she thought for a moment she might be sick.

Behind her she could hear Flossie shouting at Pups, "You could have got yourself killed!" Someone near the trees was still playing the penny whistle.

"You're in your nightdress!" Robert said, as if he had just realised.

"I heard shooting, I thought—" Evelyn's knees were shaking. "Will you put that down!" she screamed at him.

Robert dropped the gun into the grass. "We're only having fun, don't be a spoilsport."

"Have you lost your senses?"

"Oh, come along."

"Your heart!" Evelyn shrieked.

Robert's face drew tight. "My heart is fine."

"After everything! And now, guns in the middle of the night, shooting at each other."

"We weren't shooting *at* each other!"

Evelyn turned and began walking back to the group. Vikram was aiming into the rushes. "It's not even hunting season," Flossie was saying.

Pups lit a cigarette. "It doesn't matter! Old Billy here doesn't mind, do you, Billy?"

An elderly groundsman wearing an overcoat was standing in the distance, leaning against an oak tree, his hands in his pockets. A rush of shame poured over Evelyn, settling in the deepest recesses of her body.

"No, sir," Billy said. His eyes were sharp and sober.

"He knows what side his bread is buttered on," Boxer said, laughing.

Walter was there, she saw now, with a start. He was standing behind Boxer, holding a bottle of champagne that looked like it had been cut off with a sword. Next to him was Clarence. Clarence coughed, and a wet gasp of air mingled with the mist.

"Oh my God, Clarence." Evelyn held her hand out to him, and instinctively, he took it. His paw was cold in hers. Evelyn felt close to tears. "Let's go in now. Come along."

Clarence nodded.

Evelyn began to walk back towards the lawn and then paused. "Where's Lily?" she said.

"I don't know," Walter said.

"But was she with you? When you came out here?"

Walter hiccupped. "I didn't notice."

Evelyn knelt down. "Clarence, was Lily here?"

"Maybe," Clarence said. His voice was small. "It's dark."

A man in a rowing jacket, who must have been the owner of the lost shoe, since he was wearing only one, started singing "The Braes of Balquhither."

"Will you be quiet? She was drunk! What if she walked off and got shot by one of you idiots?" Evelyn said. "Lily?" she yelled into the gardens. "Lily?"

"She's probably back at the house," Boxer said.

"No—she wasn't in her room." Flossie's lips were pale. "I tried it after the first shot. Oh my God."

Evelyn addressed Clarence. "You go inside now and get nice and warm. Take off all your wet clothes and dry your hair, put some socks on. Get into bed and don't come out again, all right?"

Clarence nodded.

"Go on now, I'll watch until you get inside."

Clarence ran across the lawn and Evelyn saw the shape of his silhouette pass into the glasshouse.

"Lily?" Flossie was calling into the darkness.

"Don't overreact," Vikram said. "I'm sure she's fine."

Evelyn pushed past Boxer and the vicar and the young owlish-looking man and tramped through the mud into the marsh at the edge of the river. The water was white and silver, the clouds low; something soft and fluttery, a bat maybe, was skimming close to the water. Evelyn searched the water for any sign of Lily's fair hair, her white dress. There was nothing there. She trudged back towards Flossie. "What shall we do? Should we call the police?"

Flossie was rubbing her face. "Don't just stand there," she screamed at Pups. "Look for her!"

Pups began to call halfheartedly into the darkness.

"Do you think—" Flossie pointed to the hawthorn maze. She ran off towards the maze, and Evelyn followed. Flossie's golden pajamas were black up to her knees where they had been soaked with water. "Lily?" Flossie called into the mouth of the maze. She wiped away the fog on her glasses with her sleeve. "Why didn't I bring a torch?" She pointed to the side of the house. "I'll look here, Evie; you check the orchard."

Evelyn staggered to the orchard at the side of the house. The earth was slippery there, worms glistening in the dim moonlight.

"You're making a lot of fuss over nothing." Robert's voice came from behind her.

Evelyn turned.

"We were only having fun," he said. There was something defiant, almost churlish, in his voice.

Evelyn felt like crying. "This isn't fun, Robert."

"She's probably just asleep in the library or something," Robert said. "Heaven knows she was tipsy enough."

"What does that matter?" Evelyn spat. She was shaking so hard her jaw was juddering. There was Robert, fully dressed, and there she was in her nightdress. He hadn't even offered her his jacket. "Go and look for her."

"She's here," Vikram yelled from an upstairs window. "Found her."

Evelyn put her hand to her chest. "Is she all right?" she called back.

"She's fine," Vikram said. But there was something odd in his voice.

"You see?" Robert raised an eyebrow at her. "I told you."

Evelyn walked past him and went back into the glasshouse. The light from inside the house was bright against her eyes. Her nightgown was stuck between her legs, and grassy footsteps had been tracked on the floorboards through the hallway and up the stairs. Lily's bedroom door was open, and Vikram was sitting on the bed.

"Where is she?"

Vikram gestured to the floor on the other side of the bed. Lily was lying on the floor, facedown on a throw pillow. She had half undressed, and one of her pale breasts was pressed against the floorboards. A bottle of morphia was toppled on her bedside table, and a syringe lay in a saucer on the dresser.

"Oh my God," Evelyn said, running to her and putting her hands to Lily's neck.

"She's fine," Vikram said, lighting a cigarette. "She does this sometimes."

"But—"

"Look, she's got good colour, breathing's normal. She'll be fine."

Evelyn steadied her voice. "I think privacy would be good," she said, adjusting Lily's dress over her bosom. "Leave me with her." As gently as she could, she nudged Lily onto her side. Lily mumbled incoherently, making a sucking motion with her lips.

Robert was loitering in the doorway. "What's wrong with her?"

"Get Flossie for me, will you?"

Robert hovered.

"Go, Robert." Evelyn didn't even look at him.

Flossie's head appeared in the doorway to the bedroom, and she knelt by Evelyn's side. "Oh, dear."

Evelyn pointed to the morphia bottle, wordlessly.

Flossie rubbed Lily's feet. "She's warm enough. She'll be OK."

"Is this—is this usual?"

Flossie said nothing, so Evelyn turned to her.

"It's not unusual," Flossie said. Her mouth was pinched. "Here, let's get her on the bed, shall we?" Flossie pulled the blanket from the bed, and together they rolled Lily onto it. She indicated that Evelyn should take the top, and using it as a hoist, they lifted her onto the bed. Somewhere in the back of her mind, Evelyn was impressed with Flossie's ingenuity. Then she realised it probably wasn't her first time scooping Lily off the floor.

Flossie tucked the throw pillow next to Lily's body so she couldn't roll over. "There. She'll be fine. I'll check on her in an hour."

They looked at each other.

"Your slippers are all ruined," Evelyn said.

Flossie looked down at them and then raised her eyebrows. "Tonight's only victims. We can count ourselves lucky." She patted Lily's leg. "I'm going to go and slap Pups in the face. You can go on to bed if you like, I'll keep an eye on Lils."

Evelyn stood up, stiffly. She felt as if a month had passed since she was eating meringues in the drawing room.

In their bedroom, Robert was standing by the embers of the fire, drinking a glass of whisky.

"Don't you think you've had enough?" Evelyn said, her voice sharp.

Robert turned to her. She'd expected to see him puppyish and sorry, the wounded face he made when he knew he'd done something wrong. But he looked thunderous.

"You made an awful scene," he said.

A cold shard pierced Evelyn's chest. "Excuse me?"

"Don't embarrass me in front of these people, Evelyn."

"Embarrass you?" Rage surged through her veins.

"Carrying on like that."

Evelyn marched towards him and grabbed the glass from his hands. She almost threw it against the wall but stopped herself. That would only be proof of carrying on. "You could have got someone killed! Or yourself!"

Robert rolled his eyes. It was such a spiteful gesture that Evelyn took a step back. "No one was going to get killed."

Evelyn was trembling now. The whisky shivered in the glass. "Shooting guns in the dark? A safe occupation, is it?"

Robert sighed. He gave her a patronising smile. "I would've known."

"Known what?" In a single gulp, she drained the whisky glass and set it, hard, on the dressing table. "What would you have known?" She crossed her arms.

"The spirits would've told me," Robert said. "If Lily was hurt."

Evelyn gawped at him. "The spirits."

"Yes, Evie, the spirits. My guide."

Evelyn felt a cold terror slithering through her bowels. "Guide?"

"My spirit guide," Robert said, frowning at her as if she were an idiot. "He would've told me."

Her knees almost buckled. Evelyn sat down on the floor, heavily. She put her face in her hands.

"He always warns me, if something bad's about to happen."

Evelyn looked up at him. It was as if he were standing behind a pane of glass. "He?"

"He told me Lily was fine."

"He told you?"

"Aye, he told me."

Evelyn felt a rush of bile come into her throat. "How did he tell you?"

"What do you mean, how?" Robert said, irritably. "He said so."

"You saw—did you see something?"

"No, no, just his voice." Robert shrugged off his jacket. "Anyhow. You can't carry about making a fuss like tonight. Not in front of Vikram," he said, starting to undress.

Evelyn was shaking. "How often do you hear this voice?"

"What?" Robert said, absently, kicking off his shoes.

"Do you hear it right now? The voice?"

Robert sighed. "I don't need to," he said.

Evelyn swallowed. "Why not?"

Robert pointed into the corner of the room. "Because he's standing right there."

26

EVELYN WAS IN THE LIBRARY, PRETENDING TO READ,
when the servants came back at five thirty. She had hastily changed
into a day dress snatched from her luggage, and in the morning light
was painfully aware she had runs in her stockings. As a maid opened
the library door, Evelyn jumped. She collected herself, putting yesterday's paper aside and affecting a yawn. "Lovely morning, isn't it?"
she said.

"Yes, ma'am." The maid bobbed and knelt before the hearth. She
hesitated, a brush in hand. Evelyn recognised her cue to leave and
slunk into the hallway, where another young girl was swabbing the
floors. The scuffling sound of industry echoed through the rest of
the house: hot water pipes pinged as the boiler rumbled; the footman whistled in the dining room as he pulled back the blinds. There
was a screech as a maid discovered someone sleeping in an upstairs
bathtub. Quietly, Evelyn let herself out through the front door.

She hunched forward into the morning, her hands shaky in her
pockets, threads dancing in her peripheral vision. A man pushing a
wheelbarrow strode by and Evelyn flinched. As he passed, she hung
back, in case it was the groundsman from last night, but she didn't
recognise him. At the end of the path, she stopped and stared ahead.
Where was she even going? On her right was the gravel driveway,
the hedges either side gilded with yellow broom flowers. What if

she just started walking back up to the road? Just walked and walked and didn't stop. She could leave everything behind, every bad decision she had ever made. Evelyn rubbed her face. Behind her was the house. Robert. She looked towards their bedroom window, half expecting to see a shadowy face pressed against the glass. But the curtains were drawn. She pictured Robert, brushing fox fur from her dress, the gentlest touch on her shoulder. Her eyes burned. She couldn't abandon him, now, after everything. She didn't have the luxury of abandonment. Turning her back to the road, she trudged along the side of the house, through the orchard. Sparrows chirruped in the trees and the boughs were heavy with budding pears. The marshy turf at the edge of the river was twitching with ladybugs; a kingfisher swooped in a bow over the silver water. On the other side was a field with three chestnut horses, their flanks glossy with dew, their breath misty. Evelyn knew that it was beautiful, but she felt nothing. She closed her eyes. She pictured Dolly sitting next to her by the fire in her flat, her bun held in place with a blunt pencil. Evelyn focused on her face, the way her eyebrows pulled together when she was listening. *What do I do? Tell me what I'm supposed to do.* The image flickered, dimmed, disappeared. She opened her eyes. Why did she think she was going to get an answer, after shutting Dolly away for so long? She didn't deserve an answer.

Back at the house, Evelyn lingered by the door to the dining room, hoping that someone might be awake, that she would have a distraction. At that moment she even would have welcomed Bernice. But the room was empty. Breakfast had already been laid out along the back wall: tureens filled with scrambled egg, porridge with blackberry jam, toast, kedgeree, black pudding, sausages, rhubarb compote, teapots in knitted caps. Evelyn looked at the pots of tea and a nostalgic kind of despair churned inside her. How cosy and lovely the little teapots looked. How miserable she was. She sat at the table and made herself gnaw on a tattie scone. Suddenly, she was overcome by a spasm of hysterical hunger. She gobbled three pieces of toast, a heaping portion of kedgeree with chutney, two slices of smoked salmon, a red apple, and another piece of toast. She was just wondering if she could survive another piece of toast when Lily appeared in the doorway. Evelyn stood up, holding her crust to attention.

"Lily!"

"Morning, darling." She looked wan, her hair matted at the side. "Coffee," she said, more as a statement than a question.

Evelyn pointed to the pot. She sat down again, unable to look Lily in the eye. At once, she felt overstuffed and nauseous, her bowels tangled. She dropped the toast crust onto her plate. What was she supposed to say about last night? What if Lily knew about the spirit guide? What if all of them knew?

"I have a headache that could fell the Great Wall of China," Lily said. She pulled the cord and, when a maid appeared, said, "Gin and lime, please."

Evelyn fixed her attention on the toast rack, trying to control the bubbling in her stomach.

"Oh, don't be scandalised, darling," Lily said, nibbling a piece of parsley from the edge of Evelyn's plate. "I need it to get my engine running."

Evelyn looked at her. In the light from the window, Lily looked frail and rumpled. It was strange how little space in the room she seemed to take up in the morning, as if she shrivelled at sunrise.

"How was last night. Did it get rowdy? I woke up this morning and seem to have missed all the fun," Lily said.

Evelyn cleared her throat. "You slept through?"

"Apparently!" Lily said, cheerfully. "Although Vikram's damn parrot was in my room this morning. Scared me out of my wits."

"You didn't—" Evelyn paused. "You don't remember anything odd?"

Lily frowned. "Odd? Not other than being woken up by that owl dive-bombing my face. Flossie would have died on the spot."

Flossie. How would Evelyn begin to explain Robert's spirit guide to Flossie? Sweat tingled on her top lip.

Lily collected her gin and lime and her coffee. "I'm taking this up to bed with me," she said. "Toodle-oo." She kissed Evelyn on her forehead.

After Lily left, Evelyn pulled the window open, letting the breeze run through the collar of her blouse. She couldn't linger in the dining room all morning, wolfing down sprats and making small talk with bedraggled party guests. She took a deep breath before crossing the room and climbing the stairs to their bedroom. The door squeaked as she opened it. Robert was still fast asleep. She shifted her weight, peering into the corner at the far end of the room, near the fireplace. Robert's clothes, crumpled on the chair, the zebra-skin cushion lying on the floor. No sign of anything. Of anyone. She steeled herself before raising her gaze to the mirror. Only the top of their bed was reflected back, Robert's tie slung over the bed knob. She stepped back into the corridor and closed the door.

"Hello," Clarence said, from behind her.

Evelyn jumped. "Good grief, you frightened me."

Clarence surveyed her, his hands clasped in front of him.

"Robert's still sleeping." She didn't know why she'd said that; it was somehow just to fill the space. She shifted her weight. "Are you hungry?"

Clarence nodded.

"Well, there's a great spread downstairs," she said, with a horrible, forced jollity in her voice. At any moment she was in danger of using a word she never usually would: "spiffing," or "dashing." "Lots of porridge for a growing lad." She winced at herself.

"OK," Clarence said, starting down the corridor.

"Wait," Evelyn called after him. He turned. "Is your brother awake?"

"No, he's ill."

"Oh. Sorry."

"Why are you sorry?"

"I mean, I'm sorry to hear that. I was going to ask to drive back with you both, but if he's ill I won't bother to ask him. I mean, bother him to ask." Evelyn's face felt tight. Was this why Bernice was always flapping so much? Maybe it was a result of trying to converse with her moony sons all the time. There was something about them that demanded flapping to fill in all their queer silences.

"OK," he said. "I'm going to breakfast now."

"Clarence, wait." He stopped and gave her a cool, patient look. "Do you hear voices?" She hadn't known she was going to ask that until it came out of her mouth.

"Voices? No."

Evelyn licked her lips. "What about a spirit guide?"

"No." Clarence paused, as if he might have more to say. So she waited. "Some people do."

"But not you?"

"No."

Evelyn swallowed. "But what does it mean, to have a spirit guide?"

Clarence put a finger to the wallpaper and traced the outline of a damask flourish. "It's like having a personal spirit. They guide you through the spiritual realm. Give messages, protect you."

"Robert hears voices," Evelyn said. Her voice was steadier than she felt.

Clarence shrugged. "Some people do."

Evelyn picked at a piece of loose skin on her finger. "But it's not normal, is it, to hear voices?" She knew it was inappropriate, that she was talking to Clarence as a man, not as a child. "Houdini thinks anyone who hears voices is a madman."

Clarence was flicking the wooden panelling now. "He's right about some things."

"He is?"

"There are a lot of strange people in spiritualism. People who believe in fairies and leprechauns. And a lot of frauds."

"So—so even you think they're strange?"

Clarence blinked at her. His eyelashes were long, and his expression bored, contemptuous. "Yes. Don't you?"

Evelyn chewed her finger. "I suppose. I mean, I don't really know what to think."

Clarence sighed, as if he were profoundly disappointed in her. "I'm hungry," he said, turning and starting down the steps. Evelyn put her head against the wallpaper. She felt unwholesome. Soiled, like she wanted to scrub the top layer of her skin off.

She looked back at the door to their bedroom, and then straightened her shoulders, crossed the corridor, and knocked on Flossie's door.

"Come in."

"It's me." Evelyn put her face through the door. Flossie was sitting at the desk, writing a letter on monogrammed stationery.

"Is Pups awake?"

Flossie shook her head. "He was up at seven to be sick, and now he's back asleep."

"Oh."

Flossie blotted the ink. "Are you all right?"

"It's just—"

"Evelyn, come on in, you don't need to stand in the doorway."

She entered the room and stood with her hands behind her back, leaning against the doorknob. "It's just, I was hoping for a ride to Edinburgh."

Flossie looked at her for a long moment. "Why don't we go back together? Let the boys sort themselves out later?"

Evelyn thought of Robert, of the sort of conversation she would have to have with him, when he woke up. Her stomach gurgled. "Yes, please."

❖ ❖ ❖

EVELYN SLEPT FOR MOST of the ride back to Edinburgh, jolting awake only when Flossie beeped the horn to nudge a sheep that had jumped a slate wall and was ambling in the road. She came to herself as the motorcar slowed, thirsty, with a crick in her neck. Flossie was parking the car underneath a bank of plane trees in St. Ives Square. "Good morning," she said, with a smile.

"Sorry." Evelyn wiped her mouth. "I was a bad travelling companion."

"Not at all." Flossie got out of the car, gesturing Evelyn up towards a four-storey sandstone Georgian building. There were three bells by the front door, and a bulky dread settled in Evelyn's stomach as she saw "Janssen" was the top apartment. Eight flights of stairs later, Flossie flung open the door onto a dark foyer that smelt bitter and vibrant, like orange peel.

"I have a guest, Suzette," Flossie called into the hallway. She tossed her umbrella into a chipped ivory stand. "Suzette has been with us ever since Malacca. Mum and Papa wanted to keep her, but in the end they thought it would be good for Pups, if she stayed with us."

Evelyn nodded, trying not to show she was out of breath. How could anyone climb that staircase every day? No wonder both of them were so trim. She followed Flossie down a corridor lined with pretty but rather dull scenes of rural idyll—cows in streams, a mill, a sunset over a mill behind a cow in a stream. The room they entered at the end of the corridor was sparsely decorated. Two sofas sat along the back wall, and in the middle was a card table with a mother-of-pearl backgammon set. The curtains were a deep, mustard-coloured velvet with a darned patch at the bottom. An incongruously ornate rattan chair sat in the left-hand corner. She couldn't see either Flossie or Pups in the room. It was like they were lodging in an opera stage set.

"Have you lived here long?"

"Yes, since '21."

"Hmm," Evelyn said. "So homey." She sat on the left-hand sofa. It was meanly padded, and the coarse, bristly texture of horsehair scrunched under her thighs. At once, she was overcome with regret. She wanted to be at home, her own home. She wanted to crawl into her own soft bed, surrounded by the friendly comfort of her own things. And then she pictured Robert, pointing into the darkness: "He's standing right there." If something was trailing him, following him, it could already be at the house. Waiting. An eye, under the floorboards, watching her.

A door on the left opened and a short, brown-skinned woman wearing a black uniform entered, carrying a silver tea tray.

"Thank you, Suzette." Flossie smiled brightly. "Suzette makes the best coffee," she said, to Evelyn.

But Evelyn didn't want coffee. She wanted tea, and scones. And the newspaper. And a bath.

"Mr. Stephen?" Suzette said, pouring coffee into two miniature white porcelain cups.

"He'll be back later, he had a late night," Flossie said. She added something in what Evelyn now knew was Kristang. It was strange hearing Flossie in this other language, her face moved differently; she was given a new, gilded frame. It suited her. Flossie flicked through the telephone messages on the tray, and her lips tightened.

"Nothing urgent?" Evelyn said, hopefully. If Flossie had a pressing engagement, she could slip away without causing offence.

Flossie shook her head. "No, no." She said something else to Suzette, who nodded, and left the room.

Flossie finished her coffee and refilled her cup. "Exactly what I needed to put everything right."

With a suddenness that surprised her, a clatter of tears jangled up Evelyn's throat, her coffee cup clinking against the sugar tongs.

"Uh." Flossie looked around, panicked. "Oh, dear!"

"I'm fine." Evelyn wrestled back some self-control. "I'm fine, I'm sorry." She wiped her eyes with her sleeve. "Not enough sleep, that's all."

Flossie grimaced. "I feel partially responsible."

"You do? Whatever for?"

"Pups can be such a bad influence," she said. "He was probably behind the whole incident. He has no sense of his own safety. Or anyone else's."

Evelyn stared at her. In her haze of horror about Robert's spirit guide, she'd almost forgotten about the midnight shooting. "No, it's not Pups. Robert and I, he—" She swallowed. Saying it out loud would make it real. It would make Robert sound—it would make *her* sound—

A telephone began ringing in the hall, and Suzette's footsteps echoed along the corridor. "For you, Miss Florence," she said, around the corner of the door.

"Do you mind?" Flossie said. "It'll just keep ringing if I don't take it."

Evelyn shook her head, and as Flossie left the room, Evelyn stood up from the sofa. From the window she could see a man sweeping the steps of the communal garden. A startled pigeon rose in the air, wings arched. It was too sunny outside, too bright. It should have been raining and gloomy. It should have been as dreary and wretched as she felt. Restlessly, she paced the room, and let herself back into the corridor. Halfway down, she opened a door onto a neat study, with hardback philosophy books in a glass-fronted cabinet. A partially finished watercolour of a pineapple lay propped on an easel, with its prickly subject waiting in a copper bowl for its celebrity to be restored. Flossie had her whole life ready to be picked up again. Nothing had changed for her. She could just carry on, watercolouring pineapples and reading Hegel and drinking coffee. Carry on being normal. Evelyn crossed to the desk, where she straightened a stack of pamphlets for the Japanese Earthquake Fund. A round resin paperweight sat on the papers. Fronds of seaweed were imprisoned in the globe, little air bubbles moored in the weeds catching the light in gilt flickers. It was cold in her hands. Odd, the trinkets that people collect, the silly, meaningless objects that we give our love.

"Oh, I'm sorry," Flossie said, from the doorway, as if she had been the one trespassing.

"I like your painting," Evelyn said. Her mouth was dry.

"Can I get you anything?" Flossie said, gently. "Run you a bath? Suzette makes a fantastic potato omelette."

"No, thank you." Evelyn put the paperweight down. She wrapped her arms around her waist. "Do you believe in anything?"

Flossie started. She took off her glasses and polished them on the corner of her blouse, a tactic that Evelyn recognised as stalling for time. When she replaced them on her nose, she gave Evelyn a wary look, as if she were being baited. "I believe in science."

"Everyone believes in science."

Flossie looked doubtful. "I'm not sure about that."

"Do you believe in anything religious?"

Flossie blinked down at her desk. After a moment, she shook her head. "I don't think so, I'm sorry."

"Why are you sorry?"

"I suppose I'm not sorry." She frowned. "Is this—is this about Robert?"

Evelyn gave her a shrug.

Flossie took a breath. She crossed to the window and leant against the glass. The sunlight brushed a yellow stripe across her face. "There was this medium that Vikram was mad about for a while. Invited him everywhere. 'The Great Gupta.' Have you heard of him?"

Evelyn shook her head.

"He did séances and read palms, that sort of thing. Wore these purple turbans with a jewel in the front. Only he wasn't even Indian. He was a blond from Dundee. He had a black wig, greasepaint on his face. His real name was Christopher something."

"So?"

Flossie scrunched up her nose. "He made a fortune, dressing up like an Indian man. It made him exotic, alluring. He made a fortune, pretending to be brown. Gave him mystical credibility. Everyone gobbled it up. Even Vikram."

"But surely he knew?"

"Of course he knew! Everyone knew he wasn't Indian. Vikram didn't care. This man hung around Vikram's house for months with his beads and his gowns, and this accent." Flossie shuddered. "It was awful. The whole thing was painful to watch."

"But *you*—do *you* believe in anything?"

"My point," Flossie said, "is that Vikram wanted this man's powers to be real so badly that he ignored the lies even when they were grotesque. I can't do that. I can't accept truth that's dressed in lies."

"But the Bible . . ." She trailed off, weakly.

Flossie laughed, a short bark of a laugh. "After everything the world has seen in the last ten years, I don't know how anyone in their right mind could be religious." She looked out of the window.

Evelyn licked her lips. The coffee had left a bitter aftertaste in her mouth. "What if Pups said he saw an angel, you wouldn't believe him?"

Flossie's eyebrows twitched. "I don't believe half the things he says."

"But you know him better than anyone. If he swore to you, on his life, on your life, that he saw an angel, you wouldn't, even for a moment, wonder if it might be true?"

"No. No, I wouldn't. I'd assume absinthe was involved. Or opium."

"What if I said *I* saw an angel?"

"Did you?" Flossie turned to her sharply. Her pupils were tight and hard in the band of sunshine.

"No."

Flossie nodded, relieved. After a moment, she said, "And Robert?"

A knot of tears caught in her throat. "I don't know what is real and what isn't," she said.

Flossie took a step towards her, holding out her hands. "Maybe we could call a doctor?" she said gently. "I know an excellent psychiatrist, very discreet, a lovely older man."

"Maybe," Evelyn said. A nice, fatherly type, with a pocket watch and a garden full of prizewinning roses. A man who never had sons and talked about his patients as "his boys." "But how would I get Robert to agree to it?"

Flossie's eyes brightened. "I'll ask Pups to suggest it, or you could invite him round for dinner, casually, let them meet each other."

"I suppose," Evelyn said. Her palms started to sweat. She was going to tell her about Robert's spirit guide. Flossie would listen, she wouldn't judge Robert for needing help.

There was a knock at the front door, and Suzette's uniform flashed along the corridor.

"Damn." Flossie looked at her watch. "He's early. I told him four o'clock."

"That's fine," Evelyn said. "Maybe I should go home, anyway."

"Absolutely not! I'll be half an hour, I just need to get rid of him. Why don't you take a seat here, I'll ask Suzette to make some salmon sandwiches."

A man's tread echoed along the corridor, and as Suzette passed the open door, the visitor stopped short.

"Oh, here you are." It was Malcolm. He looked back and forth between her and Flossie. "Evelyn?"

Flossie had folded her arms. "I said four o'clock, Malcolm."

"I've been ringing all weekend," Malcolm said. "I don't want to wait any longer." Then, staring at Evelyn, he asked, "But how do you know each other?"

"Vikram," Flossie said, tossing her hand. "Have a seat in the parlour, I'll be through in a minute."

Malcolm stayed where he was. Slowly, Evelyn met his gaze.

"It was you," he said.

Flossie frowned at him. "Excuse me?"

"It was you. You were the one." He turned to Flossie. "She was the one, wasn't she? Who told you that story about the debts."

"What?" A speckled blush appeared on Flossie's neck. "It doesn't matter—and we're far beyond that argument now."

Malcolm's eyes blazed. "My God, it *was* you!" He took a step into the room. His body was taut, a purple tinge clouding the top of his ears. "What the hell is wrong with you?"

Behind him, Suzette froze. She said something in a high, panicked tone. Flossie put herself between Malcolm and Evelyn, her
hands on Malcolm's shoulders. "Mal! What's got into you?"

"Tell her!" Malcolm pointed at Flossie. "Tell her it was a lie, that
you made it up."

"Malcolm, really! Calm down!" Flossie nudged him aside, and
he looked down at her, the tension in his face relaxing.

"I didn't make it up," Evelyn said. Her voice was hoarse.

He rubbed his face, bitterly. "You're unbelievable. You rotten liar!"

"Malcolm, stop this! I'll have to get Pups," Flossie said, desperately.

"You were always like that, needing attention, needing to control everything. Dolly was always saying how fussy you were."

A cold, round nugget of pain zipped through Evelyn's body,
striking each of her organs in turn, like a game at a seaside carnival.

"Not good enough for your precious family, was I? And now
I'm not good enough for your friends, either?" His top lip curled. "I
never understood how Bobby put up with the lot of you."

"Don't take it out on Evelyn," Flossie said, sharply. "This has
nothing to do with her."

"I don't know where you get off, making out like I'm unsuitable.
I've got my own business." He turned to Flossie. "I've told you a hundred times it's my brother with the money troubles. I haven't even
spoken to him in two years. And she knows it, she's just spreading lies!"

"Your brother?" Evelyn said. Her voice was weak.

"You know damn well about Graeme. But you don't care, you
just don't want anyone to be happy, is that it?"

Graeme. Evelyn tried to cast her memory back to Malcolm's
family. He'd had a brother in the RAF, but that was all she remembered. "But—"

Flossie pointed at the door. "Malcolm, I'm serious, go and sit
next door right this moment."

Malcolm shot Evelyn a poisonous glare. "Shame on you, Evelyn.
Dolly would be ashamed of you."

As the door closed, Flossie gave her an astonished look. "I'm sorry, he's so headstrong. I don't know what has got into him. Are you OK?"

Evelyn nodded.

Flossie took off her glasses and then put them back on her nose. "I've never seen him like that." She blinked at Evelyn. "The debts—he's defensive, you can see that. Pups wanted to hire an investigator, but, Evelyn, I—you are sure, aren't you?"

"I—" Evelyn began. She couldn't find it in herself.

Flossie's body tightened. "You're not sure?"

Evelyn stuttered. "Robert," she said, at last.

"What do you mean? Does he do his accounts?"

Evelyn shook her head.

"Oh my God." Flossie put her hands to her temples. "From the spirits?"

"Clarence," Evelyn said. "They had a session together, at the Egyptian party."

Flossie sat heavily on the stool next to the bookcase. "But you *have* other proof."

Evelyn licked her lips.

"You have other proof, don't you? Your sister?"

Evelyn's throat was sore. "No, I—no."

Flossie looked up at her, her eyes pink around the edges, her lips drained of colour. "Oh, Evelyn," she said, softly.

"I'm sorry," she said. Her face was stinging. "I don't know—I thought—but then last night—I'm not sure what to think." She paused. She could tell her. She was going to tell her everything. Flossie was clever; she had an answer for everything. And she was kindhearted, all those societies. She would understand why Evelyn had had no choice back then, why she'd had no choice now. You had to fight for your safety, your happiness. Sometimes it meant making mistakes. Evelyn opened her mouth, and closed it again. It was like the moment by the river, earlier this morning, with Dolly. There was no way to explain herself. She didn't deserve an answer. She didn't deserve kindness.

Flossie was massaging her scalp.

"I should go," Evelyn said. She shuffled closer to the door. "I'll go home. You can have some privacy."

She was half expecting Flossie to try and stop her, but she just raised her head, and nodded. "Yes, I think that's for the best."

❋ ❋ ❋

EVELYN WALKED HOME IN a daze. Darting, mercurial clouds flickered over the rooftops. A circle of young boys in the park concealed their illicit Sunday football as she approached, freezing in postures of conspicuous innocence until she had passed. On Inverleith Row, she stopped at the railings outside Kitty's house. The crown of Kitty's head was visible in the parlour window, and then Alistair stood up, folding a newspaper under his arm. Evelyn took the steps and knocked on the door. Jeanie answered.

"Good afternoon, Jeanie." Evelyn realised she was hatless.

"Mrs. Hazard." Jeanie looked into the house, then back at Evelyn. "I'm not sure if Mrs. Fraser is here. I'll check for you."

Evelyn nodded, trying not to cry.

With an embarrassed expression, Jeanie shut the door slightly, and Evelyn leant her forehead against the wood. She heard Jeanie's footsteps on the tiles, and righted herself.

"I'm sorry, Mrs. Hazard; she's not here, as I thought."

"Will you tell her—" Her voice was rough. "Will you tell her I called?"

Jeanie nodded, beginning to close the door. Evelyn put a hand on the hinge. "And that, that I miss her."

Jeanie's mouth opened a little. She nodded.

Evelyn turned away before Jeanie could shut the door. She retraced her steps, along Inverleith Terrace, past the church, and then down along the Waters of Leith. The path was slippery with fresh, summery drizzle, and Evelyn let it soak into her hair. She passed the Colonies, and then wound through Stockbridge towards the market. The gutters were littered with debris from yesterday afternoon: spoiled cabbages, crumpled packets of cigarettes. A man in a ragged army greatcoat was picking through a discarded crate of green potatoes, and Evelyn looked away. On St. Stephen Place she stopped under the streetlamp opposite number two. Up on the other side of the street, a single light was on in the top flat. Evelyn closed her eyes. She would walk up to the door and ring the bell, and Dolores would come down the stairs, three at a time, a hole in her stocking. She'd take her up to her depressing, cramped little flat where it was always too warm. She'd force her to take a cup of tea and say something so horrible and mean and funny that Evelyn wouldn't be able to help but laugh. She pictured herself going to the door and putting her finger to the bell. Evelyn stood there in the street until the light in the window went out.

27

WHEN ROBERT RETURNED FROM VIKRAM'S, EVELYN leapt up and closed the guest bedroom door. She heard him first looking in the parlour and then the kitchen before he came up the staircase, calling her name. Pulling the sheet over her face, she clamped her eyes shut.

"Evie?" he whispered, opening the door. "What are you doing in here?"

She lay as still as she could.

"Evelyn?" Gently, he shook her shoulder.

She kept her breathing as relaxed and steady as possible. He was silent for a long moment. What was he waiting for? Acid rose into her throat. What if he started to talk to someone in the room? What if he could see his guide here, now? As the minutes went on, her pulse throbbed in her eyeballs. Still, he said nothing. Eventually, the hinge squeaked as he let himself out. She waited until she heard his footsteps along the hall, and then rose and crept, on tiptoe, to the door. Holding her breath, she grasped the key and, as softly as she could, turned it in the lock. Back in bed, she daren't put the light on in case he saw it. Instead, she watched under the door, where the shadow of his figure across the hall was flickering. She fell into an uneasy sleep, dreaming that she was groping through a hedge maze in the dark; somewhere at the centre of the maze, a baby was crying.

When she woke the next morning, it was past nine. It was a Monday, so Robert was likely already at work, but she dawdled in bed until she was certain she couldn't hear him in the house before dressing and going downstairs. The sun had come out, laying down a square of light by the window in the parlour, and absently, Evelyn raised the back of her dress, allowing the sun to warm her buttocks. Marty appeared in the doorway, holding the tea tray, and Evelyn yanked down her dress, pretending to search for a loose thread in the seam.

"Here you go, ma'am."

"Thank you, Marty." Evelyn reviewed her invalid's breakfast: weak tea and a dry piece of toast. She tapped her teaspoon against the cup, then let it fall to the saucer in a puddle of tea. In the coin of liquid, her own wavering eye reflected back at her.

Marty was loitering by the door. "So they'd closed off the bridge for nothing. Just awful," she was saying.

"Hmm," Evelyn said.

"And my sister said the police were around again this morning."

At the word "police," Evelyn broke out of her distraction. "Pardon? What did the police want with your sister?"

"Checking the coal shed again. She's had them there twice already."

"Checking your sister's coal shed? For what?"

Marty frowned. "For the wain." She gestured to the newspaper on the tea tray. "The laddie that went missing. Someone telephoned up, thought they'd heard a noise from in there. Only mice, it was."

"Oh." Evelyn stared down at her lap. "What does your sister's shed look like?" She now remembered the drawing session at Greg Bailish's atelier and wondered, for a moment, if the black spirals indicated a pile of coal.

"Well, like any coal shed, ma'am," Marty said.

"Of course."

Marty sighed. "The police'd be better off searching the water. I've said to her a hundred times, that's what you get, living by that river. Children will be drowning in it. And if she doesn't keep an eye on her wee ones, the same thing will happen to them. One minute they're there, next they're dead in the river." Marty was talking to herself now, walking along the corridor back to the kitchen.

Evelyn picked up the copy of the *Scotsman* from the tea tray and flicked through the pages. There it was, on page four, "Rewards Sought in Case of Missing Boy." Following a £5 reward offered by wee Charlie's local church, Edinburgh police had been overwhelmed by callers. One individual, a Mr. Murray, from Granton, claimed to have seen the boy sleeping by Portobello Boathouse, but when the police investigated, the individual identified proved to be a seal. The article was accompanied by another picture of the boy; this time, he was riding a donkey on a beach. Behind him, day-trippers paddled in the shallows by a pier next to a lighthouse. The boy had a confused, suspicious expression, as if he wasn't sure if he was being teased or not. His feet were bare, his toes pointing into the sand, and something about the naked arch of his foot made Evelyn's heart hurt. She looked closer at the picture. That sand—that lighthouse. It was Whitby.

"For my beloved," Oscar had said. On his palm was a silver ring set with a black stone. Evelyn drew back, almost toppling the jug of lemonade onto the picnic blanket.

"It's jet," he said, encouragingly. "Whitby jet."

Evelyn nodded. She knew what it was, but the shadowy gem made her think only of mourning.

"Here, allow me." Oscar slid the ring onto her finger, kissing her knuckle. "And once I've spoken to Mama, it shan't be long until we replace it with a different kind of ring." He smiled. "Ivy Cottage on the estate will need some time to be prepared."

The expression on her face must have given her away.

"What's wrong, isn't the ring to your liking? I know it's only small, but I thought it would be the perfect keepsake to commemorate how we met." He gestured over the hill towards the top of the lighthouse.

"It's very nice." Evelyn toyed with the stone. It looked like a tumour. She pictured herself sitting side by side with Oscar on his family's estate, endlessly debating the virtues of marmalade versus jam. "But what would we *do* here?"

He laughed. "What does one do anywhere?"

Evelyn smiled, but her face was tight. She picked up a jelly and let it wobble in her hands before placing it back on the tartan. "It would be a day's travel to visit with my family."

"Don't worry yourself about that, it won't be long until we have our own family," he said, lying next to her on the blanket. He stretched to caress her knee. "At least two boys, and a girl. Perhaps two girls. You like having sisters, don't you?"

Evelyn's blood turned to slurry. Every day of the rest of her life with Oscar. Living on his father's estate, talking of his father's money, bearing his children, raising his children. She looked down at his hazel eyes, the black curls, the dimple on his cheek. "Oscar, I think perhaps we are due a conversation."

Later, when the bombing strikes against the town were all anyone could talk about, Evelyn felt a silent, secret kind of relief. The Gaskells had emigrated to Virginia by then, so there was no danger to them personally, but it was like the fates were selecting to destroy the location of her closest mistake.

Evelyn ran her finger over the picture of the lighthouse. Her eyes were smarting. What if the boy was injured somewhere, calling out, and no one had heard him? With a snap of her wrist, she folded the newspaper and slumped back in the chair, reaching for her cup of tea. It was cold, but she forced herself to drink from it.

"Marty," she called, without getting up.

Marty appeared in the doorway. "Yes, ma'am?"

"So your sister knows the wee boy, the one that went missing?"

"Aye. He's the neighbour's bairn."

"How awful." She wanted to know more, but it also felt risky somehow, to get too close to the tragedy.

"That it is. Mind you, the police poking around in the coal shed every two days doesn't help either. Now everybody this side of Australia thinks they've seen the boy. If you ask me, he'll be hiding somewhere, too embarrassed to come back now, after all the carrying on. That, or he's dead."

"You should leave early today," Evelyn said. "Go, be with your sister."

Marty ran her thumbs along the pocket of her apron. "The stew needs making."

"Don't worry about the stew." Evelyn tossed her hand, and her teacup clattered against the saucer. "Go on now. It's the least we can do to be helpful. We'll see you back tomorrow."

Evelyn watched from the parlour window as Marty made her way down the road, and got to her feet. Slowly, she opened the door to Robert's study. On his desk was a tin of barley-flavoured boiled sweets and she picked one out, letting it rattle behind her teeth. She took a deep breath and pulled open the bottom drawer of his desk. His blue notebook was filled with scribbles and doodles. Loops and circles, a few telephone numbers. A cruel, but surprisingly accurate, caricature of Mrs. Wrigley across the street. And his notes. At least, they appeared to be notes. Half-written sentences, abstract words. "A sense of foreboding around the 5th August." And later, "Water? Drowning/can't breathe. Child. Litening strikes." There was a horrifying drawing of a sort of fiery angel, with lacy wings. She went through the rest of the book. "Sufocation, or smothering"; "Bridge unsafe"; "Death by bees." Her stomach roiled. This Dadaist collage of horrors. This was what occupied Robert's brain? This was what he was doing, in his study—scribbling about drownings? Inking ghoulish illustrations of angels?

Leckie's coal truck rolled by the window and Evelyn sat up with a fright, pushing the notebook back into the drawer. She climbed the stairs and paced their spare bedroom, chewing on her finger. She would know, wouldn't she, if Robert was insane? She would know if he was unwell. His messages were so accurate—there *was* something there. There had to be! Fine, so Malcolm's brother was the one with the debts. Well, that was close, wasn't it? Messages from the spirits were confusing, weren't they? It wasn't her fault the message wasn't exactly correct. She gave Flossie the information she had, and Flossie made her own decision about what to do with it. A vinegary taste rose in the back of her throat. But it hadn't been Robert's message, about Malcolm. It was Clarence who had known about the debts. But even so. Evelyn straightened the lampshade next to the bed. Yes, it was true, she had been frightened when she saw Malcolm. She'd been worried, yes. But that wasn't why she'd told Flossie about the debts. Her stomach bubbled, and she coughed up a belch of air. No, she was looking out for Flossie's best interests, that was all.

Evelyn pictured Robert, his cheeks flushed, irritated, matter of fact: "He's standing right there." An involuntary shudder passed through her body, and for a moment, she thought she might retch. That was all part of it, wasn't it? Connecting to the spirit world. Receiving wisdom. Maybe Robert got confused sometimes, but he wasn't demented. Was he?

She came back downstairs and roamed the corridor for some minutes, before finally picking up the phone and asking for the connection to Dr. Greitzer's surgery.

"He's just going out for lunch," his receptionist said, "but I may be able to—" She broke off abruptly. Evelyn heard the tapping of shoes on tiles, and then, a moment later, Dr. Greitzer's voice.

"Afternoon, Mrs. Hazard."

Evelyn gripped the receiver. "Oh, thank God, Doctor."

"What can I do for you, Mrs. Hazard?" Evelyn could hear in his voice that he was distracted. There was a faint scratching sound, and she had the sense he was signing papers.

"It's Robert," Evelyn said. "I think he may need your help."

The scribbling stopped. "Bobby? How can I be of assistance?"

Perversely, she was satisfied that she had his attention now. "I've heard him talking to himself before, at least, I thought it was himself. On Christmas. And I thought, I don't know what I thought. But now—"

"Mrs. Hazard, talking to yourself is hardly an illness," he said, with an avuncular chuckle. "Or else most of the country would be in grave danger. Myself included."

"No, you don't understand." She squeezed the earpiece. "It's not just talking. Now it seems it's a person. An imaginary person!"

"Yes, Mrs. Hazard, well, an imaginary friend is not necessarily something to get yourself worried about. Unless, is his friend instructing him to burn down the house? Or murder the King?"

"No, no," Evelyn said, shaking her head until her hair rustled against the earpiece. "No, nothing like that. He says he's given warnings, if something bad is about to happen."

"That does sound useful," Dr. Greitzer said.

"But it's not just that. I found these drawings of angels, monstrous angels. And these notes—lightning strikes!" She took a gulping breath. "Death by bees!"

"Mrs. Hazard, calm down." Dr. Greitzer said.

She gritted her teeth. "I'm perfectly calm, it's Robert who is uncalm!"

"Mrs. Hazard." Dr. Greitzer's tone sharpened. "Perhaps you should take some time away to relax. A week in the countryside, maybe."

"No, I don't need to relax. And when we called you here and you saw him, you said he'd be better soon, after he'd slept, but he's slept plenty and since then he's only become stranger. And I encouraged him, or I didn't stop him, because I thought it *seemed* true. It *was* true, somehow, but now—and I don't know . . ." Evelyn trailed off, aware that she had been rambling. "I'm worried about him," she said, finally.

"Mrs. Hazard, in this moment, you're the one I'm worried about," Dr. Greitzer said, gently. "Why don't you let me write you a prescription for some Luminal, it'll help you sleep."

A horrible chill ran over her. "There's nothing wrong with me."

"Of course not," Dr. Greitzer said.

"It's *Robert* who's acting odd. I don't need help."

"Not help, but a little rest, perhaps."

"No, I don't need a little rest."

"Why don't I call over and see you this afternoon?" She heard the clink of his watch chain against his cuff links. "I could make some time between—"

"No thank you," she said. "I'll be out then. I'm going out. Thank you, goodbye." She pressed the lever, and stood breathing, into the static.

"Would you like another connection?" The operator's voice made her jump. Evelyn pictured her cold, pretty ear listening at the receiver and prickled with shame.

"Yes please," she said, and asked for Kitty's extension. When Jeanie answered, it took a long few minutes before Kitty came to the phone.

"It's me," Evelyn said.

"Yes, Evie, I know it's you," Kitty said, with a hint of amusement in her voice.

"Can we meet? Please?"

Kitty sighed.

"Please." Evelyn's voice broke.

"Mama is here," Kitty said. "We were about to go for a walk at the Botanics."

"That's fine, that's good, that's great. I can meet you there."

Kitty paused, and Evelyn crossed her fingers. "At the gate in half an hour?" Kitty said.

"Yes, yes, thank you."

✦ ✦ ✦

FORTY-FIVE MINUTES LATER AND Evelyn was pacing back and forth in front of the East Gate, nibbling her finger. When Kitty appeared, she was pushing the perambulator, Mama walking beside her in a new gingham jacket.

Mama embraced her. "Evelyn, finally. I was beginning to forget what you looked like."

Evelyn squeezed Mama, tighter than usual. "I missed you, Mama."

"Hmm," Mama said. "Not enough to sort out that Bobby of yours, apparently."

Evelyn pulled back, already exhausted. "Must we begin so soon, Mama?"

Kitty offered her cheek for a kiss, which Evelyn provided. She peered down into the pram. Margaret grabbed for her nose, blowing a bubble of spit. Dutifully, Evelyn kissed the baby, with a treacherous disappointment that they hadn't left her with Abigail.

They strolled towards the pond in silence. At the fence, a nursemaid was helping a boy in buckled shoes to scatter bread crumbs for a swan through the bars. Evelyn hoped that Mama didn't remember the fence was only put up after Dolly fell in while feeding the ducks, or it would make her even more maudlin than usual. She raised her hand to her mouth, but Mama seized it, tutting. "Evelyn, really? Still chewing on your fingernails?"

Evelyn put her hand behind her back.

They followed Kitty up onto the slope where the rhododendron bushes were blooming.

"I saw a picture, I think, of Robert, in *Pictorial*," Kitty said, at last. Evelyn turned to her. Her tone was pleasant, but detached. "At the Beauchamp Rooms for a jazz evening."

"That, yes." Evelyn hesitated, wanting to bring up the photograph of her at the Egyptian party. She wanted Kitty to see it, to acknowledge that Dolly would have liked it. But it wouldn't be the same if she had to force it.

"I don't know how you girls enjoy that music," Mama said. "Impossible to dance to."

"I think my dancing days are behind me," Kitty said, with a smile. Evelyn felt stung. Did she mean it as a rebuke? That she was too old to be dancing, making a fool out of herself?

"And have you—" Kitty began, but Evelyn interrupted her.

"I saw Malcolm."

"Malcolm?" Kitty said, looking to Mama.

"Malcolm Holmes?" Mama frowned.

"Yes of course, Malcolm Holmes," Evelyn said, irritably. "I've run into him a couple of times, now."

Kitty sniffed. "That's unfortunate."

"And is he still running that business?" Mama said. "What was it, horses? Raising them or racing them or something."

"Apparently, yes." Evelyn swallowed. "He was due to be remarried."

There was a moment of silence.

"Is that so?" Mama's lips tightened. "Well, let's hope the next girl he meets has more common sense than to say yes."

"That's not fair," Kitty said, gently. "It was hardly *his* fault that Dolly went off him."

Evelyn was startled. Kitty, talking back to Mama?

Mama pouted. "Perhaps not. So foolish of her, though."

"Not foolish," Kitty said. "Romantic. Like you, Evie."

And before Evelyn knew what was happening, she was crying.

"I'm sorry," Evelyn said, into her sleeve.

"Oh my goodness! What's wrong?" Kitty said.

Evelyn shook her head. "Nothing."

"Mama, will you push the baby for a minute?"

Mama gave them both a hard, suspicious look, but after a moment she sighed, taking hold of the handle. "Fine. Have your secrets."

Kitty steered Evelyn towards the nearest bench. "What's wrong? Is it"—she lowered her voice—"is it Robert?"

Evelyn nodded.

"Is he not behaving?"

"I don't even know anymore." Evelyn pulled out her handkerchief and dabbed her face. "I thought I understood him, but I'm not sure." She sucked down breaths in big, greedy mouthfuls. "Death by bees!" she managed, eventually.

Kitty grimaced. She glanced over to where Mama was jiggling the pram. A pair of swifts were dipping in and out of the pool, shaking beads of water from their feathers. She looked back at Evelyn. "Are you getting enough sleep?"

"Sleep? Yes. Well, maybe not. Last night I thought I should stay up, to listen, you know."

Kitty cleared her throat. "Evie, why don't we go to my house, and Jeanie can fix you a lemonade? A nice bath, tidy up your hair." Evelyn felt Kitty's eyes travelling over her hair, and she put her hand to her head.

"I'm not—no, it's not *me*," Evelyn said, with more venom than she'd intended.

Kitty gave her a sympathetic smile. "Take a nice, calm breath."

Evelyn obliged.

"What has changed? Since the last time we spoke?"

"I don't know. Not much, objectively. He was shooting at night, out at Vikram's estate."

"Boys and their guns," Kitty said, rolling her eyes.

"No, it wasn't like that." Evelyn tried to find the right words. She felt suddenly removed from Kitty, like they were different species, facing each other in an exhibition room. Robert's spirit guide now seemed so bizarre, so grotesque, it would be like admitting to a byzantine kind of crime. "It was horrible. He was acting so strangely, more strangely, even, than he has been."

"But what has he done?" Kitty said.

"Well, he hasn't *done* anything," Evelyn said, her voice hoarse. "It's just—how much abnormal does it take to cancel out a lot of normal?"

Kitty patted her shoulder. "Oh, dear."

Evelyn looked desperately into her eyes. "He *is* normal, isn't he?"

"Of course he is."

"You do think so, don't you?" Evelyn twisted her handkerchief, willing to be convinced.

"Yes, I do." Kitty took a breath. "And actually, I've been thinking a great deal, and I owe you an apology," she said. "For what I said before. I didn't mean to be cruel."

Evelyn burst into a fresh spasm of tears. She gripped Kitty. "I'm sorry, too, I didn't mean it, any of it." And she renounced all the resentment and annoyance, although she could still feel it lingering over them, like a bad odour.

"I understand now that Robert is only trying to help people."

Evelyn nodded. "He is, isn't he?"

"Yes, of course he is."

"And I'm right to support him, aren't I?"

"Absolutely, you are," Kitty said. "He's been a good, solid husband to you."

Evelyn pictured Robert as a statue, carved out of pine. Sturdy, reliable. He *had* been a solid husband. A good, solid husband.

"And you've had all sorts of lovely jaunts," Kitty said. "Treasure hunts, the Cadogan Club."

Evelyn looked at her, surprised. She felt a sting of something like sorrow. Kitty had been following her social calendar? How? Marty and Jeanie must have been gossiping. Evelyn felt her bowels contract. What else had Marty seen and overheard?

"I think, maybe, I was a little envious," Kitty said, looking down at her gloves.

"Envious?" Evelyn croaked. "Of what?"

"The parties. Meeting important people. Doing something I can't understand. And you never invited me. I suppose I felt a bit left behind."

Evelyn stared at her. "But you didn't need an invitation. You could have come with us anytime," she said, and now she saw all her plans differently. Kitty, in costume at the Egyptian soirée. Kitty, at the opera, pearls gleaming at her throat.

Kitty chuckled. "I don't think I'd be much good on roller skates.

And the truth is, I don't have as much energy as I used to. It's a shame . . ." she paused.

Evelyn held her breath, hoping that Kitty was going to finish her thought; that she was going to say something about Dolores. Kitty licked her lips. "Dolly would have loved all of that," she said.

Evelyn nodded, not trusting herself to speak. She ached for her to say more.

"Anyhow, I realised, you know, I have my family." She touched her stomach, in a meaningful way. "And this is what you have."

Evelyn's chest squeezed.

"I'm expecting again!" Kitty said.

"Oh." Evelyn's eyes throbbed in their sockets. "I'm so pleased for you." She reached out and embraced her, tight. But it was as if Kitty were travelling on a train that Evelyn was watching pull farther out of the station. "That's very happy news," she said, as convincingly as she could manage.

Kitty smiled, a real, delighted smile, and Evelyn was sorry that she'd been so easily fooled.

"And it made me understand that you need to have your occupations, as well," Kitty said. "People will say what they're going to say." She shrugged. "But we've pulled through gossip before. And you and Robert, well, you're doing your part. So even if he's acting a bit eccentric, well, just weather the storm."

"Yes," Evelyn said. "Weather the storm. I can do that. I can weather a storm." She saw herself steering a chipped sailboat through dark waters. Ahead, waves crashed onto the warm sands of a Mediterranean island.

"All this will pass, anyhow, when it's time to settle down."

Evelyn snapped back to attention. How was she supposed to reply to that? She was settled. They were already settled. She resisted the urge to say something prickly, and nibbled her finger instead.

"And of course, you know about Alistair's nightmares."

Evelyn nodded.

"What I mean to say is, all the boys have odd moments now, don't they? Strange frights. Panicky spells. It doesn't mean they're unhinged," Kitty said.

Evelyn let out a breath, the tight place in her chest finally unwinding. Perhaps all this talk of spiritual guides was only that. A heightened sense of feeling. A modern man, reacting sensitively to the modern age.

Mama approached, pushing the pram. "The birds here are so fat," she said, as if they had just been talking about it. "It's the fault of all those old men who had nothing better to do during the war except come here to feed them."

Evelyn and Kitty shared an exhausted look. "Mama, I think all the birds are dead that were here during the war," Evelyn said.

"Well, they should put a sign up. Terrible to be feeding those birds starches, imagine what the tourists think, with all these fat birds."

"What tourists?" Evelyn said.

"Anyway, I need to sit down. Whatever you are whispering about, you'll just have to tell me."

"We're not whispering, Mama." Kitty put her hand on Mama's arm.

Mama raised her eyebrows. "Robert again, I suppose?"

Evelyn shrugged.

Mama lifted the baby out of the pram and peered at her face. "Did you give her the liniment?"

"Yes, Mama, at one."

"One a bun and four to come," Mama said, then she laughed.

Kitty laughed too, and Evelyn forced a smile at their private joke, her face pulsing.

"You're not divorcing him, are you?" Mama said, suddenly.

"What?"

"Robert. We can't have another divorce in the family—people already think we've gone to Gomorrah."

Evelyn pressed her fingernails into her palms.

"That would never happen," Kitty said, sounding alarmed. "Robert's helping people! And you know how much Evie loves to help."

"I do?"

Kitty laughed. "Yes, of course you do. You should have been a nurse or a headmistress. Getting everyone in shape."

Evelyn smiled. She quite liked the idea of herself as a headmistress. A line of young girls, all smartly dressed, their heights measured against a wall. Marching up and down a courtyard, conjugating Latin verbs.

Mama patted her knee. "Don't worry about Robert, he'll settle down in the end. You both will."

Evelyn didn't reply.

Mama leant closer. "You've got awful dark shadows under your eyes. Are you getting enough iron?"

"Yes, Mama."

"Too much champagne, that'll do it. It's ageing for the skin, you know, French champagne. It's the acids."

"No, Mama, I haven't had too much champagne."

"Get Marty to make you some of her Cullen skink when you go back home. That'll mend you right up."

"Marty's not there," Evelyn said.

Kitty and Mama frowned. Their expressions were so identical Evelyn almost laughed.

"Her mother, again?" Kitty said, pursing her lips. "Surely she can't expect to—"

"No, no," Evelyn said. "Her sister lives in the Colonies. I gave her the afternoon off because of that missing boy."

"That poor wee lad," Kitty said, breathlessly.

Mama shook her head. "I can't believe how slow the police have been."

"Mama has been calling every day to see if Alistair has updates," Kitty said.

"Why on earth would Alistair have updates?"

"He might hear something at work," Mama said, defensively.

"How would a railway engineer hear anything about a missing child?"

"Only ten, he is," Mama continued. "But what can you expect, in those tenements? He's probably been down the mines since he could crawl."

Evelyn laughed, and then stopped herself, as Mama's mouth fell open, appalled. "Mama, he's the son of a greengrocer. Probably weaned on oranges. It's just bad luck, that's all."

Mama tutted. "It's an epidemic, child snatchers. The Lithuanians take them, you know."

"I don't think so, Mama," Evelyn said. "There was that boy who ran away last month, and he was only visiting his cousin on Skye."

Kitty gave her a pitying look. "Oh Evie, you wouldn't understand. You're not a mother."

Evelyn bit the inside of her cheek.

"The idea of a missing child—it's like losing half your body," Kitty said.

Mama was nodding, solemnly. "You'll understand when you have a family."

"I have a family," Evelyn said, woodenly.

"Yes, but a *real* family. It's a whole different kind of love," Kitty said.

"I know how to love!"

Kitty waved her hand. "Not like this. It's—and when you imagine another mother . . ." She stopped, putting her hand to her throat.

Mama reached out and held Kitty's hand.

"Yes," Evelyn said, watching their intertwined fingers. "Well, I can still imagine how it feels. I still have empathy."

"I can't even read about children being in trouble, or injured."

"And I can?"

"Oh, Evie," Kitty said, a hint of exasperation in her voice, as if Evelyn were being deliberately obtuse. "I just mean it doesn't affect you in the same way, it isn't on your mind all the time."

Evelyn pictured the boy on Whitby Beach, the arch of his bare foot. Clarence's cold hand in hers in the darkness of Vikram's garden. She thought of the baby, crying, at the centre of the maze. "It is on my mind," she said.

"Of course." Kitty patted Evelyn's knee. "You just don't *care* as much."

Lightning crackled inside her. She sat up straight on the bench. "As a matter of fact, I do care. Many of my friends have been involved in helping with the search. The artist Greg Bailish?" Her cheeks flared, as she imagined what Kitty and Mama would make of Greg Bailish's particular attempts to help.

Mama squinted. "I haven't heard of him. Not one of those nude painters, I hope?"

"And I myself will be arranging a charity collection for the family. To help," Evelyn heard herself say.

"You are?" Kitty blinked at her.

"Yes. I shall be organising it with my friend Florence, she works with all of the Edinburgh charities. And Margrit, who is a countess. And Vikram, the Hero of the Highlands. He knows everybody. Influential."

"Good for you, Evie." Kitty squeezed her leg. "That's exactly what you need, something to keep you busy."

"Yes," Evelyn said, forcing a tight smile. "You know me, keeping myself busy until Robert and I get settled."

28

AFTER SHE LEFT KITTY AND MAMA, EVELYN COULDN'T face going straight back to the house. She strolled aimlessly through the West Gate of the Botanics as the sun trailed behind her, stretching her shadow onto the paving stones. The wind picked up, tweaking leaves off the trees, scattering yellow laburnum flowers into the road. On Boswall Drive, she hopped a puddle, hearing as she did the clink of a penny falling through the lining of her pocket. She looked down at it, swimming in the fetid liquid. Was it worth putting her hand in the puddle to retrieve it? Sitting in front of one of the new houses on the other side of the road was a man in an army greatcoat selling song sheets, and their eyes met. She was aware he had seen her deliberate, and was now compelled by shame not only to retrieve the penny but to walk across the road and set it in his cap. Too embarrassed now to pass him again to go to the oceanfront, she turned and went home. When she arrived, it was past six, and the house was empty. She washed her hands several times, then even though it was mild, she set and drew in the fire in the parlour with yesterday's *Scotsman*. Taking a seat in the armchair, she put her hands in her lap, and resolved herself to wait for Robert.

He came through the door just before seven, shaking a twig from his hat. "Blustery out there," he said.

Evelyn stared at him, trying to evaluate who was standing in front of her. Her good, solid husband? A lunatic? Or was there something else entirely, something malicious, lurking in his heart? But he just looked exactly as he always did, except his cheeks were pinched pink from the wind, and his nose was running.

"Where's Marty? Nearly tripped on that carpet beater again," Robert said, taking off his coat.

"It's her half day. Will you come in here?"

He looked at her oddly, but took a seat in the other armchair. The clock on the mantelpiece chimed the hour, a messenger boy rattled past the window on a bicycle. Evelyn licked her lips, hearing, in the stillness of the room, the movement of her tongue around her mouth.

"This weekend," she began, but Robert cut her off.

"This weekend was a disaster."

Relieved, she looked up at him. "You agree?"

"You won't do that again, will you?"

"Excuse me?"

"It was humiliating, Evie, getting scolded by my wife like that."

Evelyn's skin prickled. "I humiliated *you*?"

"Fussing in front of Vikram." Robert waved his hand.

Her eyes were watering. "Shooting into the dark? Bringing a child out with you? Dragging that poor groundskeeper out of his bed?"

Robert laughed. It was a pompous, cruel laugh. "His job is to be taken out of bed. He's lucky to be employed in the first place."

Evelyn shook her head. "That isn't the point." She measured her breath. "I'm worried that this is not—that you are not healthy."

Robert leant back in his chair. "So you're the minister for health now?"

"Robert, please." Evelyn's eyes filled with tears, and at once, he lost the cruel mask. Her abashed, puppyish husband was back.

"My love, please don't cry."

Evelyn wiped her face, relieved that he had broken out of his callousness. That he was recognisably the good, solid version of himself. "I'm frightened," she said, in a small voice.

Robert reached over and took her hand. "Of what, my love?"

After a moment, she said, "Of you."

Robert chuckled, and then stopped. His expression sharpened. "What do you mean?"

"The spirit guide," she whispered. Evelyn was aware of watching him, but neutrally, as a camera might. She could see the filaments in his eyeballs, the crumpled handkerchief sticking out of the top of his trouser pocket.

Robert looked down at his lap. "He told me not to tell you."

An icy trickle ran down her spine. "About him?"

He nodded. "He said you wouldn't understand." He leapt up, and Evelyn shrank back from him. "But you do understand, don't you, Evie?"

"I . . ." She trailed off. There was no possible way to finish that sentence.

He stooped to look earnestly at her face. "You do understand, don't you?"

Evelyn put her hand on his cheek. He hadn't shaved yesterday, and his whiskers were bristly on her palm. "Explain it to me," she said.

Robert's face relaxed and he sat down in his chair, motioning for her to sit on his knee. Reluctantly, she climbed onto it.

"It's a man, that you see?"

Robert thought for a moment. "It's more like I have a sense of him, than I see him. I just know when he's trying to tell me something."

"Is he here now?" she whispered, into the parting of his hair.

"No," Robert said. "I don't know where he gets to before dark."

"But at night?"

"Oh, he's around at night." Robert leant back in the chair. "Last night I felt for sure he was in the room."

Evelyn shuddered. "Our room?"

"Yes, the bedroom."

"And?"

"He was just sort of hovering by the bed, watching."

She swallowed. "You're sure it wasn't a dream?"

"It's hard to tell sometimes," Robert said. When he turned his face to look at her, there was a puffiness around his eyes that she hadn't noticed before. She felt a little dart of sympathy for him. If he really was seeing spirits, how horrifying it would be, to have even his dreams invaded.

"What does it look like?" she said.

"Well." Robert cleared his throat. "He looks rather like me."

Evelyn bit the inside of her cheek. "Does it tell you things?"

"Of course." Robert frowned.

"What kind of things?"

Robert jiggled his knee. "He reassures me, provides sympathy, advice, that kind of thing."

Evelyn took a deep breath. "So, it's more like a manifestation of your conscience."

"If you like." His tone was exhausted now, almost diffident.

Evelyn looked at him. "But you can understand, can't you, why this would seem strange?"

"Not really," he said, wrinkling his nose. "Not after everything you've seen. Not now that you believe in the spirits too."

Evelyn nibbled her finger.

"Evie?"

The evening when they were shooting into the dark like that, it felt like all of them—Lily, Vikram, Walter, Robert—as if they were all madmen. That they had all gone insane, and they'd done it so stylishly that Evelyn hadn't even noticed. "Yes," she whispered. But an uneasy tickle of doubt lingered in her belly. Was it possible, like Flossie had said, that she saw what she wanted to see? But Robert's readings, the things he knew! Clarence's cool precision, the level of detail in his messages! It wasn't a guessing game. She had felt it— felt something, drawing closer. She pictured the carved *D*, growing warm under her fingertip.

"Yes, I do," she said, again, with more conviction.

"Then surely it makes sense I'd have a helping hand, on the other side?"

Evelyn hesitated. "I suppose so."

"And it never bothered you until I mentioned it."

He was right. If he hadn't told her about the spirit guide, she would have carried on, quite happily. That dark night with the guns would have been an inebriated mistake. A young set getting carried away.

"Robert, it's important that you don't keep anything from me," Evelyn said, looking into his swollen eyes. As she said the words, she felt a sickening sense of her own hypocrisy. "We need to be allies. No surprises."

"No, I promise, no surprises," Robert said, reaching and tucking her hair behind her ear.

"And can you ask it to stop?" she said. "Not let it come to you?"

"I could try," Robert said, with a grimace, "but it would affect my readings. All the great mediums have a spirit guide."

"Not Clarence."

Robert nodded. "That's true. He's a genius, though, Evie. I'm not a genius. I need help. I need help from the spiritual side." He leant forward, kissing her neck, her cheek, her jaw, her forehead. "And I need your help."

There was a hard lump in her throat.

"You know that I need you."

"I know," she said, softly.

"I'll try and put him off, I'll do whatever you like. Only, I don't understand." Robert paused, his eyes watering. "Don't you trust me, Evie?"

Evelyn looked at him for a moment. On one side, a gravel pathway, leading up to the road. On the other, the house, the curtain drawn across a darkened bedroom. She pulled his head against her shoulder. "Of course I trust you."

29

THE NEXT MORNING, WHEN EVELYN AWOKE, HER NECK was stiff, her limbs aching, as if she were recovering from a long illness. From the gap between the curtains, she watched a black cat slinking along the fence and towards the chicken coop.

She nudged Robert. "It's gone six, Robert. Your birds will need feeding."

He moaned. "Already?"

"Yes, come on, Marty will make you a lovely cup of tea." With effort, she propped herself up in the pillows and took a large sip of water from the glass on her bedside.

Robert groaned, rolling to the edge of the bed, where he sat for some minutes, scratching his scalp. Evelyn retrieved the long-abandoned biography of Brahms from her nightstand and pulled from between the pages yesterday's copy of the *Scotsman*.

"Look at this." She opened it to page four.

Robert yawned. "Do you *need* more galoshes?"

"No, not the advertisement." She tapped the page. "Wee Charlie."

Robert put the paper on the bed and stretched, his shoulder joint cracking.

"Marty is distraught, her sister was close with the boy's family." She wasn't sure why she wanted to elevate Marty's relation to the tragedy, but somehow it felt important to place it in the right category of near, but not too near.

Robert tutted, sympathetically.

"I saw Kitty yesterday, and she said everyone has been talking about it."

"I'm sure they have."

Her stomach wobbled in an odd way, as if she were riding a bicycle too close to the kerb. She took a breath. "I think we should get involved. You should talk to Vikram, see what he can do."

Robert turned and frowned at her. "About Kitty?"

"About the boy." Evelyn shook the newspaper. "Put pressure on the government. Demand answers!"

"Answers about the boy?"

"Yes, Robert."

"If you like, Evie." He searched her face. "Would it make you happy?"

There he was: the good, solid man. "I keep picturing him out there; a wee boy, with no one to help him . . ." She trailed off.

Robert's face was solemn. "I didn't think of it that way."

"He's so young, Robert," Evelyn said, trying to keep the quiver out of her voice.

"Not that much younger than Clarence," Robert said. "And look at him, out in the world!"

Evelyn put her hand on his knee. "This is different. Clarence has lots of adults to look after him."

Robert gave her a sad smile. "That must be nice."

"You know the police don't take these things seriously," Evelyn said. "Children in harm's way. But *we* could help him."

Robert squeezed her hand. "You're right, my love. I should have thought of it myself. I'll see what we can do to help."

After Robert left for work, she called Mrs. Downie at the hall and requested a collection to be arranged on Sunday for the family of Charlie McBride. She walked along the Waters of Leith to the

Colonies and strolled around, not sure what she was looking for. It was nice enough, really. All the front gardens trim and planted with geraniums, the windows spotless. When a redheaded child kicked a muddy ball in her direction near the Gleongle Baths, Evelyn reconsidered the sacrifice of her outfit and turned for home. When she returned, she drew a bath and washed her hair. She took her time with her toilette, working up the nerve to call Flossie. Eventually, her hair was dry, brushed, and set, and she had run out of excuses. She positioned herself by the telephone and steeled herself before requesting Flossie's extension.

"It's Evelyn."

"Oh, hello."

"How are you?"

"I'm fine."

There was a horrible pause. They both started to talk at the same time.

"Evelyn, I'm not sure what to—"

"I'm sorry about what happened," Evelyn said, swallowing. Flossie fell silent, so she took courage. "I know the information about Malcolm wasn't correct, but it wasn't completely wrong either, was it?"

"What do you mean?" Flossie's voice was flat.

"Well, if his brother has debts, then the message was almost right. You know, sometimes these things get confused." Evelyn twirled the phone cord around her finger.

Flossie took a deep breath. "Evelyn, I really don't want to talk about this. In fact, I'm not sure that I want to be talking to you at all at the moment."

"I know you're annoyed," Evelyn said.

"Annoyed?" Flossie laughed, bitterly. "I'm not annoyed. I'm angry, and I'm hurt, and I'm concerned about you."

"Oh."

"I think you've been—hypnotised or something. I don't know how to help you."

It was Evelyn's turn to laugh. "Honestly, that is very dramatic. I'm fine."

"You weren't fine the other day. I think you should talk to that psychiatrist, both of you."

Evelyn balked. "No, no, we won't be needing anything like that. I'm managing it, and everything is absolutely fine."

"Evie—"

"Listen, I was calling because of the missing boy case, Charlie McBride."

"What about it?" Flossie sounded wary.

"Well, we have a duty to help, don't you think? So terrible for them. I'm arranging for donations to be sent to his family. And I thought you could advertise about it to your poverty society." Evelyn paused. Her ears were tingling.

Flossie sighed, and there was a rustling sound; Evelyn had the sense she had moved the earpiece to her neck. "You can write me details of the donation," she said, at last. Her voice was heavy, almost resigned. "There's nothing else you wanted to say to me?"

"Such as?"

"Nothing," Flossie said. "Such as nothing. Take care of yourself, Evelyn."

✦ ✦ ✦

THAT SUNDAY, THERE WERE fewer people than usual in the mews outside the Spiritualist Hall. Evelyn felt almost affectionate for the regulars. It was nice to be back in the company of usual people. No artists or musicians or men in white tie, no languid girls taking morphia on the kitchen counter. Annie McCloud spotted her in the crowd and gave her such an enthusiastic kiss that Evelyn could feel the chapped skin on her cheeks.

"I thought you'd emigrated," she said, squeezing Evelyn by the elbows.

Evelyn laughed. "How is your aunt?"

"Still alive, despite my best attempts," Annie said.

They filed into the hall. Mrs. Downie stifled a yelp when she saw Robert. "Did I see your picture at the commemmoration ball?" she said, gazing at him. Evelyn looked around for Walter or Clarence but couldn't see them, which was a small mercy. Just a few hours of normality. Relative normality. The service itself was, by its standards, fantastically usual. A woman from Stirling was talking about crystal gazing, and in the row in front of her, Annie was discreetly filing down her fingernails. After the final hymn, Mrs. Downie came back on stage.

"I have an announcement from one of our members." She was holding a piece of paper in her hands. "I'm sure you've all heard about the terrible tragedy of the little boy, Charlie McBride, who went missing back in February. One of our members, Mr. Hazard, has volunteered to help."

Evelyn turned to Robert, who was radiating smugness.

"He's proposing a spiritualist conference to help the investigation. Any sensitives who wish to be involved, please speak to Mr. Hazard after the service." She folded the piece of paper and smiled into the audience at Robert. "And I must add how honoured we are, such a generous thought."

As soon as Mrs. Downie left the stage, Evelyn fixed him with a look.

"Well?" he said. "I wanted to keep it a secret."

Evelyn said nothing. Her face was running hot and cold.

"You're welcome." He planted a kiss on her forehead.

She twitched away from him. "We agreed, Robert, no more surprises."

"But this is a lovely surprise," he said, pouting. "I know how much you wanted to help."

"And will this help?" Evelyn said. "It would be better, wouldn't it, to put money to the police. Or the reward fund. Or my collection."

"But this will make everyone aware of the poor lad," Robert said, adjusting his suspenders. "Imagine: a room full of sensitives, searching for him. We'll be more help than the police."

Death by bees flashed through Evelyn's mind. Her stomach burbled. "But one can't go to the police and say, 'A *C* or an *S* sound,' or 'Angels and demons.'"

Robert laughed. "They'd be lucky to have us. It seems Vikram does know the chief constable. He'll fix it all."

Evelyn winced. The chief constable, sitting around the table, while Boxer drank champagne from his shoe. While Clarence pencilled his freckles on. While Lily vanished into a bathroom with a bottle of morphia. "I'm not sure this is a good idea," she said.

"Nonsense," Robert said. "You said you wanted to help, didn't you? This is the best idea I've hatched yet."

Evelyn pictured Robert's chickens in their coop, crooning in their nests, as the black cat watched, patiently, through the fence. "Yes," she said. "Helping."

30

VIKRAM'S ESTATE HAD BEEN TRANSFORMED. PLAC-ards bearing Charlie's face were propped up in the entrance hall. The library was now a reception room where people were queuing to leave their coats and write their names into the visitors' book. A wheezing greyhound was tied by a piece of string to a tapestried armchair in the dining room. Two unattended children were slid-ing down the banister while Matthew watched uncomfortably. The glasshouse had been swept and furnished with long wooden benches on which older ladies were resting their legs. In the garden, motorcars were parked in the grass, and a line of men were not so discreetly urinating into the oak trees at the back. The maze had been mowed down to stubble, and in its place was a series of small tents in which pale, long-fingered women wearing cheap hats milled in and out, whispering.

Evelyn retreated to her room. Motorcars pulled into the gravel driveway, and the servants unloaded folding tables, fabrics, crystal beads, feather talismans, fumsup dolls, dried flowers, lucky horse-shoes, dream journals, charm rings, electric head-massagers, tarot cards, French foot salts, Irish wishing stones, books on flowers and clouds and fairies and composting. Doors slammed in the building, and the loose tread on the stair squeaked. Quick, merry rain show-ers darted between sprinkles of sun, and a gust of wind whisked a sodden pamphlet about transmutation against Evelyn's window before peeling it off again. She dragged the blanket off the bed and wrapped herself in it. She was strangely cold, in an achy, feverish way. She checked hopefully behind the fire screen, but the hearth had been set for summer with a pot of lavender in the grate. Evelyn sat back at the window, chewing her finger. A car at the far end of the driveway was tooting its horn impatiently, and a slim, hatless figure leapt from the front seat and stalked towards the building. Evelyn pressed her nose against the glass. It was Lily!

She loitered in the gallery, intending to jump and cheer when Lily appeared, but she still felt so frozen and stiff, all she could manage was a terse wave.

"Darling, what are you doing, standing there?" Lily said, coming up the stairs and kissing her on the cheek. "Where's Vikram?"

Evelyn pointed towards the back of the house. "In the garden with Robert." Her voice was hoarse.

Lily marched towards her usual room and, crossing to the bedside table, pulled open the drawer. "Thank goodness," she said, seizing a pair of spectacles.

"You wear glasses?" Evelyn said.

"What? No, they're not mine," Lily said. The comment hung for a moment, and Evelyn felt the blood rush to her cheeks.

"Oh."

Lily opened the window and roared into the drive, "Diggles, is that you? Why weren't you at the lake swimming last week?"

Evelyn leant against the wall by the door. The maid had missed a spot of dust at the top of Lily's cupboard. They must have the short maid with the black hair cleaning this room. If she were in charge of a house this size, she'd hire only the tallest housemaids. Girls with long arms who could get right into the corners for cobwebs.

"Evelyn?" Lily was saying.

Evelyn focused on her. "Sorry?"

"I've been talking to you for two minutes. Are you all right? What are you doing wrapped in that blanket anyway?"

"Sorry," Evelyn said, pathetically.

Lily put her hand out to Evelyn's forehead. "You feel fine. Do you have your monthlies?"

Evelyn flinched. She looked down at the floor.

"If that's all it is, you might just be a bit low on iron or something. Ask Mrs. Potter to make you some liver for supper tonight."

"I'm fine," Evelyn said. She went to chew her finger again, and then caught herself.

"Good. So, drop off the shroud and let's go, shall we?" Lily said, ripping the blanket from Evelyn's shoulders and tossing it over the armchair. "I've been looking forward to this all week." She scooped Evelyn through the arm and led her down the stairs. They dodged a shamefaced Asian man apologising profusely as a maid brushed up a broken china cup, and filed into the glasshouse.

"Is Flo coming?" Lily said, stepping aside as a blond child banged on the glasshouse window with its fists.

"No." Evelyn blinked into a flash of sudden sun. "You know how she feels about all this."

"Oh, she's a spoilsport," Lily said. "She has no sense of fun, that girl. You know she threw off that young man of hers?"

Evelyn's cheeks burned. "I heard something about it."

"I'm surprised at her being so picky, but then the clever ones often are." Lily lit a cigarette. "Look, let's get our tea leaves read," she said, pointing to a tent where a dark-haired older man was chasing a squawking chicken out of a sack of tea.

"Can we keep walking for a bit?" Evelyn said.

"Good idea," Lily said. "See what else is on offer."

They wound between the tents. A psychic bookshop was selling jam sandwiches and cups of hot Bovril. Stalls advertised palm readers, spirit photography, rocking chairs that promoted good sleep. One tent held a painter who was providing "spirit portraits" from descriptions of the deceased. A man claiming to be an "Eastern healer" was diagnosing trouble with a man's gallbladder by examining his tongue. Men were rigging up a generator to one of the tents advertising an immersion bath-heater for arthritis, where a young girl in a flowered cap and bathing suit was performing a series of acrobatic manoeuvres.

"This is the one," Lily said, tugging Evelyn towards a low, poky tent where a macabre puppet show was taking place. A doll with a white face was trapping another doll in a net. The ensnared doll was screaming for help, while a circle of children jeered, gnawing on barley sugars and wiping their noses onto a tartan blanket.

"Really?" Evelyn frowned at her.

"Yes, just a moment."

As they entered the tent, Evelyn saw Clarence was sitting there, almost invisible amongst the other children. He had a slightly gormless expression of enjoyment on his face, his mouth open. Her chest pinched. It was so strange to see Clarence just being a child. A horrible flash of pity for him overcame her. How infrequently he must be allowed to be a child. And on the back of her pity came a wave of sickness. If Charlie McBride were there, he would have been here too, just sitting in amongst the children, watching a gruesome puppet show. All of this was just window dressing, diversion; and a real child was out there somewhere, calling for help. Evelyn's head thumped.

"I don't really want—" She turned to Lily, but Lily was weaving through the children to the adults lined up at the far end of the room. It took a moment before Evelyn realised Walter was among them. He gave Lily a tight smile—a smile that was not exactly warm, but still strangely intimate. Lily pulled the glasses from inside her pocket and handed them over to him.

All at once, Evelyn felt excruciatingly lonely. She was a lighthouse at high tide. Watching on as everyone else followed their paths to their places. She backed out of the tent and stood, disorientated, by a woman selling paper roses. Wasps swarmed over the crushed petals lying in the grass. She should go somewhere, be somewhere, shouldn't she? But there was nowhere for her to go, to be. Her eyes stung. She wanted to stow herself away somewhere dark and safe. A travelling trunk. A cupboard. Maybe she could slip back into the upstairs corridor, take refuge next to the *D* in the shut-up room. No one would think to look for her there. Through a gap between the tents, the back of Vikram's head appeared. Filled with a glittery sort of relief, Evelyn stumbled towards him.

Vikram turned the corner and smiled at her, opening his arms. "Hello, darling Evelyn," he said, kissing her on both cheeks. "I've been looking for you!" he said, gently nudging her aside as a flute player pushed past.

"You have?" Someone had been looking for her. Someone cared.

"Yes, I really have to apologise for the other weekend."

"Oh." Her heart tumbled into the pit of her stomach. He didn't really want to speak to her; he was just assuaging his conscience.

"No, no, it was quite unforgivable," Vikram was saying, as if she had tried to disagree with him. "We just got a little overexcited, that's all."

Evelyn nodded. She felt floppy and weak. It had been a mistake, to come down from her room. She should have got into bed and stayed there.

"Are you looking for Bobby?"

She hesitated.

"He's preparing for the reading tonight in the meeting tent. I'm on my way myself, allow me to escort you?" he said.

"Thank you," Evelyn said, at last.

She followed him through the stalls to the larger meeting marquee on the banks of the river. The view of the water was obscured by vehicles, warm rain sparkling on the bonnets of the idling cars. People had trampled down divots into the grass.

"I'm surprised you allowed all this," Evelyn heard herself saying.

Vikram plunged his hands into his pockets. "I have the space."

"Your beautiful garden, though."

Vikram laughed. "My beautiful garden isn't going to solve any crimes by itself."

Evelyn almost tripped on a badger hole in the grass, and Vikram put his arm out to steady her. When she righted herself, she looked at him carefully. "Do you really think this will help find him?"

"Some of the most spiritually attuned minds in the country in one place. We're bound to come up with something."

"But—" Evelyn paused. Her tongue felt heavy, her thoughts slow and sludgy. "You could give to a more reasonable cause."

Vikram raised his eyebrow at her. "Evelyn, I'm the benefactor of Tollworth Hospital, and the war memorial. There's a new roof on Arair's children's library. Last summer we had tuberculosis inoculations lining up out of the dining room."

Evelyn's ears were hot. "I'm sorry, I didn't mean—"

"You did mean," he said. "But I'll forgive you." He gave her a smile. "I know you're not exactly a supporter of all this."

Evelyn stopped walking. He turned back to look at her.

"Is that how it seems?" she said.

Vikram observed her. His eyes were kind and clear. "Well, are you?"

"Am I?"

"A believer."

Evelyn's tongue was stuck to the roof of her mouth. "I thought I was," she said, at last. "I suppose I don't know how this can really help." She motioned towards a woman in a black dress sprinkling salt around a three-legged stool.

"The constabulary is out searching as we speak," Vikram said.

"But—" Evelyn's bowels squeezed. "But it's not right, Vikram. Robert, Clarence—we can't allow the police to search on their authority. They aren't investigators. They can't possibly—the police might be following their—impressions, and searching in the wrong place, and the boy is in danger, we're putting him in danger. If anything happens to him, it will be all my fault." It was as if all the words that had been clogged up inside her were tumbling out at the same time.

"My darling Evelyn, how could it possibly be your fault?" Vikram said, softly.

"I don't know." There was something burning in her chest. "I don't know." She blinked back tears. "He'll be out there all alone, I should have tried harder to stop—" There was a spasm in her throat. "I don't know. I just, I know it's not right."

"Have faith, Evelyn," Vikram said, putting his hand on her arm.

"Faith in what?"

A voice inside her begged him to have the answer, to know exactly what would soothe her.

"In your husband," he said, gently.

31

THE MEETING TENT WAS AS BIG AS THE SPIRITUALIST Hall, large enough to fit maybe a hundred people. Despite the size, it smelt cramped, like stale air and damp carpet. At the far end was a flimsy-looking wooden stage on which six policemen were sitting, their chairs drawn into a circle. In the centre of the circle was Robert.

"You can't be in here, madam." A frizzy-haired young officer approached her. "This is a closed area."

Evelyn pointed at Robert. "My husband," she said. Her voice was croaky, and even to her own ears, it sounded unconvincing. The man scrutinised her.

"Who is your husband, madam?"

"This is Bobby's wife," Vikram said, from behind her.

"I see." The policeman still looked doubtful. "Well, you still may not want to be present, ma'am. Might be a bit delicate for a lady's ears."

"Evie's made of stern stuff," Vikram said, patting her arm. "Aren't you?"

Before Evelyn could summon an answer, Bernice and Clarence entered the tent. Bernice had a pincer grip on Clarence's shoulders, and he was wearing a distinctly sulky expression, no doubt annoyed that he had been wrenched away from the puppet show.

"Master O'Grady, so nice to meet you," the policeman was stuttering.

"He'll need a glass of milk," Bernice said, imperiously.

"Of course, of course." The policeman nodded to them both and scurried off.

"Shall we go up?" Vikram gestured to the back of the room.

On stage, Robert was rosy-cheeked and bright-eyed. The policemen had taken off their caps and were sitting hunched towards him, expectant. One policeman produced a slim book from his top pocket and passed it shyly to Robert, who signed it with a flourish.

"I'll stay here," Evelyn said, shaking her head.

"We won't be long." Vikram shot her an excited smile, ushering Clarence and Bernice towards the stage.

Clarence took a chair next to Robert, and Bernice sat behind him. Evelyn lingered by the open side of the tent, where an unmoored peg was flapping in the wind. She kept her eyes on Robert. It was as if he were on the other side of a moat. How far they had travelled since November. Robert, commanding a room. All attention on him. All deference to him, to his gift. Robert, enjoying it.

"Right, well, we're all here, so let's begin," Robert said. "If you could all hold hands, and keep a moment of silence while Clarence and I contact the spirit world."

The policemen exchanged uncertain looks before tentatively reaching out and taking hold of each other's hands. Robert and Clarence closed their eyes. There was a long moment of silence. Evelyn's heart was thumping in her ears.

"I see him near water," Robert said, eventually. "There is a bridge."

Clarence wrinkled his forehead. "It's cold. And there are some trees nearby, tall ones."

Evelyn's stomach slithered. Water? A cold place near some trees? Her head was tight. How could Robert think this was a good use of police time? Water. Trees. Out there was a child, crying for help. And Robert was on stage, signing autographs. Her guts made a rebellious gurgling sound, and she ducked under the tent awning. A cloud shifted, and a warm spot of sunlight beat down on the crown of her head. She took three long, deep breaths. She would

·go back to their room, close the door, and wait for the weekend to be over. If she didn't actually *witness* it, she might not feel so awful. So complicit.

Evelyn slipped behind three "scrying" booths next to the meeting tent and walked in the direction of the house. But somewhere near a phrenology stall, she got turned around. The top of the house was visible above the tents, but each time she walked towards it, the path was blocked, and she had to turn back. She told herself not to panic, but a fluttery sense of unease was rising in her chest as she wound through the exhibits of dowsers and magnet wielders. A dream psychic. A teenage girl holding a doll who was far too old to be holding a doll. A lemon, squashed underfoot. A couple huddling together, crying. Finally, she saw the open door of the glasshouse and ran through it, skidding on a milk token from St. Cuthbert's Dairy abandoned near the wooden benches. She put her hand to the wall to steady herself; her pulse was jolting in unsteady little bleats.

One of Vikram's maids walked past carrying a tray of empty tea-cups, and Evelyn squeaked at her. "Please, can I have a glass of water?"

The maid turned to her with an expression of annoyance that quickly vanished. "Oh, Mrs. Hazard, of course." She bobbed to her and then turned back. "There was a telephone message for you, Mrs. Hazard, only a few minutes ago. I took a slip under your door."

"Telephone?" Time was so fractured and odd, Evelyn thought, wildly—*Dolores*. She wrestled it back, taking a gulp of air. "Who was the message from?"

"It was Stuart who took the message, ma'am," the maid said, blushing. "I'll fetch it."

Evelyn realised the maid might not even be able to read. "Of course, thank you."

She backed up against the wall. Her climbing sense of panic was slowly ebbing, and she concentrated on a child who was pounding on Vikram's rosewood chest like a drum before being pried away, wailing, by its mother.

When the message was delivered, she saw the telephone call had been from Flossie. Evelyn nibbled on the edge of the card. Why would Flossie be calling? Maybe Flossie had forgiven her? But even thinking about having another conversation with Flossie about Malcolm made her ears ring. It was like a big bright light: she couldn't bear to look directly at it.

Evelyn carried her glass of water into the telephone alcove by the dining room and pulled the folding door closed. In the cramped little space, she felt more snug and more sane than she had all day. Maybe she should just wait out the rest of the conference here? Evelyn rested her head on the lip of the shelf, and took a deep breath. She dialled for the operator.

"Evelyn?"

"It's me."

"Are you alone?"

Someone walked through the entrance lobby, chanting and ringing a handbell. Evelyn put her hand over her free ear. "I'm at Vikram's," she said.

"Yes, I know that, I called you there, didn't I?"

"Oh. Sorry."

"I mean, is Robert with you?"

"No." Evelyn twirled the cord around her finger. "He's in the meeting tent."

"Listen." Flossie cleared her throat. "They found the boy, Evelyn. Charles McBride."

Evelyn squinted into the receiver as if that might help her to hear better. "They found him?"

"Yes, about an hour ago."

A roar of relief lapped over her, a wave of warm cocoa. "Thank God," Evelyn said. "He's safe?"

"Yes, perfectly safe. I, well, I just thought you should know," Flossie said, quietly.

"Thank you." Evelyn put her hand to her heart. "Oh, I'm so relieved. I was so worried. But where was he?"

"Apparently working in a hotel kitchen in Aberdeen under a false name. He's being driven back now."

The warm cocoa feeling curdled in her stomach. "He wasn't near water, then? A lake or something?"

In the background of Flossie's apartment, Evelyn could hear Pups talking to someone, another man. "I don't know," Flossie said. "I mean, it's Aberdeen. I don't think there are any lakes around there."

Evelyn chewed her lips.

"Is that what Robert said? That he was near a lake?"

Her face felt numb. "Not exactly."

"Evie," Flossie started, but Evelyn said, "Don't." There was a moment of silence. "Listen, you need to speak to Vikram," Flossie said. "We've been trying to reach him nonstop."

"Speak to Vikram?" Evelyn said.

"About Charles McBride being found," Flossie said, exasperatedly. "I don't want the papers to get there first. I don't want him to be taken by surprise. Embarrassed."

Evelyn's eyes prickled. "Oh. Yes, of course."

"And you should speak to Robert as well. Before, you know, before he, um, *predicts* anything . . ." She trailed off.

There was a long pause.

"Do you know where Vikram is?"

"No," she said. "Actually, yes. He was with Robert. I can find him."

"Good. Thank you," Flossie said. "And Evelyn, please know, I understand you may not have had much choice, but this whole conference, I hope you can see now how disruptive—"

Evelyn cut her off. "I have to go, sorry, bye."

* * *

BACK AT THE MEETING tent, wooden chairs had been placed in rows facing the stage, and visitors had already taken seats at the front, reading novels to pass the time before the session started. Robert and Vikram were nowhere to be seen. Evelyn travelled up the space between the rows, dodging women who were strategically draping their shawls over the backs of the middle seats so they could return and claim them later. At the far end of the tent, Evelyn put her head out towards the muddy patch of grass near the river, where a generator was groaning, puffing steam. Robert and Walter were standing in a stubby patch of shorn nettles, talking to a policeman.

Evelyn walked towards them. "Robert?" He was laughing at something Walter had said, his cheeks pink. "Robert!" she said again, louder.

He turned to her. "Hello, my love." He gripped her, hard, by the elbows, and kissed her on the side of the head.

"I need to speak to you," Evelyn whispered.

"Yes, darling?"

She glanced at Walter and the policeman, who were watching her with a polite irritation, as if they were being forced to humour her intrusion. "Over there," she said, pointing around the edge of the tent where an abandoned fishing rod was hanging into the river. Walter and the policeman exchanged a conspiratorial, amused look.

"Right you are." Robert motioned for her to go first.

Evelyn walked until they were out of view of Walter and the policeman. She pulled Robert closer to her, and he smiled, misinterpreting the gesture. She batted him away as he leant in for another kiss.

"They found the boy," she whispered.

Robert blinked at her.

"The boy. Charlie McBride. The police found him. I just heard it from Flossie."

Robert beamed. He clasped her to him. "Oh Evie, that's wonderful!"

"He was working at a hotel in Aberdeen under a false name," she said. Her voice was tight from being squashed against him.

"How fantastic." Robert kissed her on the forehead. "We've got to make an announcement!" He went to pull away from her and she tugged him back.

"The police, they have him."

"Good," he said. But she could tell his mind was already on something else, his eyes shining. She had the urge to pinch him, hard.

"That means you were wrong," she said.

He smiled, perplexed. "How so?"

"You said he was in the water," Evelyn said, incredulously. "You said it yourself."

Robert laughed, tipping back on his heels. "I said he felt near the water."

"But—"

"Aberdeen, Evie, just as we thought. Right on the water!"

"That's not—but that's not what you said." Evelyn's head was pounding. Was that what he had said? That wasn't what he had said. Was it?

"Evie." He tweaked her nose, playfully. "What does it matter? He's been found! What a success!"

She gripped his wrist. "But you didn't do anything."

"Didn't I?" He gave her a wry smile.

"No." Her heart was beating hard in her ears. "No, you didn't."

Robert chuckled.

"You didn't do anything!" She could hear a hysterical pitch in her voice. "He wasn't in danger, thank God—but what if he was? What if he was and they were looking for water? A lake? A river? Trees, Clarence said. Trees!"

Robert wrinkled his nose at her, in a kindly way. "My love, it's hardly a coincidence, is it? Us putting our minds to tracing the boy, and now he's been found!"

Evelyn stood frozen, as Robert let go of her and clapped his hands. He turned back around the edge of the tent, and she heard his voice boom out.

"Officer, Walter, I've got an announcement. My wife has just told me the boy's been found!"

"He has?" Walter gasped.

"I'll have to call my senior officer to confirm," the policeman said, sounding vaguely put out.

"What's that? Who's been found? He's been found?" Bernice's voice twittered from inside the marquee. She appeared at the edge of the tent. "He's been found, has he? And he's safe?"

"Safe as a button," Robert said.

Bernice turned and embraced Clarence, who was trailing behind her. "Do you hear that, darling? He's found! He's safe!" Bernice pinched Clarence's cheek before embracing him again. "My darling, darling, clever boy."

Clarence's face was very still. "That's good," he said. Over Bernice's shoulder, his eyes focused on Evelyn's.

"Don't you want to know where?" Evelyn heard herself saying. Everyone turned to her.

"Where?" said Walter.

"In a hotel, in Aberdeen."

Walter strode over to Clarence and patted him on the shoulder. "Somewhere cold, just as you said."

Evelyn cleared her throat. "But—"

"And the bridge!" Walter gripped Clarence's shoulder, hard. "The Bridge of Dee!"

Everyone was talking at once now.

"Wait," Evelyn said, but Robert was marching into the tent, waving at someone she couldn't see.

"Vikram, there you are," Robert bellowed. "Did you hear the good news?"

As soon as Robert walked into the tent, the others followed him, Bernice and Walter grinning at each other. Evelyn lingered at the back.

Vikram was hurrying through from the other side of the tent. "I was coming to tell you the same thing!" he said, breathlessly. "You've already heard? I just spoke to the chief constable on the telephone."

"A hotel in Aberdeen—by the water, just as I predicted," Robert said, as they embraced.

Evelyn's stomach lurched.

"And it was the Royal Oak Hotel," Vikram said. "The oaks! As Clarence said!"

Evelyn gripped the edge of the stage; the room was lilting.

"Ring the bell," Walter was saying. "Let's start the session early, tell everyone all together."

Vikram and Robert were embracing again, and Walter was pacing up and down the stage excitedly. The people reading novels in the front row had put their books down and were whispering to each other. Outside the tent, a bell was being rung. As it pealed, people began lining up, hopeful, expectant.

"Come in, come in," Robert was shouting. "Take a chair!"

The tent filled up with people muttering between themselves, their faces bright with anticipation. More people were crowding in now, jostling for space at the edges of the stage, dropping candied apples, and waving at friends. Evelyn backed out of the tent and paused by the "mirror scrying" booths near the entrance. Tentatively, she pushed on the saloon doors of the far-right booth to find an empty cubicle with a stool and a flimsy tin mirror hammered on the wall. She sat on the stool, putting her head in her hands. Through the gap at the bottom of the doors, the queue for Robert's meeting shuffled past. Evelyn leant forward. She heard herself sniff, with a funny little sob that came from nowhere. "Don't cry, don't cry," she said to herself, rubbing her temples. "Don't cry, everything's fine."

"Are you feeling all right, hen?" A woman's voice came from the other side of the doors, and Evelyn jumped.

"Yes, I'm fine," she yelped, although her voice broke.

"Here you go, love." A freckled hand offered a handkerchief at the gap at the bottom of the doors. After a moment, Evelyn took it.

"It's clean, you can keep that one, hen. I always bring extra hankies with me to a meeting."

Evelyn put her eye to the chink between the doors. It was a short woman in an ugly orange hat. She vaguely recognised her. The woman was middle-aged, drab, unthreatening in a spinstery way.

"What's your name, love?" the woman said, adjusting her hat. "I'm Mrs. Young."

Evelyn remembered now, speaking to her on the first day of Robert's tour, at Paltern Hall. She'd been sitting with Bernice. Maybe all of Bernice's friends were fond of ugly accessories. That was their favourite subject of conversation. They attended special fetes that only sold hideous adornments. A manic giggle squirmed in Evelyn's throat and she fought to control herself. She looked at the tent fabric over the top of the doors. She couldn't bear to have to claim Robert, to have to defend Robert.

"Hawk," she said, with a sort of squeak. "Mrs. Hawk."

"Nice to meet you, love. Dizzy spell, was it?"

Evelyn nodded, before remembering that Mrs. Young couldn't see her. "Something like that."

Mrs. Young sat down on the hay bale near the stand with a neighbourly sigh. "Will you be coming in for the session?"

"In a minute," Evelyn said. Her throat was dry.

"Did you hear, they found the wee boy?"

"I heard," Evelyn said.

Mrs. Young shook her head. "What a relief. His poor mother."

Evelyn twisted the handkerchief.

"I'm hoping to make contact with my nephew, Albert," Mrs. Young said. "Are you hoping to reach anyone?"

"Um." Evelyn scrabbled. "My cousin. Ed. He's dead."

"Oh dear, I am sorry." Mrs. Young tutted sympathetically. "You poor wee love."

"Thank you," Evelyn said, prepared in that moment to accept the sympathy, the kindness. Her eyes watered.

"The war, was it?"

Evelyn hesitated. "Yes."

"Albert too." Mrs. Young pulled out a hand mirror from her purse. Through the gap between the doors, Evelyn saw with a strange satisfaction that it was indeed ugly. Pink, decorated with a ribbon made from poor-quality clay. "Passchendaele."

Evelyn stuttered, realising she was expected to supply her own tragedy. "Oh. He fell. In a well."

Mrs. Young shook her head. "How awful." She examined herself in the mirror, trying to catch a loose eyelash on her fingertip.

"Yes," Evelyn said, weakly.

"He would've been near the same age as my Albert, then? Twenty-five?"

"I—yes."

"I'm sorry, hen." Mrs. Young grimaced. "I know how hard it is." She held the eyelash up. "I've got an eyelash here. I tell you what, I'll blow it, and you can have the wish."

Evelyn blinked. A wish? What would she even wish for at this moment? To go back in time? Her throat ached. *Dolores*, she thought. *I wish Dolly was here.* With a wheeze, Mrs. Young blew the eyelash into the hay. The sound of applause and cheering came from the tent, people were whistling and clapping their hands.

"There, everyone's heard about the boy." Mrs. Young smiled. "A bit of good news! That's what we all need, isn't it? Maybe your wish already came true!"

"Please, go on in," Evelyn said, suddenly. She felt ghoulish, corrupt. Exchanging fake tragedy for the sake of a moment of sympathy. She didn't deserve it. She was rotten for sitting there, pretending, with this real, grieving woman ministering to her lies on the other side of the door. That ugly pink mirror. Mrs. Young was probably poor, desperately poor, and that was the nicest trinket she could afford. And there she was, judging her. Evelyn's stomach burbled. "Please go in, please don't wait, I just need another minute."

"Of course, hen," Mrs. Young said, standing from the hay bale and stretching her lower back with a groan. "I'll see you in there, love."

"Perhaps," Evelyn said, her cheeks flaring.

After watching until Mrs. Young was out of sight, Evelyn let herself out of the booth and paced in the grass alongside the tent. She just had to get through the afternoon. That was all. Get through the afternoon, and get Robert home. Just a few more hours. As soon as Robert was done with the session, she would insist on going home. At home, she could explain it to him. Maybe call someone in, someone sensible. Could Alistair talk to him? Evelyn was sweating into her bust bodice. The fact that Robert even needed a lesson in moral equilibrium! All the attention had gone to his head. He was too enthusiastic, that was his problem. She just had to get through the next few hours, and get him home.

Inside the tent, Clarence was holding an elderly woman's hand. "And I can see that it's a handwritten piece of paper, not from a typewriter. That's right, isn't it?"

"That's right," the woman said, dabbing her eye with a yellowed handkerchief. "Her handwriting was always hard to read."

"But Elizabeth is telling me clearly that it's not a letter."

"No, it's not a letter." The woman smiled.

"I think she's saying that it is a recipe, is that right?"

"My goodness, yes!" the woman gasped. "That's amazing!"

Evelyn took a seat on the edge of the back row. Was Clarence now reading first, ahead of Robert? Did that mean that Robert was better known now, even than Clarence?

"Elizabeth is telling me that you had better take good care of this recipe, because it was important to you both."

"It was, it is," the woman said.

"She's telling me that it's very delicious, this recipe, she wants to make sure everyone knows it."

The crowd laughed, amiably.

"Ah, I understand, she's telling me that it's a recipe for clootie dumplings, is that right?" Clarence said.

"That's exactly it!" The woman laughed, pressing her handkerchief to her face.

There was a gasp of appreciation in the crowd and a burst of applause. Evelyn watched Robert, sitting at the edge of the stage. It wasn't good for him, being famous. He needed moderation in his life. Temperance. He needed to feel less bold, less brave. Henry! She would telephone Henry Campbell. Good old Henry, with his Swiss Army knife and his waterproof jacket. When they got home, she'd call Henry and Alistair, and she *wouldn't* call Dr. Greitzer.

A young man at the back of the tent had set up a camera and was taking photographs of the audience. Evelyn shrank back.

"Thank you," Clarence was saying, embracing the woman. As she returned to her seat, the audience clapped for him, and he bowed.

Clarence walked to the side of the stage. There, Bernice passed him up a glass of milk. They exchanged a few words, and Clarence nodded, seriously. He took a sip from his glass and Bernice patted the drop of milk on his tunic; he waved her away. Clarence returned to the front of the stage and climbed onto the stool. He cleared his throat. "There is a spirit here who wishes to make a connection with someone close to him. His first name begins with an 'Ed' sound," he said.

There was a flurry of murmuring in the audience.

"His name might be Edwin or Edward?"

A horsefly landed on Evelyn's cheek and she swatted it away.

"He's trying to reach someone who is very dear to him. A relative, I believe, a young woman. She has an unusual last name, like a bird—Hornbill maybe, or Hawk? Mrs. Hawk?"

A flush ran along Evelyn's body. It tingled over her skin, from her fingertips to her toes.

"He was young when he went, maybe midtwenties. It was a terrible accident, I'm seeing. He fell somewhere, dark, into a shaft perhaps, or maybe a trench, or a well?"

Evelyn stood up, slowly. Her body was numb. Wooden. She was a puppet, a white-faced puppet, ensnared in a net. There was noise around her, people. A goat, chewing a pamphlet, a child with a balloon. There was a blue crystal, shining in the grass.

And then she was in her bedroom. How had she got there? Her hands and knees were muddy, but she didn't remember falling over. She walked along the gallery to the bathroom. Downstairs, people were cheering and clapping; the radio was on. Evelyn's face was pale in the bathroom mirror. She soaped her hands. An eyelash was caught at the edge of her eye. She licked her finger, dabbed it on the lash, and held it in front of her. All at once, her stomach gave a sloshing noise, like a milk bottle being shaken from side to side. She ran to the toilet and reached it just in time to vomit into the bowl.

She sat on the tiled floor. A single coral earring was lying under the sink. Someone must have snapped the catch without realising. And they would notice it was missing later in the day and be searching for it. She pictured Dolly's earring, under the floorboards, watching her.

Evelyn's stomach lurched again, and this time, she hovered over the bowl, but nothing came out. She coughed, wetly, and started crying. Her sobs were broken and hard. Did Robert know? Had he known? He must have known. But he couldn't have known! Did it matter? She sank back onto the tiles and put her face on her muddy knees. It had all gone too far. She had let it go too far. She had believed it! God, what she had told Flossie! She had ruined Flossie's life. Ruined her chances for happiness. And why? Because she couldn't bear to see Malcolm—watch him living, watch him being happy, not without Dolly. Another life ruined, because of what she did. Because of what would happen if people found out what she did. Women were supposed to want to be mothers; what did it make her that she didn't even regret her choice? That she had gone to such lengths to protect her choice? And if the spirits were all a lie, then none of it had been real. That *D* was nothing, like Flossie said. Just a scratch in the wall. Dolly never was watching over her, protecting her. She was still gone. She would always be gone. Evelyn put her head in her hands. It was all her fault. She was floating on a marsh. Everything was sinking.

32

TWO HOURS LATER, PAPA'S MOTORCAR PULLED UP IN the driveway, and the passenger door opened. Evelyn stood up from the front step, her knees stiff, the seat of her dress sticking damply to her thighs.

"Evie?" Kitty climbed out of the car. She was wearing a moss-coloured wrap jacket, the little swelling in her stomach covered by a cream georgette dress.

Evelyn gawped at her, unable to move. Kitty, in green and white: a little angelica bonbon. The sweetest, loveliest thing she had ever seen. And there she was, rotten, spoiled. It felt wrong, dangerous, to even get near to Kitty.

"Evie?" Kitty's eyes widened. She walked towards her cautiously, the way one might approach an unfamiliar dog. Kitty moved to embrace her, but Evelyn flinched back, instinctively. Kitty dropped her arms by her sides. Her eyes roved over the state of Evelyn's attire. "Is that all you have?" she said, after a moment, gesturing to the case on the gravel.

Evelyn nodded.

"All right then, come on in, let's go, shall we?"

Evelyn crawled into the back seat. Her knees were still muddy, and they left a smudge on the leather.

Alistair caught her eye in the mirror. "Should we wait?"

"No," Evelyn said. "We aren't going to wait."

Alistair and Kitty exchanged a look that Evelyn pretended not to see. As they drove out of Colbreck, Evelyn blinked into the sunlight. The hedges along the road flashed ruby with wild poppies, sheep in the fields gambolled in the fresh clover. Evelyn swallowed hard, feeling tears run over her chin and drop into her lap.

"Pull over, will you?" Kitty said.

"Dear me, already?"

"Don't be ridiculous, Alistair," Kitty snapped. Alistair swerved the car to the edge of a slate wall. Kitty got out of the front passenger seat and climbed into the back seat beside Evelyn. She took her hand. It was warm, soft.

Evelyn heard herself make a glugging noise. Her nose was running, and Kitty pulled a handkerchief from her pocket and handed it over.

"Go ahead, drive on," Kitty said, to Alistair. "And sing."

"Pardon?"

"Sing something. Go on, occupy yourself," Kitty barked.

Alistair cleared his throat and began an off-key rendition of "O Waly Waly."

"Whatever has happened?" Kitty said.

Evelyn shook her head.

"Are you all right?"

Evelyn nodded. "I can't explain. It's too—I can't."

Kitty's eyes searched Evelyn's face. "Tell me what to do," she said. "How can I help?"

Evelyn stared at her. Kitty, her wholesome, normal sister. With her wholesome, normal babies and her wholesome, normal husband.

"I can't," Evelyn said.

"You can't what?"

"I can't stay with him," Evelyn said. As the words passed through her, they cleared something out in their wake, like a chimney brush. She wasn't sad anymore. "I can't stay with him," she said again, louder.

A pulse ticked in Kitty's left eye. She nodded. "What do you want to do?"

"I can stay with you, can't I?"

Kitty licked her lips.

A rush of terror seized Evelyn, swirling through her like radio static. Kitty was what she had. She was all she had left.

"We—" Kitty began, and then she stopped, reading the panic Evelyn felt shivering all over her body. "Of course, you can stay with us for as long as you need."

◆ ◆ ◆

WHEN THEY RETURNED TO Kitty's house, Evelyn went straight up to the spare room. Jeanie had left the window open for airing, and Evelyn sat on the edge of the bed, absently watching a pigeon roosting on the eaves. She took off her dress and crawled under the covers. The sheets were trimmed with apricot-coloured furbelows, and from next door she heard baby Margaret crooning in the nursery. Downstairs, someone was shaking a cloth from the kitchen window and a cloud of flour rose in the air, catching the late afternoon sunlight in speckles. Evelyn lay perfectly still. She felt like a cracked egg that has been boiling in the pan, and all its insides have come out and jellified. A rush of self-pity and sorrow came over her. She was so tired. She wasn't supposed to be the oldest sister, to be the example, to be strong. If only Dolly was there to look after her, to make everything better. With a gentle knock, the door opened, and Jeanie's hand, up to the wrist, appeared, to slide a tea tray discreetly along the floorboards. Evelyn ate the corned beef sandwiches in bed and slept in the crumbs, dreaming of a jewelled mermaid on a far rock that was calling her closer, closer.

◆ ◆ ◆

"EVELYN." KITTY WAS SHAKING her.

She sat up with a rush, confused about where she was. Her slip was so damp with sweat, for a horrible moment she thought she had urinated in the bed. "What is it?"

"Evie, he's downstairs," Kitty said.

"Who?"

Kitty gaped at her. "Robert. He knocked at seven this morning and I told him to come back and this time he says he won't move until he's seen you."

"I can't." Evelyn pulled her knees to her chest. Her sweat was cooling now, and she was chill and sticky.

Kitty's lip twitched. "Please, Evie, the neighbours. He's been there for an hour."

Evelyn looked at her. "Kitty—"

Kitty shifted her weight from one foot to the other. "Please, just tell him yourself you don't want to see him, maybe he'll go."

Evelyn threw the flounce of beribboned blankets aside and stood up. She set her teeth, a swell of anger rising inside her. Robert didn't even have the sense to leave her alone. After everything, he couldn't just let her be for one day? She strode towards the door, and Kitty made a squeaking noise from the corner.

"What is it?" Evelyn turned to her.

"Your slip," Kitty said, in a small voice.

Evelyn looked at her for a long moment, before pulling on her muddy dress from yesterday. She stamped down the stairs, knowing that her hair was knotted, that her dress wasn't buttoned, that her knees were dirty, knowing that she looked monstrous, ready to be monstrous.

"Evie." Robert was standing on the front doorstep, his hands worrying his lapels. His face was puffy and his eyes pink, as if he had been crying. Evelyn's heart wobbled, spun, settled.

"You have to go, Robert."

He took a step towards her, and reached out.

She looked down at his hand until he lowered it.

"Evie, I don't understand. They said you left yesterday, and you weren't at the house, I've been going out of my mind!"

"Good," Evelyn said.

"What do you mean, good?" His voice broke.

"I'm going to stay with Kitty for a while. I won't make a scene. I'll come get my clothes later. We can tell Marty I'm helping with the baby."

"I don't understand." Robert fiddled with his lapels again.

"You don't understand?" Evelyn said. The blood roared in her ears. "You really don't understand?"

He winced. "No. I'm confused, Evie."

"Should we start with Bernice and Clarence? The spectacle—the sham, the *evil* of it." Evelyn was spitting.

"What?" Robert looked frightened. "Evie—"

"Do you know—do you know what Dr. Greitzer said to me?"

"Is he in there?" Robert's forehead crumpled. "Are you ill?"

Evelyn swallowed. "He said that either you were insane, a fraud, or telling the truth."

Robert shook his head. "I don't understand."

Evelyn gripped the doorframe. "Which is it, Robert? What is it? Which one is it?"

"What?"

"Which is it?" She was almost screaming. Her voice echoed off the tiles.

Robert took a step towards her. "It's true, my love," he said, softly. "Of course it's true."

She stared at him for a moment. The faint scar across his lips, the curly hairs in his eyebrows. Her body shook, tears ran down her face. "You know, I don't even think it matters anymore. I don't think it even matters. I can't be part of this—the strangeness, I can't. I can't do it. I can't talk to you. It's all too much, it's making me lose my mind. I can't. I can't be near you."

Robert was crying now. He rubbed his face with the back of his hands. "Evie, please, my love—"

"Leave me alone," Evelyn said. Her lips were wobbling so much she could hardly get the words out. "Just leave, Robert, please."

"What can I do? I can give it up, I can stop, we can go back to normal," Robert said.

Evelyn shook her head. "We can't."

"We can!" His eyes lit up. "I'll stop with the spiritualism. I'll just stop. We can take a holiday. Paris? Algeria? Just come home now, we can talk."

She steadied herself on the doorframe. "We can't, Robert, there isn't a normal. It's too much. It's come too far away from normal."

Robert looked desperately over his shoulder and back at her. "But you have to listen, Evie, I don't understand. Last night, when you were gone, I didn't know what to think, I tried to find you—"

"Please leave, now," Evelyn said. "The neighbours are listening, Kitty doesn't want it."

"But Evie, I need to say something, I need to tell you something."

Evelyn stood behind the door and rested her head on the frame. "No, thank you," she said, stupidly.

"Evie, please," Robert was saying, as she began to swing the door closed. Her heart was dark and blank as a slate. "Please, it's important. One more thing. Please. And then I'll go, I swear. Evie?" Robert stepped forward, his face squashed against the glass. "Evelyn, for the love of God."

"Stop it, Robert. I've had enough."

He pushed back on the door, enough so that she could see him properly. His hair ruffled, his silly, lovely face. He took a deep breath. "It's a message," he said. "I didn't know how to tell you—it came through last night."

Evelyn began to shut the door. "I don't want any messages from you, Robert."

"It's not from me." He put his hand around the doorframe. "It's not from me. It's from Dolores. Don't you want to hear it?"

ACKNOWLEDGMENTS

Over the last two years, I have asked everybody I meet to tell me their ghost stories. I've been overwhelmed by people's generosity to discuss grief, to disclose the darkest and strangest moments of their life, sometimes with a perfect stranger. Thank you to all the people who have shared their spooky encounters with me, and thank you to everyone who has listened to me talk, endlessly, about ghosts.

I owe a great deal of thanks for my sanity to my WWF comrades: Daisy, Elizabeth, Francine, Hannah, Imogen, Jessie, Kiran, Kirsty, Rachelle, Sophie, and Nell. It has meant so much to have you all as a resource and respite.

Love and thanks to Fiona Murray, for her local expertise.

To Hattie, my champion, I would be lost without you! I can't thank you enough for your continued wisdom and guidance.

To Jade, thank you so much for believing in the book, it has been such a gift to have your insight shaping the story into its final form. Thank you to Zulekhá Afzal, Ellie Bailey, Alice Herbert, Megan Schaffer, Drew Hunt (my original Foyles crew!), Ellie Wheeldon, Diana Talyanina, Laurence Cole, Caroline Westmore, and the whole team at Baskerville. To Jack Smythe, thank you for the fabulous UK cover.

Thank you so much to Catherine Drayton, my tireless US agent, for all your support.

To Masie, I am so thrilled to be working together, thank you for your turbo-charged edits and revisions. I feel so lucky to have your sharp eye and perceptiveness on my team! Thank you to everyone at Tin House for all your enthusiasm and hard work: Win McCormack, Craig Popelars, Becky Kraemer, Nanci McCloskey,

Anne Horowitz, Joelle Kidd, Alyssa Ogi, Elizabeth DeMeo, and Jae Nichelle. A particular thanks to Beth Steidle for the gorgeous design.

To Ruhi, my most encouraging writing companion, thank you for being you.

To Struan, the thank yous have no end—for listening to my constant ghost stories, for the editing parties, the extra hours, days and nights of boon-wrangling. Thank you for your love and your belief in me.

Finally, I wrote this book thinking of, and wishing for Rebecca. I love you and I miss you.

READER'S GUIDE

1. What do you think about Robert's gift? Do you believe him?

2. What role does truth play in this novel? Which character would you say is the most honest?

3. Who do you think Evelyn trusts most? Does that person change over the course of the novel?

4. In what ways are Robert and Evelyn's actions an effort to compensate for something in their pasts?

5. Evelyn feels that "ghosts are in every corner of every room." Do you believe in ghosts? Do you think what people consider "ghosts" has changed over time?

6. How do you feel about Clarence and Bernice's operation? Could it ever be justified?

7. Is Evelyn judgmental? What changes do you imagine WWI might have made to the way society considered social class?

8. What challenges arise when two people in a romantic relationship have different beliefs?

9. Discuss the book's title. What are the possible meanings?